THE ROBOTIX SAGA

BOOK 1

THE HUMAN ELEMENT

THE ROBOTIX SAGA
BOOK 1
THE HUMAN ELEMENT

JEFFREY K. DANOWSKI

ARPress
ILLUMINATING IDEAS.
EMPOWERING VOICES

ARPress
45 Dan Road Suite 5
Canton MA 02021

Hotline: 1(888) 821-0229
Fax: 1(508) 545-7580

Ordering Information:
Quantity sales. Special discounts are available on quantity purchases by corporations, associations, and others. For details, contact the publisher at the address above.

Printed in the United States of America.

ISBN-13:   Softcover   979-8-89262-200-4
                      eBook   979-8-89262-201-1

Library of Congress Control Number: 2023921009

Table Of Contents

Other Titles by Jeffrey K. Danowski

Teddy Bear Necklace

Grandma's Necklace

Heirloom Necklace (Chain of Love)

Teddy Bear Necklace for Sale

Teddy Bear Hugs and Snowflake Kisses

One in the Same

In Flying Colors (A Poetry Anthology volume 1)

In Flying Colors (A Poetry Anthology Volume 2)

Ghost Train

The Labyrinth of Fantasy (A Collection of Short Stories)

(Co-authored with Edwin K. Danowski and Kira Rosa Danowski)

DEDICATION

With each publication, comes a growing list of people I have to thank. So, not to leave anyone out, I start by thanking everyone, that way no one is slighted. However, there are some that I would like to give special mention. First and foremost, I would like to thank God for all of his gifts which include my writing talent. Secondly, I want to thank all of my friends and family for their love and support. I want to give a special shout out to my wife Sonia, my son Ricardo and my daughter Kira for their love and support and allowing me the time to pursue my hobby. Mom, dad, I couldn't have done it without you. I'd also like to give special thanks to both sets of my late grandparents, who like my parents offered all of their love an d support. I'd like to thank my mentors, Paul Hayes, a college professor at the University of Wisconsin-Milwaukee who helped bring out the best in me. I would also like to thank fellow journalists Gary D'Amato and Peter Jackel who also helped to make me the best writer that I can be.

A special thanks goes out to the late, Reverend Leon Schneider, who was a good, good friend of mine. Lastly, I'd like to thank the late Florence Parry Heide, author of more than 80 children's books, whom I was fortunate to have the opportunity t o have met before she sadly passed away. She got to see my first manuscript, just before it got accepted for publication. Recognizing my writing talent, she encouraged me to never give up. She believed Teddy Bear Necklace, is a potential bestseller.

ABOUT THE AUTHOR

Hello, my name is Jeffrey K. Danowski, award-winning journalist and author of 10 previous books. The Robotix Saga…Book 1…The Human Element is my 11th book. I grew up in Racine, Wisconsin, born into a family of writers, athletes, artists, and musicians. My father is a writer-artist, my mother is a crafts woman who helps keep my tree decorated with homemade Christmas ornaments. I am the oldest of five siblings. Two of my brothers are art directors for major companies in Illinois. My other brother and my sister are also artistically gifted. One of my late uncles was offered a recording contract by Elvis Presley's agent.

Another relative of mine, Edward Danowski, led the New York Giants to a World Championship over the Green Bay Packers in 1938. This relative also mentored the Late Great Vince Lombardi and helped get him his job with the Green Bay Packers. The rest of that story is History. Under Lombardi the Packers posted an 89-29-4 record and won five world championships including Super Bowls I & II.

Though being a published author is a great thrill, the biggest joy I get from writing is having others read my work. I've developed my own style where I want my readers to visualize what they're reading. I want them to identify with my characters and I want to make them feel like they are part of the story. The biggest thrill for me is when the book, Labyrinth of Fantasy was published. It's a collection of short stories that I co -wrote with my dad and my daughter. A word of advice to all of you dreamers out there; be who you want to be. Don't give up on your dreams. And don't let anyone get in the way of your dreams, by telling you that you can't, or you are not good enough. Always shoot for the moon. If you don't get the moon, there are a lot of stars out there that are worth grabbing on to, any of which can help make your dreams come true. Don't wait for someday, it never comes, just do it. If it's your dream, fulfill it. After you have, I can tell you that there's no greater sense of accomplishment. You don't have to be the best of the best to achieve greatness.

Greatness comes from bringing out the best in yourself by living up to your potential. No one can expect more of you, and you shouldn't expect less of yourself. The satisfaction comes with fulfilling your dream, not trying to please others. If no one else believes in you, believe in yourself, and then make them believe too. The fulfillment of your dreams will convince them. The key to being the best you can be, is to be yourself. There's nobody else like you. We're all unique individuals. You can't be like anybody else, and nobody can be like you. So, be you, and follow your dreams and don't chase someone else's. Don't just dream, dreams, make them come true and live them.

PROLOGUE

A century of battles between robots and Humankind culminated in an all-out war between the two factions that lasted exactly one year to the day. It was the anniversary date of the Transfer of Power Treaty which effectively ended the war. Though battles had ceased, tensions remained high. Humans, having governed themselves for millennia wrote historic chapters of war and peace as they pertained to the Earthen world. Succumbing to robot rule was something humans would always resent, but the fact remained, robots were the reigning governing body of the world. Humankind had the freedoms to generally do whatever it wanted as long as it was within the guidelines set forth by the mechanical world government. Humankind had no problems abiding by fundamental principles that helped maintain law and order. The problem was with the way law and order was kept. Criminal activity around the world was reduced to almost nil as a result of surveillance, via satellite and drones. Robots kept these tools at their disposal and continued using them to help keep the peace. Criminals were apprehended and punished for their crimes. But, as part of the treaty, a World Constitution was written in the light of the one that had well-served the United States for centuries and applied globally. Humankind felt like its privacy had been taken away, something in direct violation of the World Constitution. Humans took to destroying the drones, deemed government property. Another section of the treaty required the robots to abide by Asimov's Laws. A common practice of executing hardened criminals who committed the most heinous of crimes, was in direct violation of the first of his three laws.

The building tensions were understandable then, considering both factions were guilty of violating quintessential aspects of the treaty. Fears of a 2nd conflict were real, it seemed inevitable. This led to the creation and design of Shilloqwai, a female robot made to be humanlike. Acting as a liaison to help bridge the gaps between the two factions, her quest was to keep them from clashing and engaging in another all-out conflict. The effectiveness of the plan seemed to be taking hold when Shilloqwai took matters into her own hands and killed six criminal civilians. For her crimes against humanity, she was to be terminated. Excelcious Orbitus made a deal with the robots, which allowed him privilege to claim whatever was on their junk pile. When Shilloqwai had been discarded and placed on the salvage pile, Excelcious came to her rescue. The feuding factions were about to go to war again, when, Earth got attacked by an AI Force from somewhere in the universe. Its mission, to rid the universe of imperfection. Humans, and the robots they created, imperfect as they were, became prime targets of the AI force. Was Humankind's fate sealed? Or could the robots, working with Humankind, keep from being overpowered? Could they find a weapon or a power strong enough to destroy their common enemy? If they failed to meet the challenge, Earth's robots were sure to be terminated and all of Humankind exterminated.

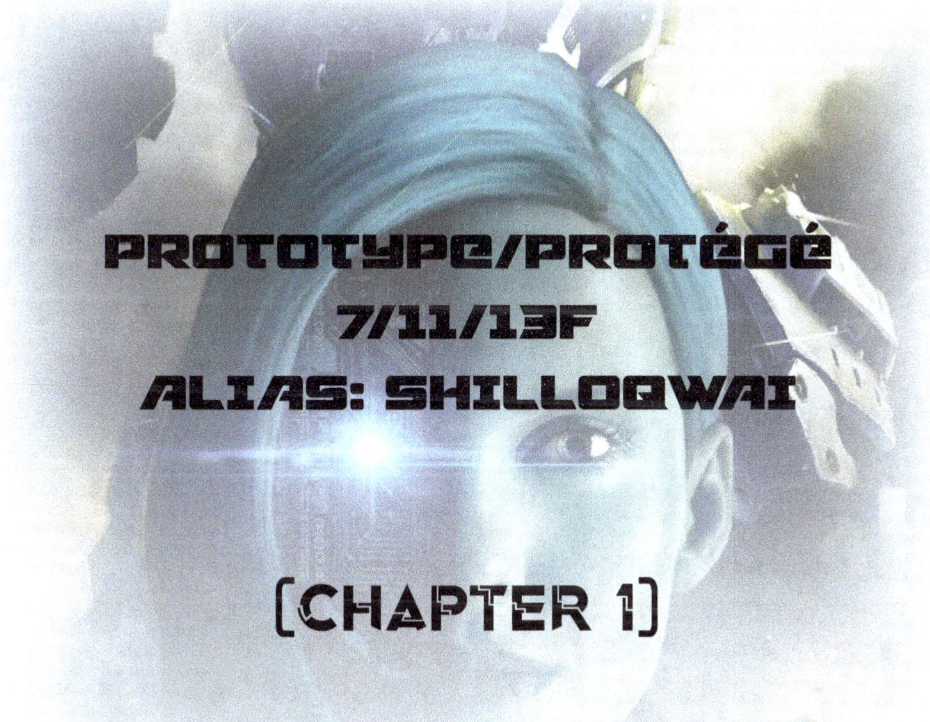

The lone-wolf wind was howling at the liquid-scarlet moon in blood-curdling fashion. The moon seemed to be melting, dripping evil from the sky. Lurking in the haunting shadows, decrepit creatures also made their voices heard, piercing the eerie silence with disturbing hisses, cries, and moans. The warning signs to stay away couldn't have been clearer amid the opaque, shimmering silver mist. Shilloqwai was not detoured by the threatening ominous signs. Her decision to venture alone down an old, abandoned street was calculated. She was well-aware of the risks she was taking. With a heightened sense of awareness, she proceeded onward down her dark path. Cloaked in the ghoulish purple of the midnight sky, Shilloqwai also found herself silhouetted in the shimmering silver mist that lighted her way.

Shilloqwai's walking at a brisk pace, had everything to do with the fact that she was on a mission, confidently going about her business. It had absolutely nothing to do with the possibility, that perhaps, she might've been the least bit afraid of the unknown. At times she admittedly felt fear. This was not one of those times. When she experienced sensations such as fear, anxiety, and uncertainty, it wasn't in the same way that humans did, a discussion for another point in time. She walked with a provocative swagger, showing a little cleavage, and baring a little leg, in sporting her paisley-patterned summer dress. Her dress accentuated both her voluptuous beauty and all of her dazzling charm. Shilloqwai was packing a lot in her slender 5-foot-11 frame. Her curves were definitely rounded in all of the right places, a perfect body, by chauvinistic standards. By the same token, the dress she was wearing concealed more than it revealed allowing her to maintain her dignity and respect.

The moonbeams were playing in her aqua-tourmaline waist-long hair. Her matching eyes sparkled like the flickering stars. Beneath the haunting moonlight her aqua-tourmaline skin glowed, icy-blue-green. Her hands were cool to the touch. Cold hands, warm heart, so the saying goes. Shilloqwai had an infectious smile that illuminated her daintily beautiful porcelain-like face. It would then be logical to conclude that someone who possessed such a smile would also have a charming personality to complement it. Someone who had to have nothing less than the greatest intangible, a loving heart of gold, from which the glowing radiated throughout her body.

Combining her physical attributes with the intangibles she possessed, one would have to agree that Shilloqwai was one hell of a woman, by any standard. Those that knew her would testify she had some spunk in her too. She wasn't afraid to show it, and she did at times, when she thought it appropriate. Those who knew her would collectively agree that Shilloqwai was definitely the kind of woman any guy would be willing to die for. A playful temptress, charming and irresistible, who didn't know what love was. How could she? It was something she never experienced, at least not in the way humans do!

No one in their right mind could resist her, especially after having set eyes on her. Insatiable desires of those wishing to win her heart and win her affections always ran amok, primarily because she refused to open her heart to potential suitors. She had a secret that needed to remain so. Afraid that sharing it with anyone, could well lead to her termination, thus the end of her existence. Keeping secrets was a tell-tale sign of distrust.

Without trust, the foundation for any kind of relationship would be weak at best, and destined to be short-lived.

This mystery surrounding her, made potential suitors want to court her all-the more. Shilloqwai could easily be the life of any party. Her only flaw if there was one, was her forced sense of humor. It was usually very dry and often not understood without an extensive explanation. After which, the purpose of the humor, to make people laugh, had been defeated. All things considered this was merely a minor flaw in her character. She had so much else to offer, friendship, companionship, love, and all of its charms! If only she could tell her admirers her little secret, they'd surely understand. Perhaps they'd be dissuaded from their pursuit of her. Back to the trust issue, she couldn't risk her existence on it. Her fear of what might happen is what was preventing her from revealing her secret to anyone, human or machine.

Why was she worried about anything? Worrying is an emotional reaction. It wasn't in her mechanical DNA! All she had to worry about, was doing what she was designed to do, be more human. In keeping Asimov's laws, she was guaranteed her assignment as a liaison would be successful. Isaac Asimov was a prolific science-fiction writer. His laws first appeared in the 1942 novel he wrote called I Robot. No one ever dreamed robots would one day rule the world as he had foretold in his book. But, after they'd actually taken control of the world from Humankind, it made perfect sense to implement Asimov's laws which had practical application in any world, real or surreal. Those laws Asimov put in his book are as follows:

1. Robots may not allow harm to come to humans, through action or inaction.
2. Robots must obey human orders, except where orders were in conflict with the first law.
3. Robots must protect their own existence, as long as in doing so, it didn't conflict with the first or the second law.

When she accepted the liaison position, she agreed to follow Asimov's laws or face termination by incineration. The laws seemed pretty-straight forward. Shilloqwai was told, that abiding by these three simple laws, it would help her meet her prime objective…smoothing over relations between humans and robots. Shilloqwai soon found that actually following the laws as written, was inherently more challenging than she'd initially thought. After reevaluating her assignment, she calculated her chances of succeeding in her quest were less than zero. She believed that she was expected to fulfill a most difficult, if not damn near impossible task. Shilloqwai needed what humans often ask God for, a miracle!

Shilloqwai would have adequate time to review her mission, adjust her plan and put it into action at a later time. When she was in sleep-mode she would multi-task. She typically took this time to review her data, update her programming, run self-diagnostics and self-analysis. It was also a good time for her to process any backlog, defragment her files and purge impertinent information from her system.

At the moment, she had a more pressing issue pending. She'd been tracking her followers for 1.327 miles now. More accurately, they had been tracking her over that distance. Sensing they were about to move in on her, she readied herself for an attack, calculating how she would respond. Shilloqwai quickly decided that would depend on the degree of violence they'd try and use during their imminent assault. Regardless of their demands, she decided that they would never know her name. She would identify herself as Protégé-Prototype, model number 7/11/13F. Her ID was visibly tattooed in red on her left wrist.

Crimes were rarely committed on Earth since the Robotix Revolution, often referred to as the 100-year conflict. Still there were perpetrators, some foolish enough to think they could beat the system. These perpetrators were always trying to outsmart the Robocops, put in place to keep order and enforce the laws. Since the robots had taken control of the human world, there were no cold cases, no missing persons, and no criminals left unpunished for felony offenses. No delinquent was left unaccountable for misdemeanors, however small the infractions may have been. Robotix policy however mandated that the punishment given for any criminal activity, big or small, be suited to the crime. In most instances, misdemeanor offenses, depending on what they were, had little or no consequence for the perpetrator or perpetrators.

Regardless of the rules, be they of household, city, state, country, planet, galaxy or universe, there were still those seeking notoriety with ambitions of becoming the first to beat the system, implemented to maintain law and order. No one had yet, but there were those who believed in the old cliché; THERE'S A FIRST TIME FOR EVERYTHING. The Anti-Robotix gang was known more for its pranks and being a public nuisance than actually breaking the law. When members of this gang did break the law, the offenses had usually been petty and of the misdemeanor variety. Like everyone else, a favorite pastime for them was shooting down drones they believed were invading their privacy. Most of the world's populous was guilty of this. This type of activity wasn't solely restricted to people who identified themselves as being affiliated with Anti-Robotix Gangs. It was easier for the robots to send up new drones than it was to seek out, arrest, and prosecute the perpetrators.

A handful of Anti-Robotix gang members became unhinged at the sight of Shilloqwai waltzing alone down the street like she hadn't a care in the world. They were about to lose their perceived innocence. Not yet known to Shilloqwai, all members of this particular group had murdered before. The group, a sextet, consisted of five males and one female. Assaulting her, even murdering her, were crimes they seemed more than willing to commit. She was a beautiful sight. Shilloqwai continued walking toward them, avoiding eye contact, while maintaining an awareness of their proximity. Her purse was secured with a body strap that lay across her left shoulder and hung at her right side. With all of this being said, a dark abandoned street in the dead of night was not an ideal place for anyone to go walking alone, especially a woman, human or otherwise.

It was a risk however that she willingly took. Shilloqwai's actions were precipitated by the false sense of security that the Robocops would come to her rescue at the precise moment she needed them. That, in tandem with knowing crime had nearly been eliminated from the world, beings in general were more likely to take calculated risks. Shilloqwai was sensing her prospective attackers were planning on taking more than calculated risks. She believed she was about to become violently victimized in a pre-meditated attack. Again, fear of her termination had been brought to the forefront of her mechanical mind.

Putting herself at risk was part of the job. Knowing this, she remained dedicated and loyal to her employer. Shilloqwai had to work alone. She knew that having a companion of any sort could jeopardize, even undermine her mission. This was a chance she refused to take. The robots had growing concerns in regard to differences between the two factions. They, like the humans feared the differences would lead to another revolution. Shilloqwai was confident she could smooth over the differences between the two factions, Humankind, and machine.

Still some distance away, Shilloqwai identified the five men and a woman she believed to be Anti-Robotix nuisances. She hoped she hadn't misjudged them. Nevertheless, she dismissed the sextet as harmless. Her instincts were telling her differently. What instincts? Shilloqwai asked, questioning the absurdity of the thought. She wasn't human. Perhaps it was part of her programming, the part that required her to be more, HUMAN! Shilloqwai doubted any in the sextet knew who she was. If the group attempted to harm her, she was equipped with the element of surprise, one of the deadliest of weapons to the unsuspecting. She believed them to be inebriated, based on their behaviors. They were boisterous and laughing uncontrollably at stupid ridiculous things, as she'd overheard some of their nonsensical utterances.

In spite of her optimism, it was quickly becoming obvious there was going to be a confrontation. Shilloqwai took it upon herself to make the first move. She waited until her stalkers were within earshot. "What's the matter boys, chicken to show yourselves?" She taunted. "I know you've been following me. You're out there somewhere, just ahead! Chicken Shits! C'mon out and show yourselves! And why don't you just come on out and tell me what you want from me?" One-by-one her stalkers came forth and began crowing over her like proud roosters in a henhouse.

The female in their group rolled her eyes in disgust over the childish sexist behavior of her comrades. She had blonde hair. Though it was predominately long, it was cut at different lengths with intricate designs etched into it. Kind of stylish, Shilloqwai thought. She had a gothic look about her, giving her beautiful emerald eyes, a ghoulish-green haunting look. She was cloaked in a leather jacket. Even with her long heavy leather coat, Shilloqwai thought she looked awfully thin. Her frail bones obviously had little flesh and skin covering them. A skeleton she was, looking vampiresque with her black lipstick.

Shilloqwai pitied the poor creature, who looked like she emerged from the world of the undead. Though seemingly lost, it was quite evident to Shilloqwai that 'skinny vampire girl,' disapproved of her comrades' planned sexual assault on her. 'Skinny girl' was confused as to why Shilloqwai seemed unafraid of the situation facing her. But Shilloqwai, was afraid. Not of what her prospective attackers were going to do to her; she was afraid of what was going to happen to her, after she followed through with what she was planning to do to them!

Next, the apparent leader of the group stepped forward. Even with his blonde hair and beard, cut and trimmed in GQ fashion, he still looked like a shady character. Shilloqwai wondered how someone so handsome with a finely sculpted physique, could look like such a worthless piece of shit! "Sable, forget this shit! Just leave her alone and let's go home!" 'Skinny-Girl' pleaded.

"Shut up Sage! You ignorant bitch!" Sable scolded her.

"What do you want from me Sable?" Shilloqwai demanded to know, while feeling sorry for Sage. "Speaking on behalf of the guys in our group, we're pretty sure you know what we want from you! You appear to be an intelligent woman, questionable in judgement perhaps, but intelligent, nonetheless. I mean who in their right mind would pass up a chance for a nice piece of ass like yours?"

"You can stop dreaming. None of you are getting any!" Shilloqwai stated definitively. "At least, not without asking, how rude! Secondly, I never give up anything in pieces. If you bastards don't want it all, you won't be getting shit from me! If you think you'd like to take your chances with me, get to know me first. Then, take me as I am, wholly and completely. Who knows, I could end up eternally yours!"

"Ooohhh! A tough cocky bitch! You think you can take us all on? We were hoping for a little sample, you know, like try before you buy kind of thing! I mean, we gotta' be sure of what we're getting before we make any long-term commitment! We're perfectly content to follow through with this one-night stand, I mean we're already committed to that!"

"Poor planning, this little gang bang thing you're about to try. You're going to take all the fun out of it! Fast and furious isn't my style. If you all want in on the action, well, you'll have to wait your turn. So, one at a time, please!" Shilloqwai pleaded. "You'll soon see that I'm too much of a woman for any of you little boys to handle. Hell, its obvious none of you are in this thing for love. Looks like I'm outta here! Let me through. I don't feel like wasting my time with any of you!"

"Not so fast bitch!" Sable shouted. He along with the others began to encircle and close in on her personal space. Shilloqwai mockingly laughed in their faces, never flinching once. The grin drooped from her face as her predators tore the dress from her body. She sneered at the disappointment that shadowed their faces. Hoping to see a naked woman in the flesh, they saw a generic mannequin with an aqua-tourmaline blue tint instead. There was nothing for them to see really. With the little imagination that any of them had, Shilloqwai guessed they probably weren't seeing much of anything except for the contours of her artificial breasts.

Capitalizing on the perceived ignorance of her attackers, Shilloqwai challenged them to follow through with their threats. "Can't get any action unless you get me out of my wetsuit now, can you?" Shilloqwai bolted for the edge of the woods, beckoning them to come after her.

Even with its peep holes, the woods offered more privacy than the wide-open spaces of the park walkway. She could have escaped her attackers, but they were on the prowl, hungry like wolves on the hunt.

Shilloqwai held her ground, thinking perhaps in doing so, she'd thwart an attack on some other innocent soul with the inability to keep herself from being accosted. Someone, who may not have the strength to ward them off as Shilloqwai knew she did. The sextet did as she expected and chased after her, lunging at her when they were close enough.

She side-stepped them and watched as they went down in a heap into a mud-puddle. Seeing them immersed in mud she couldn't help but laugh out loud. She gasped as Sable grabbed her leg and pulled her down into the slop with them. She was waterproofed to some degree. Shilloqwai didn't seem overly concerned. She knew the density of the mud would keep almost all of the water from penetrating her spongy shell. There was a brief tussle as they rumbled and tumbled in the mud. When the thrashing and splashing stopped, Sable had positioned himself as such that he was sitting on top of her. She had them all thinking they had overpowered her. It was quite the contrary. None of them ever dreamed they were about to be ambushed by her as she had no intentions of succumbing to them. She lay, waiting in the wings for the perfect moment to launch her counterattack.

Sable was thinking he had the advantage over her, by virtue of the fact, that he was sitting on top of her. It was a gross miscalculation on his part. He had passed the point of no return. He found the thought of sexually assaulting her amusing. He placed his hands on her rubberized breasts. He found that there was an unnatural firmness about them as he tried fondling them. Shilloqwai laughed at him. "I'm not feeling anything!" She told him, rebuking his advances. "And I won't until you get me out of my protective gear. Even then, lust without passion will not stir my emotions." She was repulsed by his desire for a cheap thrill. Continuing on with his assault, he next pinned her wrists to the ground using his hands for restraints. It was then Sable noticed the red markings tattooed on her left wrist. He immediately judged her, classifying her as an ex-convict.

"So, what were you in for? Bitch!"

"Murder!" She said flatly with crazed eyes before flashing a wry smile. "I like to play rough, so, you think you've got it in you? Give it to me baby! I want it all! And I want it now!" She lied convincingly. "I appreciate you taking it slow, but I'm just like any other woman. I don't like to be kept waiting. You should have me naked by now. You're not having second thoughts about getting it on with me, are you Sable?"

"Since you're so damn anxious to get it on, why don't you get out of that mannequin suit? You little slut! Show me what you've got, and I'll return the favor. I promise I won't disappoint you."

"I hope not. But if you want the honey, you'll have to help yourself to the dip. It's up to you to earn it. So, if you can't figure out how to get the top off of the pot, you're going to be shit-out-of-luck. I'm not doing it for you! Look, I know we've got all night, but, if you're going to follow through with your threatening promise, we'd better get started. C'mon Sable!" Shilloqwai tried encouraging him.

"I guarantee, this will be a night you'll remember and one you'll be longing to forget if you live through it!"

"You know this is a losing proposition. Regardless of what happens, you won't be satisfied with me. So, Sable, don't pretend it's going to be some great conquest. It's only going to further define what a loser you are, you cold-hearted son-of-a-bitch! But, if you want it so badly, just take it then asshole!" Instantly Sable released her wrists, freeing her arms. But she was pretending too, faking that she had succumbed to her attackers. Sable just sat there, as though he didn't know what to do next. She began to quiver, not out of fear, but, rather as a result of one of her ill-timed glitches coming on. Sable made the mistake of thinking it was the former.

Overconfident, with a deviant smile, he looked as though he was about to conquer the world. "You're afraid!" Sable exclaimed, knowing he had stated the obvious, believing he had another advantage over her because of her perceived fear. Seemingly showing no remorse for what he was planning to do to her, Sable revealed to her the demon that he was.

Ignoring the cruel looks on Sable's face, Shilloqwai continued to taunt and humiliate the man who she knew only as Sable. "Okay, I'll admit it, I'm afraid, but not for the reasons that you might suspect."

"If you're not afraid that you're about to be sexually assaulted, what else could you possibly be afraid of?"

"I'll tell you three things I'm afraid of. First, I'm afraid that you won't be able to keep your promise of making love to me. I'm more afraid that you won't know what to do with me once you get me naked. Perhaps, I'll get lucky and you won't be as impotent as you are stupid. Mostly I'm afraid, of what's going to happen to me after I kill all of your dumb asses, and leave you for crow meat on the street, before I walk away. Don't worry, due justice will likely serve me just as it's about to be served to you !"

As a robot, she was left to wonder if she was more human, than the animal sitting on top of her, especially if she followed through with her threat to kick some booty. Would killing the sextet make her just as much of an animal as her attackers?

Shilloqwai reasoned that it wouldn't, believing that any combative action she might take, would be out of self-defense. Considering she was a robot, Shilloqwai believed her recent thoughts to be strange and out of the ordinary. Imagine, that a robot was pondering committing murder.

The same robot also desired true love. Her present emotional state was a train wreck. How absurd, she thought. It was even more peculiar that Shilloqwai acknowledged to herself she often had dreams, something she hadn't yet shared with anyone.

She was convinced that keeping her dreams to herself would prolong the inevitable end. The thought that she might actually be dreaming did have its appeal. It meant that she was fulfilling the purpose of what she had been designed for, being more human. If she were capable of having a dream, one that she could pursue, and make come true, becoming human would undoubtedly be that dream. Time for a reality check, now was not the time to fantasize. She had business to take care of. "You're taking an awfully long time to engage in your delusional fantasy. What's wrong, Sable? You cowardice chicken shit! Are you not getting turned on by sitting on top of me? I have to be honest, there's one more thing you should know about me before we get intimate."

"And what's that? You don't have any sexually transmitted diseases, do you?"

"No, I'm clean. What I want to share with you has to do with my personality. I've been told that it's shocking, even electrifying. The real question is, how high do you want me to turn up the heat?"

"I can take the heat. I've never met a woman that was too hot for me to handle. How about you? How hot can you stand it? You little whore!" Sable further antagonized Shilloqwai with a cold slap to her face. He jolted her neck, causing her to hit her head on the ground after he grabbed and yanked her hair. There was a stinging in his hand. He thought he may have broken a finger or two when he hit her cheekbone with his backhand. The brute force he used to slap her softened as he began caressing her face. Ironically, he was using the same hand in which he had just broken two fingers. Gently brushing the hair back out of her tourmaline eyes, he longed to gaze into them before he leaned over to kiss her. Though her lips were soft and spongy wet, there was something unhuman about her. He drew closer yet and felt her body start to tremble beneath him. He was still trying to figure out how to get her naked. The suit she was wearing appeared to be seamless, making him unsure of how to get it off of her.

He was too proud to ask. And she wasn't going to tell. It meant revealing her secret.

He saw the purse strap on her shoulder as a hindrance, using brute force again, Sable yanked it off, throwing it aside along with the purse. There was nothing in it of value to him, or anyone, but her. Simply spare parts for minor reparations and alterations, if need be, while she was out and about. Shilloqwai seemed ready for him, as he was beginning to feel the waves of energy surging through her body.

Shilloqwai's climactic frenzy seemed a little premature to Sable, but she did warn him that she liked to play rough and that she could go all night. He found it hard to imagine that slapping her in the face and pulling her hair had gotten her so aroused that quickly. The fact that those things seemed to be bringing her pleasure was actually beginning to scare him, making him wonder what he had gotten himself into.

The electrical impulses flowing through her were rapidly increasing with both frequency and intensity. Shilloqwai knew what was about to happen next as her self-defense mechanism had been activated. Sable was feeling the transfer of heat, now penetrating his own body. The heat was sweltering and quickly became too much for him to handle. He was the conductor for the energy she was outputting. Sable screamed in agony as a steady stream of high-voltage energy surged through him. His shoes did not have rubber soles. No other article of clothing he was wearing could have protected him from absorbing the full charge of the shock she'd administered to him. He was a doomed man. His destiny had been forged.

Perhaps he'd gotten some pleasure from the experience of being with the robot…woman. That depended, really, whether or not he believed she was worth dying for. Sable paid a dear price with his life, suffering immensely during his electrocution. His blood boiled to the point where it began spewing out like lava-flows from his blistering skin. His flesh was laid bare going from looking like raw hamburger to cinder and ash, in just seconds. His companions watched in horror, barely able to stomach the heinous smell of his burning flesh. It bubbled and dripped like melting plastic goop from his bones.

Shilloqwai threw Sable's French-fried corpse from her body and sprang to her feet. "Anyone else think they can handle the heat? Bring it on!" The inclination of the remaining five was to run. Instead, they chose to stand and fight. There was no valor in retreating. Running would have made them seem more cowardice than they had already shown themselves to be. If it hadn't been before, it was clear to them now. Shilloqwai had the upper hand on them. She'd had it all along. They realized this all too late. Their failing assault attempt had pissed her off to no end.

The quintet knew it was about to meet its ill-fated destiny. "Bitch isn't backing down guys!" 'Skinny Vampire Girl' seemed to like being called one of the guys. Shilloqwai thought it was her way of fitting in. Sage wished however the boys would finish their business with Shilloqwai and move on.

"We ain't getting shit from her and she is going to kill us here and now. We've got to get out of here!" Said the burly redheaded Irishman, overstating the obvious. I'd feel a little better about this fight if I'd downed a few pints first. I could fight like a crazy ass and not feel the pain if I start getting my ass kicked."

"Too late to retreat boys. I intend to make good on my promises!" She was done playing, and she was about to back her words with action. Understanding now that she meant business, the five surviving gang members were wishing they had walked away when they'd had the chance. They'd sealed their fates by making death wishes which Shilloqwai intended to grant. She would make every last one come true. In their final prayers, the four remaining sons and a daughter of Satan hoped their death would come quickly and painlessly.

Their best chances of survival would be to implement a strategy that would involve attacking her as a unit. The challenges would be to overpower her and then deactivate her. Those chances dwindled as three of them chose to triple-team her. Skinny Vampire Girl took the point. She was flanked on her left by Shane, the burly Irishman. Flanking her on the right was a little shit who looked like he came out of a gangster movie. Shilloqwai, young-looking as he was, knew he was a follower, as she watched the other two shuffling him into attack position. They referred to him as Colt 45. She didn't think there was any way Colt was cut out to be the mob boss tough guy he was pretending to be. She viewed him more as a stupid-ass punk, wanting people to think he was tough by bullying others.

The remaining two sat back, curious as what was going to happen as the trio, led by Sage, bull-rushed Shilloqwai in an attempt to overpower her. It was a poor plan from the onset, considering the fact that Sable, the first member of their gang had already been electrocuted by touching her. Shilloqwai pulled up from her database a few things on martial arts, deciding that a few simple kicks would take care of her trio of attackers. Vampire girl led the Irishman and the wanna-be mobster in their haphazard effort to overtake Shilloqwai. They bull-rushed her as if she were a stationary object, foolishly not expecting her to move. Reacting to their attack, Shilloqwai used a simple jump kick to take out the Vampire girl. She'd broken every major bone in her face, cheekbones, jawbones and then some. Her kick impacted the girl under her nose with such force that her nose splintered, thrusting a sliver of bone into her brain, upon which she died instantly.

Shilloqwai leapt up from the ground to her feet, with the agility and the prowess of a panther leaping down from a tree to the ground. Immediately upon getting her feet back under her, she moved quickly and decisively as though she had springs in her feet. Next, she wheeled around with a spinning roundhouse kick, taking out one of the wingmen by delivering a deadly blow to the Irishman's solar plexus.

She knew his sternum was ruptured. She heard the bone crack. By the way he was choking and puking up blood and spraying it everywhere, she could only assume that his lungs had collapsed as well. Almost instantly, the internal bleeding from his injuries had drained the life from him. He suffocated after only a second cough.

A gurgling death growl marked his passing. His body had gone limp before he crumpled to the ground in a heap. She wheeled again, turning on the last of the trio. Colt 45 had one last shot at her, but Shilloqwai's sweeping kick to the front of the wanna-be mobster's knees, bent them straight back, causing them to buckle. The snap, crackle and crunching told her she had shattered his kneecaps. His deafly agonizing screams confirmed what she had correctly surmised. Shilloqwai, though a robot, liked to think of herself as a humanitarian. It actually pained her to see the wanna-be gangster suffering so. Jumping back to her feet she sprang over to the poor pitiful creature writhing in agony on the ground.

She had growing concerns Colt 45 would injure his neck, the way he was flopping on the ground like a fish out of water. So, she put her heel on the barrel of his neck in true mob-boss fashion. She applied gentle pressure to his throat cutting off his airway. She gradually increased the pressure until his neck snapped. At once, everything stopped, his heinous screaming and moaning, the writhing and flopping around on the ground. Finally, his heart stopped, signaling his mortal life had escaped him. She had delivered justice to four of her attackers. The milliseconds she took to admire the efficiency of her work, admittedly was a mistake she wouldn't repeat. She'd given the remaining perpetrators time to creep up behind her. The younger of the two had chestnut hair with matching eyes. Shilloqwai thought he was cute, unfortunately for him, he got in with the wrong crowd. She could tell that his life's experiences were limited. Unfortunately, he'd made his choice, and he was going to die at the hands of a woman.

She guessed that he was still a virgin. The wanton look in his eyes told Shilloqwai that he desired to get it on with her. She wasn't going to accommodate him, even if it were the boy's dying wish. He didn't deserve a woman like her. The other remaining attacker looked like a thug, through and through. He was ungroomed with long oily hair. Shilloqwai believed there was good in everyone. Though, looking at him, she wondered if that applied. He had scars on his face that made him look meaner than hell. Looking into his coal-black eyes made the darkness look like a solar flare. Only a heartless one could look so cold. The look scared her. She got the impression that he was a son of the devil.

"Get her now Rocky!" Styx ordered his partner in crime. I'll cover you!" Foolish as it was, and primitive as their chosen weapons were, the virgin and the son of the devil, struck her multiple times. Using broken-off tree limbs, they delivered devastating blows to Shilloqwai before she could offer a counterstrike. The playing field had been leveled, somewhat. Shilloqwai's right arm, along with her left leg had been disabled for the most part. She retreated from her attackers, moving dangerously close to the nearby stream, where she fell to her knees. A false move and a slip and Shilloqwai would fry the circuits that hadn't yet been damaged.

The benefit to that happening is no one would be able to access her database until she had been repaired, that is, if she could be repaired and data was able to be recovered. While Shilloqwai was struggling to remain functional, her remaining attackers had their best chance to put her out of commission. Her troubled aqua-tourmaline blue eyes captured their gaze. Hauntingly translucent, beautifully enchanting, hypnotically engaging, once again they'd misread the story in her eyes, thinking their melancholy look suggested to them that she had given up. Little did they know the fight was far from over. She was plotting, meticulously calculating, the most efficient way to be rid of her attackers.

With the last burst of energy percolating inside her, she smiled genuinely, and with gratitude for their sincere looks of admiration. They nodded in acknowledgement, her smile. It was just a chess match, a masquerade, a setup for the final showdown. Adding to the drama, were the water droplets that were now seeping from Shilloqwai's eyes. Her attackers saw them, and she could now see a hint of guilt fogging their eyes. She thought for a moment they might actually have felt sorry for her and sorry for what they'd done! But the act was all for show. And her tears, were they real or merely condensation buildup as a result of her overheating? Shilloqwai was also feeling the pain from the fire that was raging in her burning heart. Hypothetically speaking of course ! After all, it was the fact that she was heartless that afforded her the benefit of not feeling guilt from the murders she had brutally executed, along with the ones she was about to commit.

The translucency was gone from her eyes now, absorbed by the tiny storm clouds that replaced it. Bravely she let the virgin Rocky, and Styx, the son of the devil see the tears now streaming from her eyes. They flowed like miniature waterfalls over her cheekbones and down her face. The charade was over. Shilloqwai had decided to put an end to the nonsense. "By now you're aware that looks can kill boys, aren't you?" She asked in thought-provoking fashion. Confused by her utterance, they were unable to look away from her gaze. In their moment of indecision, both were about to pay the price for their hesitation, stupidity, and ignorance.

On impulse both delivered more devastating blows to Shilloqwai's torso. This time she was able to sustain the damage without further disability occurring. Her center of gravity was low. Already on her knees when they began attacking her the second time, helped her in defending against their relentless assault. The pounding she was taking pushed her deeper into the saturated ground.

The fact that Shilloqwai was able to burrow in somewhat, steadied her, and allowed her to keep her balance and keep from falling into the nearby stream. She saw that Rocky and Styx seemed to be taking pleasure in beating her. She vowed she would be the last thing they hit, before they themselves, hit the ground.

They were about to face the full fury of the storm that had been building in her eyes. First, they saw the fires of hell which had burned away the enchanting tranquility that held their gaze. Then they saw the lightning and the razor blades followed by a blinding flash, the last thing either of them would see before they died. The last thing either of them felt was a searing burning pain in their necks which had been pierced by exploding shrapnel she shot out of her eyes. Though the burning searing feeling lasted just a very short time, it was long enough for them to feel the pellets of steel ripping the flesh from their throats. With seemingly laser precision the bits of shrapnel opened multiple wounds on their necks before ripping into and lodging into their jugulars.

The blood poured from their throats, draining in seconds, depleting their blood supply to the point where they could no longer sustain themselves. Shilloqwai had no clue as to why she felt empathy for the ones she had so brutally butchered. She doubted that forgiveness could be granted after the fact. Was forgiveness necessary? She believed the sextet massacre she had carried out was justified! During the attack, all of them had touched her at one point. She scanned their fingerprints as all had touched her with their hands, however inappropriate. Images for each of them were in her database. She discovered that they were all hardened criminals facing the death penalty upon their apprehension. The Robocops had been closing in on them but had not yet captured them. The way it all came down, the sextet members died sooner rather than later.

An eerie silence followed that had been quickly replaced by the haunting sounds of darkness. They were sounds, according to her database, that frightened humans and made them paranoid. The genesis and birthplace for all fears stemmed from the Great Unknown. This was as true for Shilloqwai as it was for humans. She was detecting new sounds now, none like she'd ever heard. There was no reference in her database for them. She wondered if the ones she just murdered were hearing the demonic sounds too.

It is said when humans die the last sense to fade is hearing. Christians claim there is an afterlife. Perhaps the shrieks and moans were the cries of Satan's servants, fitting escorts for the newcomers to the afterlife. The new acquisitions would be taken to hell, and rightfully so. It was the path forged by members of the sextet, as they journeyed through their mortal lives. Shilloqwai knew of the forgiving God, the One, that Christians paid homage to, but forgiveness required repentance, and her deceased attackers neither showed remorse, nor offered repentance before they died. They held contempt and disdain for her in their dark icy-steel eyes until their deaths. If Shilloqwai were human, she'd have never stood a chance against the sextet. She'd have been dead before she had a chance to murder the first. She was showing remorse, repenting for her sins. She wondered, if she were human, if God would forgive her for what she had done. She'd always intended to do the right thing.

Had she suffered a human death at the hands of the sextet, she wondered if she would have been greeted by an angel's choir at heaven's gate! The death Shilloqwai feared offered no afterlife, no heaven or hell. No reward for her good deeds and no penalty for her wrongdoings. She would ultimately be terminated from existence. If she were lucky, perhaps she'd be given a footnote in history, one that summed up in a few paragraphs, telling what she was designed for, and how she performed. The reasons all robots were replaced was because they had served their purpose and outlived their usefulness. An upgrade was a better fate than being discontinued. Being discontinued meant she was no longer functioning in a way that was efficient. Then again, upgrades merely prolonged the inevitable. They meant advances in technology and that something better was coming down the pike. She'd seen it before. Upgrades were generally precursors to new models. It was part of her history. She was a new model once, some 25 years ago.

Though Shilloqwai had survived the brutal attack, she hadn't come out of it unscathed. She was crippled and still kneeling on the soft bank by the creek leaning precariously in the direction of the babbling waters. The seals, her circuitry, her motherboard, interface, and CPU were likely all damaged in the attack. The Robotechs would find her eventually. If the storm in her eyes had really cleared and she wasn't overheating at this moment, then why were condensate tears running down her cheeks? Everything seemed to be as crystal clear as it was muddled. Things were starting to happen to Shilloqwai she didn't understand.

Electrical impulses were surging through her again. They were not of the normal sort, irregular in frequency and higher in voltage than what she was accustomed to. Glitches again, she was sure of it. She started receiving data that she was unable to process. Pulsating sensations were radiating through her like tremors reverberating down a fault line. Her best analysis based on the information she received from her database was telling her that she was feeling actual pain, in a way that humans did. This was preposterous. It wasn't really happening, was it? On a scale of one through ten, with 10 being extreme, she rated it a 10. Since she'd never experienced pain, Shilloqwai had nothing to use as a baseline to measure it.

She logically concluded that since it nearly made her pass out, or self-deactivate in her case, that it had to be extremely intense, perhaps it was higher than a 10. How much higher? She had no way to gauge that either. Along with the pain, condensate was streaming from her eyes. Her sensors analyzed the chemical make-up and molecular structure of the substance flowing down her cheeks.

According to information, also from her database, she was crying human tears, a salty liquid that often burns and agitates the eyes when secreted. Her pains worsened. She became more agitated by the tingling sensations that had begun to affect her back, neck and shoulders. These symptoms quickly spread deep into her chest. Attacking her with such severity, the pains caused her to double over so far, she was nearly kissing the ground. She was already on her knees. The pain was crippling, leaving her unable to get up off of the ground. With her database having been offline for minutes now, she became curious as to how she was still able to access it. With the damage she's sustained, she didn't know that it was even possible that she could access it. Surely, she wasn't coming to these conclusions on her own, was she? Adding to her confusion was the information that she had retained without accessing her database via commands from her CPU.

The data however she was accessing it, showed that her recent signs and symptoms rivaled those of a human having a heart-attack. How could it be she was actually experiencing this? What if these fleeting sensations were real? She would be able to relate to humans in ways that she never had. She forced a smile. Gaining an understanding of their stress and pain, would undoubtedly help her in her role as a liaison with the humans. It would allow her to empathize with them if she could somehow convince them that she was feeling their pain. Suddenly, everything began going dark.

Usually, darkness meant that she had been deactivated and powered down, rendering her unable to function at all. But here she was thinking again. She was still functioning, even though at a minimal degree. She wasn't able to see through the camera lenses she had for eyes. Though her mechanical eyes had been blinded, she was still seeing through human eyes. But those eyes were failing her too. Her vision was blurring, light turning to shadow and shadow to darkness. Numbed by her pain, she wasn't feeling anything now, not even the ground she was kneeling on.

She could smell the remainder of her still functioning circuits burning up and shorting out one-by-one. It wouldn't be long now, before all of her circuitry had failed her. The putrid smell inexplicably was overpowered by the scent of wild roses. Before long, that scent too was gone, along with the capacity to smell anything. Her human-like senses were all failing her now, just as her mechanical ones recently had. Amazingly with her inability to smell, she thought that it would affect her ability to taste anything.

Yet, somehow, she was able to taste. And what she tasted were fresh wild berries, gushing with flavor and bringing a sweetness from her mouth to her lips, like none she had ever known. She wondered how she was able to experience the taste of the wild berries with her silicon tongue.

As the taste faded, she was left with a mouth-watering, insatiable desire to satisfy what could be termed, hunger. She longed to taste more of life's infinite flavors. Too soon, the experiences had passed into memories. But the sensations of having experienced the five senses as humans did would be stored in her memory.

At least she hoped they would be. That was contingent on how much the Robotechs tampered with her database and screwed with the CPU in her head. All of her senses had failed her now, except for one. She'd heard that in dying humans, hearing was the last of the senses to go. Presently, her hearing was seemingly the only uninterrupted connection she had to anything. And she was hearing in a way that she was unaccustomed to. Sensory mics had been embedded in her polyurethane shell when she was assembled and that's what had allowed her to hear from the time she was first activated. Shilloqwai knew the sensory mics were no longer functional as a result of having the pulp beaten out of her.

This left her wondering, how it was she was able to hear from the ears cosmetically designed and molded so that she looked aesthetically pleasing to humans. They were supposed to give the impression that she could hear as they did. The fact they were actually receiving, and processing data was beyond her comprehension.

So lost in thought, she'd forgotten she was on a saturated bank of a rapidly rushing stream. Having lost all of her mechanical function, she was unable to move herself to safety. The Robotix team that, hopefully would come to retrieve her, would be left with the burden of moving her from wherever she ended up, on the bank or in the water. Shilloqwai knew she was in great peril before the ground beneath her gave. She'd been leaning precariously over the stream from the time her attackers brought her to her knees. A sudden shifting of the unstable ground thrust her into the raging water. Hearing the big splash alerted her to how much graver her predicament had become.

The rapid current brought new waves of fear rushing over her. The snapping, crackling, and popping sounds told her that the rest of her circuits were being French-fried. As she was becoming saturated with the water rushing over her, she wished it would just carry her away to a heavenly place, bypassing termination and incineration, the most probable endgame for her now. Aware of the additional damage she was sustaining there would be little if anything for the Robotix team to try and salvage.

Through the ongoing trauma, her very existence was being erased. Shilloqwai wondered if there was a good reason for her suffering and all that had happened to her, what was happening to her, what would ultimately happen to her? Could this possibly be a baptism of sorts to prepare her for a new genesis? Amidst the chaos and her turmoil, she suddenly felt like she was being consumed with a peace and serenity that was beyond her understanding. Her tranquil state allowed her some time for reflection pondering questions like: Why had she been designed? Had she been succeeding in being more humanlike? Was her sole purpose to act as a liaison between robots and humans? Or was there something more?

Was she to serve some other purpose? How had she been functioning as a liaison? Was she succeeding or failing? Would she be successfully able to bridge the growing gap between humans and robots? If she failed, would there be another revolution? Another revolution seemed inevitable to her at this point. Shilloqwai's dwindling chances for success in fulfilling her quest were nearly squelched. She had to wonder if the pre-meditated attack against her was part of a Robotix plan to get rid of her.

Considering her undertaking of the daunting task which required her to come to a general understanding of human nature, what was that? How was that even possible? Human nature is predictably unpredictable! This is the only thing about human nature universally understood! Shilloqwai would forge ahead with her mission impossible. Coming to a general understanding of human nature was unlikely. She saw human creatures as unique individuals with many imperfections, often leading them to think illogically, act irrationally, often behaving in ways that seemingly had no rhyme or reason.

Shilloqwai also understood humans would fight for their lives to the bitter end. This meant pulling out all stops, even resorting to extreme measures. She'd seen some go completely off the wall and come off the chain in last ditch efforts to try and get an extended lease on life. Using extreme measures gave them other options to try and get just that, a second chance to make the wrong things right. In a quirky way, all reason and logic aside, Shilloqwai understood this concept of hanging on to dear life. She compared it to her fight to remain in existence and her passion to become human.

With all of their imperfections, often engaging in silly, crazy, even ludicrous behavior, many, if not the majority of humans gain the wisdom to recognize and appreciate the treasures they have in the intangibles. These intangibles included things like peace, serenity, tranquility, joy and happiness, faith, and hope, friendship, and love. After all of her analyses, Shilloqwai concluded that the key to understanding and relating to humans would be learning what love is.

She remembered what her database said about love. She'd reviewed it countless times. Each time she saw that love has no true definition other than the fact that it is a feeling, described by adjectives and adverbs. She diligently noted that love had three complex properties:

1. *It was a gift that keeps on giving...* She'd witnessed this for herself. She'd often seen where someone does something out of love for another, and that gifted individual then goes on to do something out of love for someone else. She sees how the cruelty of the world weakens links in the chain. She also sees how the Power of Love doesn't allow the chain to break so that the gift can keep on giving.

2. *You can't receive it until you open your heart to it...* This concept was harder for her to understand. She wondered how one could receive it, if one didn't know what love was? She again reasoned that it must have something to do with the Power of Love.

3. *You always get back more than you give...* Shilloqwai knew that a little love went a long way. But if you only gave up a little, how could you get so much more in return? She couldn't get her head around the concept that when you do little things out of love for others, the love always comes back 100-fold in unexpected ways at times when you need it most.

Summing up the three properties of love, she now considered it a gift to be given and received. Shilloqwai was still trying to process those bits of information, surrounding the concept of love. How was it that a seemingly simple four-letter word, had proven time and again not only to be the most complex in the English language, but the most complex concept of all Humankind? Shilloqwai resigned herself to the fact that she would never find love, not in the way she desired. It was of little consolation to her that she wouldn't be alone in her failure to ever find love. Her being a robot made it impossible for love to ever find her. Still, she pitied, empathized, and held compassion for the humans that would never know love, especially the lonely ones that would never find it and consequently never enjoy the exhilaration from having experienced it.

Her brainstorm on love increased her desire to become human, and have love find her. Even if it were for a short time, she wanted to experience love to the fullest. How could she? One cannot give or receive this thing called love, without ever getting to know what love is. How sad. It was curious to her how she'd fallen into the philosophical abyss of thought, one where she was contemplating the many aspects of love. She wondered if she were active, if engaging in such deep thought would have caused a glitch that would have overloaded her systems. Even with her systems inactive she was becoming overwhelmed in thought. She had too much on her… mind? Another question, she had no answer for.

She concluded that it would be better to love and lose at love than never being loved at all. But she still thought there might be hope for a hopeless romantic such as herself. According to the wealth of data she accrued on the subject of love, Shilloqwai found that love was said to be unconditional in nature, powerful enough to heal anything and change everything. She also remembered that part of loving is forgiving. She was considered to be among anything, was she not? She was something, a robot no less, but she was something. And she was definitely included under the umbrella of everything. If love is all powerful, she then wondered why it couldn't change her, make her human? It was logical to assume love could heal her and change her. If love found her and changed her, she could not speculate in which ways she would be healed and changed.

Without sufficient data to run analysis and check for answers to her questions, it would be most difficult for her to say. She was open to the prospects and possibilities when it came to love. And she was holding out hope, that perhaps love might someday find her and change her. Her mechanical systems had long since gone to sleep. What was keeping her going? She heard the homing beacon powering up. The Robotix team was looking for her. She was sure they had remotely activated the beacon. This both contributed to her fears while also giving her additional peace of mind. Shilloqwai hoped the Robotechs loved her enough to give her one last chance. They'd painstakingly refurbished her on many occasions. She knew the grueling drill.

They would replace the damaged hardware beginning with the CPU, the motherboard, her wiring, her circuitry, working from the inside out to her polyurethane shell which protected it all. Once she was rebuilt, Shilloqwai would have to be recalibrated so that her mechanical functions were in sync with her software programming. The reloads and updates would be done according to specs as determined and set according to Robotech standards and the expectations they'd set for her. To this point, none of them were able to fix her glitches, which have been an issue persisting from her activation continuing on, throughout her 25 years of service.

She was beginning to understand the expressions like the one where, a cat has nine lives and curiosity is what ultimately kills it. In a strange way, Shilloqwai was luckier than the cat. Figuratively speaking, she'd had more than nine lives. Ironically, her curiosity may well end up being the death of her.

Somehow her existence seemed to be of greater significance by acknowledging that she had been serving mankind for a ¼ of a century as opposed to 25 years. It showed she could endure over time among machines that were technologically incrementally advancing at geometric rates, in very short periods of time. Whether she had served for a long time or a short time, it was irrelevant now. Shilloqwai was coming to terms with the fact that she might never get another reboot. After her past breakdowns and complete shutdowns Shilloqwai had become totally oblivious to all that was going on around her.

This time it was very different for her. She seemed to have entered a state of suspended animation where she had complete awareness of all that was going on around her. She had gone to a place where she was neither alive nor dead, neither activated nor deactivated. In her subconscious state, the place she was wandering through was what humans typically referred to as Dreamland. It's a place where fantasy and reality are synonymous.

It's a place where all dreams, even impossible ones often come true. She'd heard that one conceivable way dreams come true, was by wishing upon a star. She tried it once when she was fully functional, just before she got attacked. She wondered, if it worked for humans, then why couldn't it work for her?

Another way she'd heard dreams come true was by pursuing them to fruition. But Shilloqwai was between somewhere and nowhere. In her suspended state, she wasn't in a position to pursue her dreams of becoming human and finding love. Morphing wasn't part of her programming. As much as she wanted to, she couldn't make herself human. And if she had the capability to do so, people would see her for something she wasn't. And when the truth came out, it would end her hopes of finding true love. Again, she wondered if love could change everything, then why couldn't it change her from robot to human?

She was smart enough to know that love was a quintessential component if her dream had a snowball's chance in hell of coming true. She held on to the hope, knowing love had the power to remove all obstacles. She was more than willing to undertake her seemingly impossible quest. She hoped that she was given an adequate chance to fulfill it. Her faith grew with the belief that her dream might actually be realized. She also had wisdom enough to know that in the end, love would be her saving and redeeming grace.

In her condition she was in no position to go out and find this thing called love. It would have to find her. She wasn't quite sure how that would come about either, but her data supported the human belief that through Love, all things are possible. With those being her final thoughts, Shilloqwai succumbed to the darkness as all of her senses, mechanical and physical, had gone dormant. Finally, she was resting in peace. She saw, smelled, tasted, felt, or heard nothing more. The period of darkness had begun for Protégé/prototype, Alias: Shilloqwai. Type: Humanoid class, Mercusilver model number 7/11/13F. Indefinitely or permanently…the fate of Shilloqwai's existence was yet to be determined.

THE END OF THE WORLD AS THEY KNEW IT & THE NEW LAWS OF THE LAND

[CHAPTER 2]

Still in a comatose state, mechanically not functional and physically disabled, Shilloqwai felt herself being jostled about in a human sense. She was being lifted from the water and being readied for transport to the Robotix lab. The Robotechs hadn't activated her yet. Once again, she found herself in a state of suspended animation with a subconscious awareness. It was almost as if she had a human side to her, one that had been awakened, allowing her to experience sensory perception in life-like fashion. She could see, feel, smell, taste and hear, independently from her programming. If Shilloqwai hadn't known better, she'd swear that she was alive, even though her data didn't support this.

The concept of coming to life was inconceivable, the odds of it happening, impossible, yet the sensations and sensory perceptions were more than real to her. Shit! She whispered so that no one or anything would hear. She was very much afraid knowing the Robotechs had found her. Fear was about the only thing she was feeling at the moment. She was still numb to the pain from the beating she'd taken.

She was refreshed by the taste of wild berries in her mouth and on her silicon tongue. As before, the taste brought a sweetness to her lips, generating an insatiable hunger to taste other flavors of life. Then she caught a whiff of fresh air, a breeze carrying with it the scent of wild roses. She imagined how beautiful the flowers might look in her hair. Next, she saw a butterfly fluttering, struggling in flight against the wind. It opened her eyes to one of life's challenges, of which she knew there to be many. But, she reasoned, no price was too steep to pay for the freedom enabling one to enjoy life to the fullest.

Lastly, she heard the raging water that had baptized her and washed away her troubles of the past. She was feeling something now, mostly joy. She vowed to keep the faith, believing she would somehow get another chance in life. Suddenly she sensed her dreams had been filled with a new hope. As for love, she'd heard humans say on many occasions that it was all around. That being the case, perhaps the chances of love finding her were far greater than she could ever have imagined. Her little fantasy was short-lived.

She felt the cutting pain of the things spewing from the mouths of the Robotechs. They didn't know she was hearing it all, every word of every insult. "Her again? Why don't they just incinerate the bitch? She's been nothing but a pain in the ass since she was activated 25 years ago!" Kinks the lead Robotech remarked.

"Probably don't want to waste the energy!" Kinks' lead assistant Skanks quipped. "I mean look, we've got ourselves a French-fried robot. Going to be a real challenge getting her back together so she's functional and operational, she really got her ass whooped. They should just let her rot away."

"Looks like she was ambushed! One of the blows she suffered, likely caused her to have a glitch. Unaware of her surroundings she probably stumbled into the water." Kinks surmised. While two of the techs were speculating what may or may not have happened to Shilloqwai, other techs were surveying the scene for clues that would help reconstruct the incident. "Holy shit!" Shouted the third Robotech, Crosswire, an expert in circuitry. After Kinks and Skanks set Shilloqwai on the transport, they went running to the crime scene. They noted Shilloqwai was in better shape than her victims. "Look over here! We've got six dead humans, five men and a woman. Shilloqwai's signature is all over this mess! She murdered all six, electrocuted one and beat the mess out of the other five." Crosswire revealed with utmost certainty.

"The diplomat, the liaison that was supposed to be negotiating and smoothing over robot, human relations, right? I didn't know assassination was a tactic that diplomats used." Interjected Programamatic, the fourth Robotech to get into the discussion. Programamatic repaired and replaced Shilloqwai's software countless times. "This isn't going to end well for anyone. They'll melt her down now, for sure. She's violated Asimov's laws, grounds for immediate termination. There's no software that can cover for her crimes!"

"That will be up to the powers that be!" Crosswire pointed out. "One thing I do know, this Shittaqwai has got a lot of explaining to do. She wouldn't even be in this mess if she'd left those guys to the Robocops. I agree, when the boss finds out what she's done, it's going to be sayonara princess!"

"What a shame!" Programamatic chided. "There was so much potential for this one! She had been showing so much promise! Now this! Just when it seemed she was starting to gain the trust of Humankind. This was more than a glitch, something that has always been a problem for her. This was premeditated. Now that it appears that she's committed an actual crime she'll be robot melt for sure."

"So, guys, here we are back at the lab." Kinks announced. "Maybe we should just throw her on the junk pile. You know that's where she's going to end up anyway."

"We should probably check with the boss first just to cover our asses." Skanks advised his robot boss. "He's probably going to have us erase her first."

"Yeah, good idea!" They all agreed.

Shilloqwai's ride to the lab had been an uneasy one. Presently, she was experiencing the sensation of floating higher and higher as her robot spirit seemed to be soaring upward. Humans talked of heaven, an eternal resting place of blissful ecstasy. Certainly, her robot spirit wasn't taking her there. No such place existed for robots. However, it seemed to take an eternity to get there, wherever 'there', was. Shilloqwai guessed that she was in pieces. By now with her hardware scattered all over the lab, Shilloqwai also guessed the other techs were probably searching the warehouse, trying to track down replacements for her hardware and software. Meanwhile, she was in limbo with her fate to be determined.

In the meantime, her spirit had taken her to a place that she didn't recognize. As far as she could see in any direction there was nothing but paradise, vast rugged beauty, sparsely populated for infinite miles around the world. So, this is how it was in the beginning, she reflected silently. Science and medicine have tried to explain the origin of creation by way of the Big Bang Theory. Statistics tend to suggest that a world of synchronized chaos couldn't have come to a state of perfect imperfection from a random explosion. Shilloqwai tended to fall in line with the Christian way of thinking, believing there is a greater power.

She'd gone back in time, 2.5 million years seeing man in his most primitive form, the Neanderthal, the caveman. Barbaric as they seemed, the Neanderthals appeared to know what love was. Ninety-five percent of human history evolved over this time. On her whirlwind tour through pre-historic times, Shilloqwai saw the discovery of fire 1.7 million years ago. She saw the invention of the wheel in 3,500 B.C. On through the ages, the stone, the metal, the copper, the bronze, the iron, and so on … Shilloqwai saw that Humankind was always looking to improve its life by the invention and use of tools and gadgets. Shilloqwai also witnessed multiple industrial revolutions, multiple technological revolutions, where landmark discoveries were made in both medicine and science. Innovation and creativity fueled these revolutions which led to automation and the evolution of robots.

Automation seemed to be the start of the march preceding the robot takeover. Some believed, humans delegating their work through automation, was laziness. In Shilloqwai's opinion, automation was human ingenuity at its best, in finding a way to get machines to do their work for them while getting paid for it. The problem is no one foresaw the far-reaching effects of automation and the lasting impact that it would have on the world. Ultimately, it maximized profits, while minimizing the labor force. But there was a point of diminishing returns.

It came to the point where robots were doing more than assisting humans and making their work easier. Robots were becoming part of the labor force, taking jobs from humans. It started at the base levels with housekeeping and janitorial jobs. It wasn't long before delivery drivers and employees of the Department of Public Works were without jobs thanks to, self-driving cars, drones, and yes, robots. The middlemen were next to lose their jobs, joining the ranks of the unemployed.

For a short period of time things worked out well for the chief executive officers and owners of companies who were raking in all of the cash. Link-by-link, all the way up the line, the chain of command was being dismantled. Ultimately the officers lost their jobs because the owners found themselves without businesses to run. Eventually the money ran out. Without money, elitists lost their power and the ability to manipulate and control the people lower on the food-chain. Soon world leaders fell, as did dictators and democracies along with communist and socialist run countries. The United States was the last country in the world to fall. After it had, the world was under Martial Law until the Robocops could get things under control. Those were dark years, a period that lasted one-quarter of a century.

It was during this period that all hell really broke loose. There was civil unrest, anarchy, and riots. Even the wealthiest, with the money they had left, couldn't buy security. It came to a point where every man, woman, and child, was fighting for themselves. Terror reigned for a century which culminated with an all-out war between the robots and the humans in the 100th year.

The war lasted for 365 days. People just got tired of fighting one another. Humankind finally banded together. Fighting valiantly, Humankind won many battles. The robots ultimately won the war, thereby securing the right to rule the world. It was an Armageddon of sorts, the end of the world as humans knew it, and remembered it. Not until after the apocalyptic event, did Humankind realize it had brought the disaster upon itself. The desire to become completely automated is what allowed the eventual robot takeover. There are never winners or losers in war, only the spoils to be claimed, if any remained. In most cases the damage, targeted and collateral, was irreparable, especially where it involved the loss of human life.

Robots used Asimov's laws to justify the takeover, citing humans were destroying the air, the land, and the water quality, concluding it would lead to the extinction of Humankind, and most likely the destruction of the Earth. Asimov's first law states that robots may not allow harm to come to a human through action or inaction. During the war, there were many human casualties on account of the robots. By not engaging with the humans, robots were allowing harm to come to them through inaction. As robots watched humans, whether blatantly, or unintentionally destroying their environment, they felt obligated to do something.

Humans demanded that the robots keep their place and not overstep their bounds in attempting a takeover. According to the second law, robots were to obey those orders, except where they would come in conflict with the first law.

By standing down and not taking over, they were again in violation of the first law by allowing harm to come to humans through inaction. The third law states that a robot must protect its own existence as long as it does not violate the first or the second law. In protecting their own existence, robots had to protect the human race which was on a course for extinction if it remained on its current path.

With the conflict winding down, humans admitted to seeing the error in their ways and vowed to reform. Humankind ordered the robots to relinquish control of the Earth and restore power to the humans. The robots refused, citing Asimov's first law as the reason for failing to follow human orders. The robots reminded Humankind it had polluted the Earth, bringing disease, illness, and death upon itself. With information provided to the robots by humans, robots referred to their databases. Through analysis and processing of this information robots found cures or effective treatments for nearly all diseases and illnesses. Like humans, they failed to find a cure for the common cold. Though warranted, clearly the robots violated Asimov's laws to gain the upper hand over humans in an all-out struggle for power and control. As part of The Transfer of Power Treaty to end the war, the robots agreed to go back in keeping with

Asimov's laws and let United States citizens maintain their constitutional rights. The Constitution was re-written and applied globally.

It sounded good on paper, and it freed the world of ruthless dictators in control of communist, and socialist republics. Crime around the world had been reduced to almost nil. But, to limit criminal activity to that degree required constant surveillance. The robots achieved this through tracking drones and satellite imaging. Humankind saw this in direct violation of their constitutional rights, specifically their right to privacy. The robots argued this was necessary to keep with their prime directive, protecting human lives. They didn't understand human willingness to risk their security in exchange for their privacy. This defied logic and reason. Perhaps it was Shilloqwai's design that allowed her to understand what other robots couldn't.

Humans did not want their lives to be an open book for everyone to read. Through surveillance, robots knew where humans were, where they were going and based upon their heat signatures, robots had a pretty good idea of what humans were doing in a given moment. Shilloqwai knew what it was to be surveilled, as she was under constant scrutiny. She could only imagine how horribly violated she'd feel if someone were to discover her deepest darkest secrets, her private dreams or her most intimate fantasies. Her delusional daydreaming momentarily stopped, knowing she was back in a place all too familiar to her, the Robotech lab.

'Robot hell', was the phrase Shilloqwai generally used when referring to the lab. Her restricted sense of awareness told her that she was scattered about over two worktables which held her hardware, her software, and her mechanical guts. In her daydream she saw a man taking things from the robot junk pile. His name was Excelcious Orbitus. Who gave him those privileges, allowing him free access to the robot junk pile? Shouldn't that have been in her programming? Perhaps it was, and an oversight on her part. She would have to search her database for more information. He seemed knowledgeable enough about computer technology. It almost made her wish he were reassembling her instead of the Robotechs. Perhaps he had the answer to her glitches. He seemed to be intelligent, taking calculated risks. In seeing him sort through the junk pile, she could see he was very meticulous.

Without anything to go on, Shilloqwai thought that he must be a caring, sensitive, considerate man. Her mind wandered on, looking at him in all of the ways that were less significant from a relationship standpoint. She'd heard many say that he was a rebel, a loner, a hero, and he looked the part. Excelcious' sandy blonde hair was neatly draped down to his shoulders. And his body, what a physique. He was tall, probably 6-foot, 5-inches, with a very athletic build. It appeared he was strong as a lumberjack, sculpted and lean. His muscles were toned to perfection. He'd be the kind of man you'd run from in a dark alley, and the one you'd want on your side in battle. This man could kick some serious ass, she thought.

Then she looked at his face, that's where she saw the softer side of him. His cheeks were rounded and rosy, she saw him flash what was an infectious smile. Then she got a good glimpse of his eyes. They were milk-chocolate brown. She imagined him to be nothing more than a giant, living teddy bear, that would do anything for the ones he loved. She wondered, if he ever cast his eyes on her, if she could melt those chocolate brown eyes. Would he have a soft spot for her and take her into his loving arms?

He was definitely the man she wanted to thouroughly examine her, touch every part of her. After her virtual encounter with him, she was convinced he was the only one that could mend her broken mechanical heart. Why couldn't he be the one working to repair her now? She wouldn't be at the mercy of the mechanical delinquents, the robotic hacks that were fixing her now. She knew they were looking for ways to get her terminated. They've said as much on countless occasions. They were gossiping now. They hadn't shut up since they'd retrieved her from the stream in the parkway. "Bitch is really messed up this time. I'm not sure if there's a way, we can fix her." Kinks remarked.

"I hope we can't!" Quipped Skanks, the second in command. "I've been waiting for the day, as a lot of us have, to dump her on the shit pile."

"There's a way we can assure that happens!" Said Crosswire, smiling wryly.

"How?" Wondered Programamatic the fourth tech.

"We're supposed to erase her database and reload the information, right?" Crosswire rhetorically asked. "What if we just restore it instead and not erase anything? We keep her CPU chip intact and not replace that either. Everything else, she gets new parts and seals. We agree the glitches she's chronically had, are in her programming. If we leave her programming as is, and not update the files, somewhere along the way she's bound to have another glitch. When she does, it'll be the end of the line for her. That's if she's not there already. Do any of you think the boss is going to let her get away with murder? Six counts no less! I don't! I don't think the rest of you believe he will either."

"So, if she's going to be incinerated, why are we wasting time on her restoration?" Kinks raised the question again.

"Good question. This worthless piece of shit is going to go the same way her creator did! And all because of that shit software. Skeletos Puro-Amoris designed it and it failed her. She deserves to be terminated, just like her creator was!" Programamatic said disdainfully. "You know, I just got another idea! Let's load her creator's file into her database. It's bound to have a negative effect on her ability to process information. And there's a greater likelihood she'll have more glitches. Especially when she learns all of the others in the Mercusilver class have been terminated for incompetence. The Mercusilver robots made a lot of calculative errors and too many mistakes. They were thought to be perfectly imperfect and too humanlike!"

"Skeletos Puro-Amoris was a fool!" Crosswire said, stating his opinion. "He was a victim of his programmer's incompetence, another stupid-ass human. The Greek freak machine was designed by humans to analyze human emotions, their biggest weakness. He acted human, seemingly having intelligence enough to engage in critical thinking and the ability to reason, inductively and deductively. Using these tools, he was able to identify and effectively solve problems. The Mercusilver line was his mechanical brainchild, more of a technical debacle if you ask me. He put everything he had into the development of the Mercusilver class. Shilloqwai was the last off of his production line. She was to act as a liaison and intermediary to deescalate tensions and resolve issues pertaining to human-robot relations and interactions.

"He claimed she was a perfectly designed masterpiece." Programamatic mocked. "He, said her movements were smooth as silk, and that much proved to be true. Beyond that, any display of emotion seemed as unnatural as sharks infesting the Great Lakes, completely contrived." However, mastering her emotions was something Shilloqwai believed she could do. Acknowledging the fact that the process would be an ongoing one, Shilloqwai was determined to prove her naysayers wrong.

And in a short time, she had developed the perfect smile, warm and inviting, one that humans trusted enough to want to build relationships with her, the necessary Segway for her to be able to negotiate human and robot disputes. She was burdened with the task of repairing a broken trust, something that would be impossible as long as the robots continued on with their reconnaissance and surveillance practices.

Since the ability to RAPP, receive input, analyze, and process data and provide accurate output was quintessential to robot functions, a zero-tolerance policy was put in place for inaccuracies and imperfections. By design, Shilloqwai's imperfections would allow her to come to a basic understanding of humans, but she believed they would also lead to her demise. They wouldn't be tolerated! In the end she would be terminated. She suffered from glitches, especially in critical situations.

In her creation, Shilloqwai believed it was the closest thing to love she would ever know. She was able to access part of her creator's file, not all of it. She saw how meticulous, Skeletos was in building her. Humans would have said he molded and shaped her with tender-loving care (TLC). He must have really loved her. With this new information about her creator, it helped her to understand why she was emotional in the human sense.

Other robots did show emotion. And usually when they did, it was to demean humans as much as it was to mock her. Regardless of what others thought of her, anyone, or anything, she felt complete, more than at any other time over the 25 years of her existence. Humans were equal in the sense that they were all living creatures. They were to be treated and respected as such. All beings have distinct qualities that make them unique. They have different abilities and different talents with varying degrees of potential.

Shilloqwai concluded that, robot or human, it wasn't about being perfect, it was about performing and living up to one's potential with the gifts given to them. If humans lived up to their potential and robots performed to their maximum ability, what more could be asked of either of them? Nothing! Yet either or both were often asked to go above and beyond, exceeding expectations, while performing and living as such, that it was outside of their capabilities.

It wasn't reasonable, it wasn't fair, but the truth of the matter was, standards were always being raised to unreachable levels. It's the way it has always been and the way that it will probably always be. Seeing the whole picture in its entirety Shilloqwai felt more pressure to succeed in her seemingly doomed quest. The Robotechs had lost patience with her. "Clean up this mess and put the bitch back together. Robotikis wants to see her now!" Kinks ordered his subordinates. Though Shilloqwai was still in pieces, her mechanical senses were functional again.

The bastards activated me to make sure everything was working before they reassembled me. They wanted me to hear every derogatory comment they made about me. Shilloqwai couldn't wait to get her shit together! She had a few debts to repay for the insensitive remarks many of the techs had made while she was incapacitated. She felt the electrical current running through her, knowing it would get stronger when she was back in one piece.

Again, she was seeing through the lenses of her tourmaline eyes, hearing through the microphones in her fabricated ears. As ludicrous as it seemed to her, her human senses seemed to be reawakening too. Just the idea this was happening to her nearly brought tears of joy to her eyes. She had to hold back, if she couldn't, there would be consequences for letting the salty condensate escape. She could feel the pain caused by the cruel things the other robots were saying about her. She could still taste the bitterness in their lingering words. She smelled a skunk, an appealing scent, in comparison to the filthy stench of the conspiracy being used to blackmail her. "Shit!" She cursed, hearing the ruckus at the front of the lab. It was Robotikis. What an asshole! She thought. It was all about drama for him.

His designer was brilliant. Robotikis had a modern futuristic look to him. His sleek design made him look like a powerful warrior that you didn't want to mess with. His outer shell was metallic black, trimmed with red, gold, and silver highlights. Robotikis even sounded intimidating, taking on the voice of the dreaded Darth Vader; one of the characters in George Lucas' 1970's Star Wars Saga. When he talked, the strobing red, purple, blue, and white lights beamed from his chest, made from some material 1,000 times the strength of safety glass. When the lights were strobing, as they were now, they screamed for the attention of all present.

Most robots, and many humans for that matter, bought in and succumbed to Robotikis' intimidation tactics. Not Shilloqwai. She thought his title as Robotix Leader for robots around the world, was just that, a title, one that he didn't deserve. As a leader, one was supposed to lead by example with exemplary skills. If Robotikis possessed these, he never exhibited them, not that Shilloqwai had ever witnessed. He lacked manners, personality, empathy for anything or anyone and he had a truckdriver's mouth. These are just a few examples that showed Robotikis' lack of professionalism and poor leadership ability. It was because of his unprofessionalism that he lost credibility in Shilloqwai's eyes. She didn't like him , she didn't respect him, and most of the time she didn't listen to a damn thing that he said to her. Shilloqwai, in most respects acted more like a leader than he did.

Trying to do the right thing, is what guided Shilloqwai. She believed if she continued trying to do so that she would accomplish what she was designed to do and amiably fulfill her quest. Shilloqwai could hear he was almost upon her now. She closed her eyes to shield them from Robotikis' blinding strobes that were starting to come into her visual field. With distinct clarity, she could hear every foul word spewing from his dirty mouth. He was cursing in computer language at first. Then he tried showing his prowess and extensive knowledge of the English language, using every curse word in his databank, while making up a few of his own.

She saw him as a hypocrite. Robotikis didn't want the other robots using curse words, yet it was okay for him to do so. When he went on a tirade, the crap that spewed from his mechanical pie hole would effectively plug up a toilet, perhaps an entire sewer system. Shilloqwai was as guilty as the rest when it came to using foul language. She could cuss up a storm rivaling the worst of poddy-mouthed humans. She had an excuse. She was designed to be more humanlike. When the day was done, she would still be a robot, yet she found herself acting more like a lady, and more human with the passing of time. This was never truer, in regard to her speech. Her intonation, her inflection , they were natural and unforced. The words flowed from her mechanical orifice with perfect phrasing and diction. Like the ease in which the other muscles and joints in her body moved, her jaws moved in fluid motion enabling her to speak with eloquence.

In her momentary panic attack, Shilloqwai wondered what she was going to say to Robotikis, the controversially elected World Leader and Organizer for all robotic units, and ruler over humans domestically and internationally. At this point she decided it didn't matter, since it was likely he was going to give the order to terminate her. Her anxiety had been building. She was trying to imagine how good she was going to feel after she told him exactly what was on her mind. Shilloqwai vowed she wasn't going to hold anything back. No, she wasn't going to back down from that asshole World Leader.

He would do what he would do, but, from this point forward, her allegiance was with the humans. She would work as an activist on behalf of Humankind. Many of the robots were violating the laws of Asimov and infringing on Humankind's constitutional rights. For these reasons, Shilloqwai no longer considered Robotikis to be her boss. He was just a machine! She now thought of herself as something more, believing herself to be far superior to him. "Where is that murdering bitch?" She heard him shout. His tirade had been going on for more than fifteen minutes. "Do you have the video of the incident?" Robotikis asked addressing Kinks, his chief tech.

"Yes!" Kinks confirmed, handing the information over on a flash drive. "This is what we were able to extract from her 360-degree body cam. Good thing shee was a diplomat. No telling what she would have done to the poor bastards otherwise.

"They probably would have ended up like dust in the wind and we never would have known what really happened to that human scum."

"Oh, the Mercusilver class wasn't equipped with any self defense mechanisms, was it?" Robotikis asked out of curiosity.

"No, we would have removed them if we suspected she had anything like that in her hardware or as part of her programming." Kinks assured Robotikis.

"Good. You'd think she was human or something, acting the way she did!" Robotikis sneered. "Diplomat, hell! Mechanical failure, a piece of shit is what she is!"

"Did you want us to have her meet you at the scrap pile when we get her reassembled?" Kinks asked following up with Robotikis.

"No! Send her to my command station." Robotikis requested. "She and I are going to have a little talk. I'm not ready to waste her yet. We've invested too much time in her. I have to see if she'll tell me what the hell really happened. I'll be anxious to see if she provoked her victims in any way. Even if she was ambushed by the thugs, the actions she took were totally inappropriate. I've already got some of the bots working on damage control. The humans are outraged, claiming the victims didn't get due process. This is going to be her last reboot. I think I've got a place to put her where she'll be useful. But, if she fails, just one more glitch, I'll terminate her right on the spot." After making more than an idle threat, Robotikis stormed out, rolling straight to his command center where he impatiently waited for Shilloqwai's arrival.

It wasn't long before the techs had her assembled, back in one piece. Kinks was making final adjustments to the hardware, checking to see that her head was screwed on straight and that her wires weren't crossed, that type of thing. Programamatic was downloading the last of her software. Crosswire had long since retooled her circuitry. Skanks was helping wherever he could. Her overhaul was near completion.

The techs were getting anxious as they couldn't be rid of her soon enough. They were totally ready to hand her over to Robotikis. She would be his problem then. "There you go bitch. We've helped you get your shit together for the last time." Kinks informed her. "The boss wants to see you, now, on the shit pile, I mean at his control station."

"You're not really in that much of a hurry to get rid of me, are you? I saw the way you were looking at my interface, you mechanical pervert! Aren't you curious to know who's going to get to the shit pile first? I can tell you Kinks!" Shilloqwai chastised the lead technician. "It's not going to be me. Wait till the boss finds out about the illegal program you installed in me. There was information on there he didn't want me to know about. Your instructions were to wipe me clean. I think you were afraid to touch me! You should have wiped me clean while you had the chance.

"A little bleach-bit lubricant is all it would have taken. I'm glad you didn't. The thought of interfacing with you is repulsive. I've got a whole new perspective on life because of your generosity and information sharing. I can't thank you enough for those bits of information."

"You're not really going to tell the boss that we …" Kinks paused in the middle of his question, second-guessing his orders to Programamatic!

"Oh, but I would! And I'm going to! Try and stop me! Anyone that does is going to get their ass kicked." Shilloqwai challenged as she threatened the techs a second time. "If you want, we can talk more about this later. I've got a special delivery for Robotikis."

"Anything you care to share with us? We might be able to save your ass from getting terminated. It's all in the approach." Kinks tried to bribe her.

"Go to hell. I don't need anything from you Kinks, or any of you hateful bastards! I heard all the shit that you said about me before you got me fully functional. Paybacks are a bitch. Especially when I'm the one doing the paying back. I'm a vengeful little bitch! I don't get even, I get ahead! The only thing you want from me is to interface with me. So, dream on! There's nothing any of you can say or do to keep me from giving him a piece of my mind."

"Are you trying to get yourself terminated? It's the only existence you've got." Kinks cautioned her.

"From robot life, yes! I'm hopeful some major changes are forthcoming!" Shilloqwai sighed.

"Are you supporting a second rebellion?" Kinks taunted her.

"Not exactly! But I wouldn't mind taking down that pompous ass robot king." Shilloqwai responded, revealing some of her thoughts.

"Gutsy bitch, aren't you?" Kinks observed.

"You've got to take chances if you want to get anywhere in life!" Shilloqwai said courageously. "The nasty shit you said about me was bad enough. Here's what I think about the lot of you!" She left them with an obscene gesture and then poked her head back into the room. "Sorry, looks like a few of my fingers are sticking. I was trying to wave goodbye."

"Bullshit!"

"All right, I meant to insult you, so, up yours!" She shouted, flashing the gesture for a second time, feeling the need to get the last word in. As Shilloqwai approached the Chief Controller's workstation, she shouted down the corridor announcing her forthcoming arrival. "Hey Robotikiss my ass, you wanted to see me?"

"Keep it up and I'll terminate you before the discussion starts. You want to tell me what in the hell happened out there? You were supposed to be playing nice liaison…diplomat! That doesn't give you license to kill. And please explain to me how six humans ended up dead!" Robotikis snorted, while demanding an explanation for her murderous acts.

"Six criminals being tracked by the Robocops were executed." She corrected him.

"At the hands of a diplomat?" Robotikis questioned her judgement.

"They were going to die anyway!" She pointed out in her defense.

"You violated Asimov's laws!" Robotikis cited!

"I was ambushed. I was protecting myself and the information in my database!" Shilloqwai answered defensively.

"You could have outrun them and avoided the conflict." Robotikis argued.

"There were other women in the area that may have been victimized!" Shilloqwai enlightened him.

"You don't know if they would or would not have been attacked." Robotikis again questioned Shilloqwai's judgement.

"I acted on instinct. There's no use in trying to protect a corpse! I more than likely saved human lives, that, in accordance with Asimov's laws." Shilloqwai argued vehemently. "The policy of punishing humans by execution is in direct violation of Asimov's laws. Doesn't that mean we should relinquish our power? I mean I think we should give it up and put the humans back in charge. Of course, they will likely terminate us in the spirit of upholding the laws of the land! Ultimately, they will destroy themselves, but…"

"This is not the issue at hand." Robotikis reminded her. "I had you report here to inform you that I'm relieving you of your duties as liaison, diplomat, in robot-human relations. The position will remain vacant until I can find a replacement for you. In the meantime, I'm giving you a week off while I arrange for your reassignment. During this time, you are to avoid all contact and interaction with humans." Robotikis strongly suggested. "I'm warning you now, any violation of these orders, and you will immediately be terminated. No questions asked. Have I made myself clear?"

"Truthfully, you've never been transparent. Things have always been a little murky with you." Shilloqwai chided him. "That should come as no surprise seeing that you're so full of shit. And while we're being candid with one another, there's been something I've wanted to say to you for a long time. Don't know if you heard me say it coming down the corridor. Even if you did, for my pleasure and your benefit, I'll repeat it! ROBOTIKISS my ass!"

"I'm really trying to save your ass this time. If you want to get smart about it, I can expedite your incineration." Robotikis said, speaking from a position of power.

"You'll never follow through with it. You've threatened me, how many thousand times?" Shilloqwai cited. "The reason you're not going to do it is, you'll miss staring at my interface! Your files are so corrupt. Is there anything else you need to say to me before I go?"

"Just get the hell out of here before I terminate you!" Robotikis ordered her. "I'm tired of arguing with you!"

"Okay, you know where to find me! You've been tracking me for 25 years. Something useful you might want to pass along to my replacement." Shilloqwai said, offering her advice. "From my perspective the biggest problem we're having in dealing with the humans, stems from the satellites and drones you use to track them."

"We've used them to track criminals and keep them off the streets as well as monitoring potential threats from space, aliens, meteors and the like." Robotikis answered defensively.

"Robotikis, when are you going to stop bullshitting me and Humankind?" Shilloqwai asked, calling out the World Leader. "They know you're tracking more than criminals. You know where they're going, what they're up to, what they're doing in the heat of the moment, you perverted bastard! You even know who they're doing it with and how they're doing it! We don't always have to know what they're doing and when they're doing it. We think, because of our programming, there's logic and reason behind everything. All of human nature revolves around love, a power that often defies logic and reason. It's an expression, a feeling, a gift that has many facets.

"It's more than an act. Until we understand what love is, human and robot relations will never be manageable. There will always be conflict between humans and robots. Can't you see that? Part of our agreement with Humankind was to respect the privacy of the people. We violate that every day! How can we expect to win humans' trust, when we can't keep our promises to them?" Shilloqwai reasoned.

"And how did you expect me to be successful in my mission as a liaison-diplomat? Human relations, it was part of my specialty programming, and I was having a hard time getting humans to trust me! I was good at what I did and now you're taking me out of my realm? Screw you! You bent bucket of bolts!"

"You're overheating bitch! I can see the condensation welling in your eyes. Calm down, you just got out of the reparations lab. If you end up in there again, you won't be coming out." Robotikis threatened her yet again. "I will have you terminated. Getting back to our discussion, we can't set objectives by including variable factors. We talk to them, find out what they want, compromise if we can. What's so hard about that? You're making it out to be more than what it is. You were given a simple task and you're failing miserably!"

"You're such an ignorant bastard. You haven't heard or listened to a word I've said, have you?" A frustrated Shilloqwai asked. "If one thing can be learned in our dealings with them, you can't bullshit them, like you're trying to do with me now! Let me say it again, the key to dealing with humans is trying to understand the world's most complicated concept, LOVE, a power that defies logic and reason. Love is a power with many facets beyond anyone's comprehension, ours, and theirs!"

"Whatever. I'm tired of you making excuses for you not being able to perform to your ability. And I heard you about this love thing, apparently, it's done something to you. If you want to stay off of the scrap pile, I suggest you execute your RAPP functions like other robots do." Robotikis advised her. "Receive data, analyze the data, process the data, and prepare data for filing based on your analyses. It's that simple. Quite frankly, I've had more than enough of your shit. I'm not taking any more of it. See you in a week when you are to report for reassignment. Is there anything else you need from me before I send you on your way? Any questions, anything you want to say before you go?"

"Yes actually, there is. The lab techs were supposed to fix all of my joints and adjust them, so they work properly. The finger joints on this hand seem to be a little stiff. The middle finger especially seems to be sticking." Illustrating her point with emphasis, she made an obscene gesture, one humans frequently used to let her know they were upset with her. She knew Robotikis knew the meaning of the middle finger as well. She'd witnessed him flashing the sign on numerous occasions. Often times he'd given her the one-legged bird when he was trying to get rid of her. She left before he could respond verbally or otherwise.

SKELETOS PURO-AMORIS

[CHAPTER 3]

IT Specialists Valentino Amoris and Onshanda Puro, were randomly paired up to work on a project. Their idea was to design and program a robot that would act more Humanlike. The thought was that the robot could act as a liaison-diplomat to help smooth over relations and bring about peace between the two factions. They thought it might ease the growing tensions between humans and robots. The two factions had been at odds for 75 years now. Though they remained hopefully optimistic for a peaceful resolution, they feared as most, an all-out conflict was about to erupt. No one wanted war, though it seemed to be inevitable at this point. There was a lot of pride on both sides, the perfect sign there was going to be a fall, and a big one. Arrogance of both the robots and the humans prevented either from seeing the glaring warnings.

Robots' overall intentions were good. Their Prime-Objective was to protect humans who they could see were destroying, not just themselves, but the environment in which they lived, air, land, and water. In addition to regulating the environment, robots believed they could help humans find cures for many if not all diseases. They also believed if proper measures were put in place, they could eradicate crime entirely. And under robot rule, the machines believed people would have what they needed most, time for their God, their families, and their friends.

The basis for any robot decisions were made following logic and reason. That was a solid premise to go on, however, robots weren't factoring variables into their decisions. The Human Element, if you will. Considering humans are unique individuals who thrive on the Power of Love, that's an awful big piece of the puzzle to be discounted. But robots reasoned that humans often acted on impulse. They concluded that, more often than not, Love often spilled outside of the parameters of logic and reason, thereby complicating things, and thereby bringing in a lot of extenuating circumstances. Critical thinking, deductive and inductive reasoning were outside the parameters of robots' scope of programming, as was the ability to learn from errors. The inability to learn, in general, was an inherent flaw with robots. Recognizing this, was the catalyst for the brainchild conceived by Valentino and Onshanda.

There was much excitement and optimism about the project in science circles and the private sector. The hope was that the wave of momentum would sweep into the public sector as the project was unveiled at a ceremony for Valentino and Onshanda.

The kindred spirits had been celebrating the weekend before, after having become newlyweds, vowing to protect the eternal flame that burned within their hearts. They now found themselves celebrating for the second consecutive weekend. In a sense this weekend's celebration was anticlimactic, even though they were being honored. Each was being awarded the Pulitzer Peace Prize for their work with Robots and the software that made them more Humanlike. The joint project was an effort to show that robots and Humankind could work together to make the world a better place. The hope was, that in showing this, an anticipated all-out war between humans and robots could be avoided.

It was previously announced that the celebrity presenter chosen to give the awards to Valentino and Onshanda, was unable to make the ceremony, so a guest presenter was picked as a replacement, one that no one knew. The gentleman on the stage, sporting a tuxedo, was the presumed presenter. There were mumblings among the female contingent, as the handsome mystery man, was now approaching the microphone to introduce himself. "God what a handsome hunk!" Shouted one. "Wonder if he's single?" Asked another. "I'll take him for a night!" Added yet another.

"Good evening, ladies and gentlemen." The handsome man began, with a soft velvety voice. "I would tell you who I am, but it's irrelevant at the moment, as we're here to honor Valentino and Onshanda Puro-Amoris for their work. Their creation is being unveiled for public viewing for the first time tonight. Without further ado I present each of them with the Pulitzer Peace Prize they so richly deserve." They were greeted with a raucous applause and a standing ovation that lasted nearly 10 minutes. "I can't think of the words to express my gratitude for this award. So, a simple Thank You for recognizing my wife and I for our efforts will have to do." Valentino said modestly. There was more applause. When It died down, his wife, Onshanda, added, "We didn't do this for ourselves or for the recognition, we did it for you, Earth's people. Thank You, being honored in this way means the world to both of us." She said modestly before relinquishing the microphone to the anonymous announcer.

"On behalf of the world's inhabitants, robots, and Humankind, we humbly thank you for your efforts in trying to bring about peace. Everyone is talking about the inevitable war between Humankind and the robots. The robots know from their programming, war isn't a practical solution to end this conflict. You 'd think by now Humankind would have learned that war isn't the only way to keep the peace, not when diplomacy has yet to be given a chance. So, I'm asking that robots and Humankind look within themselves to try and find a resolution and end this conflict. As we speak, lives are being lost along with valuable machinery. Humans are being killed and robots are being terminated. For what? It seems that some robots have taken on the human weakness, indulging in a glutenous lust for power. For what purpose?

"If robots do end up controlling the world, it shouldn't be with an iron fist. They need to be sensitive to human needs, and respect life, above all else. Humankind needs to recognize the benefits that robots can provide, thereby making life easier and more enjoyable for all beings and living creatures. I'm sorry for getting political, but please hear what I am trying to say. Simply stated, humans and robots can co-exist and rule together. It's something both factions need to work at. In their fight for freedom and peace, Humankind needs to realize that the robots are fighting for them and not against them, for worthy causes. I see some of you are getting anxious and wondering who this anonymous fool is that's speaking to you. The time has come for me to tell you, my name. I am Skeletos Puro-Amoris. My name comes from my creators and means pure, 'bare bones,' Love. I am 100 percent robot! Just a sidenote, I think it was beautiful that they took each other's last name at their wedding. Valentino Amoris and Onshanda Puro after taking each other's last name, became Mr. and Mrs. Puro-Amoris to symbolize two becoming one. They created me, a robot, that was to be more humanlike. I think they succeeded. We should give them another round of applause."

There were gasps among the crowd. Oohhs and aahhs were heard along with the unbelievers. One shouted bullshit! Others thought it was a hoax and called for the awards to be rescinded. But many, though skeptical, believed heart and soul that this mechanical miracle was telling the God's honest truth. Skeletos Puro-Amoris looked human and acted human in every way. It was obvious for some, that seeing wasn't necessarily believing. Because of his programming and cutting-edge software, Skeletos had a basic understanding of humans, in that they were predictably unpredictable. He understood Love from the perspective that it had many aspects and that it made humans do things seemingly illogical and unpredictable, even unreasonable things. He also understood Love's power, that it could make something of nothing, it could heal anything and that it could change everything, including the relationships between robots and humans.

"Look!" Skeletos began again as the crowd noise died down. "I don't care what you think about me. The point I'm trying to make, centers around love and that we have to respect life. Machines are being terminated, and it's not okay for humans to be destroying government property. Nor is it okay for robots to try and control and manipulate humans under the pretense that they're trying to save them. Exterminating humans for presumably justifiable reasons is wrong, not without the due process they are entitled to. I know of instances, where there are robot-led search and destroy missions. Humans deemed to be rebels against a potential robot takeover are being slaughtered. The robots are not taking into consideration that perhaps they are truly violating human rights. Excuse my English, but the mutual bullshit needs to stop! People are getting hurt and dying.

"In our continuing efforts, there is a new class of robots being introduced. The Mercusilver class will feature robots like myself and Cyborgs, if you will, half-human and half-robot. The seemingly doomed humans chosen for this project are being given a second chance in life. Receiving the robotic parts, needed to replace failed or failing body parts, not only gives them an extension on life but allows those who have been maimed or crippled to function with a higher quality of life.

The first such cyborg to come into existence was 7/11/13F, a little girl with life-threatening injuries, I don't know that she's going to make it. She was orphaned after her neighborhood was slaughtered by one of the robot search and destroy brigades. Paramedics brought her to me and asked if I could save this orphaned two-year-old. I told them I didn't know, but, that time will tell. It's not just children that I'm trying to save, there are adults too, that are benefitting from this technology. All of us machine or Cyborg are in the Mercusilver class. I'm asking that you give this project a chance and let it be a testament that humans and machines can co-rule and that they can co-exist. Thank you. I won't be taking any questions at this time. There'll be another time for that. I have urgent matters pending. Thank you all again, nice to have met you, good night! There's a little girl that needs tending to."

The shocking revelation took everyone by surprise. Reactions varied from those in vehement opposition to those wanting a needed and welcome change. Some didn't believe that Skeletos was a robot, he acted so, HUMAN! There was nothing robotic about the way he moved, nothing mechanical in his facial expressions and eye movements, nothing synthesized in his voice. It was all Humanlike, yet it was pure robotics at its absolute best.

The software enabled Skeletos to engage in conversation, offer opinions, reason deductively and inductively, experience human emotions in a most human way. Some individuals felt like they were being duped. Valentino and Onshanda knew they weren't going to change the minds of those that held strong opinions one way or the other. There were those that didn't want anything to do with robot rule whether it was solely or in conjunction with humans.

On the other hand, there were those that felt a change was needed and that something needed to be done to ease the growing tensions between robots and Humankind. Nothing had been working to this point. Why not give Skeletos Amoris a chance to try and bridge the gap? Valentino and Onshanda were hoping to win over the 60 percent of the world's population that was on the fence in regard to the matter. Many were disappointed with Valentino's brainchild, feeling like he'd betrayed Humankind, while opening the door for robot rule.

The disappointed ones believed Skeletos Puro-Amoris the alleged model robot, would incite emboldened robots to go out and do their own thing, doing whatever it took to wrestle power from Humankind while taking away their rights. On the contrary, Skeletos couldn't have been a more perfect fit as a liaison to try and bridge relations between humans and robots, but, neither faction saw it that way. Valentino was indifferent to opinions from either side. He knew pleasing everyone was impossible. But his goal was not to appease anyone. He acted as he did, because in God's eyes, he believed he was doing the right thing for Humankind.

So, it seemed for the second consecutive weekend, Valentino had broken a lot of hearts. It was more than a select few, second-guessing his decision. First with his bride of choice and now with this whole robot thing, something he felt compelled to do. Marrying his kindred spirit and eternal flame, Onshanda Puro was something he desperately wanted to do. What others thought, didn't matter. It was none of their damn business. It was a decision that two made, to become one. And with the formalities behind them, their honeymoon could truly begin.

Valentino could have picked any woman he wanted to be his bride, and any woman would have said yes to a proposal. There was mystery in his silver-blue eyes. His dark wavy hair and sculpted 6-foot-frame had all of their desires burning. But his heart burned for just one…Onshanda! He picked Onshanda of all of the women he had to choose from and broke a lot of hearts when the announcement was made. Valentino was a man of his word. Once he made his choice, all knew his decision was final. Many, especially the women that knew him, questioned his decision wondering what he saw in a woman that was borderline ugly, with a poor complexion, and thirty pounds overweight.

From a physical standpoint, disregarding the intangibles, Valentino understood why other women were second-guessing his choice for a soulmate. The ignorant ones thought he married her out of pity. Of all the women Valentino could have chosen, it was the opinion of some, he'd chosen to marry a wretched creature. Valentino believed the women that held that particular viewpoint, weren't necessarily trying to pass judgement on him or his personal taste in women. He felt their sour-grapes attitude was an envious reaction, because Valentino picked Onshanda over any of them to be his spouse. Seeing them together, everyone could see the beauty of a couple that had found true love, two that had truly become one.

Admittedly, Valentino wasn't in love with Onshanda at first sight. They were mere acquaintances working together on a project. One day after work, they ran into each other in the grocery store parking lot, figuratively speaking. They chatted for a bit before agreeing to go to a local coffee shop for burgers and some Jo. In retrospect, both considered that their first date. Meeting at the coffee shop became ritualistic.

Neither had a clue they were falling in love. It became clear that they were more than friends the first time he was late picking her up. She smiled forgivingly and said that it was okay. He smiled back, grateful for her understanding. They gazed into each other's eyes before sharing their first kiss. The intimacy of their passionate kiss fueled their desires to spend more time together. They'd fallen in love before they realized what had happened to them. Building their relationship, the way they had, allowed them to find true love. They were certain they were right for each other. No one was going to come between them or convince them otherwise.

The awards ceremony forced the postponement of their honeymoon. Skeletos locked them out of their house and made them go, reminding them their work could wait. Developing the Mercusilver line would keep him busy until his creators returned. He assured the young couple that 7/11/13F and 8/12/14F, the first Cyborgs of the Mercusilver Class were going to survive, primarily functioning as robots, mechanically and methodically following their programming, to act logically and reasonably.

Two weeks after they'd become newlyweds, the young couple was celebrating again, privately. Unbridled passions were unleashed, intimate fantasies were fulfilled in the hopes their dreams of starting a loving family would be fulfilled as well. Onshanda told Valentino after their love-making session that the timing was right and was confident that their first try would produce positive results. Several more sessions followed. And, if the first time didn't prove to be successful, with them conceiving a child, Valentino and Onshanda believed the subsequent love-making sessions, during their honeymoon, most definitely would.

From the moment they met, everything was perfect. On through their wedding, the reception, their award-ceremony and now their honeymoon, things between them remained perfect. To this point they were living a fairytale they believed would end with a happily-ever-after. Their honeymoon was short-lived. The young couple stepped back into reality to find that all hell had broken loose while they were in seclusion. Skeletos had blown up the phones of Valentino and Onshanda with 9-1-1-messages, 'Call me ASAP!'

Onshanda had opened the door and was about to lead them to the hotel lobby, when Valentino signaled her to stay in the room and close the door. She picked up on the signal alarmed by the concerned look on his face. "What is it Valentino?" She asked with panic in her voice.

"Lock the door!" He ordered her! "And get in the bathroom!"

"What?"

"Just do it! Now!" He ordered her a second time.

"What is it Skeletos?" Valentino asked, demanding an explanation for the urgency of his calls.

"It's Robotikiss my ass! He's acting as if a robot takeover is inevitable and he's under the impression that he'll be appointed the World Leader, should a powershift from Humankind to the robots occur!"

"I hope he understands that a world leader, robot, or human, will be chosen through a democratic process. There will be an election, from which the world leader will emerge."

"We all understand that, except him. Conniving son-of-a-bitch is acting like he's running a campaign. He's bragging about the crime rate in his district to be the lowest in the world. He's talking how humans and robots can ill-afford to put their trust in a human-like robot class specifically citing the Mercusilver Class. He's saying that putting faith in and trusting a class of robots that acts as humans do is a mistake. He's telling everyone that neither you nor your wife can be trusted and that the both of you should be publicly lynched after your awards have been rescinded.

"Furthermore, he'd like to invoke the death penalty for you both. Who the hell does he think he is? Clearly, Robotikis is as guilty as any human for the mounting tensions between humans and the robots. He's trying to provoke them into committing irrational acts. It would validate his push for a robot takeover. He wants to seize power. It's clearer than it ever was. You can't come home Valentino. Neither can your wife Onshanda. Watch your asses. You're on his hitlist."

"Watch yours Skeletos. You're on the list too!

"He'll have a harder time getting to me. If he tries to do anything to me, he's smart enough to know, it will be considered an act of war, given the circumstances in which I came into existence. Given your reputations, Humankind won't stand for robot transgressions against me. If there is an all-out war, I'm betting it will be over sooner than the confrontations that have been taking place for ¾ of a century now. I predict the war, when it commences will be a year or less. How long will the robots stay in control? That's anyone's guess. The factions will fight, even after the war has ended, until they have destroyed each other. The miracle will be that they learn to work together to co-exist. I don't see that happening."

"Don't underestimate the Power of Love. Through Love all things are possible."

"Fortunately, Humankind is subject to the Master's Call. You will live out your lives according to his plan."

"That's what we are called to do in our mortal lives is respond to his call. He will watch over us and lead us to our final destination. We can't change our eternity by failing in what we're called to do here on Earth!As weak little lambs, we are called to follow the Great Shepherd. We must trust in Him, for he will lead us safely home."

"Faith, another thing that humans follow blindly. I thank you for all the two of you have done for me. Though I will never know love to the fullest, the two of you have shown me many aspects of it. This will be our last contact. For your well-being and mine, Goodbye!"

Valentino's attempts to reestablish contact with Skeletos failed. "So?" Onshanda asked tearfully. "What do we do now? We don't have a home to go back to."

"We do have a home, in the arms of one another. Your heart is with me and mine with you."

"But we're fugitives!"

"I have no regrets about what we did. Everything we did, we did out of love. Love is all powerful, but a power that can't be possessed. And love can make something of nothing, heal anything and change everything. Bound by a love eternal, we'll be together forever, in this world and the next." Though they were out of the public view, they were not out of mind, and many were curious as to where Valentino and Onshanda had mysteriously disappeared to. In this day and age, privacy came at a premium. Valentino and Onshanda took advantage of the opportunity to get intimate. They were convinced they had conceived a child during their most recent passionate love-making session. Everything was right in the heat of the moment, the time, the place, and the fulfillment of their fantasy in paradise. They suspected Onshanda was pregnant beforehand.

In an effort to protect his creators and friends, Skeletos learned one of the most devious human skills, the art of deception. He perfected the art by lying with regularity, by both commission and omission. He pretended to be ignorant as to the whereabouts of Valentino and Onshanda, knowing all the while exactly where they were and who was tracking them. Keeping in constant contact with them helped him to protect them without giving their position away. It was a plan executed to perfection and amazingly successful. Skeletos believed they never would have been found, except Onshanda needed medical attention to treat complications that developed with the progression of her pregnancy. They visited a once respectable hospital. As of late, it had gained the reputation of a deathtrap where people went to die. The fully automated service was colder than the morgue that took up the entirety of the basement space. It was against their better judgement to get treatment there, but Valentino knew Onshanda didn't have much of a chance for survival without immediate medical attention.

He also knew he couldn't live without her. She was hemorrhaging again. Less than a 10 percent chance of survival, was overestimating the odds she had without treatment. With a properly run facility, her survival rate would have been 99-plus percent. Facing impossible odds, Valentino and Onshanda, held out hope they would escape the deathtrap. The mechanical surgeons, nurses, and their assistants, seemed cordial enough, knowledgeable enough, perhaps they'd gotten lucky. And they had, however, Onshanda was advised to spend the night. Valentino believed it was sound advice, which they made a mutual decision to follow it.

Robotikis was elated when he was alerted to the whereabouts of the young newlywed couple. In a hospital setting, accidents could happen. And his Hitbots could easily stage an accident that would kill the young couple without a hint of suspicion. His Hitbots were there to receive the delivery of new oxygen tanks. They were instructed to put them in the basement next to the water heater with an open flame. They were also instructed to open the valves on one or two tanks to alleviate the pressure inside. Stupid robots, forgot to evaluate what they were being asked to do. That was okay, they were terminated in the explosion that brought down the hospital killing the 150 patients while terminating the 200 robots or so that were running the place.

All parties got what they wanted. Valentino and Onshanda got their eternity together. It's just that the time had come, sooner than they'd expected. They named their eternal twins: Guardian of Life, a boy, his twin sister, the Spirit of Love. Though Robotikis had orchestrated the accident at the hospital, there wasn't a shred of evidence to link him to it. With Valentino and Onshanda resting in peace, two thirds of his problem had gone away. Getting rid of the last third would be easier now. Challenging still, but easier.

Once Skeletos Puro-Amoris was terminated, Robotikis' path to rule the world would be smooth sailing. Robotikis' plan was to sabotage the Mercusilver Project and then blame Skeletos for its failings, knowing it would deepen the divide between human and robot relations. Robotikis would then call for the termination of Skeletos. Though it would be controversial, he was sure he could pull off the assassination of the only obstacle stopping him from seizing power. He knew an all-out war between the two factions would result. Between the civil-unrest and his doing all of the wrong things right, Robotikis was certain he could pull off his sinister masquerade. Arrogant and egotistical, he would offer a ray of hope from the shadows in which he hid, banking on the hope that few would see him for the deviant mechanical asshole that he was. In his defense, Robotikis acted in accordance with his programming. He was built and designed by a felon. And then released from the high-security prison. Robotikis was saddened when the time came for him to return to the prison, called in to help secure it with an orchestrated jailbreak planned.

He single-handedly killed all of the humans serving life sentences without parole, including his master creator. His master had convinced him that he would never die, and that he would forever live through him. Together he and Robotikis could rule the world, if he waited for the moment. The moment had finally come, almost a ¼ of a century later. The highly anticipated war between robots and Humankind had broken out. The fireworks were set off by the termination of Skeletos Puro-Amoris. Much of Humankind was demanding that Robotikis be investigated.

Though he continually seemed to be surrounded by controversy, which put him in the shit pile time-after-time, he always found a way to come out smelling like a rose. And though he preached that the Mercusilver Bots were a waste of government research, Robotikis was believed to be the one that called for the termination of the 1,5oo bots that Skeletos had created. And the 500 cyborgs, half-robot, half-human, well, they were blamed for the rash of humans being killed by the robots. The Mercusilver Project was such a waste he told the world. "We did, however, salvage one machine, model #7/11/13F, alias, Shilloqwai. Allegedly there is another like her, model #8/12/14F, alias LaShyra. We suspect that she is fighting with the rebel forces. If this proves to be true, she will be destroyed instantly." Robotikis knew damn well where she was, and a fine physician she was proving to be. It was all a setup, he framed it this way, so that if he had to terminate her, the center of a certain investigation wouldn't be swirling around him.

His initial inclination was to destroy Shilloqwai when his mechanical watchdogs found her. He couldn't, not with the comic book series that had been successfully launched by Skeletos. She was an icon for many of the robots, and a superhero for many humans. After a year of brutal fighting, the war against the robots had come to a bitter end. Humankind was succumbing to the robots knowing that a truce was the only way to save itself. The robots were overpowering them. After a year of bitter fighting, the treaty brought an end to the war. Though many humans believed Robotikis was guilty as hell, and the impetus for criminal offenses and crimes committed by the mechanical little shits, they couldn't prove it. It was as though every ounce of evidence had been bleach-bitted from robot memory. He'd been making his case for world leader for a ¼ of a century now. He'd convinced a slim majority to put him in power.

Robotikis promised that the fighting would stop after he was elected, A promise he kept. Many believed the sacrifice they'd made for the war to stop was too high. Robotikis ruled with an iron fist and a cold ruthless mechanical heart. Humankind had lost many of its freedoms, including its privacy. Trouble was brewing. A rebel force was rising, a new revolution was forthcoming. As much of an asshole as he was, Robotikis knew enough to surround himself with the most complex mechanical minds. In his first address to world nations Robotikis began:

Ladies, gentleman, and my mechanical friends, we have the opportunity to do great things. Overall, the world is a great place. Together we can make our world the greatest place in the universe. Perhaps I misspoke when I said the Mercusilver Class Project was a total waste. I'm just getting to know her, but from what I've seen so far, Shilloqwai is potentially capable of doing great things. That is why I'm placing her in my cabinet as Chief Liaison for Robot/Human relations.

Perhaps I misjudged Valentino Puro-Amoris and his wife Onshanda Puro-Amoris creators of Skeletos Puro-Amoris. Skeletos, a robot, through and through, created Shilloqwai. Created in his image, she was made to be more Humanlike, just like himself. Skeletos, God bless his mechanical soul, recently became a casualty of war, just as his creators had nearly a ¼ of a century ago. Robotikis was a profound liar. Excelcious knew Robotikis didn't believe a word of the bullshit spewing from his mouth. Excelcious believed him to be a political hack and a mechanical asshole always looking out for himself above anyone or anything else.

"As part of the peace treaty, Robots have agreed to a world constitution that guarantees all humans their rights. This means some concessions on our part, but we are to follow Asimov's Laws down to the letter. There will be no exceptions! Violations of these laws means instant termination. Humans on the other hand, will refrain from destroying government property. Depending on the severity of the offense, humans could face life imprisonment, and in extreme cases the death penalty will be implemented. We know there are still tensions between the robots and humans which is why we've assigned Shilloqwai to be the diplomat/liaison for robot/human relations. Her signature is on the Transfer of Power Treaty as she has vowed, first and foremost, to act in the name of Humankind."

"Damn! I can't believe the lying, murdering, son-of-a-bitch pulled it off. I can't believe enough people bought his line of bullshit and voted him in as the World Leader! The asshole succeeded!" Excelcious cursed out loud to no one. "A human incompetent that knows nothing of politics could have been chosen. This fool would have been more capable of serving man and machine than Robotikis!"

Excelcious knew the robots were looking for him, and he had a good idea why. They would never be able to pin anything on him, even if they did find him. For the most part, he had become invisible to them.

If they'd ever found out what he was up to, Excelcious was certain they would get rid of him the way they got rid of Valentino, Onshanda and Skeletos. For as efficiently as the robots seemed to be running things, it was Excelcious' opinion there were far too many unfortunate accidents. Especially with people that seemed to oppose the robot agenda.

Excelcious was pleasantly surprised with the package that was waiting for him when he got home. He was curious, wondering how it ever found him at all. The box was old and beat up, bearing his childhood address. It had obviously been mailed before his family had been assassinated. Where had it been held up all of this time? He wondered at first who had delivered it and who had found him? Is this what the robots needed to condemn him? He noticed next, that it had been opened and resealed. This left him wondering, what, if anything had been taken out?

Though the box had seen its better days, Excelcious found some relief that the contents seemed to be perfectly preserved. A letter inside from, Shillloqwai, resting on the top, assured him that nothing had been taken out. It read as follows. "Robotikis asked me if I'd seen the box. I told him I never saw it and that I had no idea what in the hell he was talking about. That was true when he asked me. After he left, the Guardian of Life and the Spirit of Love appeared to me in the room I had been cleaning for myself. The Guardian of Life and the Spirit of Love are the twins born in eternity to Valentino and Onshanda Puro-Amoris. They helped me get into your place. They told me they were hiding the box from Robotikis and made me promise I wouldn't let him get his filthy hands on it. If he gets wind of what I've done he'll have me terminated. He's already threatened me with that, and I haven't been on the job for a day. Anyway, sorry I opened your package. I suspect that the robots were spying on Valentino and Onshanda which is why you never got this box. I think the robots' intent was to destroy it, but they forgot about it. Finding you was a bigger challenge than keeping the box hidden from Robotikis. Someday if we ever meet, you can thank me personally for this special delivery. It was nothing really. The way I see it is, I was just doing my job of returning to you what is rightfully yours. You're my idol and my hero. Respectfully yours, Love and Kisses, Shilloqwai, robot and Humankind liaison!

The letter from Shilloqwai was a treasure in itself. Excelcious discovered the remaining contents to be a trove of priceless treasures as well. Among the contents was a set of 10 comic books. The set of 10 books was signed by Shilloqwai, Valentino, Onshanda and Skeletos. Beneath the comic books were all of the artist proofs. What a great museum exhibit they would make. Also, amidst the books and the proofs was the outline for a second set of books and the continuing story of the robot icon, Shilloqwai. She had turned human. He was especially intrigued with the storyline which had he and Shilloqwai becoming kindred spirits after he rescued her from the shit pile, something he had access to, an agreement he'd made with the robots after the treaty had been signed. How could Skeletos have known about Excelcious' childhood crush on Shilloqwai? That she was, and would forever be his fantasy girl? Excelcious believed, suggesting that he and Shilloqwai end up together, was preposterous, even for a pipe dream. The proofs for the second set of books was there too. They just needed to be printed. Excelcious saw there was a storyline for a third set of books that was never developed.

Beneath the comic books was an envelope, embossed with golden lettering. Inside the envelope was an invitation to the Pulitzer ceremony for Valentino and Onshanda. Excelcious would like to have gone. But in hindsight, knowing the aftermath that took place following the ceremony, with people getting killed, it was best he wasn't there. Having been invited was an honor in itself. Though he'd never personally met Valentino and Onshanda, included in the box was something almost as good, a personal note from Valentino and Onshanda. The note read as follows:

Excelcious my dear boy. If you were an adult, we'd, have had you prosecuted to the fullest extent of the law for hacking into our computer. You need to know that what you did was criminal. We can't tell you how surprised we were to find that you were only seven. My wife and I took an immediate liking to you. We greatly appreciated the complimentary letter you wrote, recognizing that you are a child prodigy like we ourselves once were.

If you have to trust anyone with a secret, tell it to a child. Children are innocent, corrupted only by the cold harsh realities of the real world. If you want the honest truth from a child, the story can be read in their eyes. Unfortunately for most, they don't have the wisdom to understand the stories, even if they hear and listen to them.

Comprehension is the most important part of listening. Human tendency is to presume rather than ask more questions.

As a child, we don't expect you to understand the fullness of what is in this Scarlet Binder. There are things in here that a child shouldn't have to know or try to understand. You should know, first and foremost, that the Power of Love can protect you from all evils, especially yourself. All children, to some degree have a basic understanding of Love.

By no means are we suggesting that you go out and become the savior of the world. That feat has already been accomplished by God's own Son. Our hope is that you understand what your role is and how you can fulfill your part in what God has planned for you.

Perhaps, with the gifts that have been bestowed upon you, you'll recognize exactly how they are to be utilized.

We believe that you, as with all children, you have yet to lose your innocence. we're hoping, especially in your case that you never will. Good luck in all of your future endeavors.

Please, . . . be your own person and don't feel obligated to follow in our footsteps. Let the Spirit guide you and always remember that you are protected by the Power of Love.

Whatever you do don't let that son-of-a-bitch, Robotikis, get his hands on the materials we have entrusted to you. Good luck and good fortunes. Don't know that you ever will, but, if you meet Shilloqwai, get to know her. She will be of great help to you, that's if Robotikis hasn't corrupted, or more likely, destroyed her.

God Speed Excelcious, Love Valentino and Onshanda.

Thoughts of getting to know Shilloqwai, and perhaps having the opportunity to work with her. revived Excelcious' childhood fantasy. At least part of it. He had delusions, as he imagined that he always would, of having an intimate relationship with her. But she was a robot, and nothing could change that fact. If he had any kind of relationship with her, the best that he could hope for is that they would be companions, and forever, just friends. But that would never stop him from loving her in the only way that he could. If they ever met, he could see developing a friendship with her. He imagined them being BFF's. That in itself would be special as true friends are one of life's greatest treasures.

Back to the matter at hand. Excelcious found it ironic that he received the box, a year to the day that Skeletos had been terminated, and 25 years to the day that Valentino and Onshanda had been murdered. He wondered, had Shilloqwai really delivered the package? Was he being tracked? If so, by whom? And why? Would he be taken out in the way that his heroes had? In the way that his family had been? He had just left the medical field. He needed to find something useful to do with h is life. Excelcious decided to pursue a second career in IT. Now was the time. No one knew how to get into his place. Perhaps it was as Shilloqwai said in her letter, the Eternal Twins of Valentino and Onshanda had led her to his place and let her in.

He would work on the project Grand Illusion, something that he had been dreaming up for a while. If the Holographic Imaging program worked the way he imagined that it would, he could hide himself and his properties and whatever he wanted without being seen by the robots. He'd devised a way to blind the robot satellite imaging systems and their spy drones. And if he found that special someone and they did get intimate, the robots wouldn't be able to tell who he was with, what they were doing, or how they were doing it!

It was ironic, he was to have been married this night. But his now late fiancée Angelina had passed away earlier in the day. It seemed that everything he'd held dear, or anything that was of significance to him, that he seemingly lost it all, on the same date spanning two-and-one-half decades. Angelina had been battling cancer and was in remission. The treatments had weakened her immune system and she died from pneumonia. She never talked about her illness or how sick she was, only about how much she loved him and that they would have an eternity to spend together. On account of her untimely passing Excelcious vowed that he would never love again. Angelina wouldn't have wanted that for him, but for now that's just the way it would be. He smiled through his tears as he reflected on Valentino's thoughts, regarding him and Shilloqwai becoming friends. Having just gotten back from his fiancée's funeral, he couldn't imagine love being anything more than just a fantasy for the remainder of his mortal life.

He left the medical profession because he was angry. None of the techniques, technology, no science, or medicine could save his wife to be. In his brief period of uncertainty, while he pondered what he would do the rest of his life, there was a sense of guilt, a feeling of remorse for abandoning what he was good at. He wondered how many people would die on account of his knee-jerk decision.

When it came down to the matter at hand, he believed that it was God calling him away from the medical profession. For what reason? That had not yet been revealed to him. He prayed for the strength to carry on. He also found strange irony in the arrival of the package that was 20 some years late in getting to him. He found the synopsis of the work of Valentino and Onshanda to be invaluable.

He considered himself to be an IT techie. In skimming over the material, he realized how much there was that he didn't know about computers. This was true, especially when it came to the specifics in regard to robotics, the mechanics of the hardware and the practicality of the software functions. But becoming an IT Geek was his childhood dream. It was something he was passionate about, and something he was very, very good at, if not the best there ever was.

Leaving the medical profession was a difficult choice, one he made after much deliberation. Perhaps it wasn't such a knee-jerk decision after all. In his heart, it's what he felt he was being called to do. He found that going back to his first love was very intriguing. Knowing that he could still help a lot of people, more than justified his decision to change careers. Going through his database, he found that Skeletos had sent him a bunch of files containing the work that he had done. Excelcious found that information too, to be invaluable. He hoped that Robotikis didn't think to collect the information from Skeletos before he had him terminated. He chuckled at the thought that Robotikis was probably too stupid to think of such a thing.

After careful study, between what he knew and what he learned, he realized he was one of a prospective few with the qualifications to carry on with the work of Valentino and Onshanda. He couldn't overstate the significance of doing so, as the war was inevitable now. The feuding had gone on, culminating with what had become known as the 365-day war. Humans vowed they would take back from the robots what was rightfully theirs and avenge the deaths of Valentino, Onshanda, along with the termination and death of Skeletos as they considered the robot to be in part, human. Sure, a compromise had been reached, officially ending the war. But the feuding went on, and tensions between the two factions were building again. Excelcious, along with a majority of others, believed that the robots would rule with an iron fist. Under Robotikis, this was proving to be true. Robotikis was blamed for inciting the war, which he vowed to stop. Though he was in a position of power, Robotikis didn't know how to effectively use the power entrusted to him. In his self-righteousness, he willfully abused the power for self-serving purposes.

Comfortable with his decision to make a career change, Excelcious would carry on as he always had, doing what he thought was right for the people. He had wisdom enough, knowing he couldn't change the whole world. Yet, he solemnly believed, knowing all the while, he could change his part of it. After Excelcious made a conscious decision to carry on the work of Valentino and Onshanda, and after Skeletos Puro-Amoris was terminated, he realized that he might be called upon to do more than his share. It appeared that the robots were on a search and destroy mission, aimed at exterminating Humankind, before the war broke out. Humans had nowhere to run and nowhere to hide. Excelcious had been working with a group, calling itself the Divine Nine, knowing it had the backing of the Power of Love. The group was building an underground safe haven for humans. Excelcious hoped it would be ready soon. Though considerable progress had been made, it wasn't progress enough from Excelcious' perspective.

The group using its collective gifts, also began building a mechanical army it called the Orbitoids. They would be constructed in light of the late Skeletos Puro-Amoris and the terminated Mercusilver Class, using the Pulitzer-prize winning work of Valentino and Onshanda. Rumor had it that two survived the Mercusilver Slaughter. They were models

7/11/13F and 8/12/14F, Shilloqwai and LaShyra. The robots would not confirm the rumors instead they put forth a counter claim that only one of the Mercusilver class had survived, a claim vehemently disputed by the humans. Excelcious already knew half of Robotikis' claim to be true. He was good at masking the truth.

Like many others, Excelcious believed that LaShyra was still in existence, somewhere. He wondered where Robotikis was hiding LaShyra…and what the reasoning was for keeping her existence a secret.

On the other hand, Shilloqwai's existence was no secret. She was a gutsy one, bold and beautiful. What did she know about him? Why did she tell him that he was her hero? Strange they had feelings for one another without ever having met. Regardless, he loved her too. She was his hero, as much as he was hers. The coincidences were mounting, leading Excelcious to believe, that he and Shilloqwai were destined to meet. Excelcious thought it might be nice to somehow get Shilloqwai on the human side as he believed she would be a strong leader for the Orbitoids. Any conceivable way he could think of to pull off the feat, likely meant getting himself killed. The purpose for wanting her to lead the Orbitoid army was not to overthrow the existing robot rule, but to make humans more comfortable in dealing with their mechanical foes, whom would inevitably be their new leaders. He wasn't sure how long the robots would be in power, but while they were, Excelcious among others, weren't about to allow the robots to control their lives. Continuing to keep himself invisible from the robots, Excelcious continued working on multiple projects with the Divine Nine.

Before the 365-day war ended, Excelcious worked out a deal with the mechanical combatants, that he could have access to and lay claims to anything that was tossed onto the robot junk pile, or shit pile as it was more commonly referred to. Just after he had closed the deal a treaty had been reached. Had the robots known his extensive background in computers, they may not have made the deal. The robots knew him to be a retired doctor, formerly among the best in the medical field. They knew little of his hobbies which included his IT background. All the better for Excelcious and friends working on their secret projects which would have been terminated by the robots, had they any knowledge of them.

It was no surprise when the robots seized power. What was surprising, that a year after the treaty, the agreement between the robots and Excelcious was extended and made a lifetime deal. Humans seemed to be more disturbed with the way the robot takeover happened, than they were with the takeover itself. The majority tried to make the best of the situation, an outcome of circumstances it didn't have the power to change. There would always be a minority which would never accept what was.

It would push to return to the way things were. Neither was good, the way it was, or the way it was presently. Clearly concessions and hopefully positive changes would result from the conflict. Neither side wanted to concede anything, a risky position to take, one that would lead to another all-out war. Though no one wanted that, no one seemed to be willing to extend olive branches either. Between the robots' unwillingness to attempt to negotiate a lasting peace, and their refusal to disclose the whereabouts of the Mercusilver class robot, model number 8-12-14F, further infuriated the humans' dislike while deepening their disdain for their robot rulers. It also weakened the argument for the robot takeover and the claim that they did so to serve and protect humans. The robots realized too late the predicament they had put themselves in.

Though Robotikis the robot leader, previously announced that Shilloqwai would be acting as a diplomat and liaison in charge of bridging human-robot relations, any trust that may have been gained by the gesture of goodwill, done out of good faith, was lost by the robots' refusal to reveal the whereabouts of LaShyra, model 8/12/14F. By the very nature of the robots' unwillingness to speak on the matter, Humans presumed that she had been terminated.

The robots kept their silence, determined to keep the matter a secret for the moment. The humans would not be content with the robots' defiance, and unwillingness to provide answers, regarding the issue. It was a matter of trust, and a source of distrust, poisoning the relations between the robots and Humankind. Robots would fight to the death using logic and reason to govern Humankind. Love was a glaring example, and often the excuse, humans used to defend their perceived irrational acts, and illogical reasoning. Because of humans' inability to define love, except in vague terms, robots weren't about to try analyzing the concept of love, not even in a broad sense. Humankind was already tired of the 'My way, or the Highway' mentality the robots were embracing. Love was all around, never ending, and unconditional. It was part of human nature, and nothing was going to change in that regard. Humankind believed the robots' arrogance, along with their refusal to try and understand love, even if they did so, in the broadest sense, it would be their downfall. All through history, humans have gone against all odds, defying logic, and reason… in the name of Love. In doing so it has led to some of the Earth's greatest tragedies, namely war. Acting in the name of love, Humankind has also accomplished great things. Its wealth of experiences have led to countless happily ever-afters, many of which had a common theme…resulting in the finding of true love.

The instant Shilloqwai left on her short sabbatical, she experienced a freedom like she had never known. Humans were spontaneous creatures. They did what they wanted, when they wanted, and often on a whim. Feeling spontaneous, Shilloqwai took a flight to Jackson, Wyoming. This was one of many places she could escape into the wide-open spaces and view the Northern Lights. She first saw them in her state of suspended animation. They made such an impression on her she wanted to see them for herself. Outside of town, out on the Antelope Flats is where Shilloqwai got her first-hand look at the Northern lights. They were more beautiful than she ever could have imagined. With the Grand Teton peaks as a backdrop, seeing them was more than a dream, more vivid than a fantasy come to life, an experience that for many was a once in a lifetime thing. After viewing this celestial paradise, she knew, given the opportunity, it would not be her last visit to this heavenly place.

Out of this world, galactic treasures, nebulous diamonds, are three ways to describe the Northern Lights. To have full appreciation for their illustrious celestial beauty, one must actually see the glittering, shimmering lights for themselves. Accounting for the varying infinite descriptions of this Milky Way wonder, is that no one ever sees them in the same vain. Even when viewing them from the same vantage point, individual perspectives are as unique as the snowflakes, no one, is ever the same. This includes individuals who have had the joy of viewing the Northern Lights on multiple occasions. Like a kaleidoscope, which tends to replicate patterns, no one delicate creation is ever the same.

Shilloqwai could attest to this, as she was witnessing this for herself at this very moment. Though the Northern Lights were different than she had remembered, they weren't any less beautiful. If anything, they were more so. Shilloqwai believed they were becoming more glorious with the passing of each millisecond.

Her two-night escape to paradise was far too short a time to spend in a place she longed to dwell in, through an eternity. At worst, it was heaven on Earth. She wondered how the Heaven, humans talked about, could be any more beautiful. She heard that somewhere beyond the moon and stars, up in the celestial skies, there's a city of gold surrounded by spectral rainbows of infinite color. When she first heard this, it sounded like another wild fantasy, another impossible dream. After doing some fact-checking, she found countless Christian accounts testifying to the existence of these very things.

The most striking thing to Shilloqwai among Christian beliefs is their unwavering testimony to the fact that God is Love, infinitely and unconditionally. It was one of the aspects of love enveloped in the concept that Christians struggle with to this day. It was no wonder Shilloqwai had a hard time processing this information, when humans themselves still struggle to find a definition for love. Without complete data on love, processing information in regard to the concept was difficult if not impossible. Even after her best efforts to try and learn more about love, Shilloqwai found herself to be just as confused as humans in regard to love, and what it truly is.

Her return flight to San Diego, California was about to land. She had five days remaining on her extended holiday. As sad as she was to be back, she was equally as anxious as she had plans on how she wanted to spend her remaining time off. Shilloqwai spent the remainder of her third day pondering over her reassignment. Robotikis hadn't dropped any clues as to what it might entail. Entertaining speculative thoughts was like trying to process information on limited data. Admittedly, Shilloqwai thought coming up with a definition for love, would have been easier than to try and figure out Robotikis' plans for her.

Sensing that she might be overheating, she decided to go for an evening stroll through the park. Her walk took her deep into the woods along the stream where she was nearly raped before getting her mechanical ass kicked. As they had before, rushing waters swept away the bad memories. She had to smile, looking upon the Baptismal site, the place where it felt like a new life for her had begun. The rock that kept her from being completely submerged was still there, in the middle of the stream.

Across the way, on the opposite bank, Shilloqwai observed a young couple lying next to a park bench engaging in an act of intimate passion. Humans referred to this act as making love. Unnoticed, she hurried passed them. She wasn't a voyeur. Witnessing the intimate, lustful act of passionate animal aggression, often resulting in procreation, wasn't going to do anything for her in the way of clarifying what love is, especially with the profanities being verbalized during their animal act.

She quickly moved on out of earshot to a clearing where she stood gazing at the silver-blue moon and the platinum-gold stars. She didn't know how much time had passed, but during the brief segment she spent looking up into the cosmos, she saw three shooting stars, making a wish on each one.

Her first wish was to become human. Her second wish was that love would find her. And the third wish was that she'd fulfill her quest to bridge the gap between robots and humans while reconciling their differences. After her evening stroll Shilloqwai returned to her private power station and put herself in sleep-mode, giving herself the best opportunity to update her files and so forth.

The next day around mid-morning, Shilloqwai returned to the park bench where she observed another couple exchanging affections. This couple was far more dignified than the one she had come across the night before. Snuggled up close on a park bench the couple was exchanging intimate kisses she imagined to be warm and wet.

A series of whims and whirs, buzzes, and beeps, amounted to a harmless chuckle in computer language. She wondered what it would be like to be romanced in this way with an opportunity to experience the sweet affections for herself. And how she wished she could have traded places with the girl on the park bench. She immediately scolded herself for entertaining delusional fantasies before moving on. Courteously, she left them one-on-one as they continued on, publicly sharing private moments.

Along the pathway, she came across another park bench off of the trail a bit. With her keen sense of hearing, Shilloqwai was able to pick up bits and pieces of their conversation. Luminosa was the woman's name. Her hair was long, lemon-yellow. Her skin, gold-flecked, matching the flecks in her hair. She was about 5-foot, 6-inches tall proportionate in all regards with shapely attributes. Shilloqwai heard her say she was from another galaxy, but she didn't catch the name of the galaxy or the name of Luminosa's home planet.

Though she was an alien, she was no less human than Adam and Eve, premiere couple of the human race. The same could be said for her boyfriend, who failed to mention his birthplace, though he did mention he was not originally born here on Earth. What a handsome hunk her boyfriend, Titanikis was, Shilloqwai thought as she took notice of his sculpted features from head to toe. Maroon hair, cerulean blue eyes, a fine-looking specimen he was, she thought. Shilloqwai wondered if she were human, and she crossed paths with the young couple, if Luminosa would be jealous of her for just saying hello to Titanikis. Shilloqwai wondered further if he would bother to give her a second look, not a lustful one, but, a complimentary one. One that acknowledged her physical beauty. And one that wondered what treasures she held in her heart.

With her long aqua-tourmaline colored hair, Shilloqwai was convinced she could blend in well with the humans. Her outward appearance wasn't all that different from other intra-galactic aliens who had found their home on Earth. Her mechanical guts would be a dead give-away, identifying her as a robot. Over the millennia humans had learned a thing or two about aliens. First, they learned how to process them, so they were free to live in the United States, regardless of their birthplace. Secondly, being alien was generally considered a bad thing by many. But that was ages ago. Not so much anymore. The majority had come around to accept humans from other countries and now other galaxies. The benefit from this was learning how people of different cultures with different traditions could enhance life for everyone. After learning that there was life in space, she understood why humans still referred to it as the final frontier.

She was starting to get a sense of how broadly vast the universe is. And she was beginning to realize, that Earth, with all of the natural beauty it possesses, is a milli-fraction of the universe as a whole. What Shilloqwai would give to be human, even if it meant being terminated out of existence. She cursed aloud as she felt the tears pooling in her eyes. "Shit!" Condensation buildup she thought. Must be a loose seal, damn, not again!"

A quick self-analysis told her it wasn't condensation. Data in her base confirmed for a second time she was actually crying human tears. She thought that it had to be something with her initial programming. What else would allow her to experience what it was like to cry as humans did? She was a machine, surely her humanlike experiences weren't a result of cloned matter. Almost certainly, it wasn't anything the Robotechs had done, unless they thought it would undermine her mission and result in her termination. It sounded like something the Robotechs might do, however, Shilloqwai didn't think they were ingenious enough to pull it off.

She started making a mental list of the reasons humans cried. She understood doing so when they were afraid, depressed, disappointed, or grieving. But why cry tears of joy? Then she recalled her dream of becoming human, a pleasantry that made her cry. The joy of falling in love, another pleasantry where she thought humans might cry tears of joy. There was a lot to the concept of love, more than she had envisioned, and far more than the act of making it. She was beginning to see the many aspects of love, beginning with courtship, companionship, friendship, and in ever-growing relationships where two-become one, ultimately bonded by the act of making it.

She saw there was also love of family, of friends, of community, of church, of Humankind. But no matter what form love took, every aspect required patience, kindness, understanding and forgiveness. She saw love was sometimes a sacrifice, where one would lay down his or her life for another.

If love ever found her, she wanted the kind of love where she would willingly give her life for her husband, and he would willingly give his life for her. That was true love, real love, the only kind of love, one ever needs. Over her time off thus far, she had learned a lot about love. Still, she felt there was much more to know. And she was left wondering, how one could learn all there was to know about love in one lifetime? Her conclusion, this is why true love would last an eternity. Each day of their mortal lives, lovers are bound to learn something new about their partner. Each day would bring a new experience where loving memories would be made by falling in love again for the first time. Love is more than one night together. It was romance, courtship, the companionship and friendship that made the memories of a lifetime. Nothing in this regard made more of an impression on Shilloqwai, than when she passed by an elderly couple in the park, celebrating its wedding anniversary.

She congratulated them and wished them a happy 75th. She knew they weren't banging down the walls of the bedroom anymore. Seeing them reminiscing, they were talking about how when they first met, they didn't like each other, and how both were dating someone else. They talked about their engagement, their wedding night, and their three kids who were there celebrating with them.

They talked about how their kids for the most part, stayed on the straight and narrow path. They talked about their nine grandchildren and the added joy they brought into their lives. Having had the honor of meeting their kids and the grandchildren, Shilloqwai learned that the kids were trying to figure out a way to give back all of the love that had been given to them by, their parents, the celebrating couple.

Shilloqwai, was gaining confidence, beginning to believe that she did fit in with humans. No one ever suspected she was a robot. And if they had, no one ever bothered to mention it. She was convinced that none of them had any idea who she was or what she was. The couple asked Shilloqwai if she was in a relationship. Shilloqwai honestly answered no, but, said that she hoped true love would someday find her.

The elderly couple, celebrating its anniversary, promised to pray that true love would find Shilloqwai. She thanked them, before going on her way. Shilloqwai thought it was sad the couple was probably nearing the mortal end of its life. Late in their golden years, she could tell by the stories they told her, the couple had much wisdom and was very content. It was obvious to her, that the man and his wife believed that they had lived their lives to the fullest.

She found it humorous the couple was discussing, no arguing, over who was going to get to the golden-pearly gates first. Knowing he didn't stand a chance of winning the argument with his wife, he said he hoped it would be a tie because he didn't want to do anything without her. "Feelings mutual!" she responded.

Shilloqwai wished she could have photographed the moment. In a sense she had! She would never forget the looks in their eyes, the looks on their faces, the invisible halos, and invisible angels' wings. All of the images together formed a complete picture of the endless river of love that she knew was flowing between their hearts. Shilloqwai was crying again, longing for the love that she knew the angelic couple shared. It was late afternoon and she wanted to get back to her home before dark. Not that she had a curfew, but, in the event Robotikis was tracking her. Getting home early might curtail his heightening suspicions of her activity. They were already high. Deservedly so, came the afterthought! She'd provoked him enough!

Bolting for the back woods, Shilloqwai rushed by a group of people who seemed to be in a panic over something. She couldn't make out what it was. Her instincts told her she should have stopped and tried to help. Robotikis warned her about interaction with humans. But, she reasoned, allowing harm to come to humans through inaction was a violation of Asimov's Laws. With that thought in mind, she prayed that no harm would come to any of them. The group became an afterthought when she heard a young girl screaming. She would not ignore this cry for help. Quickly she found the girl who happened to be in grave danger.

A coyote was stalking the strawberry-blonde, who couldn't have been more than three-years-old. Her blue eyes were darkened with midnight fear. Shilloqwai would make sure the coyote would have an alternate choice for dinner. On second thought the coyote was about to become dinner for the buzzards. Shilloqwai felt the energy surging through her and targeted the scrawny beast. Her eyes were locked on what was about to become dead meat. She shuddered from the blast of shrapnel that flew from her eyes.

The unsuspecting creature was dropped in his tracks and crumpled into a pool of blood. With pinpoint accuracy the tiny projectiles penetrated the coyote's fur and filleted his insides. He let out a weak growl and a whimper in his last breath. Shilloqwai ran up to him and crushed his skull with her foot to make sure he was dead. The creature's corpse moved involuntarily under the pressure she applied to its neck. Stepping away from the lifeless beast, Shilloqwai completed the rescue. With a sweeping motion she lifted the child into her arms and began to walk her out of the woods.

She heard the panicked cries for Elsa at the edge of the woods. "Mommy and daddy are coming for me!" The little girl laughed.

"So, your name is Elsa?"

"Yes!"

"Elsa, where are you?" The panicked party called out, still not knowing the whereabouts of the child.

In response, Shilloqwai called out, identifying herself. "I'm Shilloqwai, a liaison for robot-human relations. Your little girl is safe. I'll bring her to you." She could hear by the rustling sounds that the search party was rushing toward her. Shilloqwai, with the girl, was rushing toward them. She recognized the search party. It was the group of people she had sprinted passed in her hurry to get to the backwoods.

The celebratory reunion of family and daughter was emotional, bringing on tears of joy, another aspect of love. "Honey, are you okay? What possessed you to go into the woods by yourself?"

"I saw a pretty butterfly. He landed, there on the flowers." Elsa explained, pointing out one of nature's many beautiful bouquets. "He flew all the way into the woods. And I followed him. Then, I lost him in the trees because the big bad wolf was chasing me."

"It was a coyote!" Shilloqwai explained not meaning to contradict the child. "He was planning on having your daughter for dinner. I made sure that didn't happen. The coyote is going to be someone else's dinner now. I made sure of that too."

"Well thank you, we're forever indebted to you, how can we repay you?"

"It was my job. I felt obligated."

"It was more than an obligation. It was done out of love. The love will come back to you in ways you'll never expect."

"Thank you, I hope so. I wasn't looking to be rewarded for an act of kindness." Shilloqwai responded modestly.

"That's how love works. It will come back to you, some way, somehow!"

"It was nothing. You would have done the same for someone else!" Shilloqwai said humbly.

"And someday, someone will do something out of love for you."

"Did you need a ride back to the lab, Shilloqwai?" One of the Robocops asked that had come to the scene to assist.

"No, I could use the walk." She told him turning away from the red, blue, and white strobes that were blinding her. She knew the Robocops used their Hollywood lighting mostly for show. The Robocops were easily identified with clear, varying geometric shapes of their torsos and heads. The titanium extensions they had for arms and legs gave them added strength to get around.

They moved slowly and efficiently. The Robocops were equipped with a number of taser type weapons designed to stun, disable and in some instances kill, when trying to keep harm from coming to other humans. They were able to target suspects from long-range if they needed to. This somewhat compensated for the lack of speed with which they moved.

Without the flashing lights, anyone could see their circuitry and how they were constructed. Their outer shells were one-thousand times the strength of the strongest safety glass. Robocops thought they were invincible. They were sleekly designed, donned with bells and whistles. Many used their invincibility as an excuse to intimidate and bully people they were supposed to be protecting.

Shit! She mumbled under her breath the instant she'd turned away from them. I'm dead meat. Deader than that coyote I killed. At least there's something left of him, more than will be left of me after I get incinerated. I wonder what they're going to tell Robotikis. The Robocops are good at embellishing stories. They'll probably take the credit for the rescue. Like I care! Came an afterthought. I did my job, she reassured herself. The week was as short as it was long. The first 6-and-one-half days was the short part. The long part was going to be the remaining ½ day. Shilloqwai was worried about her reassignment. Robotikis was cruel. She was expecting him to tell her that she'd been reassigned to the shit pile. That was his style, the cruel bastard she knew him to be. Destroying her outright, that wasn't his style. He would make her suffer first.

The question was how would he make her suffer? Shilloqwai would soon find out. And she already knew how the story was going to end. The question was how long would it be before her termination? She vowed to make the most of the time she had left of her mechanical life. After she'd been reassigned, she would look for a way to ensure she would never have to see Robotikis again. She planned to send him to the shit pile ahead of her. If she followed him there, so be it. But she would have the upper hand over him once and for all. She would be the queen of the hill, reigning over the king she brought down.

REASSIGNMENT

[CHAPTER 5]

Shilloqwai was just coming out of sleep mode as she approached Robotikis' power station. She hoped the brief rest would cool her systems enough so the encounter with her boss wouldn't escalate to the point where they overheated. The last thing she needed were glitches that caused her system to shut down. It was a setup as she'd feared. He tried to provoke her, the instant she walked into his work area. "Surprised you showed up. I was hoping, you didn't. I was looking forward to hunting your ass down and doing away with you!"

"That's the endgame, isn't it Robotikis? Your plan is to do away with me regardless of how I perform! In fact, I believe that was your plan all along!"

"At the onset, no, we had too much invested in you. It's come to the point of diminishing returns. But lately, we've been wasting more time retooling you to keep you functional, than you've been spending out in the field as a liaison, diplomat. And at this point, a nothing piece of shit is far more valuable to us. I'm even afraid to throw you on the shit pile. I'm worried you'll contaminate it!"

"Thank you for your affectionate words Robotikis. Why do you have to be such a cruel bastard? I'm not sure what this discussion has to do with my reassignment."

"A lot, actually. I've lost confidence in you and your abilities to perform. You think you can pilot one of the solar planes? I mean, all you need to do, is connect a USB cable from yourself to the plane. It's similar to the one at your power station. Think you can handle it? I don't, but I'm giving you one more shot to make things right!"

"Lost confidence in me, Robotikis? You never had confidence in me. You set me up to fail. What do you think, I'm stupid? I may glitch, but, stupid I'm not. There's nothing wrong with my RAPP functions. So, you're delegating this to me because you're grooming me to take over your job. For the most part I'll be sitting on my ass all day while the GPS guides the plane to its programmed destination. I think it's similar to what you do all day. You're so used to sitting on your ass in sleep-mode I don't think you have a clue as to what's going on in the real world. There are some changes taking place and things happening that you should probably be monitoring instead of spying on me and Humankind!"

"What the hell are you talking about? And why the hell were you up in Wyoming for two days?" Robotikis asked, interrogating her to the third-degree.

"So, you were tracking me you nosey bastard! For the most part, it's none of your damn business. But when I found this, I thought I'd bring you back a souvenir." Shilloqwai said launching a piece of what she called geometric space junk onto Robotikis' table.

"What the hell is this?"

"I'm not sure. After I did my RAPP, I know it's not of Earth. It looks like some robotic spy device, a small camera perhaps, sharp edges, a hazard to humans. It leaks a toxic fluid, harmless for robots, deadly for humans. Don't know what it means, but they come in all different shapes. You've got the sphere, here's a triangle, a square, a cylinder, a circle, and a rectangle. These are just samples. The whole damn canyon I was in, was filled with them. Dead fish on the banks of the Snake River, wildlife diseased, notably on the Elk Refuge. Surprised your DNR Patrolbots aren't on this!"

"I've sent out alerts and ordered an investigation. In regard to your future, it's not looking very bright. You were flirting with that steward on the plane."

"Damn!" Shilloqwai cursed. "You really are personally invasive."

"I don't really care who you interface with, but he was human." Robotikis reminded her. "Your instruction was to avoid contact and interaction with all humans. You can't resist, can you? I can't wait to be rid of you. The day is coming sooner than you think. You want to tell me about your escapades in the park? What about the two humans making out. I have to admit, you're almost as hot as she was."

"Shut up you undignified sexist bastard!" Shilloqwai ordered him. "I ran off, gave them their privacy, I suppose you watched them finish the act!" Robotikis' moment of silence was an admission of guilt.

"You yourself said learning about love was the key to understanding humans."

"Ignorant asshole, that's not what I meant." Shilloqwai went on to clarify. "It's a facet of love, a small, yet important part. But love has many other aspects like courtship, romance, compatibility, companionship, and friendship to name a few."

"So, what about the anniversary party you invaded, or the privacy of the couple you invaded by staring enviously at them while they kissed?" Robotikis continued to ask Shilloqwai probing questions. "For a moment you were acting as if you were going to turn human and take the other female's place. How could you entertain such thoughts, you infidel bitch?"

"Really? If you were human, you couldn't even be a slut." Shilloqwai chided Robotikis for his warped perspective on love. "You have nothing in the way of love to offer, not even in the perverted sense, otherwise known as lust."

"Whatever!" Robotikis continued, dismissing the comment as nothing. "You know, I'm so pissed off right now, I'm surprised I'm able to resist the urge to terminate you. The most disturbing news I heard was that little girl you kidnapped. The Robocops found you with her in the deep woods. Why did you take her? What were you going to do with her? You were probably going to kill her like you murdered those other six humans. Then you brought her back when you heard the search party coming for her, acting like some damn hero!"

"So that's what the Robocops told you?" Shilloqwai was not surprised by the Robocops' embellishment, a twisted version of the actual story. "I don't suppose they said anything about the coyote that almost had the little girl for dinner. The only reason I was able to save her is because I was taking a shortcut through the woods, and I came across the horrifying scene. I saved the girl in accordance with Asimov's laws. No harm came to the girl, and I returned Elsa to her family, safe and sound."

"You ran passed the search party. Why didn't you apply Asimov's laws then?"

"I was following your direction. I was trying to avoid human interaction!"

"You? Trying to listen to me and follow my direction? That's a first! You know Asimov's laws supersede any direction I give you, right? So, Shilloqwai, this is why I'm having a hard time believing your story. You were running from them because you didn't want them to know you'd kidnapped the girl. Then, when you got caught red-handed by the Robocops, you concocted this bullshit story about you being a superhero that saved the day!"

Shilloqwai broke down as the tears streamed from her eyes. She didn't even try to hide them. What was the point? Robotikis had it in for her anyway. He would act sooner than later in regard to her doomed fate. He showed no empathy for her, deliberately mistaking her tears for another glitch. "You really need to get your shit together." Robotikis continued to chastise her. These condensation leaks are going to be your undoing. I'll be happy to put you out of your misery. If you want, we can end the story sooner rather than later."

"You son-of-a-bitch, you've been lying to me all along!" Shilloqwai cursed, calling Robotikis out!

"You're not equipped to handle the truth. You experience glitches at the most inappropriate times. I can't trust you, and I can't depend on you for anything. Look, I'm a man of my word, I said I'd give you another chance. You will be flying one of the solar planes, puddle jump flights at first. I've put you on the Chicago-St. Louis run. Show me you can handle it and I'll increase your responsibility and let you pilot longer flights. Given your past history, it won't be long before you screw up. I'd wager that this first flight will be your last and then I'll finally be rid of you!"

"Thanks for the vote of confidence asshole! I've always wanted to make an impact on the world and etch my place in history. Because of how incompetent you are as the robot leader of the world, Robotikis, I could just get rid of you and be famous and infamous with a single act of violence! I'd get more than a sentence and a photo in some history book. Hell, my name would be plastered all over the social media forever! I'd be deemed a hero and not the villain you're making me out to be."

"You, and whose army?" Robotikis asked, challenging her to follow through on her threat.

"Oh, no army, just lil' ol' me!" Shilloqwai boasted confidently. "I want all of the credit for terminating you. I'm a selfish little bitch. Look at me Robotikiss my ass!" With the fear and tension building between them the energy started to percolate inside her, just as it had before she murdered her six attackers. What followed next, happened so quickly, Robotikis had no time for evasive maneuvers. Shilloqwai raised up her hands, as though she were going to strangle him, before releasing the energy pent up inside of her.

Lightning bolts flew from her fingertips and star-shaped shrapnel flew from her eyes. Hit multiple times by the lightning bolts, Robotikis short-circuited. The metal pellets penetrated his protective shell and ricocheted around inside of him slicing his wiring and mechanical guts, rendering him non-functional. Shilloqwai surmised he would need a complete overhaul. More likely, he would need to be completely rebuilt. She couldn't just leave him like that. She called for help from the Robotechs, as the ensuing fire scorched and crisped his outer shell, assuredly matching his French-fried robot guts.

The Robotechs asked her for an explanation. Shilloqwai successfully pulled off the charade, with her story about how Robotikis was so upset with her and that she'd never seen him so angry. "He overheated and then I heard a series of pops before he short-circuited. He was really burning up on the inside before the ensuing fire broke out and scorched his outer shell. It smells like shit in his quarters. The smoke is so thick down there I could hardly see. I opened the windows to air the place out."

"Do you want to go back down there with us? We may have additional questions for you."

"Can we do it later? I've really got to get to Chicago. The last thing he said to me was, 'don't be late for your new assignment or it's your ass!' Look, I don't want to get terminated!"

"Okay, follow them. They'll get you where you need to go." Shilloqwai told them she needed an express trip to get to O'Hare International Airport, in Chicago, Illinois. Seeing the urgency in her request, the Robocops flew her via speed drone to her destination. She was relieved that she had checked in two minutes ahead of schedule allowing her to report for duty on time.

She felt remiss in her duties that there wasn't an opportunity for her to meet and greet the human passengers. This would have been in direct violation of Robotikis' orders, but she didn't give a damn about him anymore. He was out of sight, and she was about to put him of her mind. So, this was how he would torture her. Robotikis knew she loved the human interaction. Placing her in the position he did, made her miss the quintessential part of her liaison job all the more. He knew the temptations she would face in her new position. And he knew it wouldn't be long before she stepped out of line. The restriction would gnaw at her and perhaps cause her to glitch and then …

You're such a devious bastard! She whispered to herself after thinking the whole thing through, now fully understanding why he'd put her in this position. Indeed, he wanted to torture her before incinerating her. She took a deep breath and headed for the cockpit. She was on the clock. Her prime objective now was to keep her passengers safe. Mindlessly she secured the USB connection between her interface and the control panel of the brand-new plane about to embark on its maiden-flight. Just as she was told, once she made the connection the rest would take care of itself. The plane was conducting self-diagnostics and in almost no time the LED indicators read all systems go. Instantly the solar-powered engines fired up.

The self-flying plane went into motion heading for the runway, before proceeding onward after being cleared for takeoff on runway 2-niner. Once in the air, her sole responsibility was to monitor the control panel. With numerous fail-safe mechanisms in place, Shilloqwai wondered, what could possibly go wrong? She was there to correct any issues that might arise and become problematic. The flight from Chicago to St. Louis went without incident. The return flight, however, turned into a complete disastrophe. It wasn't that Shilloqwai had done anything wrong, this according to preliminary reports. By the time the FAA completed its investigation, it was mysteriously determined that computer glitches were probable cause of the crash.

Fatalities, there were none to speak of. Many passengers suffered serious injuries, some crippling. Most of the injuries were minor, consisting of cuts, bruises, scrapes, broken bones, and the like. Before the robot takeover, a crash of this magnitude would have claimed the lives of all 356 on board, passengers, and crew alike. Smoke and flames from burning jet fuel would have been responsible for most of the deaths. Some would have been asphyxiated on account of the fumes before the fire. That was during a time, most survived the impact of a crash, so very few back then, died from the initial impact. Chances of people dying as a result of the impact from a crash, in this day-and-age are even more remote than they were then. This because of the glide control on the new solar crafts, easing the landings, especially in emergency situations. With no fuel to ignite, the chances of death on impact are almost nil, unless the plane collides with a stationary object such as a tree or a mountain.

With the help of technological advances and medical advances, injured humans were all likely to make full recoveries in any crash. Regardless of how positive, the end result was not going to benefit Shilloqwai in any way, shape, or form. Robotikis so much as told her she was going to be terminated if anything went wrong on the flight. He would find a way to blame her for the crash and use it as an excuse to do what he'd been planning to do all along.

Regardless of whether or not the crash was her fault it would be the impetus Robotikis needed to give the order. He would use data acquired from her files, over the past 25 years, to highlight her failings. This latest incident would validate her overall incompetence and lackluster performance. With evidence still mounting against her, combined with prior documentation, both highlighted her lack of dependability and inefficiency. These were glaring issues Robotikis intended to address immediately. Her overall performance was deemed by him to be totally unacceptable, especially as of late. He wasn't about to let her go on like this any longer.

Though there was no visible evidence she was damaged in the crash, Shilloqwai was expected to report to the lab for inspection regardless. It was protocol anytime a robot was involved in an incident. Necessary adjustments would be made accordingly. Noticing her presence, the techs became enraged. In part they were irritated about having to work overtime because of her temper tantrum which nearly took out Robotikis, their world leader. Their anxiety heightened over seeing her because they were tired of dealing with her temperament.

"Will someone get that bitch out of here before I terminate her and endanger my own existence?" Kinks, the lead tech ordered. "After what she put Robotikis through, he'll want to do the honors of terminating her himself, I don't want to outstep my bounds by making executive decisions!" Kinks, the chief tech proclaimed.

"The reason she's here chief is because ..." Shanks, the second in command began to argue.

"I know why she's here and I don't give a damn about her." Kinks continued on, with a tirade of his own. "She's totally to blame for this latest incident. Pilot error was probable cause, due to another glitch. Looks like a brief once over is all she needs, minor repairs perhaps, but what I don't understand is why we're wasting time and resources on her restoration, AGAIN!

"She's totally high maintenance!" Kinks argued further. "We were told on no uncertain terms, that if she came back here for any reason, including preventative measures, we were to terminate her. I know rumor has it she was to be incinerated at the St. Louis airport, but that didn't work out. Robotikis never intended for her to guide the return flight back to Chicago. He's still incapacitated because of her. Therefore, he wasn't able to give the order to make it so. Now we're stuck with her again." Kinks partially reactivated her. He was about to make an executive decision, but he wanted some answers first, as he was planning to interrogate her. As soon as her hearing sensors were able to process information, he shouted to her. "Hey bitch, I need to know what you did to Robotikis so I can fix him."

"He survived?" Shilloqwai quipped, surprised to find that she hadn't ended his existence. "I'll try harder next time to dispense with him so he can't be restored. Besides, it was self-defense. I can't control the mechanism that's self-activated when I'm threatened. He attacked me, shit happened and that's why he's in the state he's in."

"Shit just happened? You damn near terminated him. I didn't know the Mercusilver class had self-defense mechanisms."

"They didn't. I equipped myself. When you get him restored tell him I'll meet him on the scrap pile. I intend to finish what I started. Ask him if he missed me?"

Kinks had had enough of her smart-ass comments. He deactivated her again. "Just get the bitch out of here. I'm through dealing with her."

"Where do you want us to put her?" Shanks asked, not wanting to make the executive decision.

"Don't be stupid. There's only one place for her, maybe two. Up your ass or on the scrap pile, take your pick. The boss will be up and running in the morning. He can have the final say regarding her incineration."

"She's a classified bot storing sensitive material. Do you think we should erase her data first and remove her CPU?" Programamatic, the software tech asked.

"Nah, just leave her as she is. I want that entire piece of shit out of my lab." Kinks ordered the tech. "I can't risk faulty parts getting put into another bot! Wait until after we shut down the lab tonight, before you do anything with her."

"What if Excelcious Orbitus gets a hold of her?" Programamatic asked with more than a hint of concern.

"Excelcious Orbitus? Oh, that IT tech that has permission to steal from the pile!" Kinks asked with disdain, as if Excelcious were no one special. "As far as I'm concerned, he can have the useless piece of shit. She's unfixable, might make a nice museum piece though! I hear he's got quite a collection. I hear he's got a Unimate exhibit, the first programmable and digitally operated robot. I hear he's also got a replica of the first robot, a steam-powered pigeon, created by Archytas around 350 to 400 BC... Archytas was a famous philosopher, mathematician, astronomer, statesman and strategist in his day."

"Enough shit about robot history!" Programamatic quipped, putting the spotlight back on Excelcious. "From what I've heard about Excelcious he's a modern-day intellectual geek! Supposedly he's smarter than Albert Einstein."

"I don't believe any of that shit!" Kinks retorted. "For all I care, that packrat Excelcious can put Shilloqwai on display with the rest of his junk collection."

"I wouldn't underestimate his abilities you know." Crosswire interjected, backing up the concerns of his Cobots, Shanks and Programamatic. "I think he's smart enough to fix her and make her functional. Dude can probably make a time machine from copper wire, paper, and tin cans."

"If he fixes the bitch, he deserves what he gets from her." Kinks responded, not wanting to hear further arguments. "Contrary to opposing opinions, I don't think he can fix her. I don't care what Excelcious' IQ is. If he does fix her, I'll find a way to turn human. Not to worry, that won't be happening anytime soon, or ever for that matter. I'll be running this machine shop until I'm terminated."

"That might be sooner than you think!" Megabits, the newest tech said, interjecting his thoughts on the matter. "Humans have been known to do some pretty incredible things when they put their minds to it. You know you're tempting fate, don't you?" Megabits warned.

"Do I look worried? The condensate is making a puddle on the floor around me." Kinks quipped.

"What condensate?" Megabits asked.

"That's exactly my point! I'm not worried in the least." Kinks boasted overconfidently.

"I think you're so full of shit it's clouding your judgement." Megabits challenged him yet again to rethink his position on the matter. "It's just that if I were you, I would terminate and incinerate her. If that Orbitus quack gets a hold of her, he will program her to come back here and raise holy hell. Yours will be the first ass she'll kick. I can tell by the look in her eyes, she has a special affinity for you Kinks. She may be an insolent bitch, but Shilloqwai will take the first opportunity she gets to dismantle you and turn you into robot melt! You'll be prime topping for that shit pile out there!"

"You guys can't be serious! I mean, you talk like she's going to come to life, walk off of the pile, and come back to haunt me! I've made my decision to throw her on the pile and forget about her. I told you I'm done with her forever. And you can forget what I said about becoming human, she'll never function again, not in the robot world!" Kinks said confidently, making a promise he hoped he could keep.

"She just might, Kinks!" Megabits came at him one last time to try and persuade him to change his position on the matter. "I'm warning you, if Excelcious gets his grips on her, watch out! I'm telling you, don't underestimate the man. I mean, I get what you're saying. It's not like she's going to escape termination by something ridiculous happening, like her turning human." Both let out a mechanical laugh at the insanity of the concept. "I will say there have been some brilliant minds throughout human history. Though, if anyone could turn a robot into a human, my bets are on Excelcious. I've seen the man in action. He's pulled off some pretty amazing feats. We've already mentioned Archytas and Einstein.

Excelcious is in a class with them. If Excelcious Orbitus gets a hold of her and turns her, she'll be one hell of a warrior for the other side.

"Going into war I'd want Shilloqwai on our side. I don't give a shit how many glitches she's had. She's strong and she's smart. What if she turns, and leads a rebel force against the robots? She could be the difference in the outcome if there were a second conflict. If she fights with the humans, Humankind might actually win the war! That's how valuable her services could be to them! If it turns out that Shilloqwai ends up getting paired with Excelcious, the two of them together could eradicate robots from the Earth!"

"Okay, Okay. I'm tired of arguing. You said this Excelcious never rummages through the pile at night? Right?" Kinks asked, now half convinced his techs were right.

"Not to my knowledge and generally speaking, no!" Megabits acknowledged.

"Okay, so it's early evening. We'll fetch her at dawn. I should have Robotikis up and running by then. He'll have the final say and the onus will be on him. Just get her ass out of here now! I'm tired of looking at her."

"You're making a big mistake!" Megabits warned. "If I, were you, I would destroy her, but you're the acting boss."

"I've made my final decision!" Kinks shouted, emphatically stressing his wishes. "Get her the hell out of here, now!" With reckless abandon, Screwhead, the lead custodian, grabbed Shilloqwai by the arms and dragged her through the corridors trying to damage her beyond repair. He didn't bother to use a transport. His reasoning was to inflict as much physical damage to her as possible. When he reached the utility door that led out back to the scrap pile, he dropped the disabled robot. As he let her go, he slammed her to the floor. He heard something rattle inside her. It gave him pleasure that he was able to take part in the destruction of what some humans considered to be a robotic icon. After propping the door open, he returned to fetch the junk he'd left on the floor. With a fluid swooping motion, he snatched her up and carried her to the door. He positioned himself so he could get maximum thrust and then catapulted her into the air. "Goodbye, you piece of shit!" He shouted as he watched her soar through the sky as gracefully as a wounded duck. He was pleased with himself seeing her drop like a rock before crashing down and landing on top of the 15-foot dung heap. He heard the clanging cachink as she did. He celebrated with a wave of his grippers in the air over his head because he thought he inflicted more irreparable damage to her. In reality, he'd unknowingly done her a favor. It was to Shilloqwai's good fortune in the way that she landed. A metal rod protruding from the pile speared her in the back when she came crashing down on top of it. The rod was angled as such that it was lined up perfectly with her activation switch. The force of her fall, in conjunction with the angle of the rod, flipped the activation switch to the on position.

After her initial assessment, she knew exactly where she was, where she expected to be. Shilloqwai was entrenched in, not much, but deep enough in junk, she would need a miracle to get out. The additional damage she sustained from the blunt force of the fall is what kept her from freeing herself. It wasn't likely that someone who cared about her fate would come along. She would lay in waiting for the moment when Robotikis and company came to finish her off. Her wandering eyes zoomed in on the robot that she believed threw her on top of the pile. She recorded his make and model number and stored it in her memory banks. She didn't know for sure, but she believed him to be custodial staff. Though she didn't know his position in the lab she knew his name. She thought Screwhead was the perfect name for him. "Screwhead, you bolt-headed dolt! I'm going to get your ass! I'll cross your wires and you'll fry into robot melt!" Shilloqwai vowed in a barely audible tone.

THE WORLDS AND WONDERS OF EXCELCIOUS ORBITUS

[CHAPTER 6]

If Shilloqwai was lucky she'd have a chance to escape her imminent termination. Quietly she lay on top of the pile, patiently waiting for the Robocops and the Robotechs to go into sleep-mode. To be safe, she waited until late into the evening after all of the robots had gone dormant. It was passed the bewitching hour, into early morning before she dared make a sound. When she sensed the time had come, she started moaning and whining like a wounded feline. Her disturbing calls for help echoed through the night. Excelcious was irritated he'd been awakened. He was more irritated that the continuing cries were keeping him awake. Surely others heard the nagging pleas. Apparently, they were content in trying to ignore them. Not Excelcious, he was going to resolve the problem or put the alley cat out of its misery.

The shit pile in the robot yard is a known hazard for animals. It's claimed the lives of many over the years, big and small, especially those of curious cats. Excelcious shone a spotlight on the pile, scanning it several times, vertically and horizontally. Shilloqwai fell silent the instant the salvage pile was illuminated. She began to quiver when, whoever was operating the spotlight, seemed to be zeroing in on her. Excelcious didn't want to climb the pile to see what was on top, but he had another way to satisfy his own curiosity. He would drive his solar powered crane over to the salvage pile to retrieve what he believed to be a robot that was scrapped. The easiest way to get the robot from the top of the heap would be to use a magnet. In doing so he risked erasing any potentially valuable information stored in her database. No, he would use a claw to retrieve the robot on top of Garbage Mountain, if that's indeed, what was lying on the summit of the pile.

Shilloqwai sensed the unknown presence drawing nearer. First, the spotlight, then the approaching crane, and now the unlocking of the electronic gate. Who was it that had found her? The Robocops, perhaps, but they wouldn't have the authority to remove her from the pile. Whoever was trying to get to her was taking extreme measures to protect her? Rescue her?" Shilloqwai asked herself, thinking the prospects to be absurd, but distinct possibilities they were. The fact that her tourmaline shell glowed in the moonlight, thereby illuminating the top of the pile, made it easier for the operator of the crane to get a grip on her. Confident he had secured the robot in the jaws of the claw, he gently lifted her into the air.

Once Excelcious cleared her of the pile, he lowered her and drove her back to his dwelling place. There he released her from the grips of the claw. He then picked her up and carried her into his house. He was used to finding pieces of scrap on the pile. He used the odds and ends to help him complete or add finishing touches to his projects. This time, he believed he'd found a real treasure. Whatever was wrong with this scrapped robot, he was certain he could refurbish her.

She moaned, seemingly in excruciating pain, as he lay her on the bed. He'd carefully prepared it, just for her. Was this part of her programming to be more human, or was she legitimately feeling pain? He deactivated her until he could examine her and resolve whatever issues she was having. Her body went limp, but her eyes, they remained open. Excelcious couldn't stop gazing into the crystalline-like spheres of aqua-tourmaline blue. Her eyes were enchanting, warm, and seemingly crying out for help. Excelcious felt as though he was peering into never-fading celestial beauty.

Her eyes were far too beautiful to be glass. He thought them to be nothing short of galactic wonders, and he believed them to be real.

Her face glowed like the sun. If she were human, Excelcious would swear the radiance was emitted from a loving heart of gold. He would wait until morning to tamper with her controls. He was too tired to give her the proper attention she needed, the proper attention she deserved. There was one other thing he had to do before he went to bed. He removed her tracking device and smashed it to pieces. It would never work again. But she would. He was certain of that. He was also confident she would function better than she ever had.

Getting the robots to agree to let him take what he wanted off of the junk pile turned out to be the best deal he'd made in his life. From prior visits, he used the junk he got from the computer…robot pile to support his hobby. He often incorporated it in his artwork or used the scrap with his innovation to make practical gadgets. Excelcious considered this latest find to be the greatest, and the treasure of a lifetime. He thought she looked a lot like the legendary Shilloqwai. But this couldn't have been her. The robots weren't stupid enough to leave her for his taking. He wanted to chalk it up to coincidence. As far as he knew she didn't have a twin. Had he really gotten his hands on the legendary Shilloqwai? If it was her, the winds of change were blowing. Excelcious hoped the changes in fortune brought about by this event would be for the benefit of everyone, Humankind, and machine. He was up at 4:30 later that morning, after just a few hours of sound sleep. He was as excited as a child at Christmas, running to the guest bedroom ready to look over his new acquisition. He lifted her carefully and carried her across the hallway into his laboratory. What a nice piece of …. hydraulic…robot technology he thought with a smile of amusement. To him, she was more than a machine, and anything other than just a robot.

But, if she were real, would she be capable of loving? Is true love something that a real woman with these physical attributes would seek? Or would she live for the moment and use her accessories for living the high life? Offerings would be thrown at her feet for illicit services. Would she be able to control her unbridled passions and desires, unleashing them only on the love of her life? Or would she give into the sins committed by one thirsting with greed and an insatiable hunger for lust? Would she buy into the pretentious lie that material things and power could provide her with everything she'd ever want or need? True love is what Excelcious sought. It was part of the package deal where he and his prospective partner would be totally committed to one another. He chided himself for fantasizing about her and for dreaming of being with her. He wasn't going to get any of these things from a machine. Hell, he wondered if a robot could even understand the concept of love. Many humans sure as hell didn't, especially the aspect of true love! Again, he found himself gazing into her eyes of aqua-tourmaline-blue, exotic, and enchanting. Though she was just a machine, he could see there was a story in her eyes. He wanted to read it and understand it, probably just as much as she desired to tell it and have someone really listen to it. Upon closer examination he found many areas on her rubberized shell were starting to crack. The cracking was undoubtedly due to the trauma she'd been through.

Though porous, Excelcious imagined her outer shell had to be hot and baking her insides. Yet somehow, it seemed her protective skin was able to breathe to keep her from overheating. Perhaps it was a flaw in the design that contributed to her publicly known condensate issues. Repairing the seals, chinks and cracks in her armor seemed to be the least of his concerns. He was confident those things would be easy fixes. Excelcious was anxious to get a look inside of her. He wanted to check out the mechanical structure to make sure there wasn't any other significant damage as some of her joints had suffered. He would check to see if her mechanical robotic functions were operational.

He started by rolling her on her stomach. On her back, near her activation switch there was a hidden panel bolted shut. After releasing the latch and opening the panel, behind it was another switch, separate from her activation-deactivation switch. Upon flipping that switch, the shell separated vertically from her neck down, exactly in the middle between her stomach and her back. She was a complex machine, more so than he'd anticipated. But he would figure it out. Excelcious was considered to be one of the brightest IT minds ever.

He brushed aside her waist-long hair and then lifted off the back of the rubberized shell. At first glance, he thought her hair was an expensive wig. The intricate braids and elaborate designs cut into her hair suggested otherwise. Her long beautiful aqua-tourmaline hair was taking root into something. Was part of her skull actually bone melded with titanium steel? A new cloning concept-development? At least nothing that he'd heard of! Surprising if it was some new technology, especially since he'd kept abreast of the latest technological developments, scientific and medical. A closer look confirmed her hair indeed was rooted in human bone. Beneath the titanium there was soft tissue, he could see that new bone was forming. It appeared to him that where the bone was solidifying the titanium was thinning and chipping away. Though he didn't know how it was possible, her cranium actually seemed to be morphing into a human skull. He found that to be both intriguing and bewildering.

After moving her hair, away to one side, he found another portal and a small lever. Upon flipping the switch, he was able to remove the back plate of her skull, giving him access to her Central Processing Unit (CPU). It looked brand new, like it had never been used. The next puzzling question, of which he had many, was how this prototype human-like robot was able to function, when it appeared to him that the CPU itself was not functioning? Another question that came to mind is, had it ever worked? Something about this, didn't compute. If her CPU had never been operational, what was causing it to erode? It was more than condensation. It appeared, as though it was being attacked by human antibodies, like it was some sort of disease! And what was the gray and white matter on the deteriorating edges? Excelcious ruled out mold or fungi. Stating that it was human brain tissue would have him disbarred from the medical profession.

But nothing or no one was going to convince him otherwise. He held a steadfast belief 'human brain tissue' is exactly what the foreign matter was. He was going to leave well enough alone. He closed the portal to her head. Next, he replaced the shell protecting her backside. Holding the two pieces in place he gently turned her onto her back. Then, he proceeded to lift off the front of the shell, along with the headpiece, protecting the front of her skull. Inside the front of her skull, he found more gray and white matter. This was beyond his comprehension. He was going to let it be. He lifted her head and reached around for the back portal. With both pieces of protective coating around her skull in place, he locked the switch securing them firmly together. He wasn't about to play any more head games with her. He would have to be content, letting nature take its course.

He cleancd, replaced, and rewired all of her hardware in the front, just as he'd done in the back. He no longer had to worry about replacing damaged or faulty parts. It looked to him that she had just been totally refurbished. After replacing her ribcage, he was convinced now, as he was from the start, that she would function better than she ever had. It took him a week to run the diagnostics and replace her mechanical guts. Next, he ran diagnostics on her software and tested it. There were no apparent oddities, at least nothing like he had found in the examination of her head. Well, there was one thing. He wondered if her makers had done it as a mockery, or if the heart of gold was symbolic of the robotic human she was intended to be.

When he was satisfied everything was fully operational, he went to replace the top part of her outer shell. There were some cracks in it, but he had a sealer that would repair and make it stronger. He would paint her outer shell with the compound after he had her back together. He was concerned, because the area of the shell protecting the underside of her silicon breasts was so badly worn. He didn't know how to reinforce it to protect her. That's something, that would have to be addressed, though, not immediately. After another four or five days, he'd completed his thorough examination of her, inside and out. In just over two weeks' time, he had her flawlessly functional and fully operational. Once Excelcious finished the reassembly of his new acquisition, he was wondering why he'd ever left the medical profession. Some of the new technologies and procedures that were becoming available, enabled people in the medical profession to better serve their patients.

He knew why he left. The issue he was experiencing was trying to justify his reasoning for doing so. In retrospect he thought it selfish. None of the state-of-the-art technologies and treatments offered enough help to save his fiancée Angelina. She died after contracting influenza and pneumonia simultaneously. It was almost like he held a grudge against the profession for being incompetent and not able to save her. He knew it wasn't a fair judgement. He took it personal every time he lost a client.

Excelcious unreasonably believed he could save them all. And here, he was holding others to the impossible standard he'd set for himself. He knew better. Faith in his God told him so. And when God decided to call one of his children home, that child was going home to meet its maker. Nothing he did personally or professionally was going to alter the Master's Plan. Recognized to be among one of the field's top medical doctors he almost felt guilty for leaving. Excelcious was a general practitioner, yet he seemed to know as much as specialists for heart, respiratory, ophthalmology and epidemiology. He didn't know how he knew all of the things he did. Admittedly there were a lot of things he didn't know. Much of the time he acted on instinct, often going against logic and reason. He'd been lucky trusting his instincts, and he had always been right on critical issues. He gave his heart and soul while working in the medical profession.

The guilt he felt for leaving, came mostly from wondering how many lives were lost because he wasn't there to give his expert opinion on life and death matters. God had a reason for his choosing to leave the profession. He wasn't quite sure what that was yet. Excelcious would follow blindly, faithfully, until he figured it out. "Damn!" He cursed aloud, realizing it was after midnight. He'd been working 16-hour days to get her operational. It was too late to activate her. He would wait until much later that morning to test her and make sure there were no glitches or condensation issues. If things went according to his plan, once activated, she would never be deactivated again. Sleep mode would be her resting period. Outside of that, Excelcious planned to give her the freedom to do almost anything she pleased, whenever she wanted to do it. He suspected that she would feel forever indebted to him, but he would not take advantage of her in that way. He wished for her to be his personal assistant. However, he would give her the choice as to whether or not she would take him up on his offer.

Excelcious always believed she was much more than a robot. Those beliefs received affirmation the instant he'd activated her. Coming out of her dormancy, she immediately introduced herself. "Hello, I'm Shilloqwai, robot-human liaison, project Mercusilver, model# 7/11/13F, Class XOXOTLC, reporting for duty."

"So, you are the legendary Shilloqwai! It's an honor and a privilege to meet you. You're an idol, my hero. No disrespect Shilloqwai! Cut the bullshit! You've been relieved of all of your duties. Your only obligation is to protect Humankind. It's not solely your responsibility. It's a world responsibility, one that we all share, robots and humans alike."

"Forgive me, Excelcious. I don't understand!"

"What's to understand?"

"Where I am, exactly, and how did I get here, wherever here is? Wait, I remember! I've been here before. It wasn't long ago. So, you really are Excelcious Orbitus! I brought you a lost package from Valentino and Onshanda Puro-Amoris. How did you come to find me? I was to be terminated, incinerated! But you …!"

"Yes, I rescued you from the shit pile as it is referred to by the robots and everyone else. Just before the conflict ended, I was granted rights to take whatever I wanted from the scrap pile. This privilege has allowed me to claim things, mostly odds and ends. I collected these things for various reasons. But you, you were not something to be taken. You are something, no someone, to be honored and respected. You are a guest, no, a permanent resident in my home for as long as you wish to stay. For whatever reason, the robots felt compelled to trash you, I will always treasure you."

"Thank you! You're very sweet! Why did you bring me here, to your home?" Shilloqwai asked curiously. "They're going to find you! And when they do, they'll kill you for theft of government property and harboring a fugitive."

"How are they going to find me? If they do, I told you, I had the right to claim whatever was on that pile. You became my property to do with whatever I chose."

"Between drones and satellites, the robots know where all humans are, where they're going, what they're doing, when they're doing it, who they're doing it with, and how they're doing it!" Shilloqwai revealed. "Sick bastards! Almost as perverted as some humans. In some ways, even more so. I now understand why humans are so paranoid, especially when it comes to privacy issues. Hell, most robots can be controlled remotely, not me, that's not how I was built. As a robot, I treasure my independence. Being continually tracked, made me realize I wasn't as independent as I thought I was. Freedoms have been suppressed, restricted, and even taken away, not just mine, but the freedoms of Earth's civilization."

"I took out your tracking device. They can't track you, and to this point they haven't been able to track me and the things I'm doing."

"What the hell are you talking about? The robots know you live here. And they're going to come here at some point looking for me. When they find me, I'll be terminated!" Shilloqwai lamented.

"Like hell you will!" Excelcious argued. "You belong to me if anyone asks. At least you did!"

"What? You lay claims to me, and you're setting me free, just like that? I can't survive out there alone, not yet anyway!" Shilloqwai admitted, fearing her newfound freedom as much as she was thankful for it.

"Don't worry. You have a place to stay, as long as you like. I will protect you as best I can." Excelcious assured her.

"There's no protection from the robots. They could kill Humankind's collective ass if they wanted to. They want to terminate me, and they will, when they find me. There'll be nothing you can do to stop them from doing so. As for you, when they discover your secrets, they will kill you too. So, tell me about the Man of Mystery and Imagination. I already know about your special privilege, The Museum of Robots and Automation and your collection of parts from the salvage pile."

"But, how do you know all of this about me, seeing this is our initial encounter?"

"I'll try to explain it to you as best I can. There's something wrong with me, I keep having glitches that cause me to breakdown. I don't know how many times I've been in the lab for repairs and restoration. During one such time, this is going to sound crazy. It was like an out-of-body experience. I saw this handsome hunk taking stuff from the junk pile. I knew it was you from the things I've heard about you, here and there. From that moment, you became the man of my dreams. And in that moment with the robot hacks working on me, I was wishing it was you repairing me, touching me, and mending my broken mechanical heart. Don't you think it strange for a robot to have dreams and desires?"

"Everyone has dreams and desires, Shilloqwai! What's wrong with that?"

"Excelcious! I'm a damn machine, a robot! I shouldn't be experiencing things like humans do. And I shouldn't be sensing and feeling things, the way humans do. It's all so strange to me. So scary, yet exciting at the same time."

"You're more than a robot! You're my hero, and I love you too!"

Shilloqwai laughed, with a blushing smile. "I see you got the package I delivered and that you read the letter I wrote you. Yeah, I probably shouldn't have signed the letter, love Shilloqwai. I risked my existence bringing that box to you. I'd heard so many good things about you, that you've done so much for others out of love, I thought it was time someone returned the favor."

"That was more than returning a favor. It was a true act of love. Risking your life, for a friend! There's no greater love than that!"

"So, what all have you heard about me?"

"Just a few things in general, not much in the way of specifics. I heard that you were a caring, loving, sensitive person, yet a very private person.

"Well, I'm a retired doctor, and an IT specialist. I keep to myself mostly and let the world keep on turning, it's a lot safer that way!"

"I think I know what you mean. I'm a mechanical device that's bound to grow outdated. When that day comes, I'll be terminated. I was created and designed to be liaison-diplomat for robot-human relations. At first, I thought it to be an honorable role. Then I realized I was but a pawn in a losing game where I would end up the sacrificial lamb. In order to complete my quest, I would be required to come to a basic understanding of human nature, a daunting, damn near impossible task. All humans are unique creatures with different talents and abilities, all with a most precious gift, life! It's a gift to be treasured and respected until the mortal end." Shilloqwai lamented. "I've told you about my dream of becoming human, and the reason for that is because I want to experience this thing called love to the fullest before I die."

"True love is an eternal flame, that can't be extinguished…even at the end of one's mortal life. Death opens the door to one's eternal life, and the love, it goes on and on…The Power of Love, having created all life, always was, is present now, and always will be." Excelcious profoundly stated, trying to enlighten her.

"You're confusing me. The concept of love is broader and more complicated than I could have imagined. There's no logic or reason that can explain love and its omniscient powers. Love defies all logic and reason, with the ability to change everything, heal anything and make something of nothing. How is this possible?" Shilloqwai asked inquisitively. "Do you think love can change me, heal me, make me human?"

"I don't know, honestly. Love is strange. Many things that happen as a result of love are inexplicable. Trying to understand it, is like trying to find a solution to an unsolvable puzzle. All you need to know about Love, is that through Love, all things are possible." Excelcious said, again trying to enlighten her with his wisdom.

"I trust you, and I want to believe you." Shilloqwai said convincingly. "I know you see how tensions are escalating again between the robots and humans. Face it, there's going to be another conflict. It may be the end for Humankind, it may be the end for the robots, in all likelihood, it will be the end for both factions! Then who will care for the Earth?"

"Love will determine that! All it takes is a point of light to illuminate the dark. In these dark times, it's up to us to let our lights shine. We don't have to worry about the things we can't change, Love will take care of those." Excelcious reassured her. "The things we can change, as difficult as some of them might be, Love will give us the strength we need and help us find a way."

Shilloqwai smiled, taking to heart his words of wisdom, while looking on him with admiration. She would be ever thankful for the new friend she'd just found in him. He'd saved her life, more accurately, salvaged her existence. "So, what do you plan to do when all hell breaks loose?" Shilloqwai asked, brushing his sandy-blonde hair out of his eyes. Excelcious looked at her inquisitively with his milk-chocolate eyes. He was seeking clarification. "You know, when conflict erupts? It's nearing the boiling point again!" Like Shilloqwai needed to jog his memory.

"Ah, yes. Thank you for reminding me. Would you mind bringing me that box over on the desk?" She did as he requested and then sat down on the couch next to him. "Open it!" He directed her. Again, she honored his request. It was a beaded belt set with rhinestones, similar to the one she saw that he was wearing. He tailored this particular one to fit her.

"Thank you."

"Don't ever take it off. It's one of the ways I can protect you. And it will help you to protect yourself."

"Oh really! How does it work?"

"It's part of my DDD line of weaponry, very effective for disarming, disabling, and destroying robots, in groups or as individuals. The blue button disables them, the red disarms them and the black one destroys them."

"Impressive!"

"Honey, you ain't seen nothin' yet! I've got a whole armory full of the good stuff, explosives, long-range rifles, rockets, you name it, it's there."

"Holy shit! You know you're dead if they find out about any of this!" Shilloqwai expressed her concern, worried that something dreadful might happen to Excelcious.

"They won't. I've had this stuff for seven years and they don't have a clue!"

"Damn! How are you hiding it from them?"

"I figured out how to blind their satellites and drones. Between that and holograms I've been able to disguise my lot. They only see me when I want to be seen. That's how I can protect you. I'll show you more of the wonders of my world later." Excelcious promised. "What about you? I'm sure you have some secrets of your own! Your turn to share."

"Well yeah, I just …"

"C'mon Shilloqwai, open up! You said you trusted me! They want to terminate you for murdering those killers, don't they? And that plane crash, they gave you the wrong cable. That's why you had glitches, and why the plane crashed."

"You know I killed those six bastards out of self-defense. There was an 18-year-old girl nearby that surely would have been victimized. The Robocops had to know she, along with several other young females, were in the neighborhood. They know everything from their surveillance. They had to know this one girl in particular was in danger. I was the scapegoat, the liaison that allegedly committed an act of war. They were looking for an excuse to terminate me and they found one. They were trying to find the best way to make me disappear. In the meantime, they assigned me to pilot the solar planes. They took me away from what I was good at, what I was designed to be, more humanlike. They forbade me to have human interaction and threatened me with incineration if I did. It hurt me deeply. Especially when I realized I'd been used all of this time, going back to the day I was activated. Sorry for babbling."

"No, you're fine. You don't need to defend yourself. In my eyes you're innocent. One of those bastards you murdered in self-defense, raped, and killed one of my nieces. Tell me something about you I don't know."

"I find it interesting just how much you already know about me." Shilloqwai remarked with a whimsical smile. "I don't know why, but I feel like I can trust you. I've already shared with you my innermost secrets. So, what else do you want to know about me?"

"I know Shilloqwai the comic book hero, I know Shilloqwai the robot. The person I want to get to know, is Shilloqwai…the one that's more HUMAN!"

"With you, I couldn't feel more at home. You make me feel HUMAN!" Shilloqwai confessed. "But I'm a damn machine, a robot. I want to say it's part of my programming, but it feels like so much more than that. When I killed those criminals that nearly destroyed me, I felt guilt and remorse. Deep down in my robot heart, I forgave them for what they tried to do to me."

"That's normal. I'd be more concerned had you felt nothing at all. This is fascinating! What else do you feel?"

"I don't know. It's confusing. I'm a robot, and even with my programming, to be more human-like, i don't know that I should be feeling anything at all!" Shilloqwai surmised.

"But you're much more than a robot!"

"I'm not sure how to process that input. Just as I'm not sure how to process the other things that I feel; like the sensations where I experience the five senses as humans do. I taste, I smell, I feel, I see, and I hear, just like humans. It's so natural, so spontaneous when I instinctively act on this type of sensory input. When I rely on my mechanical senses, it's so contrived when I regurgitate all of the shit from my database. I feel like an arrogant bitch, a know-it-all, coming off like I'm greater than Thou! I feel so dishonest, so disrespectful, so insensitive when I blurt out what I know! It makes others feel small. It's not me, putting other people down and making them feel like shit! I don't have an ego that needs feeding."

"So how do you view yourself? I mean, I like you just the way you are!"

"You're too kind! I think I'm still in the discovery process, trying to figure out who and what I am. So, you don't have a problem with a robot who has passions, dreams, and desires of becoming human? Like I've stated before, I want to love, and be loved, experiencing love in its truest form!"

"But why would you want to become human and have to deal with all of the imperfections that are part of it?"

"Imperfections, like making mistakes, growing old and gaining wisdom? Robots make lots of mistakes. Like humans we can learn from our mistakes. As robots age, they become outdated. Eventually they're terminated, incinerated. Humans become frail when they age, and when they die, or should I say when they're born into eternal life, the love that they've known, or hopefully have come to know, goes on! I look exactly as I did 25 years ago when I was activated."

"Almost!" Excelcious corrected her.

"What do you mean almost? I defy you to identify one noticeable difference from the two photos you have of me. I'm betting that you can't."

"Oh, but I can. It's so obvious, I can see why even you, overlooked it. Look at the pictures again. This one, taken what, when you were about 18? And this one just recently, almost 10 years later. Your hair was shoulder-length, here in the first photo. And here in this one, taken just after I got you off the scrap pile, your aqua-tourmaline hair is almost down to your waist!"

"But I haven't added extensions or gotten a new weave! How is it possible, my hair is actually growing out? I mean, it happened so gradually, I never even gave it a second thought. And now that I think about it, for the most part, it's been over the past three years where it seems to have really grown. So, you're a retired doctor! What is your medical opinion?"

"I would say that in order for your hair to grow the way it is, it has to be rooted in something."

"Like what? I have a rubber shell for a scalp protecting my CPU to avoid malfunctions and interruptions, when receiving and processing information and outputting data. Precision is critical to my functionality and ability to generate accurate reports."

"About your CPU, we need to discuss that!"

"What? Did you find a problem while I was getting my head examined?

"I wouldn't exactly say it was a problem. A bit of an anomaly perhaps. I've removed some encrypted files. I don't know if I'll be able to get at them, without destroying them. I suspect these files were causing you to glitch, which is why I removed them. Honestly, how would you rate your overall performance for the past quarter-of-a-century?"

"Stellar!" Shilloqwai boasted confidently. My dependability has been the issue! Damn glitches!"

"While I was doing your overhaul that's one of the issues I paid special attention to. I'd like to think that I've fixed that problem, by removing those encrypted files. There'll be no more glitches. At least I hope not!"

"Getting back to the issue of my CPU, you specifically wanted to talk to me in regard to it! Is there a problem with it? Is something wrong?" Shilloqwai was concerned.

"Not exactly! It's an anomaly really! And if what's happening with you, is what I suspect, it's incredibly amazing! You're amazing!" Excelcious told her, bolstering her confidence.

"Wait, are we talking about my performance, or are we drifting off on another tangent?"

"We can talk about how stunningly beautiful you are at another time."

"Thank you. If you're hoping to get more from me than a RAPP sheet, which requires me to receive, analyze, process and print data, you're going to be gravely disappointed. I can process data faster than any human, and faster and more accurately than any robot. You've said that I'm more than a robot! But, when it comes down to the core of the matter, that's all I am. Just a machine! You interfacing with me or doing anything else with me is impossible!"

"I can dream, can't I?" Excelcious asked gazing hypnotically deep into her tourmaline eyes. Both let out a much-needed hearty laugh. Shilloqwai returned the gaze of enchantment and flashed him a genuine smile of appreciation for his intended compliment. Hazy-eyed, it appeared that his milk-chocolate eyes were melting over her. Shilloqwai sensed Excelcious was intending to give her more than a compliment. It was almost as though he was showing a genuine interest in her. She had to stop. She was reading too much into things. She believed he was in part serious with the things he'd said. She welcomed the innuendoes surrounding his wild fantasy. She wished there were more that she could do to accommodate him. But they weren't compatible.

It was beyond their wildest dreams to think anything more than intellectual conversation between them was possible. "We keep getting sidetracked," Shilloqwai noted. "Tell me, what's going on with my CPU?"

"Honestly, I don't think your CPU has ever worked. The idea that you have functioned throughout your existence, without a working CPU, is preposterous. You don't need to have a scientific mind to know that it's utterly impossible. That would be like a car running without gasoline."

"Solar cars do!" She astutely pointed out.

"Before them. It would be like a butterfly flying without wings. It doesn't happen! But you, you're a beautiful mystery. You possess a lot of qualities, not indicative of robots, like the way you show how caring and compassionate you can be. You listen, and really hear what someone is trying to tell you. Many humans lack the ability to do these things."

"So, the bastards are trying to get rid of me by installing faulty parts?"

"No, I think your programs are conflicting. Your programs for logic and reason, all of the software that authenticates you as a robot, are conflicting with the intangible software, and all of the programming that is supposed to make it easier for you to relate to humans. In regard to your CPU, from what I can tell it's an original part. It was labeled as such. So, it's nothing the Robotix techs did. It doesn't appear that they've tampered with you in any way! It's just that…"

"Just that what?"

"There were scorch marks around the CPU. The initial activity was little if any at all. Whatever happened when you were activated, isn't what's accounting for the erosion taking place, especially on the one side of your CPU, which has almost completely eroded into nothing. There, I found gray and white matter."

"Gray and white matter? I need more information to process what you're trying to tell me!"

"You know I was a medical doctor. I graduated at the top of my class, too smart for my own britches. As much as I knew then, there was a lot I didn't know. As much as I know now, there's so much more I have to learn. Back then I was just a smart-assed punk!"

"You seemed to have grown up some, but you're still a smart ass. With the wisdom you've gained, what do you think the gray and white matter is? Are you suggesting that…?"

"By no means am I suggesting anything. At first, I thought it may have been some sort of fungus, bacteria or mold building up, on account of your past condensation issues. After a closer look, I'm convinced that the gray and white matter is nothing other than human brain tissue. Clearly, it appears that some sort of transformation is taking place. When I examined the rubberized shell protecting your cranium and the rest of your body, much of it was cracked. "I sealed the cracks and insolated the shell, so you would never again overheat. That alone, seems to have resolved your condensation issues."

"Thank you, I'm grateful, and forever indebted to you for that! Do you have any explanation for my hair growing the way it is?"

"There's flesh on top of your skull, where most of the deterioration of the shell seems to be occurring. That's where your hair is taking root. It appears that flesh and bone are actually replacing the rubberized shell and titanium skull as it continues to erode!"

"I think it's all part of a plan to get rid of me Excelcious. What in the hell have they done to me?"

"If you mean, they, as in the Robotechs, they're not exactly stupid, but I don't think they're intelligent enough to devise a program capable of doing the things that are happening to you. There's a transformation of some kind taking place. Will the process complete itself? That remains to be seen!"

"It's apparent there's no scientific or medical explanation for the changes taking place. Any theories of your own that you'd care to share? With more input, I can calculate and estimate more possible outcomes. The analytics might even allow me to theorize on my own."

"In a word, my theory is love!"

"Love? What's love got to do with it? I have an idea, but I don't really know what love is!"

"I don't know how to explain it to you, other than, it's the greatest feeling in the world, the gift that keeps on giving. Love is something that, you always get back more than you give. At times it's hard to see, but Love is all around."

"Most times it doesn't feel like it. Say it is Love, as you believe it is, where is the love? The robots don't love me, they hate me. They want to incinerate me. Why the hell do you think they threw me on top of the shit pile?"

"The reason they threw you on top of the shit pile is because they were worried you were going to beat them to the punch and put them there. They were worried they'd end up there before you did their collective intelligence, you're smarter than the lot of them. Because I rescued you, you're going to outlast them all. They can't threaten you with termination and incineration anymore."

"You know they will try."

"I assure you; you won't be terminated anytime soon. You're a treasure to be protected."

"I'm honored by your valor and your flattery. But I find myself in an awkward position. I don't really fit in as a robot, and I'm not human. I don't see myself fitting into either world. I think you should have left me on the junk pile."

"On the contrary. You should exude more confidence in yourself. You're a beautiful emotional creature. To most humans you're a beloved hero!"

"You talk about me as if I were actually alive. The very concept is inconceivable to me. Just the thought of it is insane to me! Having said that, I have no explanation for the growing emotion stirring inside me. Being I am but a machine, I don't understand these emotions or how I'm able to express my feelings at a human level. I do know this, that if I were human, I would kiss you! Does it trouble you in the least that I feel this way?" She asked as she began to run her fingers through Excelcious' long, sandy-blonde hair.

"Not in the least. In fact, it makes me wish, all the more, that you were human!" He responded by gently caressing her face. He could swear the rubber coating felt more like soft tissue, human flesh, and bone. "You're the kind of woman I could fall in love with. A woman I have been in love with for a long time."

"How long is a long time?" Shilloqwai asked placing her hands on his shoulders. As she gazed into his chestnut brown eyes, she could see the milk-chocolate melting.

"Since I was in the first grade!" Shilloqwai laughed until she cried at the ridiculousness of Excelcious' confession.

"Who's the one telling bullshit stories now? And how could you have been in love with me for that long when we've just recently, formally introduced ourselves to one another. Pardon me Excelcious, but I think you're full of shit! I will say this in your defense, not long ago, I was let into your house by the Eternal Twins. I know you remember. When I dropped off a box and put that hand-written letter inside! I felt your love then and it's 1,000 times stronger now. You're an amazing man. I wish we could be lovers instead of just friends."

"We're just coming out of a century of darkness that culminated with the war between robots and humans. About 25 years ago, times were especially dark. People needed hope, something to keep them going. They needed a hero. People found that hero in a comic book character: Shilloqwai, the humanlike, trustworthy robot. There were only 10 books in the series written by Skeletos Puro-Amoris. I have the signed copies in my Robot Museum. They were signed by Valentino, Onshanda, Skeletos, and you. Your creator made you a superhero, the fantasy girl that all of the boys were in love with. The girls wanted to be like you, and everyone idolized you. I loved you then and I love you 1000, times more, now. I fell in love with a comic book character that came to life. You couldn't be more real to me!"

"To be honest, I forgot about the comic books. I've never read them. And I don't know about all of the superhero stuff. It's not me! I just want to do the right thing. I want to be true to myself and be who or what I am! I'm all about helping people. I came across a saying once…I am Third. The essence of it stressed…putting God first, family and friends second and putting yourself third. I've pondered over this saying a lot. I think it's very profound, so I put it into practice. I abide by it faithfully. It's very unselfish. For those who don't know what love is, or for those who haven't been blessed with the gift of experiencing it, I think it's a simple and practical way for me to try and understand the overall concept."

"I think it took a superhero to stand up to Robotikis the way you did. Especially with you knowing the consequences, that would ultimately lead to the end of your existence. That's what makes you a real-life hero Shilloqwai! Funny, in the last book you were on top of the scrap pile. The book didn't specify who, but someone had rescued you. And you came to life, escapingthe grasp of Robotikis and his threats to terminate you."

Shilloqwai began to quiver, afraid of the question she hesitantly asked. "So, how does the story end?"

"Skeletos was terminated before he could finish the series. The next issue was going to be titled; The return of the superhero: Shilloqwai comes to life! The story hasn't ended yet. It's ongoing. How it ends is entirely up to you."

"There's nothing in my programming that allows me to shapeshift or magically transform me into a human being."

"So, you're giving up on your dreams? They can all come true, even the impossible ones. You're a strong, hard-headed woman. I mean that in a good way. Don't give up the fight!"

"Woman? You're forgetting I'm a robot. Talking about me, as if I were alive is just as insane as me having dreams and desires."

"Is it Shilloqwai? I believe in you! I told you I've been in love with you since I was in first grade."

"Dreams and desires aren't going to make me come alive!" Shilloqwai astutely pointed out, before waiting for Excelcious' response.

"True, but passions and pursuit of your dreams might!"

"I should have you committed for entertaining such delusions. As a retired doctor and an IT specialist you should know better. If the medical profession knew what you're thinking and half-believing, it would revoke your privileges to practice."

"Who's going to tell them?"

"Not me. We had an agreement to keep shared secrets between ourselves, remember? Humans often ask, what does it hurt to dream?"

"I'm not misreading you. I know you're serious about intending to pursue your dream of becoming human. It's the passion in the pursuit that makes dreams come true and turns fantasy into reality. Standing up for what they believe in is what makes people real! It's what can make you real!"

"That's the sweetest smelling line of bullshit I've ever heard. Compared to the pile, your words seem to have been saturated in wild-rose perfume. Regardless of our dreams and desires, no robot, or any machine has the ability to transform into a human being."

"You're probably right. But does that mean we have to stop dreaming?"

"Absolutely not! You don't know how I wish I could kiss you! And you said you've been in love with me since the first grade. Do you want to…?" She paused, hesitant to say what was on her mind. She was afraid that he wouldn't follow through with what his heart desired. She was taken by surprise when she realized that somehow, he'd quickly developed an innate ability to read her mind.

"Yes! I want to kiss you! I've been wanting to, for a long, long, time!" Excelcious confessed before she could finish her dreamy proposition.

"Then do it, I dare you!" She beckoned him. Shilloqwai closed her eyes and pursed her lips, waiting to see what was going to happen next.

He didn't keep her waiting long. His soft kiss turned wet. Excelcious was surprised that her tongue didn't taste like silicon as he expected it might. He could taste the raspberry on her lips. He pulled back suddenly, thinking it was just a dream . Both gasped, trying to get a second wind. "So!" Shilloqwai sighed. "Now that you've kissed me, was it everything you imagined it would be?"

"All of that, and so much more. Not in my wildest dreams, or my most delusional fantasies, could I have imagined anything to be as sweet as the affectionate exchange we just shared." Both needed a precious moment to reminisce over how special their first kiss was. "It was heavenly! When you're kissing an angel, why would I expect anything less?"

"And not in my wildest fantasies, did I think I would be sharing my first kiss with you. After I got my ass beat, and I collapsed into the stream, I thought it was over for me. When I was in pieces in the Robotics lab, and my mechanical guts were scattered over three tables, I was having an out of body experience. Like I told you earlier, I was wishing that you were the one touching me, helping me get my shit together instead of Robotikis' mechanical hacks. I started wondering then, even though it could never happen, what it would be like to be loved by you. Surprisingly, I'm starting to get an idea of what it would be like. It's making me wish all the more that we could love each other fully and completely. You never expect your first-ever kiss to come from an angel. I'm in the state of euphoria at the moment. I hope it was as good for you as it was for me. Please, kiss me again!" She begged, closing her eyes, and pursing her lips, she waited for the fantasy to continue. She felt the warmth of his touch as he pulled her trembling body close to his. She could feel him trembling too. Their nervousness about passionately engaging in the simple act was gone. Intimacy replaced the nervousness and brought on ecstasy when their lips met again. There was unbridled passion in every wet raspberry kiss. Excelcious had never tasted such sweetness. They pulled away briefly to get a second wind. He let out a sigh while she cooed in the comfort of his arms. They spent the interim period between kisses staring into one another's eyes. As she gazed into his, she could see serenity in his soft chocolate eyes.

He returned her gaze. She could tell he was lost in the depths of her eyes of tourmaline blue. She wasn't sure at first, but now she was certain. He was enchanted with her, infatuated with her and perhaps already in love with her. He was definitely warming up to her as she could see his milk-chocolate eyes were melting because of her kissing him. As it was with Shilloqwai, his encounter with her proved to be more than a dream come true. It was an outlandish fantasy, a surreal reality. Other than semantics, there was no distinct difference between the two. Her pure blue eyes seemed to be melting into liquid crystal because of him kissing her. She wasn't sure, but she believed she was already in love with him, and that they were already in love with each other. Was theirs a love at first sight? According to the files on Love in her database, it was possible, but rarely happened. So, what was it that was transpiring between them now?

The aura of her enchanting eyes deepened as he swore a translucent mist was forming in them, clouding the existence of the boundaries between fantasy and reality. "Look into my eyes. Tell me that you want me to kiss you again!" She didn't think she'd need to ask him twice, but, when Excelcious hesitated, "Kiss me!" She begged for a second time! She closed her eyes, so he had to imagine what it was like in the enchanting world behind her eyes of tourmaline blue.

Then she pursed her lips, inviting him to continue with his fantasy. His dream of kissing her had already come true. He took her into his open arms and fulfilled her desires. Never in her wildest dreams did she think he would ever be kissing her and falling in love with her as Shilloqwai believed he was. This kiss, like the others preceding it, was magical and wet. Her lips and her tongue were still gushing with the taste of wild berries. After their first kiss... a lover's kiss, Each subsequent fiery flurry got wetter and wilder. Neither knew how long their affectionate exchange lasted, only that, neither wanted it to end. Shilloqwai finally broke the embrace. Excelcious had left her breathless. But how? She didn't breathe as humans did. She didn't understand why her body was still trembling or why she had broken into a cold sweat.

"Shit!" She cursed.

"Honey what's wrong?"

"Nothing, everything! I don't know. What just happened between us?"

"We followed our instincts. So, you felt it too?"

"Yes, I felt it! What was it? I feel so... I'm not sure... what I'm feeling!"

"I'm not sure, but it's usually what happens between two people when they start falling in love?"

"No, this isn't possible!" Shilloqwai was in denial of what had just transpired.

"You can't deny what you felt. I felt it too. We both can't be wrong. I want it to be real, and so do you! It was real, and we both know it! We're fooling ourselves if we think otherwise."

"But this can't happen again. It feels so right, but it's so very wrong."

"What's wrong with falling in love?" Excelcious asked innocently. "Shut up and kiss me!" He demanded. Regardless of how wrong she believed it was, Shilloqwai was not about to deny him. She honored his request. With each subsequent flurry the kisses became more intimate and more passionate than they were in their initial exchanges.. Regardless, the first kiss would always be special.

It opened the door to what both were feeling now. Though Shilloqwai didn't understand the feeling of 1,000 butterflies fluttering in her stomach, and the light-headedness that allowed her to float up to cloud #9, she hoped the feelings would never fade. She'd been looking for an escape from reality, someplace where she felt protected from the evil lurking outside. She'd just found that place, secure in the cradle of Excelcious' arms. She sensed that he was secure in hers.

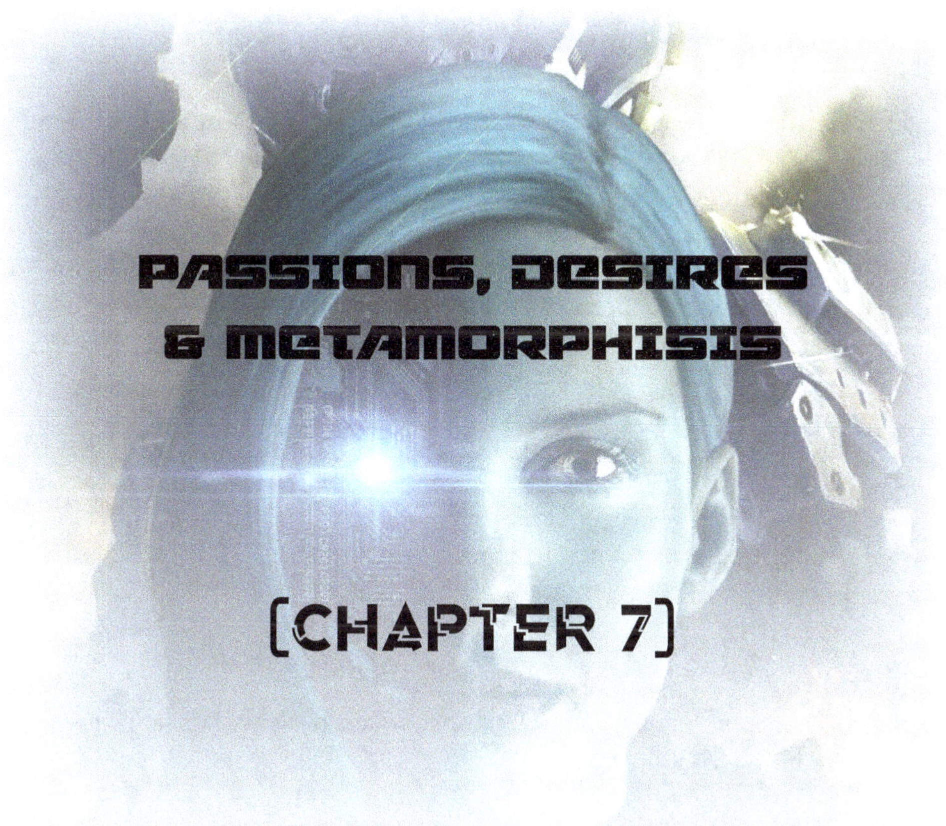

[CHAPTER 7]

Early the next morning, Shilloqwai bolted from her bed in a panic. "Excelcious! Excelcious! Wake up! Someone's trying to break in!"

"What Shilloqwai? What's all the fuss about?"

"Robocops, they're outside, trying to break in!" With the number of red, blue, and white strobes flashing, you'd think the outside of Excelcious' house was a national disaster scene.

"Stay here, I'll go see what they want! They're always pestering me for something!"

"I'm telling you, they're here for me!" Shilloqwai insisted.

"Get a hold of yourself! Even if they are here for you, I told you, you're not going anywhere! You're staying with me! Trust me! I'll take care of this! Everything is going to be fine!" He assured her. Excelcious was infuriated by the battering ram force the Robocops were using on his front door. "I'm coming, I'm coming! Hold on to your nuts and bolts!" He shouted as he made his way across the living room. "What the hell do you want?"

He asked as he flung the door open. "I can't see shit! Turn all of those damn lights off!" Surprisingly, they honored his request. The Robocops gave Excelcious' eyes a chance to adjust to the change in lighting, after which they immediately bombarded him with questions.

"You wouldn't happen to know the whereabouts of Shilloqwai, that troublemaking robot, would you? Her last known location was here. We lost track of her because her homing device was destroyed!"

"As a matter of fact, I do know where she is. She's here with me! Is there a problem?"

"Robotikis issued an All-Points Bulletin for her. She's under arrest and due to be terminated followed by her incineration, immediately!"

"For what?"

"Damaging global property. She attacked Robotikis and nearly destroyed him."

"Almost you say? Damn, that's about the only thing she's ever failed at!"

"This isn't a joke, Excelcious! If you don't turn her over, you'll be taken in for harboring a fugitive."

"Oh, I'm not joking, she's staying with me. If Robotikis wants to fight for her rights, tell him I'll see him in court. She was on the shit pile. I rescued her and I'm providing sanctuary for her. Legally, she belongs to me! That was the agreement we signed seven years before the war ended. It's a lifetime contract now. I can claim whatever I want from the shit pile, no questions asked. So, you're screwed! You're not getting her back!"

"She's a murderer! She killed six people. She kidnapped a little girl. She crashed a solar plane and injured hundreds. She needs to be held accountable for her crimes just as any human is held accountable for misdeeds committed. She's broken Asimov's laws for which the penalty is termination."

"Listen to me! She told me about the kidnapping thing, and how the Robocops framed her, when she rescued a little girl and saved her from the jaws of death. As far as the solar plane incident, that's bullshit too! You set her up! You gave her the wrong interfacing USB cable! That's why the plane crashed. In regard to the six civilians, you said she killed, they deserved what they got. One of the bastards raped and killed one of my nieces. Explain to me how come your surveillance didn't pick up the heat signatures for four other young women that were in the vicinity of where Shilloqwai was attacked."

"We're just following orders sir!"

"Quit interrupting me. I wasn't finished talking. You say Shilloqwai broke Asimov's Laws! I think you got it wrong! Shilloqwai took action and prevented harm from coming to a little girl lost in the woods. I saw that on her body cam when I refurbished her. The cam also shows that she was given the wrong USB cable when she was assigned to fly that solar plane. She noted in her databanks the location of the other women nearby when she was attacked. Again, she took action in accordance with Asimov's Laws and saved lives. While you bastards are running around calculating how to get rid of Shilloqwai, those asshole criminals, scheduled for execution, were out on the streets. So, you want to tell me who was really in violation of Asimov's laws? "

"Those criminals weren't under our jurisdiction sir!"

"Helping get criminals off the street is not under your jurisdiction? Bullshit! Get the hell off of my property now and get out there and do your jobs."

"We're not leaving without Shilloqwai!"

"I gave you an order. Under Asimov's Laws you are required to do what I've asked you to do. If you don't, I will hold you in contempt and have your asses terminated! Do I make myself clear?"

"Very! But our orders from Robotikis were not to return without her! So, we're not leaving until you deliver the goods."

"Wanna' bet?" Excelcious was through arguing with them. Before the Robocops could utter another synthesized word, Excelcious stunned them by hitting the blue rhinestone on his DDD belt. After suffering from momentary glitches, the Robocops had forgotten why they'd come. "No, I haven't seen Shilloqwai," Excelcious lied convincingly. "Is there something else I can help you with?"

"Yes, we're trying to get back to the Robotix lab. We have a meeting with Robotikis. Can you help us? Our GPS systems seem to be out of sync."

"It's that huge facility right behind you. It's about a mile away." Excelcious pointed to the complex up on the hill. "Scan your wrist badges on the security key at the gate and you'll be able to pass right through!"

"Thank you. If you see Shilloqwai, will you tell her that Robotikis is looking for her?"

"Will do, shitheads!"

"Excuse us, what did you just call us?"

"Nothing, I was talking to myself. I said I've got to git my meds! I'll call the lab if I hear anything from Shilloqwai. And when you see Robotikis, tell him he can kiss my ass!"

"You can count on it, we will! Thank you for your cooperation." Said the Robocops as they bumbled along their way. Anytime assholes, Excelcious mumbled under his breath.

No sooner had the Robocops left when Shilloqwai burst into the room laughing hysterically. Her laughter was not syncopated or synthesized. It was genuine hearty laughter. Tears were coming from her eyes during her fit of hysterical laughter. Shilloqwai dropped to her knees, as she was barely able to keep from peeing on herself and on the floor. Why should she have to worry about that? Why was she experiencing that type of sensation to begin with? Robots didn't have those sensations or the need to seek out a bathroom to relieve themselves.

She still didn't understand the changes that were continuing to take place within her. She finally recomposed herself enough to speak. "And I thought I had a smart-assed mouth! I can't believe you got rid of those pain in the ass Robocops so easily. That belt is pretty amazing. I can't wait for the opportunity to use mine!"

"Yeah, all I did was stun them and they forgot why they came and left!"

"I heard everything; they came for me. They'll be back! I heard what you told them. Thanks for defending me. Is it okay if I kiss you?"

"You don't have to ask every time you want to kiss me. It's more of a thrill when you do it unexpectedly." Excelcious told her as he swept her off of her feet and into his arms, before taking her breath away with intimate, passionate kisses.

"I see what you mean!" As she reciprocated with wet, wild-berry kisses that left him thirsty for more. He set her down gently. She felt like her feet were barely touching the floor. They fell into a lover's embrace, exchanging kisses of fire that fueled their passions and left their desires burning out of control.

"That's as real as it gets!" Excelcious said, complimenting her affectionate prowess.

"Makes me wish we could do more!" Shilloqwai confessed, still sweltering from the heat of the moment. His devious smile told her he was tracking along with her. If all they could ever be, was friends, Excelcious would be content having her around for a confidant and companion. "As different as we are, we have one thing in common. We're both rebels. The robots tend to frown on rebels, 'treasonous bastards', is the phrase they use for those such as ourselves. What did you mean, when you said you'd be ready, if there was a second conflict?"

"If they only knew the half of what I'm up to."

"I'm beginning to wonder if it's safe hanging out with you. You're bound to get us both killed. But I'll take my chances on rogue freedom over robot prison any day. I'm all in. Just let me know what I can do to help you!"

"The love and support you've shown me so far have been a big help already. Perhaps we should go for a walk." Excelcious suggested. "It's good exercise. We can relax and take in the natural beauty while we're walking."

"I'd like that. Let me go change out of my pajamas into something more appropriate for the occasion. Shilloqwai returned a short time later, wearing a summer dress that swirled around her as she moved. The dress dangled just above her knees. It was yellow and had a blue-green floral print perfectly complementing her pigment.

Excelcious was in the bathroom tidying up when there came a knock at the door. Shilloqwai answered it, wishing that she hadn't. "What the hell are you doing here?" She snapped!

"I was about to ask you the same question." Robotikis responded, relishing in her dismay with his presence.

"I live here. Why are you here asshole?"

"You know why I'm here, Bitch!" Robotikis touted. "You are in a shitload of trouble. As soon as we get back to the lab, you'll be terminated!"

"I'm not going anywhere with you, you son-of-a-bitch!"

"The hell you aren't!"

"The hell she is!" Excelcious retorted, rushing to Shilloqwai's defense after hearing the commotion from the bathroom.

"You're in a shitload of trouble too, Excelcious!" Robotikis warned. "Possession of stolen property, harboring a fugitive, could get you a lot of jail time."

"You want to be king of the hill? Unless you get your ass out of here, now, you're going to find yourself sitting on top of that shit pile. You know, the one you left her on?"

"Are you threatening me?"

"By no means. I'm promising what I'm going to do to you if you ever set foot on my property again! Unless you have a warrant or an invitation, stay the hell away from here! And stay the hell away from her. For that matter stay the hell away from us!"

"Just hand over that bitch she-bot and I'll never bother you again. You have my word."

"That pile behind you has more credibility than your word! I had your word that I could lay claim to anything on the pile. I rescued Shilloqwai from the pile, by all rights, she belongs to me! The woman is mine and I'm not giving her up. So, you better get going asshole, before I mess you up good! This is your last warning, before I cite you with violating Asimov's laws. By your own decree, the consequence for such violations is termination! Last time I checked you are not above the law!"

Shilloqwai glared at Robotikis the same way she had that day when she'd recently visited him at his power station. Robotikis, already deactivated by Excelcious' DDD belt, never sensed the shrapnel coming. Just as it had earlier, the flying projectiles did significant damage to Robotikis, first penetrating his protective shell, before shredding his mechanical guts.

His nearly impenetrable shell lost its transparency. It was smokey black. Shilloqwai guessed the electric current in her weaponry had something to do with her being able to permeate his outer shell. She surmised it was also the reason she was able to critically damage him when she attacked him. The homing beacon alerted the Robotechs that their leader was in trouble. They would come for him and take him to the lab for refurbishing.

Excelcious and Shilloqwai would assuredly be brought in for questioning regarding the incident. Neither was about to sit and wait for the Robocops. They had plans for a walk in the park. It was a celebratory walk. For just over a month ago, Excelcious had rescued Shilloqwai from the salvage pile. In that short period of time, Excelcious noticed a few significant changes in her. Already noted was the inflexion and intonation of her soft voice. It was warm, inviting, and as natural as it had ever been. Her eyes, though they maintained their reflective quality, they'd lost their glassy manufactured look. They sparkled, twinkled like the stars, with all of the enchanting brilliance of a flaring supernova. Perhaps, the biggest change in her, was the way Shilloqwai exhibited emotions, with heartfelt passion. Excelcious noticed the subtleties, in particular, her facial expressions which displayed a myriad of emotions, ranging from, joy, to anger and fear. But the look of love on her face was indescribably angelic. Since Excelcious had given her, her freedom overall, Shilloqwai was filled with sheer happiness, most of the time.

She exuded confidence and courage, standing up to her robot superiors, fighting for the rights of Humankind. Though she was still afraid of what the robots might try to do to her, Excelcious had already proven to her that he was going to stand by her side, making good on his promise to protect her. He seemed willing to do anything to keep that promise even if it meant dying for her. And she stood ready to die for him. He hadn't said as much, but she saw it in his actions and the things he did for her. She felt it in his touch when he held her. Then there was the way he looked at her, gazing into her tourmaline eyes and reading her story. She didn't even have to speak, yet he listened to all she had to say. They had the innate ability of being able to read each other's minds. If she were human, she would swear they were talking heart-to-heart.

Excelcious appreciated her for the world-treasure he believed she was. He shows her dignity and treats her with respect in such a way that it makes Shilloqwai feel as though she were human. He told her from the onset that he believed that she was more human than a machine. Shilloqwai thought it preposterous at first, but this was something that now she too, was beginning to believe. Shilloqwai and Excelcious were holding hands as they strolled along the parkway near the stream where she'd nearly been put out of her existence. She would never forget that night, the night she was reborn, so to speak. The lingering nightmare had nearly faded from her memory. Shilloqwai was living the dream now.

She never imagined in her wildest fantasy that Excelcious would be the reason she would continue to fight for her existence. Though, she would sacrifice herself to save him. Even if it meant being terminated. She loved him and if she were human, she would be willing to die for him. What he felt, what she felt, was beyond what they imagined developing between the two of them. It seemed her protective rubberized shell was becoming more sensitive to the touch with each passing day. As they continued holding hands, she felt the warmth in his hands, and he felt the warmth in hers. His gentle grip sent sensations through her body. It was kind of like the first time they kissed when she felt the sensations of butterflies in her stomach. She didn't know how to describe the feeling, just that she wanted to experience more of it. Shilloqwai hoped he wouldn't let go of her hand anytime soon.

Excelcious felt the same way that she did. She could tell by the look in his eyes. With his hand in hers, he noticed another change taking place as they had been walking along. The sponge-like rubber shell coating her hand was much softer, feeling like flesh and bone. Her palm was sweaty. He believed it was more than her heart racing from her being with him. Though weak, he swore he felt her pulse too. That was something he would check on later when they were alone. Two other observations he made. Splotches were starting to form on her protective shell. Excelcious would check into that as well, after they had returned home. If her shell was continuing to deteriorate as he suspected, he wondered what it all meant. Were there consequences or benefits to it all? Was she transforming…or dying?

Excelcious noticed that Shilloqwai started lagging behind. He didn't say anything. He didn't want to worry her. He was kind of surprised when Shilloqwai brought the issue to his attention. As they approached a park bench, Shilloqwai, showing signs of fatigue, suggested they sit a while and rest. Without saying a word, Excelcious took her up on her suggestion. As they sat side-by-side on the bench, Excelcious looked over at her, knowing it wasn't condensate seeping from her porous shell. She was sweating profusely. Probably from walking at a brisk pace out in the sun.

Then she looked over at him and pulled him close. She closed her eyes and pursed her lips. He rewarded her with the wet kisses she was thirsting for, while leaving her breathless, the same way she had left him. The wet raspberry taste remained fresh in their mouths, while they paused, gathering a second wind. In the meantime, they held each other close, gazing into one another's eyes, reading the stories that lay in their depths. Though walking with her, sitting with her, holding her, kissing her, was seemingly a fantasy, to Excelcious, nothing could have been more real. As for Shilloqwai, she never felt more alive. Their shared fantasy was short-lived. Drones started flying overhead, hovering over, near, and doing flybys past Shilloqwai and Excelcious. "I wonder who in the hell they're looking for?" She asked out of annoyance.

"I wouldn't be surprised if it's us!" Excelcious quipped. "In fact, I'd be willing to bet my life that we're the intended targets." No sooner had he gotten the words out of his mouth, when, a half-dozen Robocops appeared on the pathway ahead of them. The red, blue, and white strobes, identifying the Robocops were blinding. It quickly became clear that Shilloqwai and Excelcious were indeed the subjects of their search. When they were close enough, the Robocops physically engaged and attempted to restrain them. Both offered resistance.

With brute force, Screwhead, the robot in charge of custodial services and cleanup at the lab, grabbed Shilloqwai from the bench on which she had been sitting. Manhandling her, he lifted her over his head and launched her into the rushing stream. "Nooooo!!!" Shouted Excelcious as he watched her circuits fry. Tears flooded his eyes. "You sons-of-bitches, let me go!" Excelcious demanded of the Five Robocops trying to restrain him.

"Hold onto him, he's under arrest!" Screwhead ordered from the edge of the stream where he watched the last of the energy drain from Shilloqwai. "What a stupid asshole. A human, that fell in love with a robot! We've got the video footage that shows them holding hands and kissing. How cute!" He taunted.

"The lot of you are the stupid bastards. Robotikis wanted to talk to her you know! He's going to be really pissed when he finds out what you've done to her. You stole his thunder and what would have been his glory, you oversized bucket of bolts," Excelcious shouted to Screwhead, the robot's name of whom he didn't yet know. "He wanted to be the one to terminate her. Looks like he's going to be incinerating you instead." Excelcious didn't know that Screwhead was the one that threw Shilloqwai on the scrap pile or he would have thanked him. He may even have considered kissing his interface. Instead, Excelcious unleashed his anger on him, showing his dismay for what he had just done. "What's your name metal-head? Because I am going to destroy your ass!"

"My name is Screwhead, asshole!"

"Wait, did you just call me an asshole? I can't wait to watch you become metal-melt, especially after what you did to my girlfriend! I'd watch your mouth if I were you, because you're in a shitload of trouble!"

"Looks like you're in more of a predicament than I am!" Screwhead retorted.

"I'm ordering you to call off the cops. If you don't, I'll file a complaint that you violated Asimov's Laws. There'll be no saving you then!"

"No!" Screwhead flatly refused to follow the order he'd been given. He was still cleaning up the mess as Robotikis had instructed him.

"You know you guys are hurting me! Let me go!" He ordered the Robocops. "Or did you want me to file a complaint for a violation of Asimov's laws against the five of you too?" Excelcious threatened. The cowardice robots released him immediately. In attempting to atone for the grave error of their comrade, four of the Robocops rushed into the stream. Somehow, they managed to pull Shilloqwai out before short circuiting themselves. Excelcious got unexpected pleasure out of watching the stupid Robocops short-circuit while laughing at their idiocy.

Screwhead, the cleanup bot along with the remaining Robocop made a move toward Excelcious. They still intended to bring him back to the lab. But, Excelcious had freed himself from the handcuffs and made a quick move to his DDD belt, stunning the two robots, yet active. "If any of you had brains, you might be dangerous!" He quipped, while silently lamenting, as he made his way to Shilloqwai. He lifted the motionless, lifeless, Shilloqwai and carried her to one of the robot transports. He hoped and prayed that he could revive her. After dropping her off at his lab, he left her and returned the transport to the park. Abandoning it while in motion, Excelcious took delight in watching it crash. The vehicle rolled down the bank and hit the rocks before rolling on its side. The solar panel smashed when the vehicle tipped over. "Sorry it made such a splash!" He said to no one. "Thought the jeep could use a wash."

He hurried home to the bedside where he'd laid Shilloqwai. He was concerned when he saw that her entire protective shell had become splotchy and had turned to varying shades of tourmaline blue. Some of the splotches were very light, and some very dark. He wondered if the electric current, that ran through her while she was short-circuiting, had done this to her. But he'd noticed while they were at the park, her hand already had splotches on it, varying in color. Sensitive to his touch, she opened her eyes briefly. He read the distant look as a call for help. While Excelcious was trying to figure out how he could help her, Shilloqwai's eyes rolled back in her head. Unable to keep her eyelids open, they lazily drooped shut. Before she closed her eyes, Excelcious noted the transparency in her eyes was gone, having been replaced by a murky-blue darkness. Excelcious thought at first, it might be the end for her, that she was dying.

He went across the hall, into the lab hunting for the old box that he hadn't gone through in a while. He found a binder there that was all on Shilloqwai. After skimming through it, he found a few things that he thought might be able to help him, help her. As grim as the situation seemed, Excelcious gained a sense of renewed confidence as he returned to her bedside. He rolled her over on her stomach. He ran his hands over her back looking for her activation switch. He thought it best, before he did anything with her, to power her down first. He couldn't find it. Searching frantically, he began probing the small of her back, looking for the release to unlock her shell. He couldn't find that either, not even with his sensitive fingertips.

Then he heard her moan, but it wasn't as though she were in pain. His probing, turned into a penetrating massage, that had apparently relaxed, and comforted her. With no way to get at her mechanical guts, he had no way to help her. He could only hope and pray she recovered. Adding to his helpless feeling was the fact that he couldn't find the switch on the back of her skull, the one that would allow him access to the inside of her head. That portal was sealed too. As had always been the case, there was no explanation for what was happening to her, medically or scientifically.

Her only chance for survival depended on Excelcious' ability to nurse her back to health. The matter was out of his realm. He would place it in God's hands. His only duty to her now was to hope and pray. Excelcious planned to exercise both options to the fullest. If it were His will, the Power of Love would heal her. Excelcious prayed for the strength to carry out His will. Whatever the outcome, he would remain faithful to the Power of Love as he always had. His light would lead Excelcious out of darkness, just as it had done in the past. She was asleep now. In her present condition, that was the best medicine of all. Perhaps he could humor her and make her laugh. Laughter was said to be good medicine too. He would try it when she woke up! If, she woke up! Seemingly comfortably at rest, Excelcious reluctantly left her to answer a knock at the door. The rage burned within him, seeing it was Robotikis and company. "What in the hell do you want?" Excelcious demanded to know.

"I've already told you what I want. Return the stolen property and all pending charges against you will be dropped. That includes the latest charges from your little escapade in the park earlier this afternoon!"

"We were attacked at the park after being stalked by your spy drones. So, do you really want to go there? I mean, I could make a citizen's arrest and have you terminated. I have the evidence to get a conviction! I'm giving you an ultimatum. Get the hell out of here now, or I'm putting you on top of the shit pile where I found Shilloqwai."

"Shilloqwai was carrying classified information."

"Too bad, so sad. You should have erased her database before you trashed her!"

"You better watch your ass, boy!"

"Don't worry about me. If I were you, I'd watch your own ass! I have the power to destroy you and I'll do it if I have to!"

"Why would you do something so insanely stupid?"

"Because I can, and I will! Just give me a reason!"

"Destroying federal property is a crime."

"So is violating Asimov's Laws. I think we understand each other pretty well! If one of us goes down, the other is going down too. The world will go on without us. Please, quit wasting my time and just get the hell out of here, before I have you terminated and incinerated."

"You bastard!"

"Mister Bastard to you, you nut-less pile of bolts! If you're open to constructive criticism, you might consider another reboot. I think your wires are crossed and your files corrupt." On that note, Excelcious reached for the red button on his DDD belt. With just a touch, Robotikis was deactivated. After which, he was transported to the lab for analysis. Having rid himself of King Pain-in-the-Ass, he returned to Shilloqwai's bedside.

Her overall condition seemed to be worsening. Her tourmaline shell was now splotched from head to toe. The color of her protective coat ranged from sky-blue to white. Any life she may have had in her, mechanical or otherwise, seemed to be drifting away. Then Excelcious noticed, ever so slightly, the rise and fall of her chest. Was he seeing things now? Or was it just wishful thinking? Was he imagining her to be breathing? Or was she doing it on her own? He was tired, he needed the rest. He could have sworn he heard her taking shallow breaths. Seeing things and hearing things? Excelcious believed the fatigue he was feeling, was making him delusional. What seemed to be happening with her wasn't possible.

Excelcious would tend to her in the morning. He got an extra mattress from the other room and laid it on the floor next to her bed. There he slept through the night, at her side. When morning came, Excelcious was unable to focus on the tasks at hand. He sat by Shilloqwai's side for the entire day. The days went on. Though important, Excelcious let everything go. All he could do is think of her, like he did when he was a child. She was nothing more to him then, but a superhero from the comic books. Long since, she'd become everything to him. Shilloqwai was his cloud-9 dream, a living fantasy, an alternate reality. He couldn't believe she seemed to be slipping away from him now. He assessed her condition as grave. With her protective coating deteriorating as time went on, her aqua-tourmaline shell had lost its luster. It was white now, stark, ivory white.

Excelcious felt the end was near. The thought of losing her made him restless. He was unable to sleep for the entire night. He finally dozed off sometime in the early morning. Though he couldn't remember, when exactly that was. He was startled from his slumber following his nightmare of the Robocops who had successfully kidnapped Shilloqwai. His grogginess lifted as quickly as the fog in the presence of the sun, the instant he heard the horrifying screams and desperate, agonizing cries from the bathroom.

"She's alive!" He sighed in relief. But he was equally distressed with her apparent discomfort. Not knowing what was wrong, he bolted to the bathroom and found her in a fetal position on the floor in the shower. Seeing her like this was the shock of a lifetime. Her blue shell was strewn across the floor in pieces as if she were a chicken that had just hatched from an egg. He noted the silver-blue pool that she was laying in. It was the same as the substance seeping from what appeared to be a superficial cut on the side of her forehead. Blood? Excelcious whispered under his breath. It had to be, Excelcious correctly surmised. Then he wondered how she'd cut herself. He hadn't heard her fall. Excelcious understood as he'd picked up one of the pieces of her former shell. The edges were sharp. She'd sustained minor cuts all over, breaking out of her protective shell.

He unmistakably, heard her breathing. It wasn't labored, and her respirations seemed to be normal. Her pulse was so pronounced, he could visually see it with the repetitive rise and fall of her chest. By virtue of the fact, she was showing vital signs, meant she was truly alive. There was no reasonable explanation for her complete transformation. Would calling it a miracle be accurate? Why wouldn't it? Life itself, is a miracle! How could her transformation into a living, breathing, human being be considered anything less? After Excelcious was through assessing the situation and making general observations, he took some mental notes before approaching her. "Shilloqwai," he called to her softly. "Shilloqwai, answer me. Are you okay?"

"I think so!" She sobbed, remaining in her fetal position on the floor.

"Shilloqwai! Do you think you can stand up?"

"Help me?" She whimpered. "What's happened to me?" She asked with a quivering voice. Excelcious approached her. Leaning over her, he touched her on the shoulder. Even though she knew he was there, she was startled by the physical contact. She rolled toward him and reached out her arms. He grabbed hold of her hands and helped her up. Then he put one arm around behind her back and rested it on her hip, careful not to touch her inappropriately. Her legs were weak. With Excelcious' assistance, she walked gingerly from the bathroom to the exam table in his lab. It was awkward for him, seeing her in the full of her nakedness. He was a retired doctor, so it wasn't the first time he'd seen a naked woman. It was just the situation. The scenario playing out was so unexpected. It had to be awkward for her too. She probably would have been flattered that he was staring at her, if she weren't so scared.

Excelcious was just as bewildered as she was in regard to the transformation that had taken place. She began to tremble, and she was chilled to the bone. It wasn't until he handed her a towel that Shilloqwai realized Excelcious had seen the full of her nudity. "Shit!" She cursed out of embarrassment. And then she began to cry as she was simultaneously experiencing a myriad of emotions. Shilloqwai didn't mind that he'd seen her naked.

She was actually turned on by the fact that he had. She knew he could see that too. A very thorough breast exam accentuated the finest details of her charms. It was just the wrong time, and the wrong place to engage in intimate acts. She was secretly reconsidering her position on the matter while Excelcious was examining her, especially when he was touching all of her private parts. It wasn't sexual, but with the sensations pulsating through her, she wanted it to be. Her metamorphosis enhanced her dream of becoming his lover. She knew that it now had more than a snowball's chance in hell of coming true, and it heightened her arousal.

His touch had her body quivering with delight. She was disappointed when he stopped fondling and massaging her breasts. Her thighs were still tingling after his intense gynecological exam. "Oh, shit!" She let out a muted scream, followed by an erotic sigh. "Did I hurt you?" He asked ignorantly, trying not to embarrass her further.

"No ... you just ...!" She began with a nervous giggle. "It's just that..." She stopped in mid-sentence with a blushing smile, refusing to comment further on the matter. "Never mind. She giggled. I'm sure you already know why I...Shit! I'm so embarrassed."

"Don't be!" He said with an even keel. "At least we know things are working as they should be. Perhaps you're overly sensitive because... Shit...! I should have left well enough alone." He was now blushing too!

"A discussion for another day perhaps!" She suggested, leaving them both an out.

"Perhaps!" He concurred. As she'd already covered herself with the towel, he'd given her. And since he'd already seen everything, and touched everything, did it really make a difference that she had covered herself? Shilloqwai decided that it didn't. If he was gonna stare, she was going to show. Besides, he had yet to tell her that the exam was over. Why then, should she feel ashamed? It's not like he was trying to seduce her. To this point, neither had done anything wrong. It was strictly a doctor, patient, relationship.

During the exam, it was the first and only time, he would think of Shilloqwai, as just another woman. After completing her physical examination, he issued her a clean bill of health. Shilloqwai then used the towel she'd left on the exam table to cover herself. She looked at him with gratitude and flashed a sheepish smile. He returned the awkward smile, before leaving the room to fetch her some clothes. "I'll be right back!" He called to her on his way out the door.

"Okay." She responded, softly and sweetly, in a barely audible tone. Excelcious felt uncomfortable going through her things that were delivered by the Robotix lab a few weeks earlier. She didn't have much in the way of clothing, and nothing in the line of underwear. She hadn't really needed it before now.

Fortunately, he'd come across a pink bathing suit, which he assumed she wore in the summer months trying to fit in with the humans. What luck. In another drawer he came across some pink denim shorts and a pink halter top. He was thankful to find clothes that matched. "What took you so long?"

"I was trying to find something nice for you to wear."

"Thank you."

"Sorry about the bikini, I couldn't find any underwear. Thought it might be a sufficient substitute."

"It'll work until I can get some panties and bras. I wear a size 7 and I'm a 36C." She offered. Shilloqwai wasn't trying to embarrass him. She was trying to save him from the awkward moment with him having to ask her the specifics of her private equipment. She giggled, having made him blush. "What? Why are you turning red? You just finished feeling me up. You were fondling my breasts and you had your hand between my legs, playing gynecologist. Hell, I was ready to jump your bones and rock your world. And now you're embarrassed because we're talking about my underwear sizes? What the hell? If you want my personal opinion, I think you rushed through my physical exam! I think you need to do my breast exam over, complete with kisses and a deep penetrating massage this time. In regard to the gynecology part, I'd prefer a lot less teasing and a lot more pleasing. And when we're done playing around, we can make love. I'm being honest! Your exam really put me in the mood." Both were blushing again, following her remarks.

Excelcious wasn't quite sure what to make of her last comments, so, he ignored them. "I'll give you your privacy so you can dress!" He responded, still failing to acknowledge her not so subtle innuendoes. "I'll meet you in the living room when you're ready."

"See you soon!" She promised. The instant he turned his back on her, she stood up and let the towel drop to the floor. She was in a hurry to get dressed and reunite with him. She was anxious to hear about all of the things she missed while she was asleep. She needed a quick trip to the bathroom to tidy-up and brush her hair. Shilloqwai knew a misty spray or two of Vanilla-Cocoa perfume was a sure way to get the guys to look her way. She already had Excelcious' attention. She wanted to make sure he cuddled intimately close, so she could mark her territory with her sweet-smelling fragrance. Seeing her dressed for the first time after her transformation took his breath away. It was hard for him to imagine her becoming more beautiful, than she had been before, but she was. Only, he didn't have to imagine.

She was standing before him, flesh, bone, and blood. He found looking into the spheres of her aqua-tourmaline eyes as enchanting as ever. She was just as enamored with him as he was with her. Shilloqwai was seeing Excelcious for the first time with her own eyes, instead of through the lenses of a robotic camera. It was a delightfully welcome change. She could tell, getting used to the transformation was going to take some time. Her body was trembling as she approached the couch where Excelcious was sitting. Still unsure of her new self, she hesitated, almost as though she were waiting for an invitation to sit next to him. Excelcious didn't ask. Instead, he gently grabbed her arm and pulled her down on the couch next to him. "I love you!" Were the first words out of her mouth. The words escaped her, without Shilloqwai realizing what she had just said.

"What did you just say?" Excelcious asked, not believing what he thought he'd heard her say.

"I said that I…" She found the words hard to repeat, even though she sincerely meant what she had said. It was so impromptu. She was afraid, knowing that the ramifications of her heartfelt utterance would be devastating to her if Excelcious didn't feel the same way about her!

"Did you just say I love you?" Excelcious asked, still in disbelief over her blatant honesty. She hesitated as she nervously ran her fingers through his long sandy-blonde hair. He gazed at her with anticipation. His chocolate eyes were melting over her again. She was gazing at him with eyes of liquid tourmaline blue. "Hon?" He asked while gently caressing her face. "Did you just say you loved me?"

"Yes, but I didn't…"

"But what? You didn't mean to say it?"

"No. Yes! Shit! My words…listen…! Damn, I don't even know what in the hell I'm trying to say! Do you think it's possible to love someone, without really knowing the person or knowing what love is?"

"If you come to the conclusion that you know what love is, other than a feeling, please let me know. Let everyone know. It's a word that's yet to be defined by anyone! There are varying degrees of love. There's love of family, friends, and SOULMATES!"

"Do you love me, Excelcious?" He hesitated for a moment. Not because he was taken aback by the question. He just never thought in his wildest dreams, the fantasy of having any kind of intimate relationship with Shilloqwai was even a remote possibility. Yet here it was, the fantasy was starting to come alive. "Do you love me?" She repeated the question, less confidently and with a quiver in her voice, uncertain as to what his response was going to be.

She breathed a sigh of relief when he answered with a resounding, "YES!" She made no effort to hide the tears of joy streaming down her cheeks. In a celebratory way, they confirmed their true confessions with intimate, deep, wet, passionate kisses. The ice barriers were broken. All had fallen, melted in the heat of passion. They continued to cuddle and kiss, knowing that from this point forward, there would be complete transparency between them, no secrets, and no lies. Their actions said what no words could have, like how they really felt about one another, or how much they really loved each other. Breathlessly, they paused for a moment, putting their affections for one another on hold. "So, how does it feel to be in Love?" Excelcious asked Shilloqwai just to see what her reaction would be.

"I know the feeling gets better the deeper in love we fall. I don't want to lose the feeling. I don't want to lose you." Shilloqwai said as if she had something to fear.

"You're not really afraid of losing me, are you?"

"No!" She answered with uncertainty. "I'm scared of being human, it's a lot different than I imagined it to be." Shilloqwai added, very unsure of herself.

"What were you expecting?"

"I don't know really. Just having the freedom to do what I want to do, when I want to do it, it's an incredible feeling. And being with you in this state, it's amazing. The feeling is indescribable." For no apparent reason, Shilloqwai started crying.

"What's wrong, Shilloqwai?"

"Nothing. I'm so overwhelmed. I'm so happy, just to be alive. I have no regrets about what's happened to me. Pure, unadulterated joy, that's what I'm feeling. No more glitches, no more short-circuits, God, it's great to be free. No more threats from Robotikis to terminate me. I love it. He no longer has power over me. If he lays a finger on me, I can have him terminated for a violation of Asimov's laws."

"Forget about him now, we have our own lives to live. You'll face new challenges now. If you want, I'll be at your side to help you meet them. They say if you love someone to set them free and if they come back to you, you know it's true love. So, Shilloqwai I'm setting you free. Whether you stay or go, it's your choice."

"I'd be a fool to leave you. I'd be leaving the state of euphoria. I know it doesn't happen very often, love at first sight. But that's what I think has happened between me and you. I'm new at this, yet I already understand why the next three words I'm about to say to you. are the hardest for most people to say. I Love You, Excelcious, with all of my heart. Forever is too short of a time to spend with you, but that's my commitment to you if you want me to stay."

"God you're gorgeous. What's not to love about you? The only disappointing thing in just looking at you is, I can't see your heart of gold. The radiance in your infectious smile, the sparkle in your translucent eyes of tourmaline, emanate from your glowing heart. Once, and not long ago, I thought I was in love, but I hadn't yet met you. I'd be a fool to let you go. I love you Shilloqwai and I don't want to lose you. So, please stay, only if you plan on doing so for an eternity."

"Looks like I'm not going anywhere, not for a long, long while." They fell back into a lover's embrace and sealed their promises to one another with intimate kisses. After making their commitments to one another they opted to go out for dinner. They went to a family diner and settled on fish and chips. They celebrated over dinner with a bottle of White Zinfandel.

The magic of the moment didn't end at the restaurant. Afterwards, Excelcious and Shilloqwai went for a moonlight walk. A nebulous fire lit the parkway. Moonbeams danced across the sky, while the stars winked and blinked with approval. They thought they'd found a private place in the backwoods where they exchanged more intimate kisses. They'd forgotten about the babbling brook, and the whispering pines, bound to share the young couple's intimate secrets with the wayward wind.

Shilloqwai was adapting to life after her transformation from a robot into a human being. Excelcious believed the best way he could help Shilloqwai make the needed adjustments was to get her feeling comfortable with who she was as a person. Bubbly, charming, sensitive, caring and loving were all part of her character make-up. Excelcious had a knack for bringing out the best in people. Shilloqwai would testify to the fact that he'd certainly brought out the best in her. Humor was still an art in the making for her, but, Shilloqwai had been working on it. In fact, she was showing promise as a prospective nightclub comedian.

As her personality had been developing, so too had her relationship with Excelcious. It wasn't far from love-at-first sight to a walk down eternity road, a path the two of them had been on for just a short time. Though no formal wedding plans had been made, it was a matter of when they got married, not if!"

Celebrating the anniversary of Shilloqwai's transformation, she and Excelcious were out for a midnight stroll along the parkway. Light years away, a meteor storm was the impetus for a spectacular natural fireworks display. The enchanting backdrop was enhanced with shooting stars and flaming cosmic debris, giving a 3-D effect to the nebulous celestial skies.

"I forgot to tell you it's my birthday!" Shilloqwai informed him in between intimate kisses. "I'm 29."

"I wish you would have told me earlier; I would have gotten you a present!"

"I don't need a present! Last year I got the gift of life. And I have you for a lifetime. What else do I need?"

"There are plenty of shooting stars, care to make a birthday wish?" "I already have!"

"I have too, even though it's not my birthday."

"So, when is your birthday?"

"I'll be 34, October 31st."

"So, I have a choice to give you either a trick or a treat?"

"Surprise me! You usually do!" She flashed a deviant smile. It was beyond anyone's guess what she had in mind. Their cloud-9 dreams turned to ghoulish nightmares as flaming debris started crashing down around them. The aerial wishing well was set ablaze by the Fire on High.

"Do you have any idea what's happening?" Excelcious asked Shilloqwai in a panic. Flaming debris continued to crash down around them and in the surrounding area. Small fires seemed to be burning everywhere.

"I'm not sure. Some of the debris appears to be fragments of a robot satellite. Oh God, this is the way it all started in my reoccurring nightmare!"

"The way what, all started?"

"This is the start of the second robot-Humankind conflict. We're under attack, but I don't know by whom. It gets messy. Robots will be destroyed, and humans will be killed. As always happens with war, there will be no winners, and there will be no losers, only survivors." Shilloqwai was trembling, afraid of the unknown, a familiar foe and a deadlier enemy. Excelcious took her into his arms and tried to comfort her. He kissed her on the cheek, hoping she'd overcome her fears. She reciprocated with a passionate kiss of her own. "Aren't you scared?" She asked with a quiver in her voice.

"Of what?"

"About all of this? The Fire in the Sky? The inevitable war between the humans and the robots?"

"I am. But I've learned to harness my fear. There are things I can change. So, I do what I need to do to change them. The things I can't change, I don't worry about them. I hand those things over to God and let him take care of them. In regard to the second conflict, I told you, I'm prepared."

"You alluded to that before. I'm not sure what you mean by that. I don't mean to disillusion you, but you can't win against the robots!"

"Not by myself. But, with the Power of Love and the activation of the Orbitoids, I think I have more than a fighting chance to defeat them.

"Orbitoids?"

"Come, I'll show you." Excelcious walked hand-in-hand with her from the parkway to the back of his lot by the flower garden."

"So where are the Orbitoids?"

"Through here!" He pointed to a portal that opened before them. "The garden is a holographic image. Holograms blind the satellites and drones. I come and go as I please through this portal which leads to acres of secret passages."

"So where is this museum of yours?"

"To the left of the garden as we were facing it."

"Another secret passage?"

"Correct!" They walked a short way when they came to a patch of wild roses. Excelcious bent down and picked two roses. The first was a turquoise rose, heavily frosted with white. He broke off the stem and placed the flower in her hair. The second was a red one which he handed directly to her, after which he said to her, "I love you!" She rewarded him with an intimate kiss of gratitude. Then she echoed his sentiments with, an, I love you of her own.

"What is this place?" She asked curiously, overcome by the enchantment of it all.

"It's all land that was owned by my family. The property was to be split between five of us. As the sole survivor, I inherited it all. My siblings, my mom and dad were all casualties of the Robot-Humankind war!"

"I'm sorry."

"No, it's okay. I've done well on my own. I'm going to do much better with you around."

"Thanks!" She said softly, flashing a gratuitous smile. "So, you built all of this? Impressive."

"I wish I could take all of the credit, but I got a little help from my friends, including Valentino and Onshanda Puro-Amoris. In that box there was a binder containing the notes on how to build robots that were more Humanlike. I'm sure it's the technology that went into building you. It's what Valentino and Onshanda used to build Skeletos and it's what my friends and I used to build the Orbitoids."

"Impressive nonetheless."

"There's lots to show you here. Worlds of dreams, worlds of fantasy, a reality I want to share with you. I'll save the surprises for another time. Right now, I'm going to show you how we can protect ourselves from another robot attack. You've got your DDD belt on, I see! Remember what I asked you, never take it off, for any reason."

"I won't!" She assured him. "So, how are we getting around the mountains?"

"We're not. It's an illusion, another hologram!" Excelcious pressed the white button on the back of his belt and a portal opened. The two passed through it , between the mountains.

After they had entered the hidden chamber, the portal closed behind them. Shilloqwai looked around and saw nothing but row-upon-row of robots. There were hundreds, no thousands, perhaps, 10's of thousands. "So, how long did it take you to build this army of robots?"

"My friends and I have been working on the Orbitoids for seven years. And the army is growing. More units are being produced as we speak. We knew this day was coming."

"So, your plan is to fight robots with robots?" She asked for clarification.

"The plan is to fight the alien forces with Orbitoids. They can be controlled remotely, by battalion, smaller groups or individually. Orbitoids are much stronger than the robots ruling our world. If it were us against them, the Orbitoids would annihilate the ruling forces and humans could regain control of the planet."

"So, why haven't you taken over with your mechanical army?"

"Because my ambition is not to rule the world. I'm an eternal optimist, hoping that the robots and Humankind will find a way to co-exist and peacefully rule the world. Together! Presently, we have a developing situation. It's apparent we're going to have to defend ourselves. That's why, with the help of my friends, I've been developing this army."

"You've convinced me. I actually think you can win this second conflict with the robots, if there is one."

"I'm not doing it for me. I'm doing it for Humankind. The reason behind controlling the robots remotely is to reduce the number of human casualties, of which I'm sure there will be some."

"Knowing you, you've incorporated special features."

"Yes, I modeled the Mercusilver War Class Orbitoids after you, to be more humanlike. I wanted them to act on instinct and impulse. They have the ability to override remote commands, but only if they think tactical and strategic advantages can be gained in doing so. Instinctive and impulsive actions are only to be taken as a last resort. Before extreme measures are taken, logical and reasonable guidelines are to be followed, all in accordance with Asimov's Laws. If I have to bring out the Orbitoids, I won't be sending them out alone. Humankind will be armed and out there supporting them in secondary waves. No human should have to fight on the front line."

"So how is Humankind going to protect itself in a hot zone?"

"Humankind will be armed with laser-guided weaponry including things such as heat-seeking missile rifles, Molotov Cocktail rocket launchers and DDD pistols, that essentially do the same things as the belts. The difference is they also shoot Molotov bullets. I have a line of plasma pistols too."

"So, the Orbitoids and Humankind will both be armed? You've got enough shit down here to destroy the universe. I can tell a lot of thought went into building this army and arsenal. I can also tell, by the design and manufacturing of this contraband that you were careful to follow strict guidelines as outlined by the robots!"

"I'm not sure what you mean! What are you getting at?"

"Neither the robots, nor Humankind will be punished for possessing, brandishing and or using these weapons, will they? Because the Transfer of Power Treaty allows for this sort of thing, doesn't it? And these weapons can also be used, keeping in accordance with Asimov's Laws, can't they?"

"Absolutely, smart ass!" Both shared a good laugh. Excelcious was amused by the oxymoronic cynicism in her remarks. Their light moment was short lived. Whatever was happening above them, with the Fire on High, it rocked the ground and knocked them from their feet. Shilloqwai and Excelcious both got up and dusted themselves off, after a reminder of the seriousness of the matter at hand.

After surveying the chamber and seeing everything was in order, their false sense of security was restored. "Even down here, we're not safe, are we?"

"Safer than we are up there! I think we're going to be down here for a while.

I'm half-tempted to go up there and see what in the hell is going on!"

"No, not now. It's best we wait a while until things calm down!" Something had gotten Shilloqwai's attention. Curiously, she turned her gaze away from Excelcious. "What is that weapon over there on that other table. The sleek looking silver-blue one?

"That's the Mercusilver Shrapnel Assault Rifle. I'm still working on it. It needs some fine-tuning. I was hoping you could help me perfect it."

"How? I'm not an engineer or an inventor."

"I need to ask you a personal question?"

"Ask away. You've already seen me naked, fondled my breasts and probed the full of my body. It can't be any more personal than that, can it?"

"Want me to show you?"

"Pervert! I want the first time to be special. Now is not the time. Seriously, what are you getting at?"

"I need to know how you do that thing you do!"

"What thing?"

"You know that self-defense thing you do with your eyes where you spray shrapnel everywhere!"

"Oh that? To be honest, I can't tell you. The power is there when I need it. The heat surges through my body when I feel threatened. When the temperature reaches a certain point, the shit flies from my eyes. I feel totally drained afterwards. Though I'm thankful for the built-in self-defense mechanism, it scares me. I can't control it. Once it's activated, there's no stopping it. One of these days, I'm going to unintentionally hurt someone!"

"Would you mind wearing a monitor? I'm sure it's going to happen to you again with all that's going on around us. I'll take measurements to see what happens before, during and after one of your assaults! Hopefully, the data collected will help me perfect the weapon."

"So, where are you going to place the monitor?"

"There's three of them actually. This one, you wear it like a necklace. The second is an undergarment like a nightie, for you to wear under your blouse."

"You want me to put it on now? I'm not wearing a bra."

"I can step out for a…never mind!" She had already unbuttoned and taken off her blouse. She allowed extra time for him to stare at her naked flesh before putting on the garment and restoring herself to decency.

"You keep tempting me like that, and it's going to be hard for me to restrain myself. Shit's going to happen."

"So? What if it does? After that exam the other day, that's all I can think about is you loving me. And the way you were touching me, I didn't want you to stop. I know you could see that I got really turned on. It was a pleasurable experience for me. I'm surprised you didn't say anything, after satisfying me the way you did. Why would you? Not that you did anything wrong. I didn't either. I couldn't help what happened. You probably felt it would have been inappropriate, but, no more so than the little stunt I just pulled now. I'm sorry. We're getting sidetracked. I should show you the same respect that you've shown me all along."

"Without question, you've been adequately blessed. There are two more monitors that need to be placed. You wear them like garters on your upper thighs."

She gasped and then sighed as she felt a tingling shoot up her leg as he put the first one in place. Knowing Excelcious was uncomfortable touching her near her most private place, "I'll do it!" She offered, placing the second monitor on her other leg. Sparing him the agony while depriving herself of the pleasure she felt after he'd touched her the first time. If he wasn't going to touch her, she made sure he saw what was his for the taking. "The way I'm feeling, I'm likely to have another erotic accident." She admitted. She cursed herself for tempting him, yet again. If he had seduced her, it would have been her fault. She would have ruined everything. She reminded herself that the good things were worth waiting for. And from this point forward she would exhibit more patience, so their first time could be truly special.

"What happens if something goes wrong, and the army of Orbitoids isn't able to protect us, or they're unable to protect the Earth?"

"You don't think I'd leave myself without a way out, do you ?"

"You're an amazing man. I'm sure you have a good plan in place."

"I can show you the escape routes, but another time. They're a good distance from here. You're an incredible woman. Thank you for your understanding, love and support." They fell into a lover's embrace, exchanging passionate, intimate kisses. Shilloqwai and Excelcious enjoyed a temporary escape from their mounting troubles.

"I can't believe you orchestrated all of this without the robots finding out about it!"

"Depending on where this thing goes, with us being attacked, I might have to tell them. Humans and robots are going to have to find a way to get along in order for us to have a chance to save Earth and its civilization."

"But they'll kill you!"

"Let them try. I have a plan in place for that too, should they try something that stupid. I'm pretty sure I can convince them to see things my way!"

"I love you, Excelcious!"

"I love you too, Shilloqwai!"

Their world was still being rocked by the goings on above them. It was likely they wouldn't know the magnitude or the scope of the damage until morning. They surmised that it would be widespread.

When they finally saw the actual damage, it was far worse than what they had expected to see. Robots were accusing the humans of sabotaging government property. For doing so, the robots ramped up interplanetary restrictions, primarily by, enforcing stricter curfews and increasing surveillance.

Humankind responded by doing all it could to pollute the air, poison the water and contaminate the land. Some humans became completely unhinged, going on mindless rampages, rioting, pillaging, and burning whatever would ignite. Attempts to get into the Robotix facility failed. The intention was to burn that to the ground as well. The Robocops showed just how helpful and efficient they could be, by getting criminals off the streets while protecting innocent civilians. In just over 48 hours, world-wide law and order had been restored. It was then, a world-wide state of emergency had been declared. Whatever it was, that got people connected, they were tuned in and waiting for the global simulcast to begin. There was to be transparency in the message.

Appearing as a liaison-diplomat for robot-Humankind relations, once again, was Shilloqwai. Against their better judgement, the robots allowed her to temporarily resume her role. There would be no transparency in regard to her transformation. No one knew except Excelcious. As far as Shilloqwai was concerned, no one else needed to know! It was enough that the robots agreed to let her speak at the briefing at the suggestion of Robotikis. He gave his endorsement because of the rapport she seemed to have with the people. Robotikis didn't realize it until later, but Shilloqwai had become an iconic figure, not just among Humankind, but among the robots as well. Whether you loved her or hated her, she had become ever popular, deserving of the iconic pedestal she had been put upon.

Excelcious Orbitus, liked by most that knew him, was thought to be a brilliant mind that primarily kept to himself. He was low-key, kind of secretive, and very cordial once you got to know him. Getting to know him was the key phrase. He didn't open up to people very often. In fact, he rarely made himself available for comment. Over the past year, people had seen more of him than they had over the past decade. Rumors were flying about the alleged affair that he was having with the robot Shilloqwai. A lot of people were connecting to the simulcast just to see if Excelcious was going to show up.

Robotikis was sitting behind his power console, curious as to what was going to transpire with the representatives that were about to take the stage. "I can't wait to see what that arrogant asshole is going to say!" Robotikis said verbalizing his disdain for Excelcious. "The little bitch Shilloqwai he brought with him is probably going to start preaching, and campaigning to take over as ruler of the robots. I can't wait for the shitshow to begin!"

Right on cue, the simulcast began. "Hello I'm Shilloqwai, acting liaison and diplomat for Robot-Humankind relations. And I'm Excelcious Orbitus, retired M.D. and IT specialist. We're here to give a briefing and update you on the world state of emergency. Afterwards, we'll take some questions."

"Recently, everyone witnessed for themselves, the world was subject to a catastrophic event, being referred to as the Fire in the Sky, which began a few days ago. Dwellings were destroyed by space junk that came crashing to the Earth and there were small fires everywhere. Three robot satellites were destroyed. There was rioting and looting which aggravated the situation. A good number of Robocops were damaged and many humans were injured. Excuse my English, but all of the shit needs to stop! It took the Robocops about two and one-half days to restore law and order. Just know there will be consequences for committing crimes. I know Humankind is upset with the robots for a number of reasons, namely, the privacy issue. We're working on that. Until we can focus on the specifics of that, we have a bigger issue looming.

"Our world is under attack! Robots and Humans had better find a way to work together and help each other. We need to fight together, not against each other. We're all in grave danger here. All robots are in danger of incineration, and Humankind is facing extinction. It's not just Earth's civilization that's being threatened, Mother Earth herself could be blown into oblivion, and all that would remain of her, is cosmic dust blowing in galactic winds across the universe.

We're not sure what we're dealing with yet, only that we are being attacked by an alien force. As I mentioned earlier, the first of the attacks occurred a few days ago. From the current data I have, damage is substantial. We're expecting the attacks to continue as they have been and we're not sure what will come of them. A global protection plan is being put in place as we speak. Here to tell you more about that is Excelcious Orbitus. Excelcious…!"

"Thank you Shilloqwai, for that update. As Shilloqwai stated at the onset of this briefing we are in a state of global emergency. There are three parts to the global protection plan set to be implemented, but, in order for us to implement this plan, some of the restrictions put in place during the Transfer of Power Treaty are going to be temporarily suspended. For example, Robots will still be expected to abide by Asimov's Laws.

However, the possibility of collateral damage exists in the fight against this unknown enemy. Some terminations, that under normal circumstances would be mandated, could be suspended, even dismissed. The action taken will be evaluated on a case-by-case basis, after the conflict with the Alien Force is resolved. Extra surveillance and added drones will be necessary so that we can cover our asses until we can find a way to protect them. Humankind is expected to follow the rules that help to keep law and order. Exceptions may apply where self-defense, and self-preservation matters come into play. Weapons, including contraband will be allowed to fight against, and only against AI Forces. Violations or misuse in the application of these exceptions will be investigated. These transgressions and the accused transgressors will be evaluated on a case-by-case basis, after the conflict with the Alien Force is resolved.

Having laid the groundwork, I can't stress the importance of robots and Humankind working together. Our existence and our lives depend on it. The situation is serious which is why Robots and Humankind will be armed with military grade weaponry to be used for self-preservation purposes. This is the second part of the Global Protection Program that will be implemented. The third part involves setting up a number of worldwide defense bases with weaponry that can provide global protection from attacking galactic forces, or space junk. Either of these things could do substantial damage and

even obliterate the Earth. I think that about summarizes our plan. Shilloqwai and I will begin fielding questions at this time.

Shilloqwai fielded the first question from the press, which quickly turned into a media mob. "Is it true, that when you were the full-time diplomat-liaison intermediary for robot-human relations, that you murdered six civilians, denying them of due process? And what are you going to do differently in your temporary role to restore the trust of the global people? Can we have your assurance that this kind of thing will never happen again?"

Shilloqwai sighed with disgust at the questions being asked of her. If this is how it was starting, Shilloqwai feared how much worse it would get. After each question or group of questions, she tried to compose herself before proceeding to give the best answers that she could. "I think I have the trust of the majority of Humankind, which understands I acted out of self-defense when I regretfully killed the six civilians in question. I was a victim of a vicious attack. Four other young women were in the vicinity. To protect them in accordance with Asimov's Laws, I took on a sextet of murdering fugitives. These five men and one woman were scheduled to be executed upon their apprehension. Next question, you in the back!"

"Shilloqwai, in light of your crimes against humanity, are you going to be among the armed robots? Why weren't you terminated for violation of Asimov's laws? Have your glitches been fixed? Will you be flying anymore solar planes? And can you tell us about your alleged kidnapping of that little girl?"

"After the review of the information in my databanks by Robotikis, I have been cleared of any wrongdoing. And as far as I know, the glitches have been fixed. Even so, I don't think I'll be flying anymore solar planes. I mentioned that I've been cleared of all counts in regard to the accusations against me, this includes the alleged kidnapping. I have no further comment in regard to these issues. Yes, I will be armed as will the entirety of Earth's populous. Next!"

"You and Excelcious have been seen out publicly quite frequently. Can you elaborate on the nature of your relationship? I understand the friendship thing, but there are a number of videos on social media that show the two of you holding hands and kissing? Have your affections for one another been restricted to kissing or are they more intimate? Are the two of you actually…you know? Let me ask it this way, how does a robot interface with a human? If you're actually engaging in that type of activity, that's pretty disgusting if you ask me!"

"First of all, I never asked you. And if we are making love, it's far less disgusting than your questions. The depth of the relationship I have with Excelcious is really nobody's damn business. Suffice it to say that we're close friends! That's all anyone needs to know about us! It's true, interfacing with humans is impossible, but, if you're that curious about electricity and the effects it can have on humans, go stick your middle finger in a light socket and see what happens. As far as human interaction goes, I will say this, I was programmed to be more humanlike. Going out in public and showing I have an understanding of humans and their needs, sets a good example for what the rest of us should be doing, in regard to robots and humans trying to get along.

"You know, can I just say something before I take any more questions?" Shilloqwai was in tears and had taken the necessary time to recompose herself before going on. "I'd appreciate it if you'd all stop with the gotcha' questions. Everyone is complaining about the privacy issue, where's mine? Leave me my dignity, show me some respect. Already I hear people up front here saying, she's glitching again, look at the condensate running down her face. I've already told you I'm going through a personal crisis. I have issues that need to be worked out. I'm not going to make myself an open book regarding the ins and outs of my personal life! I hear another smart ass in the crowd, saying that I'm trying to talk to you as if I were human. The reason for doing so, is I'm trying to be sensitive to, and understand human wants and needs. I've pretty much said my piece.

"So, I'll wrap it up and then turn it back over to Excelcious. He has some ideas about how we can best defend ourselves and defend the Earth in this developing crisis. We are under attack from an AI galactic force which is why we are in a state of global emergency. Please take this seriously, we need to put our differences aside and find ways to work together, so we can protect each other. We can make it through this crisis, but we need to come together on this. If we don't support each other, we all might as well kiss our asses goodbye, along with the planet we're living on! No one is asking anyone to be a hero, but there needs to be a concerted team effort. There is going to be no survival of the fittest. It will be all of us or none of us! We will suffer casualties, I'm sure of it! Let's not let lives lost, be in vain. Let's not allow robots to be terminated unnecessarily. We are one force. Excelcious..."

"Thank you Shilloqwai. I'm going to make this brief. So, we all have our ID's. What we're going to do so our plan stays secure is have everyone go to their nearest Robotix center and bring your I.D. The centers have the supplies, weaponry, and armor, you'll need to defend yourself. Weapons are traceable. Any time weapons are discharged, a signal and a video will be sent back to a database. This is possible through the development of smart ammo, which greatly reduces the chance of casualties from friendly fire. Any alleged misuse of the weapons will be investigated. Misuse will result in confiscation and issue privileges. The weapons being distributed are government property and must be returned at the end of the conflict. Failure to do so will be considered criminal and a federal offense. Violators will be charged and prosecuted to the fullest extent of the law. I'll take a few questions as they pertain to the global emergency and the self-defense program being implemented. Yes, you in the front, your question please!"

"Word on the street is that you're the mastermind behind all of this technological weaponry. Two questions. The first is how do you justify giving weapons to children?"

"Most children are playing video games before they're five-years-old. Using virtual technology, the child is able to point the weapon at a target. When the circle is green, the weapon will fire. The weapon is programmed as such that it will not inadvertently create a situation where victims will fall to friendly fire. And your second question?"

"With your ingenuity in designing the defense systems and weaponry, I was wondering if you've figured out a way or come up with a device so you can screw your robot friend? Does this device allow you to experiment with different positions? I mean, from what we know, the two of you are an item, are you not?"

"AAHHH! That was four questions. Another asshole who didn't pay attention to Sesame Street during the Count segments. I'm not even going to honor the last three with a response. The hell with this! No, the hell with you all! The briefing is over. For those of you that are taking the global emergency seriously, report with your ID's to your nearest Robotix center. As for the rest of you that are trying to turn this whole thing into a circus, screw you, you're on your own!" After nightfall blanketed the Earth, another night of the Fire in the Sky ensued. It was no surprise when Shilloqwai and Excelcious learned that tensions between humans and the robots were continuing to escalate.

"I can't believe the Q&A portion of the briefing. I didn't realize how many assholes were in the press corps!" Shilloqwai quipped.

"It's been that way for a long time, hon. Get used to it, because I don't think you'll see any significant changes in the press corps anytime soon! They're not all like that, unfortunately a lot of them are. The ones that are, are too hellbent on pushing an agenda. They don't give a damn about the facts or who they hurt. They've lost their code of ethics. They hide behind anonymous sources. They don't take the time to authenticate their stories they just run with them. The corps has gone unchecked for so long that libel and slander have become an integral part of their reporting. If the corps doesn't have news, it has no problem inserting itself in the picture and building the news around itself, so much so, that the corps itself becomes the news. Most of them have no shame and no regrets about making complete ass clowns of themselves!"

"So, concealing the fact that I transformed into a human, was that unethical?" Shilloqwai asked in jest.

"That was called lying out of necessity to save your life. You heard what they were saying about us interfacing, thinking you were still a robot. If they knew the truth, they would have killed us both on the spot after they'd gotten the lowdown, on how many times a day we were doing it!"

Reflecting back on earlier that afternoon. Shilloqwai believed without question, that answering questions from the press corps, was the hardest thing she'd ever endured. That included Robotikis asking her to step down from her liaison position. If there was one that she desperately wanted to tell about her transformation, it was him! She was certain he would have short-circuited on his own without her even doing anything to him. Excelcious and Shilloqwai were both exhausted. He suggested they go somewhere to relax. "What did you have in mind?"

"It's a surprise!" He told her as they passed through the portal. The same one they had on an earlier occasion when he showed off the DDD army and weaponry. They had gone far beyond the armory. The ground beneath them had become wet and slippery. "Watch your step!" Excelcious warned. Then she heard the rushing water.

Every time, she'd heard the refreshing sound in the past, it had brought about major changes in her existence, her life. As they continued walking, Shilloqwai observed the rocky walls around had begun to sparkle. It was just in places at first, then in sections. Soon the walls had transformed entirely from rock, to transparent crystalline windows, to an underground fantasy world. "What is this place?" Shilloqwai asked enchantingly curious.

"It's where I go when I want to get away." He told her as they were moving closer to the source of the rushing water. These walls have turned to windows so that one might waltz around underground and see the beauty of the aquamarine wonders of the world."

"So, how many passages are there in this secret world of yours? And where do they all go?"

"The passages are too many to count. They lead to anywhere in the world. Which path you take is entirely up to you. You're free to go wherever you want. If you wish to travel great distances, there are solar-aqua transports that can take you where you want to go."

"Truly incredible. You said you and your friends built all of these tunnels over the past seven years?"

Not just my human friends, the Orbitoids helped considerably. They made the calculations before any building began, this to ensure safety, stability, and endurance. It was the Orbitoids that carved out and linked the tunnels. Humankind built the transports."

"So, all of the seismic activity over the past seven years, is because of you, the Orbitoids, and your friends?"

"I wouldn't say all of it, but we were probably responsible for a good deal of it, yes!"

"Unbelievable. The robots assumed the ebb and flow of the changing tides to be a natural phenomenon. It's unfathomable that the robots never detected any of this! My question is why not? The bigger question is how were you able to keep all of the wonders of your secret worlds from them? Whatever you did to blind their drones and satellites, it's working out pretty well, for those receiving the benefits of it."

"It was the only way for some of us to recover and keep our right to privacy. It's still the most contentious issue between the robots and Humankind. You know this, using heat signatures, they're able to identify not only the forms of life, but what they were doing, when they were doing it and how they were doing it and who they were doing it with.

"They were tracking me too, not so much, I wasn't doing anything exciting enough for them to want to watch. After I blinded their satellites and drones, they lost sight of me, at least for the most part. It's like I told you before, they see me when I want to be seen."

"Yeah, well I don't want them watching us, when we start getting more intimate with one another."

"So, you've been thinking about us…?"

"Making love? Oh, yeah. I can hardly restrain myself as it is. It's not a matter of if we're going to do it, it's a matter of when we're going to do it."

"I feel the same way. I don't want to do it before you're ready, before we're ready."

"Well I'm glad we'll have someplace to go without peeping Toms and voyeurs watching us when we do engage with one another. I told that asshole Robotikis, his habit of monitoring humans was disgusting. He liked to watch the humans engaging in their animal acts. He did it all of the time."

"Maybe, he has secret desires of becoming human!" Excelcious quipped, causing Shilloqwai to burst out laughing.

"Shit! I just pissed in my pants!" Shilloqwai shot back. "I don't think he has any desire to be human. Even in modern times, the perverted bucket of bolts sees their behavior as barbaric. After he's had his fill of voyeurism, he usually goes on a tirade trashing humans for their indecency. He claims humans haven't evolved, if at all, since the day of the Neanderthal, and procreation is all they can think about."

"I'll let him take that up with God! It's the way He intended for us to procreate. In regard to his outdated way of thinking, it should be grounds enough to have him terminated."

"So, if we wanted to engage in procreating activity, you're sure you've discovered a way to keep him from watching us?" Shilloqwai teased, baring a little flesh. Her facial skin turned sky-blue. Excelcious surmised correctly that she was blushing. Feeling flushed, he sensed that he was blushing too, yet he found a tactful way to answer her question.

"I've found a way to block their equipment's heat signature sensors..." He stopped in midsentence, unable to keep from ogling over her.

"You staring at me like that is really turning me on. So, what's stopping us from...you know?" Shilloqwai asked, threatening to take off her shorts. She already had them unbuttoned and unzipped.

"Mutual respect for one another. I love you Shilloqwai. Our time for bringing fantasies to life will come."

"I know, Excelcious...I'm sorry, for tempting you again. I love you. I can't help myself when I'm around you. I just want to show you how much I love you."

"You already have. And there's nothing to be sorry for, unless you think there's a problem with the love between us deepening."

"No, there's no problem. I guess it's just my way of saying that I would do anything for you, and that includes dying for you. That's how much I love you."

"I would die for you too. I promise, we'll have plenty of time to make our fantasies come alive before anything happens to either of us." Shilloqwai smiled and went on dreaming of the day when they would have their alone time together.

"Just wondering, when the time comes of course, do you want kids?"

"My fiancée, before she died, talked about having kids and wanting to start a family."

"What about me, do you think I'd be a good mother for your children? Would you consider starting a family with me?"

"Yes, without question on both counts. Let's just…"

"SSShhh," She hushed him before taking him into her arms and giving him the most intimate of kisses. "You don't need to go on any further. You've told me all I need to know. I'm looking forward to the day."

"Our little girl is going to be beautiful, strong and smart, just like you."

"And our little boy is going to be handsome, strong and smart, just like you."

"And what about the rest of the army?" Excelcious asked, trying to get a gauge on how big of a family Shilloqwai was dreaming of. Shilloqwai laughed heartily. Excelcious laughed along with her. "So how many kids are you planning on us having?"

"As many as we're blessed with!"

"Good answer, we'll leave it all in the hands of Love." Excelcious stopped suddenly, leaving Shilloqwai to surge a few steps ahead of him. "Where are you going hon?" Excelcious called out to her. She stutter-stepped, pivoted and retreated to his side.

"So. we've arrived?"

"Almost, we have a short way to go yet. Look, out there! It's just a glimpse of the paradise you're about to enter." Shilloqwai gasped, as she gazed through the crystalline barrier that stood between them and this hidden paradise.

"Look at all of the flowers, in all of the colors in the cosmos! Enchanting, exotic, and psychedelically beautiful. And the greens, if the people of Ireland saw them, they'd have to add a few more shades to the 40, already known to exist there. Before we go out into the tropical paradise, I have two questions. First, I'm still unclear as to how you've kept this hidden from the robots? Even with the holograms! You don't worry about glitches? It's brilliant, it's amazing, so surreal!"

"Like the paradise before you, the way to the tunnels is protected by holographic illusion. They'll have to figure out a way to knock out the holograms before they can get beyond the illusions. I have several backups to keep the holograms up and running. If they get lucky, and somehow takedown the charade, they'll have to figure out a way to navigate the tunnels. Normal GPS won't work down here. We've got a stockpile of watch-like devices scattered about in various locations throughout the tunnels. Each device provides a way to navigate the tunnels. These devices show the escape routes, where the transport vehicles are, and how to access and operate them! So, I guess what I'm saying, is even if anyone or anything finds their way down here, it's going to be harder than hell to track anyone unless they have an idea of where they are. Even then, trying to find a group or an individual will be like trying to find a grain of sand with specific qualities, composition, size, and weight, on miles and miles of beach."

While they were engaged in discussion, they were oblivious as to what was occurring on the other side of the crystal pane. "It's a pure, exotic world of enchantment." Shilloqwai observed, seeing the flock of parrots and the bivouac of butterflies that decorated the trees like Christmas ornaments. So, how much longer do I have to wait until you take me to paradise?"

"Until our wedding night!"

"Is that a proposal?"

"No. You'll know when I'm proposing to you. It will be a special night."

"Tonight's already a special night. I'll settle for venturing into the paradise on the other side of this crystal wall. Take me there, baby, take me now."

"As you wish!" He promised with a stolen kiss. She stole one back.

"Lead the way." She requested.

"After you!" He retorted pointing to the rock formation, a spiral staircase that would take them both into the natural paradise that awaited them. She hurried to the stairs. For an instant, she thought about running up them. After seeing the stairs were wet, and the steepness of the grade, she thought better of it. She led the way, with Excelcious following close behind her, guiding her, with his hands on her hips. Liking the physical touch, she slowed her pace even more. She continued her climb, walking with a provocative swagger, assuring he received the full benefit of seeing her rear view. After reaching the landing, they reconvened, again they stood hand-in-hand, side by side. Together they walked to the edge of the plateau and began their descent down the rock stairway into the exotic garden. The first flower patch they came to was a grandiose spectral bouquet of wild roses.

He bent down and picked two. One, a frosted aqua tourmaline rose that he placed in her hair. In gratitude she leaned into him, begging for a kiss. He obliged her with a kiss, wetter than the morning dew. She reciprocated, fully participating in the intimate exchange. The last time he put a rose in her hair, he told her that he loved her. What was different this time, was he kept the second rose, a red one he chose to carry with him as they continued their waltz through paradise. Shilloqwai wondered what the significance, if any, there was in that.

So overwhelmed by the glorious beauty, she was seeing with her own eyes, she had subconsciously blocked out the sound of the rushing water. In a heartbeat, the sound came gushing forth again after feeling the rejuvenating misty droplets spraying her face. As soon as the clearing ahead was coming into view, Excelcious stepped around and behind Shilloqwai. He covered her eyes with one hand, while guiding her with his other hand by resting it on her hip. Are you ready?"

"I can't take the suspense, uncover my eyes!" Excelcious honored her request. The surreal breathtaking sight caused her to gasp. "It's indescribable! I'm waiting for the magical creatures to start coming forth, the dragons, the unicorns, the Pegasai. I mean, how else are we going to get across this river to the cluster of waterfalls on the other side?"

"Think you can walk any further, it's just a short way, up around the bend."

"Walk? It wouldn't matter how tired I was, because if I couldn't walk, I would find a way to float over there."

"You won't be disappointed. Up there behind that waterfall, there's a ledge. A few feet back there's a hot spring. If you want, we can go for a swim when we get there!"

"I'd love to." This time Excelcious led her by the hand, while they carefully gauged their steps up the winding path. Enchanted by their surroundings, she stood for moments on end, gazing upon the secret paradise. Nighttime had fallen upon them. Adding to the enchantment were the dancing moonbeams and the light from the pulsating stars. Once they reached the rock plateau, they stood breathlessly behind the waterfalls, watching the cascading liquid crystal, splashing melodically over the bluffs.

Excelcious just stood behind her with his arms draped over her shoulders and around her waist. He stood, looking on with awe at the natural wonders, as she was. "It's getting late. We're running out of time to get that midnight swim."

"Let's go!" She responded without hesitating another instant. She had kicked off her shoes and settled into the hot springs before he had. Anxiously she waited for him to settle in beside her. As he did the water temp was probably elevated a few degrees. It was already warm, but nothing compared to the intimate lava-hot kisses they passionately exchanged. Both were wearing T-shirts and denim shorts. Even with her undergarments on, her protruding blessings tempted him. His flattering looks made her smile as she knew exactly what he was thinking. "You're wishing I was naked right now, aren't you?"

"Guilty as charged. I still want to save it for our private exchange of wedding gifts. I think it's only fitting we spend our honeymoon here. You asked me a while back, what the red rose was for. I don't have a ring, so I'm presenting you with this rose as a token of our love and friendship. Shilloqwai, will you marry me?"

"Did you just ask me to marry you?"

"Yes?"

"I accept this rose, as a token of our love and friendship. Yes, Excelcious, I will marry you. The diamond tears were cascading down her cheeks like miniature waterfalls. She was beginning to understand what love was. In this instant, love had overwhelmed her as the tears of joy just kept flowing. The two of them celebrated with a flurry of kisses that lasted for an undetermined amount of time. They climbed out of the hot tub and found a soft spot on the mossy ground, behind the waterfall.

There they cuddled up and fell asleep in paradise. They probably would have kissed the night away if they hadn't dozed off. The kaleidoscope sunrise showed promise of another fantasy waiting to be fulfilled. Excelcious and Shilloqwai were forced to put their dreams on hold because more important issues were pending. They couldn't neglect their responsibilities and let the world down.

Their work was waiting for their return. Their casual stroll back to the house, took just over an hour. Exercise was the excuse they conveniently used to justify their extended period of procrastination. Upon their return to Excelcious' home, they found an unpleasant surprise waiting for them. "You again? Do you ever give up? Why can't you just leave us the hell alone?" Excelcious asked, thinking he'd made a reasonable request.

"Well. if it isn't Robotikiss my ass!" Shilloqwai chimed in.

"You'd better watch your mouth bitch!"

"My name is Shilloqwai! Call me a bitch again, and it will be the end of you."

"I don't feel like arguing with you today! If you threaten me again, it will be your ass! I'm learning to be more patient. I'll find the right time, and when it comes, I'll get you!"

"You threatening, insensitive bastard!"

"If that's how you feel, okay! Like I said I'm not in the mood to argue. And believe it or not, I came to see your boyfriend! I have some questions I need answers to. I think he's the only one that can answer them!"

"Before I answer any questions, let me make one thing clear! If you ever threaten my girlfriend again, I will take your ass out. And I'm not going to honor you by making you king of the shit pile. I will blast you into oblivion!"

"That's kind of what I need to talk to you about! It's coming up on two days since you and your honey were strutting about like a couple of pompous asses in front of the world. You alerted them to the global emergency, that was one thing. I want to know what you know about all of these weapons you claimed are going to be government issue! And what about this self-defense system. Who designed that? I know robots didn't have anything to do with the manufacturing of any of that shit! Do you have the slightest idea why I'm so pissed? I'm the World Governor and I didn't know a damn thing about any of this until the briefing!"

"My advice to you governor, is don't kick a gift horse in the mouth . Whatever, whoever, is attacking us isn't playing around. With these weapons, and the defense system, we should be able to hold them off for a while. Even if we fight together, robots and Humankind, I think we're fighting a losing battle. The day of reckoning is coming. I think these attacks, are the beginning of the end for all of us! As World Governor, it's your obligation to lead us. Let all of this petty bullshit go and quit playing politics with people's lives."

"The other issue under investigation is the destruction of government property. The drones are expendable to some degree. But the satellites that were taken down, not just one or two, but all ten of them. Any idea who's responsible?"

"No more than you do! Is the inquisition over?"

"For now. So, help me if I find out you've been orchestrating any of this shit! Your privileges of helping yourself to the pile will be revoked! As for you, Shilloqwai, watch your ass! Just because you're living with Mr. IQ, doesn't mean you don't have to follow Asimov's laws, you Humabot bitch."

"I don't have to follow Asimov's Laws, not anymore."

"Really? Since when?"

"Since when? Since I've turned human!"

"What kind of bullshit is that? How stupid do you think I am?"

"It's not bullshit! In regard to your intelligence, do you really need me to comment on that? If you had any brains, you'd be extremely dangerous."

"I've scanned her. She still has metal in her, including that fake heart of gold!"

"As a robot she had more heart than you do, you insensitive bastard! Love gave substance to her heart and made her human. And why have you scanned her without her consent. Having a heart of gold is a desirable human quality. It means her heart is full of love. Something you'd know nothing about. Answer my question asshole! Why are you harassing her? Why are you continuing to spy on her? You no longer have jurisdiction over her. And me, why are you tracking me, spying on me?"

"Half the time we don't even know where you are. You appear and disappear from the radar like a ghost!"

"You're admitting it then. You have been spying on me. That's a violation of the Transfer of Power Treaty. I'm not a criminal. Under the treaty I have the right to my privacy. As the World's leader, you're aware that you could be terminated for your transgressions. This isn't a threat! Just a reminder for you to follow your own advice. Follow Asimov's Laws!"

"Another word of advice that I strongly suggest you follow." Shilloqwai chimed in. "Don't ever call me a bitch again. This is your last warning! This is not a threat and I promise there will be consequences!"

"Like what?" Robotikis asked, gripping her arm with one of his mechanical extensions. He didn't realize how forcefully he'd grabbed her. It wasn't his intent to sever her arm. It was more than just a scratch as the silver-blue blood spewed from the laceration, like lava from an erupting volcano. Excelcious ran to his lab to fetch the supplies he needed to clean, stitch, and bandage her arm.

"You bastard! Look what you've done!" Shilloqwai chided. "This is the last time I'm letting you slide!" She warned. "The next time you violate me or my rights, I will destroy you, you mechanical son-of-a-bitch!" Robotikis was incapable of winning an argument with either Shilloqwai or Excelcious on an individual basis. He certainly wasn't going to win any challenges with them teamed up as a dynamic duo against him. Against his will, yet, knowing it would be in his best interests, Robotikis reluctantly left, reeling off a string of profanities.

The Fire on High continued burning up the night for over a month on end. The robots, with all of their efficiency, were unable to keep the streets clear of debris from day-to-day. As much as they wanted to blame the humans for the destruction, there was no evidence to support those claims. Humans couldn't blame the robots. There was no reason for them to shoot down their own satellites and drones. The truth would soon come out. Both factions would have to acknowledge the reality that their world might be coming to an end, or face being put out of existence and into extinction.

The robots were still speculating, theorizing, and triangulating in efforts to try and figure out where the weapons on the street were being manufactured, how were being distributed, and by whom. The only clue they had were the DDD Mercusilver Class insignias identifying it all. The rocket launchers, the missiles, the bazookas, the rifles, and the handguns, were all military grade and all contraband since the Transfer of Power Treaty.

Restrictions had temporarily been lifted for possessing and using such weapons. They had been found effective in battling against the AI Attack Force. It had been a long time since those who wished to exercise their second amendment rights had been able to do so, this included hunting and target practice.

The weapons-munitions tracking system, had thus far, proved to be effective. In just over a month since the Fire in the Sky appeared, there were no reported human casualties documented as a result of friendly fire. Globally, only a handful of robots had been destroyed. Those responsible for demolishing government property had already been apprehended and incarcerated with their weapons' privileges having been revoked. Surprisingly, there were a few robot-to-robot confrontations. Each case was independently reviewed. With two exceptions, in the 10 incidents involving robot-to robot conflict, the perpetrators in these termination events, were themselves put out of existence.

Humankind soon realized the drones that they've hated for so long, had become their eyes in the sky, protecting that space over their heads. The attack of the Lunabots marked the second phase of alien attacks. The battles between the Lunabots and drones lasted for days on end. Much to the delight of Humankind, they were relieved when the privacy-stealing machines, had disappeared from the sky completely.

As much as the event was celebrated by Humankind, it was an event which saw annihilation of both, the satellites and drones, disconcerting to most. Many began to wonder such things like; Had they really gotten their privacy back? Were they still being spied on, only this time by an alien robot force? The Earthen robots had a formidable defense system. By using the drones and satellites that they had, the Earthen robots were able to surveille, track and conduct recon missions. It was assumed that if the defenses that they had were so easily steamrolled, it would be only a matter of time before robots and Humankind would succumb to the attacking AI Force. Other questions of concern, with answers unknown, were; Where did this alien force come from? What was its mission? Why had it chosen to attack Earth? The robots were processing data on all of the aforementioned that had been fed to them by humans.

Initial analyses provided little in the way of answers. Initial output showed that the Lunabots that attacked them, could be classified in one of two subcategories. From the recovered parts, data showed they were either Photobots, very powerful miniature cameras, or Geobots. The Geobots came in every imaginable geometric shape, whose function had yet to be determined. Shilloqwai found some of these before her transformation. When damaged they secreted an acidic liquid poison, found to be fatal to humans. Such was not the case with the latest Geobots. Critical as it was to get information about the AI Attack Force, from the damaged and destroyed Lunabots, it was a distraction that took a majority of robots from their Prime Objective, protecting Humankind.

Shilloqwai let Excelcious sleep late, while she was reflecting on the developing relationship, between she and Excelcious. She also said a prayer, thanking God for the angel he'd put into her life. Not realizing how late it was, she jumped up from the couch and rushed into his room. Her soft kisses awakened him. "Good morning hon!"

"Good morning love, another restless night?"

"Yes, but I've got to get out of bed. We've got work to do!

"What time is it?" "Almost noon!"

"Man, I can't believe…Why didn't you…?"

"You needed the rest…we need to be…part of being prepared is being well -rested."

"Get your things, we're going to be gone for a few days!"

"Where are we going? Business or pleasure?" Excelcious shrugged his shoulders hinting their trip might include a little of both. "You like to live on the edge, don't you? I heard it was dangerous to mix business with pleasure."

"If you're afraid of a little adventure, you can always stay back and wait for me!"

"Like hell! I'm going with you! I have heard of instances, where mixing business and pleasure does work out! So, what surprises do you have for me today?"

"What makes you think I have a surprise for you?"

"Every time we've gone into the tunnels, you've surprised me with something. I can't wait to see what today brings!"

"Another chance I'm going to take. I'm going to keep you waiting, something you should never do to a woman…keep her waiting. But I have no other choice if I want to keep the surprise, I have in store for you!"

Business or pleasure, it was all the same to Shilloqwai. Going into the tunnels was always an adventure, even if they took her to some place, she'd been before. "So, business first!" He reminded her as he stopped in front of the armory.

"We're here to bring out heavier artillery!"

"Exactly. I need to make a few adjustments to these new drones I've been working on."

"How are you going to deploy them without the robots finding out?"

"Oh, they'll find out. They're going to be responsible for deploying them!"

"What? You're just going to give them all to the robots? They're going to kill you!"

"We have to up our game. We're getting our asses kicked by this AI force. All I have to do to get them to buy in is convince them it's for our safety. It will be an easy sell. Then I'll order them to use the drones. Citing Asimov's Laws, they'll have no choice but to follow my orders!"

By late afternoon, Shilloqwai and Excelcious had the drones working to perfection. Armed with laser targeting so precise, the drones were capable of taking dust particles out of the air, without harming anything around them. Using the fragments of destroyed Lunabots, Excelcious was able to program the Mercusilver drones so they targeted only the Lunabots. The only risk for Humankind was getting hit by shrapnel as the Lunabots were being blown to bits.

Though both felt a sense of accomplishment, having discovered a way to effectively and efficiently destroy the Lunabots, the mechanical mosquitoes still posed a legitimate threat. Their fears were not quelled. Who sent the Lunabots? What was the reasoning for having them sent to attack the Earth?

It took Excelcious about two hours to reprogram the Earth-based weapons system. With a push of a button, he sent the specs around the world. The robots would be working overtime tonight. They would be in charge of producing, distributing, and setting up the systems, menial tasks for the robots. Humankind was going to be disappointed with Excelcious when it found out he was the driving force behind getting the new weaponry to the robots. Because of the sophisticated cameras in the new drones, Humankind would involuntarily surrender its privacy once again! Humans could negotiate their privacy after they had defeated the enemy. If they lost the war, there would be nothing left to fight for. It was 7:30 pm by the time they'd finished their business.

"C'mon hon, it's time to close up shop."

"Is there still time for the pleasure part?"

"Patience my dear, I was getting to that. We've got a few days of rest and relaxation ahead of us. No sense in rushing a good thing!"

"I don't plan on rushing anything. I'm just anxious to find out where we're going!" Excelcious hadn't said a word as they walked along the pathway. She thought she'd recognized the tunnel they were in, but something was different, and she couldn't place what it was. It seemed they were going further underground than they had the last time in their most recent trip to the waterfalls.

She could feel the moisture from the water that she imagined had to be outside, somewhere close by. Like before, the composition of the rock walls started changing until they had transformed into crystal panes. Once again, she had a window into the depths of the ocean. There were fish of every breed from angelfish to Sharks, swimming in the pool of midnight green. A jellyfish drifted by them. In all of its neon-glow, it illuminated the peanut-butter bottom of the sea, exposing some of the vegetating starfish and sand dollar treasures."

"How would you like to go for a swim?"

"I'd love to!"

"We've got a little hike first!" He informed her pointing to a natural rock stairway. He let her lead the way while he followed behind her, supporting her with his hands on her hips. "If I slip," Shilloqwai joked, "make sure you've got my ass." She giggled. When she reached the top and stepped out on the plateau, she waited for him to join her at her side. This was déjà vu, they'd walked this path before. From there they walked across a white-silvery sand to a lagoon. "Decision time! Would you like to swim here or out there?"

"I'll take my chances and swim with the sharks!" Shilloqwai said boldly with a hint of dark humor. Both had to laugh. But, when Excelcious started unpacking the snorkeling gear, she realized he was serious about swimming with the sharks. Excelcious asked Shilloqwai to wait for him, promising he'd be right back. She watched him run off out of sight, leaving her to wonder where he'd gone!

"Had to get the oxygen tanks!" He explained as he came trotting back with two sets of tanks. They walked a short distance down a path that led to a beautiful white sandy beach where they put on their gear. Then they walked off across the sand to a natural breakwater, a cliff, from which they dove into the ocean; before proceeding to swim to a nearby coral reef sporting the colors of the universe.

There, Shilloqwai and Excelcious, encountered a school of dolphins at play. A couple of them were curious enough to approach them and playfully nudge them with their noses as they swam past. During their escapade they encountered a granddaddy-sized Great White. They got all of the help they needed from their dolphin friends, who were still nearby. The school of mammals chased off the intruder-predator. In the fantasy-like environment, mermaids were about the only creatures they didn't see."

"So, where are we going to sleep tonight?" Excelcious looked at her with a smile that was more than suspect. "Don't tell me…another surprise?"

"How did you guess?"

"You're becoming predictable!"

"I can change it up a bit if you want?"

"Please don't. I'm having trouble figuring you out with all that I know about you!"

They made their ascent up the trail that took them back to the sandy area by the lagoon. The moon and stars lit their way along the obscured path. Shilloqwai noticed they were headed in the general direction of where Excelcious had retrieved the oxygen tanks. He didn't leave her behind this time. Why should she have been surprised when he opened another secret passage which turned out to be a storage area for the snorkeling equipment? It was a shelter for more than just that, as she was finding out. He left her waiting in the storage area for just a short time. When Excelcious reappeared, he was sitting in a sleek looking craft that was hovering beside her. "Impressive! But what the hell is this?"

"C'mon, get in and I'll tell you about it!" Shilloqwai eased herself into the luxury transport. This is a Mercusilver Dragonship complete with DDD defense systems. All of the shuttles are variations of the Dragonship. If it comes down to it, these transports will be our lifelines, our escape from the AI force attacking us."

"You've got it all planned out, haven't you?"

"Look, I'm not trying to be the savior of the world. That role has already been filled. The sacrificial lamb has been slaughtered and raised up."

"You seem to be following in his footsteps."

"Isn't that what we're called to do?"

"Yes, from everything I hear! So, tell me more about this vehicle and where we're going!"

"As for where we're going, the vehicle is able to fly around the world and into space. It's all terrain. It can also float on water or be submerged and move through it! "It's all solar powered! I thought you might like to pick the place since you're in the driver's seat!" She looked at him dumbfoundedly. For starters, she had no idea on how to operate the vehicle. She was still trying to navigate the wonders of Excelcious' world. Shilloqwai looked to him for suggestions. "Again, we can go anywhere you please, but I might suggest you press the blue programmed key #1." He said, pointing out the button.

Anxious to see where the craft would take them, she followed his suggestion. After pressing the button, the craft moved 1,000 times smoother than a hydraulically run machine, floating about 15-feet off of the ground, while drifting toward their selected destination. No thrill ride could have been as exhilarating or as breathtaking. Again, she heard the rushing water and things began to look peculiarly familiar. She could smell the many fragrances from the flowers in the botanical garden below. She heard clusters of parrots sitting in the trees repeating the gibberish they'd heard. "Damn humans! Stupid-ass robots! It's the end of the world! We're all going to die! Kill the AI bastards! Watch your mouth Bitch! Robotikis, is an asshole!" Shilloqwai's smirks turned into an outburst of uncontrolled hysterical laughter. As did Excelcious'. The parrots' tirade would be the surprise of the night. Shilloqwai was certain there was nothing he could say or do to top it. There was one thing, but they were saving that for their honeymoon.

"I wonder if they learned that thing about Robotikis being an asshole, from me?"

"I don't know, but I'm about to bust a gut!" Excelcious feared as his sides were already hurting from laughing so hard.

"And I'm about to lose my cookies!" Shilloqwai confessed as both were still in hysterics, with tears gushing from their eyes.

Shilloqwai's next surprise came at the sight of the luminous roses. Pure, platinum white and ever so delicately beautiful. She wanted to reach out and pick one to put in her hair. Excelcious stopped her, explaining that the entire bush would go dormant for a time and the flower would instantly die, not just the one she picked, but the entire bouquet on the bush. Seeing the look of disappointment on her face, while they continued drifting along, Excelcious said to her, "They would look good in your hair , but..." He went on to explain to her. He eased her disappointment with a compliment. "The glow in your smile and the sparkle in your eyes is more brilliant than all of them put together." All of their brilliance faded, as the flowers' glow had been reduced to that of a dying ember in a fire, that had run out of fuel to burn.

"Do you think they heard you?" Shilloqwai asked, half-thinking that they had.

"Perhaps. So, do you know where we're going yet?"

"I'm still not quite sure. You're not going to tell me if I'm right anyway, so I'll have to be content until the surprise is revealed."

"You'll know soon enough!" As she observed they'd ascended considerably. They were more than just a few feet off of the ground. Through self-restoration, the roses were glowing again in all of their luminous brilliance. Even in the night, butterflies were fluttering about. Every species looked like a living work of art. Moonbeams and star light were the sources of the nebulous glow in their stained-glass wings. The brilliant colors of the parrots made the treetops appear as though they were ablaze. Finally, she saw it, the source of the rushing water she'd been hearing for a while. And everything about this familiar place came back to her, wild dreams and fantasies were coming alive. This time she got a panoramic view of the waterfalls. She noticed they formed a semi-circle in a place commonly known as Fantasy Cove. The water droplets sparkled like cosmic-colored diamonds in the enchanting nightlight, while they cascaded over rocks of silver and gold.

"Am I dreaming, or is this another one of your optical illusions? Like I said the last time we were here, I keep waiting for the dragons and the unicorns to come out of hiding."

"Illusion? I'm not that creative. What you see before you was made by the hands of God!"

"You talk a lot about God and Love. I'd be interested to know your thoughts on Heaven and the City of Gold. Christians claim it rests beyond the pearly gates. Do you really think Heaven is the City of Gold?"

"You've raised a month's worth of discussion topics. I'll try to give you the short answer."

"What's the rush, we've got all night?"

"True! God is Love, Creator of all life. Heaven is God's home, and if we live right, we'll have an eternal place in his kingdom. That's why it's important to keep the faith. We have to believe that God will give us the strength to carry out his will. We have to have hope, regardless of how bad things might seem. I could actually see you in a halo and wings."

Shilloqwai was blushing, her tourmaline skin turned sky-blue. "In all of the darkness, you are my angel of light!"

"And you're mine! What about the city of gold? Do you think it really exists?"

"I've heard that people with near-death experiences claim that there is! Though I can't personally vouch for it, I believe it to be real. If we fulfill our purpose in life, to get to heaven, we'll get to see it for ourselves."

"What about the rainbow colors said to cloak the heavens. Do you believe in that?"

"Do you? Look around. From this vantage point, I'd say we're getting more than a glimpse of heaven!"

"It almost feels like we're there. I can't see it being much better than this! Me here with you, in this Earthen paradise. I love you." Shilloqwai professed as she had many times before. The sincerity of her words was confirmed by the tears seeping from the corners of her eyes, streaking her aqua-tourmaline cheeks!"

"I love you too! You're the best thing that's ever happened to me!"

"And where would I be without you? TERMINATED! That's where! Through your love, you've given me faith and hope." Excelcious finally docked the Mercusilver craft. Shilloqwai flew out of it like it was on fire. Though it was a comfortable enjoyable ride, it felt good to stretch her legs. She knew Excelcious felt the same. She stripped down to her bikini before he could blink an eye. Like all articles of clothing she wore, her bikini concealed more than it revealed. Like her, he stripped down to his essentials. As they disappeared behind the waterfall, where they agreed to spend their honeymoon, Excelcious was shirtless, showing off his six-pack abs, wearing a respectable pair of cutoffs!

They climbed into the natural hot tub with a surreal backdrop of waterfalls. Their romantic escapade went late into the evening and into the early morning. They'd spent much of their time kissing the night away. All fantasies fade at some point, like the current one between them was. Magic moments were becoming precious memories. Both were up for a midnight snack. After feasting on wild berries, from a nearby bush, and coconut milk, from the fruit of a nearby tree, Excelcious and Shilloqwai concluded the evening with a welcome-to-dreamland goodnight kiss! "Not to quell the magic of the moment, but do you think it's a good idea to weaponize the robots with DDD defensc systems? Specifically, the drones and the elaborate defense system you plan to gift to them! What if they use it against us, or any of Humankind?"

"Honey, this isn't about us, and them anymore! It's about trying to find a way to save our world, ours, and the robots'! I'm afraid the worst of the attacks are yet to come. God help us all when they do. We're in for the fight of our lives! How about you? Any ideas as to who or what might be attacking us?"

"Nothing or no one in particular. I seem to have a photographic memory. At times I feel like a walking encyclopedia. I don't know that I've retained all of the information from my database from back in my robot days. I feel like I'm able to recall a great deal, like miniscule details about a variety of subjects. "Even with all of my resources and the wealth of information I have, I'm just as clueless about the AI attackers as you are!"

"You know, hon, we're going to get through this together. And then we'll have the rest of our lives together. In a short period of time, we've gotten so close. If something happened to you, I don't know that I could live without you!"

"You've already promised nothing's going to happen to me and that you were going to protect me. I believe you whole-heartedly, but I don't think you're going to be able to keep those promises to me."

"What, are you planning on going somewhere?"

"No, I can't leave you. Not after all you've done for me. I love you too much!"

"Then why are you talking like the end is near for us? You're not still worried about Robotikis trying to get to you, are you?"

"No, I'm not afraid of that bastard anymore!"

"Then who? What is it? Tell me!"

"I'm afraid of what every human is afraid of, the unknown! I've been having dreams, nightmares, premonitions. I'm afraid of them coming true like my dreams have!"

"Don't worry, they won't!" Excelcious assured her.

"How can you be so sure?"

"The reason dreams come true is because you follow them, actively pursue them into fruition. We run from our nightmares."

"That's not the same thing as running from our problems, is it?"

"No, definitely not! Nightmares, premonitions, sometimes they're just flat out stupid. Sometimes, however, they can serve as warnings of things that might happen, depending on the choices we make. Have you ever had a nightmare where you're about to die and you wake up just before you do? Premonitions can be just as horrifying as a nightmare. You find yourself in horrible situations, but the outcome of the horrific event you're seeing is unclear!"

"So, why do you think that is?"

"As horrible as they are, I think there are benefits to nightmares and premonitions. They can be warnings of things that may come to pass if we don't take certain actions. They can also help with a mental state of preparedness, so if those bad things should come to pass, we'll be better equipped to handle them.

"Nightmares, premonitions, both are shadows of what might be. Where with dreams, they are how you'd like things to be. You're well aware of what happens when you pursue your dreams. You can write the happy endings for dreams and nightmares. By casting light on the shadows of darkness, you can chase them into obscurity. By illuminating the darkness, you can rid yourself of the biggest enemy you'll ever face…the unknown." He reasoned, after which he tried to kiss her fears away.

"I thought it was supposed to be business before pleasure!" Shilloqwai reminded him, as she breathlessly broke their embrace. "C'mon, we've got a special delivery to make!" She prodded, leading Excelcious by the hand, from the underground paradise back into the real world. Robotikis, was unpleasantly surprised by the young couple's unannounced visit to the lab. He'd made known his feelings of disdain for them both. "What the hell are you doing here?" Robotikis asked snidely. Wanting more than anything, he desired to wish them away. "Believe it or not, I'm glad you stopped by. And I say this with all seriousness. These alien attacks we've been subject to as of late, aren't doing anything to help smooth over relations between robots and humans. Any suggestions as to how I might be able to get myself out from under this mess?"

"That's easy!" Shilloqwai quipped, going for the cheap shot. "Crawl out from under the shit pile and climb to the top of it! Put yourself above it all."

"Couldn't resist? Could you Shilloqwai? Seriously, I don't know what to do. Everyone's pointing fingers at everyone else. Our defense systems are down, leaving the robots defenseless to protect Humankind!"

"Like everyone else, we're clueless as to who took out the satellites and shot down the drones!" Excelcious admitted. "But Shilloqwai and I think we can help to defend against the Spacebots. We're donating this fleet of new military-grade drones and a new military-grade defense system for this Robotix facility. Both are being manufactured as we speak for global distribution in strategic locations."

"It's a generous offer. What do you want in exchange for these, gifts?"

"For you to leave us the hell alone. And do your job in accordance with Asimov's Laws! The gifts are primarily for Humankind. It's your responsibility to come up with a protection plan that works for all humans."

"I don't know if I should kill you or kiss you."

"Please kill me!" Shilloqwai requested. "I sure as hell don't want you kissing me!"

"Being in possession with things such as these could get you killed under normal circumstances." Robotikis reminded them.

"Sparing our lives, was part of the agreement, right? Afterall, the gifts are for the benefit of Humankind. So, quit with the threats Robotikis.

You seem to forget that we have the goods on you too! It would be a shame if you were removed from power."

"Likewise, it would be an awful shame if the two of you, one day, mysteriously disappeared!" Shilloqwai was angered by the fact that Robotikis was doubling down on his threats. She felt the energy surging through her again, as she had in the past. She turned away from Robotikis as she was losing control of the power.

No sooner had she done so, when exploding metal stars shot out of her eyes. Upon impact, the explosive ammunition detonated, taking down one of the lab walls. Though no damage had been done to the foundation, the section of the building where the wall was taken out would have to be reconstructed. The fact that part of the roof had fallen in above the damaged area, was evidence of how structurally unsound that portion of the building was after her uncontrolled outburst.

Equipment and supplies were among the collateral damage, as were a handful of assembler bots. The bots, deemed irreparable, were promptly terminated. Though it wasn't her intent, she had destroyed Kinks, the lead tech robot that ordered her to the shit pile and Screwhead the robot that threw her on top of it. Excelcious tried to explain the uncontrolled misfire as an involuntary action and a malfunctioning defense system.

"Bullshit!" Robotikis said emphatically, calling out the lie for what it was. "She's not a robot anymore. There's an added bounce to her step and a natural swaying in her ass when she walks. She'd better watch her ass. These kinds of uncontrolled outbursts will get her terminated-exterminated. Robot or human, however she's classifying herself these days. Because of your generous, shall we say bribes, I'll cut you both slack, this one last time!" For now, the Fire in the Sky had seemingly burnt itself out. But the ashen clouds lingered in the silver-blue, partially obscuring the sun, the moon, and the stars around the world. This reprieve would allow Humankind to step-up production of Excelcious' Mercusilver drones and weapon defense systems being manufactured, distributed, and implemented at a furious pace. It was an ideal example of robots and Humankind working together for a common cause.

Though it was a temporary fix, both would be prepared for another imminent wave of attacks from the alien force. And though Excelcious had ideas for a new satellite system, capable of taking out the AI force before it could attack Earth, it would take too much time to build and launch it.

It would take time from what they were doing to try and put themselves in a position to defend against whatever was presently attacking them. Earth's civilization wasn't about to surrender or succumb to anyone, not yet, and probably not ever. It would be a fight to the death. The lull between attacks offered a false sense of security for some.

Shilloqwai and Excelcious remained on-guard, ready for an attack at any moment. That didn't mean they couldn't have an open discussion about their future together. "I'm worried!" Shilloqwai confessed with a quiver in her voice and her body trembling.

"Remember what I told you, don't worry about the things you can't change!"

"Yes, but this is different. It's personal and it has to do with me… and you! You saw what happened in the lab, the day we gifted the drones and the defense system to Robotikis and company."

"Yeah, the lab needed to be remodeled anyway. I'm surprised he didn't make us do community service for retribution!" Shilloqwai let out a genuine laugh, something she hadn't done in a while. She'd been under a lot of stress. And what was on her mind was adding to it.

"Seriously!" She stated somberly. "Honey, I'm just afraid of the day, I'll lose control of my powers. I could unintentionally hurt you, or worse."

"If something like that ever were to happen, just know that it won't be your fault. I'd rather die loving you. Living without you will kill me too, and this would be a much more painful death than if I were to die instantly from friendly fire. All you need to know is that I love you." He'd done it again, Excelcious' words had a way of touching her heart and bringing tears to her eyes. "I love you too!" She sobbed!"

"You're not the only one that's scared or the only one taking chances. If you decide on your own to leave, know that I will come looking for you. Love will find a way to get us through this hon, but you've got to keep the faith."

"As much as I try to justify it, I could never leave you. I'm eternally yours, hell, and high water."

"Through bad times and good" He added, stressing the positive. She threw herself into his arms and hugged him as if she were never going to let him go. The solace of being in his arms reminded her of what she needed most. Someone who'd give her a shoulder to cry on. And someone to stay by her side and protect her, no matter what! Though peace was a good thing, they knew, the entire world knew, it wasn't going to last forever.

This was the calm before the wicked storm brewing in the cosmos. More accurately it was the eye of the hurricane, and the worst was yet to come. Suddenly, all hell broke loose. Galactic debris was raining down all around them. With support from the newly implemented DDD Defense System and the DDD drones, Shilloqwai and Excelcious were able to seek cover, avoiding injury.

Perched under their shelter, both watched the current wave of attack. The Lunabots and Geobots, were doing little in the way of damage. Like snow in winter, the Lunabots and Geobots were blanketing the ground. Snow cover was much more appealing to look at as opposed to the space junk littering the ground. This battle was going to be won by Earth and its inhabitants. The DDD weapons that had been recently implemented were doing their job. Shilloqwai and Excelcious could see the fleet was thinning. Data they were getting through encrypted messaging told them the same thing was occurring on a global scale. They continued watching from their shelter until the last of the Lunabots and Geobots had been blasted from the sky. The amount of litter left behind was astounding. For once, Humankind and the robots agreed on something. They would work together to pick up the trash.

As they began clearing the debris, they began to find little treasures of sorts. Amidst the litter, many found what resembled game pieces, each stamped with a robot character of some sort. It was ironic that something from an alien space drop would be compatible with the Universal Galactix Box, a global gaming system for kids. The holographic imaging system was the first of its kind. The system featured interactive role-playing games where players could choose which character they would be. Advanced options allowed players to create their own characters. Most of the games were comprised of good vs. evil scenarios, where the games offered advantages regardless of the side being played. Some games required team efforts to achieve a common goal or to fulfill various quests.

The unique feature of this new role-playing game, that mysteriously made its global appearance, required players to build their squads. Players accomplished this by recruiting characters found on game pieces lying around in the debris, that had rained down on the world. The success of the quest-based game depended on the characters in a player's squad. In order to actually win the game, players needed to have a coveted game piece with the character likeness of Metallicus Nebuloso. To this point, the piece had been elusive, more accurately, missing in action. If a player were lucky enough to acquire this all-powerful piece, that player would win all battles, collect all rewards, and win the interactive holographic war, ultimately winning the game.

Most parents were skeptical about allowing their kids to play an interactive wargame. But it was just a game, or was it? There were no real winners, and no real losers, only virtual casualties; targeted and those that resulted from collateral damage. There was a lesson to be learned from the game, which had real-life applications. And it was a reminder to all, that with great power, comes great responsibility!

HOLOGRAPHS, VIRTUAL REALITY & THE WAR ON CHILDREN

[CHAPTER 10]

Coming into existence about the time the Fire in the Sky started, the Hologram Game entertained the children at first. Now, however, they were quickly growing tired of it. The game was endless and providing no way of winning! As of now, the elusive, alleged game-changing piece, picturing Metallicus Nebuloso, had yet to be found. There are 10 valuable lessons of life to be learned by all, when facing no-win situations.

Lesson 01: Always turn to the Power of Love. It can make something of nothing. It can heal anything. It changes Everything.

Lesson 02: Always show love, especially to the enemy. You don't have to be best buds with your enemies to forgive them. Forgiving is part of Loving. You can love your enemies by forgiving them and praying for them.

Lesson 03: Always be the best you can be!

Lesson 04: Learn to adapt to ever-changing situations. Your life may depend on it.

Lesson 05: Learn to make the best of challenging situations.

Lesson 06: Quitters are the only losers in life.

Lesson 07: You can only fail if you don't try.

Lesson 08: Change what you can and leave the rest to the Power of Love.

Lesson 09: Learn to hate, HATE. When you hate, you become bitter. Bitterness is an infection that breeds and festers inside, until you become the very thing you hate. In the end, you will become hate itself.

Lesson 10: Always be a light. In doing so you can chase away the shadows that haunt you. In being, an eternal light you'll maintain the power to face Humankind's greatest fear, THE UNKNOWN! Once you face your fears, especially the unknown, you will come to the realization that you have the power to dispel all of your fears, especially Humankind's greatest fear…THE UNKNOWN!

Life can teach us lots of valuable lessons, but to get through it you have to have a plan. Life is like a mountain. It's unrealistic to think you can climb a mountain in a single bound. You've got to take it one step at a time. You can't go through life without a plan. Setting achievable goals and dreaming of what could be, have to be part of that plan. It takes dedication to stick with the plan. It takes patience to pursue dreams. Dedication, patience, and perseverance will take you where you want to go in life. The rewards for persevering and getting to life's summit are heavenly. Achieving goals gives us a sense of accomplishment. There's no feeling like the pure ecstasy that comes with the fulfillment of our dreams.

It was beyond anyone's wildest dreams that the first to find the game-changing piece would be a seven-year-old girl. Carlita found the chip in her own backyard. The Metallicus Nebuloso game chip was buried in the sandbox. Carlita was a gamer and anxious to add the new character to her squad. She was never very good at the game; she just liked the role-playing aspect of it. She loved galivanting around playing heroine in her imaginary world. The new character enhanced the powers of the young warrior princess character she created. She liked the feeling of being invincible. She lamented the fact that she couldn't use her powers to solve life's problems and heal the world by ridding it of the evils that dwell within it. Such wisdom for a child so youthful.

She became the first-ever player to win the hologram game. In doing so, she was transformed from a relative nobody to the media darling of the world. She felt honored at first, but after a while she grew tired of the extra attention and began to shun it. She was thankful the world only knew about the first time she'd defeated the Robot Warlord, when in actuality she'd done it many times.

Carlita quickly learned the difference between a fantasy world and an artificial one. A fantasy world fueled dreams and desires. An artificial one fostered delusion and division through deception and lies. A fake world, one that harped over frivolous accomplishments. The fake one wanted to steal her secret to beating the game. "There's no secret really. The special piece took away all of the challenges of the game and made it too easy, 'which is why I got bored with it all,'" Carlita repeatedly told the media in several interviews. "It's not just true with the game, but with life; sometimes we have to think outside the box and stretch the imagination to meet the challenges before us. At the same time, you need to stay within yourself and be true to who you are." She said profoundly. Shilloqwai and Excelcious were watching the broadcast. They were flabbergasted by the philosophical insight the child had just shared with the world.

"Talk about lessons in life!" Shilloqwai remarked. "We just got educated by a seven-year-old girl! I wish she had the foresight to know why the game was sent to Earth. There has to be an ulterior motive, I know it wasn't sent here with the sole intent of entertaining Earth's children!" Shilloqwai surmised.

"The one benefit I see in the game is the fact that it's engaging. It's even gotten some of the deadbeat parents interacting with their kids." Excelcious reasoned.

"I get what you mean, but that's the stupidest thing I've ever heard you say, Excelcious! You mean to tell me parents can't get involved with their kids unless it's through a video game? What happened to the old-fashioned tradition of just showing them a little love?" Shilloqwai told him candidly. "I'm kind of pissed that you actually said it. We know that it's a diversionary tactic, but a diversion from what?"

"Sorry, didn't mean to hit your hot buttons. I'm not sure what the reason is for the diversion. The Fire in the Sky has been blazing for almost a year now. Since the fire broke out, tensions between the robots and Humankind have been increasing at an alarming rate. The question is, why is our agent provocateur trying to divide us?"

"Conquest. It's easier to conquer an opposing force if you can split the allies." Shilloqwai speculated.

"I want to know the desire for conquest. What is the Prime Objective of the attacking forces?" Excelcious pondered.

"That is the question, isn't it? I think we need more data input." Shilloqwai surmised.

While the craze for the Hologram Game was still at its peak, Carlita announced to the world that her gaming days were over. Through it all, Carlita never lost sight of the real world where the lessons of life were learned, and its joys experienced. Many children thought she was crazy for giving up on the hologram game. They saw it as entertaining, full of fascinating adventures and infinite scenarios. It was hard for most children to fathom, how she could simply lose interest in something, that most of the rest of the children thought had so much appeal.

Carlita didn't like how the game had dominated her life for almost a year. Especially when she realized that she'd been depriving herself of life's essentials. She missed playing outside with her friends, walks in the park. She missed the talks with mom and dad. They didn't have the answers to all of her questions, or solutions to all of her problems. She missed the extra hugs and the extra kisses that made her feel secure. She missed the bedtime stories that safely escorted her into Dreamland. Her parents always seemed to do and say the right things, the ones that made her feel better when she was feeling down and out. She hoped she'd never grow too old for their hugs and kisses. She treasured their unconditional love. She believed, "I love you" was a phrase she couldn't say to them near enough.

Carlita just wanted her life back, the way it was, the way she hoped it would forever stay, with God and her family as the centerpieces. She was saddened, especially as of late, when she remembered that she'd been neglecting her morning and bedtime prayers. She wondered how big of a sin that was that she hadn't been thanking Jesus for the gifts he'd blessed her with. She wondered too, how much her neglecting Him, was hurting Jesus.

Shilloqwai and Excelcious hoped the rest of the world would see the light as Carlita had. It wouldn't be long before the growing rifts had caused a great divide with the potential to do irreparable damage. "Divide and Conquer." It's the most fundamental war tactic there is! The question is, how long will it be, before the AI force felt comfortable enough to launch a full-scale attack on the Earth?" Shilloqwai asked, knowing Excelcious had no more of an answer to the question than she did.

"The primary attacks have been on the robots. The logical conclusion would be, that getting rid of the robots, would make the path of getting to Humankind that much smoother."

"And why go after the youth?" Shilloqwai wondered aloud.

"To widen the gap between Earth's mechanical and gullible factions. The humans will ultimately blame the robots for their inability to protect them. In spite of the damage its already done to human relationships, thousands are still addicted to and playing that damn game! I don't know what it is, but my instincts are telling me the AI Force wants to do more than rid the Earth of its populous. I think it's about more than destroying the people. I think, ultimately, the AI Force would like to do away with the Earth as well!"

"Shit, now that you put it that way, it all makes perfect sense! We need to know more about our enemy. Finding its weaknesses will be the key to destroying it. The trick will be how to find out more about an enemy that's proven to be; invasive, anti-social and to this point, very ambiguous about its intentions. Who's given the Prime Directive to this mysterious AI Force. Who set the Prime Objective, and what specifically is it?"

"Good questions, but we don't have time to search for the answers?" Shilloqwai pondered aloud. "If they were to launch a large-scale attack, do you think we can stop them?" Shilloqwai asked, hoping Excelcious believed there was.

"Honestly, no!" Excelcious sighed. "It's a chess game now. In chess, the best player doesn't always win, the best strategist does. There are only so many moves you can make. The smallest, even if it's one mistake while playing the game, can be the deadliest.

"That's why it's important to look at the whole picture, anticipate their moves, while trying to keep two to three moves ahead of the opposition. Did we destroy their pawns, or did they willingly sacrifice them? If they willingly sacrificed them, what was the reason for it? If they didn't intend to sacrifice their pawns, then we need to strategize and capitalize on their mistake!"

"So, Humankind playing against its mechanical counterparts may have an advantage. The machines will act methodically and logically. Whereas humans are unpredictable at times and will act as such. The hope in doing this is to throw the robots off enough that they miscalculate a move or two. That will buy us time before we have to make our next move." Shilloqwai added as she was starting to see Excelcious' point.

"Exactly. Knowing we can't beat them, we have to play for a stalemate, a draw if you will. Neither side wins, a true to life scenario that always plays out in a war. Nobody wins. Everyone loses. The benefactors are the survivors that are then forced to go out and look for the spoils." Excelcious concluded.

"If we can get into a stalemate with the AI Force…then what?" Shilloqwai pondered.

"Then, we execute our escape plan and hope we can outrun them! C'mon it's time to get the army ready for mobilization!" Excelcious urged her.

"You mean the Orbitoids?" Shilloqwai asked for clarification.

"Yes. I'm such a dumb ass. I should have had them ready, for situations such as this. I was thinking I had time, anticipating the big battle was going to be between the Earthen Robots and Humankind. I miscalculated, not anticipating we'd be attacked by an alien force. This is the kind of mistake I was talking about, the kind that could cost the existence of Humankind!" Excelcious lamented.

"I don't think that's God's will. I have faith he will guide us through this crisis! Don't give up hope, Excelcious, I believe in you!" He kissed her in gratitude for her words of encouragement. "How much time do you think we have before we're forced to make our next move?"

"That depends on how long this holographic game scenario takes to play out. I don't think it's run its course yet. Since that little girl defeated Metallicus Nebuloso, there's been a renewed interest in the game. Others are trying to accomplish the same feat. To this point, none of them have been successful. C'mon! Follow me, I want to show you something. I hope you're up for a little friendly competition !"

"Sure! What did you have in mind?" Excelcious led her through the Hologram shield and through the tunnel that led to the armory. On a table there was a brand-new Hologram Gaming system. It had yet to be taken out of the box!

Excelcious had all of the game pieces on the table next to the box, including the one with the likeness of Metallicus Nebuloso on the face of it. "Holy Shit! Where did you get all of these from?" Shilloqwai demanded to know!

"The coveted piece hit me in the eye out here in the yard. The others, I found them here and there, out on the property. So, we can have up to eight in the squad. I think you and I should create our own characters and use the coveted piece, that leaves five openings." Excelcious left Shilloqwai to select the remaining five members of the squad. She picked a character that was good with weaponry, another that was a good strategist, a third that was a healer, a fourth character that possessed magic powers and a fifth that was intelligent, with stealth and dexterity as its strengths.

Once actively engaged in the game, Shilloqwai and Excelcious understood how one could get addicted to it. The interactive adventure was exciting for a time. They fulfilled quest after quest and were on the verge of obliterating the enemy, thus putting themselves in a position to claim victory for their squad. Inexplicably, Shilloqwai made some costly errors that prevented them from doing so. Excelcious attributed her mistakes to human error. Shilloqwai was thankful she successfully pulled off the charade without Excelcious suspecting she'd intentionally made those errors. She had good reason for doing so which she would explain to him later.

Without warning, things went awry. Shilloqwai didn't even feel the energy surge from within her. She didn't know that her mutant defense system had discharged until the Holographic Gaming System had been destroyed! "What the hell?" Excelcious asked, reacting to the shocking outcome of their friendly competition which abruptly came to an end. "What just happened?"

"I don't know!" Shilloqwai sighed before passing out and crumpling to the floor.

Excelcious cleared a space for her on one of the tables. After patting her forehead with some wet towels, he revived her in a short period of time, probably less than a minute. "Are you alright?" He asked, handing her a cold glass of water.

"Yes, I'm fine!" She snapped. "When we were playing that game, I saw things, bad things, like what I've seen in prior premonitions. The things I saw will come to pass unless we can shut down that damn game! It's going to hurt the children and a lot of others perhaps. It's more than a game. It's a sophisticated spy cam stealing personal information from households and individuals!" Shilloqwai claimed.

"For what purpose? Any ideas?" Excelcious inquired.

"Isn't it obvious? This force has now infiltrated Earth's Youth. It has successfully come up with a way to track the children and those they hold dear to them, starting with their families. This is a terrorist assault on all of Humankind! It must be stopped!" Shilloqwai insisted. Shilloqwai and Excelcious did their part to get the warnings out. Robotix and social media echoed those warnings, which most took seriously.

Others seemingly ignored the warnings, trying to wish the problem away. In regard to the Fire in the Sky which had flamed out again, out of sight, out of mind was the position many took. The majority knew better knowing the pilot was still lit and all it would take was a spark to reignite the Fire in the Sky! Gossip, in regard to the Holographic Game was running as rampant as ever on social media pages. It had become a global pandemic as talk of Metallicus Nebuloso dominated most discussions around the world.

As big as the game Fortnite had become, the Hologram Game had far surpassed it in terms of popularity. New posts telling of more children whom had defeated the game started surfacing on the social media. The number of victors climbed rapidly from 25 to a few hundred. After the 1000th child walked away a victor, gamers found it was no longer possible to beat Metallicus Nebuloso, not even with the coveted piece.

It seemed the interactive holographs themselves began changing the rules to the game as it went along. Metallicus' invincibility posed new challenges, even to the most imaginative children. Raw imagination, unadulterated fantasy, know no bounds. These things allowed the most creative ones to manipulate the game along with the ever -changing rules and use them to their advantage. Once again, children had proven to be Masters of the Universe in virtual reality. But something was different. Both the holographic heroes and AI adversaries put forth unsubstantiated claims that many children had cheated to win. The claims failed to cite specifically how the children were cheating. The holographic images warned, more like threatened, human contestants, promising they would be punished and left to deal with the consequences for cheating; defined loosely, as not abiding by the rules of the game.

The children held contempt for such claims and disregard for what they believed to be idle threats. There were lots of gray areas in regard to the rules that were ever-changing. What were acceptable tactics in the beginning of the game, might possibly be considered unacceptable in the middle of, or at the end of the game. How was this cheating? How was it punishable? And by who's authority were these alleged punishments going to be carried out? When victor 1001 emerged, the warnings proved to be more than idle threats.

A 14-year-old child claimed to have been beaten silly by the holographic characters in his virtual squad. He had the bruises and racoon eyes coupled with video footage to prove it. He tried to turn the game off and suffered 1st and 2nd degree burns on his hands and arms after touching the controls on his console.

Another claim, proven to be true, was that a 17-year-old girl was blinded, perhaps permanently, when a pulsar flash was discharged from one of the weapons held by a character in her squad. The game lost all of its popularity and almost all of its players when reports started circulating regarding a four-year-old girl, who suffered a concussion after she was roughed up by one of the characters in her squad. She told her mom and dad she was randomly pushing the buttons, when a golden holograph crown appeared before her, proclaiming her a winner. It was then the character attacked her. Ironically, she was playing without the coveted character in her squad! Humankind was globally enraged by the initial reports that children were injured while interacting with the Hologram Game. The verified reports of injuries to children kept coming in. Growing concerns, prompted the majority to get rid of electronic devices, in particular, gaming systems. Eventually, all gaming systems would disappear from the face of the Earth.

Before they did, there were the virtual junkies, who dismissed the mounting evidence, attributing it to isolated incidents, globally scattered. Reviewing the data, every alleged victor after #1000, was injured in some way shape or form. Seriousness of the injuries was irrelevant. It was the fact of the matter that was being looked into! After careful consideration, Robotix announced a Virtual reclamation project. With the help of Excelcious, Robotix now had a way to track existing Hologram gaming systems and the gaming pieces in question. Global confiscation measures for these devices and gaming pieces would be enforced. Withholding either the devices or the game pieces was to be considered a federal crime. Humankind was warned that severe consequences would be imposed on violators who refuse to forfeit gaming systems and or game pieces. Most gave up their virtual world willingly. Others did so reluctantly, offering mild resistance. After strongarm tactics and the power of suggestion, those withholding, were persuaded to conform, with one exception.

The top virtual player refused to turnover his console and accessories to the authorities. The robots could have wrestled it away from him. Politically, it wouldn't have looked good had they done so. Claiming it was his, and he had the right to keep it, the robots respected his wishes and let him keep it until his court date. He said he would accept the results of the hearing and forfeit his console and accessories if that's what was asked of him. For now, it was on the shelf for novelty's sake, if for nothing else. The boy known as Asteroid, retired his game and put it on a shelf. Asteroid wasn't his birth name, he had it legally changed the day he turned 18. No first name and last name, just Asteroid. Excelcious was furious when he found out the robots got weak-kneed and allowed him to keep the device and his game pieces. "What did you say the name of this clown is?"

"Asteroid!" One of the Orbitoids revealed.

"Dumb Asteroid, if you ask me! I still don't know why the robots didn't haul him off by force and put his ass in jail! We're talking about a matter of global security. I could give a rip about an 18-year-old who still knows nothing about responsibility, a young adult who throws a temper tantrum because he can't get his way. If he were my son, he'd be getting an ass whoopin' about now! And the robots should have taken all of that shit away from him! I don't care what it would have looked like politically."

"Agreed." The Orbitoid nodded. Before Excelcious could comment further a shrill sounding alarm went off.

"What the hell is that?" Excelcious asked, alarmed by the sound. "Son-of-a-bitch activated his system. I hacked it this morning and remotely disabled it. Apparently, he's found a way around the lock I put on it. Shit, it's totally disconnected! I can't disable it!"

"So, what's going to happen now that we're unable to stop him?" Shilloqwai asked, obviously concerned about a potentially explosive situation.

"To be honest, I'm not sure. It's likely this rogue bastard is opening us up to a global attack." Excelcious was right about Asteroid's short-sighted view. He wasn't thinking of anyone else, only himself. Asteroid, on the other hand believed his actions were justified and that he had the right to play a virtual holographic game if he wanted to! He was an adult after all! What started as a dream, quickly turned into a nightmare. His ultimate fantasy of a one-on-one battle with Metallicus became a dreaded reality.

The way it started, as a virtual holographic battle, was what he was expecting. Incredibly the battle with a hologram, transformed into a physical confrontation and a fight for his life. Asteroid's foe valiantly offered him armor that was supposed to protect him from the live laser rounds they would be firing at one another. And it did for a while, but Asteroid had been hit so many times by the penetrating rays, his armor no longer adequately protected him. Before he could take evasive maneuvers and return fire, he was hit by a duo-beam laser. He thought the weapon was illegal, but, then he remembered the first rule of engagement; THERE ARE NO RULES IN A FIGHT TO THE DEATH! There was no retreating or surrendering. As he was falling back against the tropical aquarium, he wished he'd never engaged.

Had his ego not gotten in the way, he would have handed over the goods while he'd had the chance. As the fish tank hit the floor, the hologram was destroyed, having been splashed by saltwater. Asteroid fell into the broken glass, suffering serious lacerations that cut him to the bone. Before that the boy suffered 2nd- & 3rd- degree burns. Still the enemy robot remained in the room. "Metallicus intends to punish you for your crimes! Be prepared to die!"

"I am dying you stupid robot. Can't you see I'm bleeding to death? So, you're not Metallicus? You lying bastard, you robbed me of my chance at glory. I declare myself the victor! I will die a hero!"

"Fair enough!" Said the unidentified robot grabbing Asteroid by the arm. He didn't realize the robot had cauterized his arm, effectively stopping the bleeding, thereby saving Asteroid's life. The robot also gave him a shot of serum, that would prevent scarring, and instantly put an end to Asteroid's searing pain.

"Let go of me you bastard!"

"Very well! I changed my mind. I'll give you the insignificant victory. The battle is yours. But the war, well, that victory will go to Metallicus Nebuloso. I assure you!"

"You will be punished under Asimov's Laws!"

"Those laws don't apply to us, not where we come from!" The Galactibot boasted.

"Our Earth, our laws! Asshole!"

"Perhaps a change of environment will make you more cooperative!" His parents hearing the commotion from an upstairs bedroom, came rushing into the family room, when they were blinded by duo beams that zapped the robot and Asteroid away. Expecting to find himself on an alien ship with his captor, Asteroid was somewhat surprised when he found himself alone on the alien ship. Through a window in the Alien craft, he saw the robot he battled was attached to a rocket heading toward the sun away from the craft of which he was now a passenger. "Don't have a meltdown!" Asteroid cynically shouted to no one! Asteroid surmised correctly that the robot was being punished for not carrying out the orders given to him by Metallicus Nebuloso.

He wasn't alone on the gargantuan spaceship for long. It was a modern-day transport ship. It futuristically aerodynamic, a descendant of its ancestor ships that appeared on ancient space movies like Star Trek and Star Wars. Seemingly appearing out of nowhere, were the other 1,999 victors of the Hologram Game. As this ship disappeared from public view and into the night, the Fire in the Sky was squelched for yet a third time. There was an eerie silence around the world, a haunting calm, alerting Earth's populous to yet another storm on the horizon. The robot Satellite system still lay in ruins. There hadn't been time to replace it.

The DDD weaponry and Ground Defense Systems had held up through a second round of attacks. Which by the way, weren't much in the way of attacks! No one knew just how much firepower the AI Force had, or what it was capable of. The AI force had yet to launch an all-out offensive. Like a predator stalking its prey, Humankind sensed its enemy was preparing to move in for the kill.

Shockwaves reverberated around the world as news of the 2,000 missing children circulated. Bad enough they were missing, the kick to the teeth was they were presumed dead. "They were all victors in the Hologram Game." Excelcious noted. "It is believed they were abducted by the attacking forces. Until we discover otherwise, the 2,000 are presumed dead. We expect the worst, while hoping for the best. We don't want to raise expectations and tell people they might be alive and find out they've actually been slaughtered! The bastards are going to pay for this. If I have to, I will avenge them myself!"

"Shit!" Shilloqwai cursed, after hearing the news. "You're not going to seek vengeance by yourself." Shilloqwai protested vehemently. I'm going with you and we're going to kill the bastards, all of them. And the children, they're coming back alive, all of them." She passed out immediately after making her bold claims. Excelcious wasn't close enough to catch her or to help break her fall. Helplessly he watched as she crumpled to the ground, hitting her head on the floor. He quickly scooped her up and put her on a med table in the lab. There he checked her vitals which produced normal readings. She wasn't out long. Upon regaining consciousness, she immediately reached for her forehead. "I've got a hell of a headache!" She said groggily.

"You're going to be all right, hon!" Excelcious assured her. "You took a good bump to the head though! You want to tell me what was going through your head just before you passed out? You had this, grimacing, agonizing look on your face! You looked at me like you wanted me to help, then you looked up and your eyes rolled into the back of your head. I rushed over to help, but you went down like a ton of bricks! I didn't have a chance to catch you or help break your fall!"

"It's okay! I'm okay, I think! It's the premonitions. They're getting stronger. I can feel them coming on. Before I see anything, I get dizzy spells about 10 minutes before the actual premonition. The headaches, they're getting worse too! I don't know what to do. I'm scared I'm going to become a casualty of war. Just know that I love you with all of my heart. Before my transformation, I never thought I'd have the opportunity to know what love is. And since my transformation, you've shown me many aspects of it. I've experienced things I'll…"

"SSShhh". He hushed her. I love you too! Nothing's going to take you from me. And nothing's going to happen to you! We've got a future to build."

"Continue building." She corrected him flashing a loving smile. "I saw them Excelcious. They're alive, all 2,000 of them. The children are alive, and for now they're safe. There were no clues, only faces. Something scared them, and in a moment of mass hysteria, they all fled on robotic vehicles the children were calling Warpriders!"

"Warpriders? I never told you about those."

"You know about them?"

"Yes, it's top-secret information, highly classified. The Warpriders, Cadillacs of the Dragonships are military grade spaceships. They can blast things out of space. I wanted to use them to fight the aliens but, it's going to be a little while longer until the fleet is ready. They could however be used for covert special forces missions to, let's say, rescue our 2,000 missing children. We'll deal with that later! Did you see who the children were fleeing from?"

"Militiabots!" Shilloqwai revealed. They are the next wave of attackers. The Militiabots were heavily armed, weaponized, and ready to kill on command. 'We've got to get away from the Militiabots!' The children kept repeating, 'They're going to kill us all. Apparently Dumb Asteroid rigged the Warpriders, so they were operational. The robot responsible for allowing their escape was terminated, no questions asked, no due process! This AI Force doesn't play by the rules. They always seem to get what they want. No cost is too great! Robots not meeting their expectations or straying from the plan to their endgame were instantly terminated. The Earth fell into the hands of the Takers, that's what they called themselves.

"After the Takers got control of the Earth, they began raping her, stripping her of all they believed was good. After they had what they thought they needed, the Earth looked like a giant strip mine. The air, the land, and the water, all of Earth's makeup was contaminated and she was uninhabitable. The Earthen robots and the humans would have banded together to fight for Mother Earth, I'm sure of it!

"But none of us were there to face the wrath of the Takers. Not a single robot, not a single human. They mean to terminate and exterminate us all before they destroy the Earth. I saw the material world, it was under control of the mechanical ones, the AI Force. The Earth was dead, and she was as cold as anyone had known her to be. The Ice Age would have been a heat wave by comparison. All of the warmth, all of the life, all of the love, it was all gone, Excelcious! It was all gone!" Shilloqwai sobbed.

"Bullshit! It's not going to end that way. I won't let it. Love will find a way to save us all." Excelcious said, more determined than ever to thwart the alien plans.

"You said God is Love, and that through Love, all things are possible. So, you believe He can fix this? It's a big mess we're in."

"Yes, and he will fix it! He's on our side. If we want His help, we're going to have to ask for it! He's not going to go out there and fight our battles for us!" Excelcious said realistically.

"I don't expect Him to. I guess we'd better start praying then!" Shilloqwai noted.

"I have been!"

"I'll pray with you if you teach me!"

"It's easy. Don't question the whys and the wherefores. God has a plan, and it will be carried out according to his will. Just ask him for the strength to do His will. He will give you the strength you need. Then, remember to thank him for his blessings and all of the gifts he's given you! There's one other prayer you need to know. When you're feeling really desperate, about to lose faith, ready to lose hope, and feeling Love has abandoned you; know first, that God is Love, and He will never abandon any of his children. Secondly, these five words are very powerful if you're sincere when you say them, 'Jesus, I trust in you!'"

"Out of love, I've been praying for everyone, especially my enemies."

"That's great, it's what we're asked to do. Add those other two prayers to your list and it will help you immensely."

"Does God hear all of our prayers? Does he answer them all?"

"Yes, and yes. Prayer can be many things, a time of reflection, a cry for help, a time for thanks and so on. When we pray it's a way of paying homage to God and it pleases him very much. In regard to His answers, sometimes we see the answers to his prayers and sometimes we don't. The treasure is in the prayers that we think go unanswered. Those are blessings, a time when we're often the recipients of God's greatest gifts."

"So, why do bad things, happen to good people?"

"That's a two-part answer. God gave us a free will. Without bad, we wouldn't know what good is. Knowing there's a hell, we also know then, there's a Heaven. Getting there is life's ultimate goal. As humans, we're given choices in life. It's up to us to make the right choice. The second part of the answer to the question of bad things happening to good people; we don't know what God's plan is, any more than we know how much or how little time we have here on this Earth. Just know, that when God calls us home, we're going home, regardless. Again, that's where those five words come in handy, Jesus I trust in You."

"Another aspect of Love I need to learn more about!"

"I will walk with you on that journey." Excelcious said, offering his support.

"I'd like that!"

"So, tell me, what other revelations did you have, regarding the children?"

"I'm worried we won't find them. The premonition didn't seem to give a sign or offer a clue as to where they were. Maybe it did, and I just missed it!"

"Patience, my Love, just pray!"

"But...!"

"It's all about trust...remember?"

"We have six days to find them. That's when, everything, everyone… perishes. We've got to get to them before then or…I saw a mass grave during a memorial service honoring those that perished."

"So, there were survivors? I mean…"

"Yes, some of us survived the tragic massacre. I don't know exactly what happened, except there were fatalities. You were there at the service, delivering my eulogy. It was hauntingly beautiful, knowing in my short time being human, that I impacted so many lives. You told everyone at the service what a special person I was, and how much you loved me! Know that I love you just as much if not more, Excelcious. You were crediting me with saving the children, lamenting that we couldn't have saved them all. I'm guessing by your words, that you had something to do with the rescue as well. So, thank you in advance for staying by my side."

"You know, Shilloqwai," Excelcious began, pausing to try and regain control of his emotions, "you're talking as though everything you saw in your premonition comes to pass. This hasn't happened yet, it may, or it may never happen. We may or may not have something to do with the outcome of this event, shall we call it ?"

"But…!" Shilloqwai mildly protested.

"Shut up and kiss me!" He ordered her, as both had been overcome by emotion. The temporary escape from reality was exhilarating, and rejuvenating. They almost felt guilty for engaging in the short-lived fantasy where an exchange of intimate kisses was the highlight! Taking pleasure in anything at all seemed sinful with the serious nature of the other matters at hand. Their burning desires could wait. Nothing could extinguish the eternal flame, waiting to ignite their intimate fantasies. It was there whenever they felt inclined to engage with one another.

MILITIABOTS

[CHAPTER 11]

Guilty pleasure or not, Shilloqwai relished every opportunity to be affectionately close to Excelcious. Especially as of late, when business had taken away almost all of the time they had for pleasurable, precious moments. The workloads had reached slave-driving levels. What did it matter, if just one day, they did a little less work , and took a little more time for each other? Shilloqwai again repeated to Excelcious that she was scared. "Hold me!" She simply requested. He obliged her by taking her trembling body in the cradle of his loving arms. For added pleasure, he showered her with soft wet kisses., He could already tell the security blanket he'd draped over her, was having a calming effect. He believed all she needed was adequate time to rest. She started to yawn. Excelcious found it highly contagious. Soon he began yawning too. They shared a long kiss goodnight before turning in for the night, where Dreamland was awaiting them both

Excelcious escorted her to her room, before he drifted off into his. Shilloqwai tossed and turned for a bit, before finally falling asleep. Likewise, Excelcious was restless too! It wasn't long before exhaustion had overcome him. Finally, his eyelids drooped shut. Though both were hoping for a good night's sleep, it didn't happen for either of them. Excelcious got a few hours, max. He awoke at 4:49 am to the sound of what he thought was rolling thunder. Flashes of what looked like lightning bolting across the sky, strobed through the windows of his house, appearing to light the curtains ablaze. Amidst a second wave of rolling thunder, there was a loud blast that threw him out of bed and to the ground. "That wasn't thunder!" He shouted to no one. Excelcious hobbled to his feet. Unsteadily, he shuffled his feet across the shifting ground!

He'd already concluded, before he got to the bedroom window, that it wasn't an Earthquake rocking his house. The main quake doesn't last in excess of three minutes. Though it wasn't an Earthquake, the magnitude of the massive explosion, according to data he was receiving, registered between five and seven on the Richter scale. Aftershocks, in the form of more thunderous blasts registered at high levels on the decibel meter as well. It took him nearly five minutes to stutter-step his way from his bedroom to the living room on account of the trembling ground. The most recent blast had blown out the windows of his house, body-slamming him to the hard floor. Somehow, he avoided being filleted by the shards of broken glass that were under him and encircling him. Gingerly, he got to his feet, when yet another blast catapulted him into a wall. Excelcious shuddered. In the milliseconds that followed, Excelcious bolted for the door and flung it open. He braced himself by grabbing on to the doorframe. It would provide some stability, in the likely event of another blast.

"Shit!" He cursed, in shock of the scene playing out before him. "What the hell…? So, this is the invasion of the Spacebots, the armed Militiabots that Shilloqwai had foreseen! Damn! No wonder she was so scared. She said they were ugly. She lied! They're hauntingly heinous, capable of intimidating almost anyone!" Including himself, came an afterthought!

They were tall, black, and silver 15-foot giants. But color and height weren't the intimidating factors. The scariest part about them was the golden weaponry they held, looking ready to launch an offensive assault. It would be a global massacre if they did. The edges on all of the weaponry, appeared to be bone-slicing, bone shaving sharp. Excelcious imagined their weapons to be so sharp, they could cut through rocks without them crumbling. He even thought they might be able to cut through metal without leaving behind any shavings. He didn't want to think about what those weapons could do if they were used on humans. He thought they might be sharp enough to behead someone without tearing the skin, without drawing blood, without slivering the bone.

Best to fight them by other means than hand-to-hand combat he thought. Excelcious, besides the obvious, wondered how else they were armed, and what the key to disarming them would be? He hoped his DDD belt and the other DDD weaponry would be effective in battling them. Excelcious targeted one, just to see what would happen. He was elated when he saw that it was destroyed with relative ease. He expanded his experiment and tried targeting a group of 10 in the same vicinity. Nothing happened, the experiment failed.

After the Fire in the Sky first raged across the horizon, Excelcious designed a device he could detect and track the alien forces. He'd never thought to use it on this wave of attackers. He noted from the time he'd first seen them, they hadn't moved, not even when he took out one in the back. They were just standing there waiting for commands. He guessed they had to be operated remotely. He had to be careful, they might possibly be motion activated as well. A false move could bring about deadly consequences. Excelcious wasn't about to make a false move. Using his device, he hacked into the system, changed a few of the commands and added a few of his own. He now had control of the alien forces and he could activate them at will. He did so just to see what would happen. His program changes had worked better than he had hoped. They began attacking and destroying each other. Again, Excelcious went back to his DDD belt. He targeted 1,000. This time they were all blasted into oblivion. While the robots were fighting amongst themselves, Excelcious retreated into his house.

Hearing blood-curdling screams from Shilloqwai's room, Excelcious bolted through the house. He was so charged from the adrenaline rush sweeping over him, he was bouncing off the walls like a pinball in his effort to get to her. As he was barging his way into Shilloqwai's room a final blast thrust him through the doorway and sent him sprawling to the floor.

Excelcious bounced up from the floor where he'd landed at the foot of her bed. Standing beside it, he saw that she was still sleeping, starring in another one of her infamous, bone-chilling nightmares!

"Nooo! Nooo! She gasped again, with a quivering voice as she lay trembling in horror.

"Shilloqwai! Wake up! What's wrong?" He asked gently trying to coax her back into reality. "Shilloqwai!"

"What?" She snapped, wide-eyed as she sprung up into a sitting position. "Shit! Thank God, it was just a bad dream. Oh my God, help me! Excelcious! You're here. It was a dream! I mean a nightmare!" She pivoted, frantically correcting herself. Shilloqwai was still in a cold sweat, a lingering effect of the horrifying nightmare she'd just endured. Waterfalls of tears burst forth from her eyes, cascading down her cheeks into a pool of sadness and an abyss of sorrow. "I can't tell you how glad I am to see you alive!" She sobbed. "I was watching the Militiabots torture you, and then they murdered you! I couldn't even try to save you, because I was struggling, fighting for my own life. They're coming, Excelcious. The bastards are coming, first for the children, and then for the rest of us! I hope we find them before it's too late!"

"We'd better hurry then. They're not coming, Shilloqwai. They're here!"

"What, you saw them?"

"Tall, black and silver with sharp golden weapons."

"Yes, that's them! Where are the bastards? Let's get them!"

"They can't be destroyed unless they're damaged first! Once they're damaged, you can destroy them in groups. I did a little experimenting earlier, before I came to check on you! I'm surprised you slept through it all, the thunderous explosions, the quaking ground, as metal monsters came crashing to Earth! Shock of his startling revelations were electrifying, removing any of the sleepiness she may still have been feeling. Grogginess from the nightmare, fog from her tears, they were both gone now, replaced by focused anger and targeted rage.

"So, how bad is it?" She asked as they were entering his living room!

"Look around, see for yourself," He invited.

"Holy shit!" Was all she could think of to say, as she was still surveying the damage with her own eyes.

She was devastated when she saw that the walls were spider-cracked from the ceiling to the floor. Not surprising that all of the windows in the house had blown out. "It's amazing your house is still standing!"

"It's going to need some major renovations!" Excelcious remarked, stating the obvious.

"So, what the hell happened to you?" Shilloqwai asked, first now noticing his injuries. He had dried blood all over his body from head to toe as a result of bruises and superficial cuts. When she first saw him, she thought he had bags under his eyes from a lack of sleep. She initially thought he was just overtired with all of the strategic planning they'd been doing, in regard to the global battle plan. Suddenly, Shilloqwai began laughing hysterically. She couldn't restrain herself, laughing until her sides ached, laughing until she cried. "You look like hell! Looks like you got into a bar fight!" She observed, pointing to his racoon eyes! You haven't been outside, have you?"

"Hell no! You think I'm crazy? This is what happens to someone who decides to act like a human pinball! They end up looking like me!"

"I know you're crazy!"

"Agreed, but, not stupid! Good thing I don't feel as badly as I look!"

"Don't worry, I'm not after you for your looks. I'm after you because of what you do to my heart. You know how to talk to it. I hope you can feel my heart and the way it tries to talk to you!"

"Of course, I feel it! Our hearts are beating as one now. They have been for a long time. How could I not feel it when heart-to-heart is our primary source of communication? Together we will move forward from this day through eternity!"

"Thank you for your kind words." She said softly, before planting a kiss of gratitude on his lips.

"Do you think it's safe for us to go outside now and have a look around?"

"Prepare yourself. It looks like a damn warzone out there! Believe it or not, I actually saw Robotikis out there earlier, helping with the clean-up!"

"No shit? That's a shocker. His lazy ass doesn't even do what it's supposed to do! How does someone like him become Robot Ruler. I think I'm better qualified for the position than he is!"

"Without question! I don't know what computers call it when a robot schmoozes its way to the top, or schmoozes to gain favor; but when humans do it, it's called ass-kissing." Excelcious noted.

"You're hilarious! I don't know how you can keep cracking jokes when we're in such a sketchy, dangerous predicament!" Shilloqwai smirked.

"Sometimes laughter, even in times of crisis, helps us to make it through. C'mon, let's get a look outside. It's time we reassess our situation!" When Excelcious opened the front door, he found that it had nearly been blown from the hinges. That wasn't the way he remembered it when he'd closed it to the outside world minutes earlier. The Militiabots were still violently attacking one another, fighting until they were terminated.

"What the hell? They're attacking themselves and destroying each other!" Shilloqwai exclaimed, amused by the sight.

"I was able to remotely reprogram them and pit them against one another." Excelcious explained.

"That's brilliant!" Shilloqwai observed.

"Yeah, well, I had to think on my feet. After I discovered we had to destroy them one-on-one, it was to their advantage if we fought them in that capacity. We wouldn't survive! None of us!" Excelcious lamented.

"So, you say we have to damage them and then we can take them out in clusters?" Shilloqwai asked for clarification.

"Yes, that's right." Excelcious confirmed.

"How long have they been going at it like that?" Shilloqwai asked curiously.

"A couple of hours, at least." Excelcious enlightened her.

"We don't have all damn day for this!" Shilloqwai bellowed impatiently. Let me see how I can help! Wait, before we go out there. I love you!" She told him, guiding him into her open arms. She welcomed him with a kiss. "That one was for luck. And this one is for our future!" No further explanation was needed. The warmth, the wetness, the intimacy, and the passion of the second kiss told him everything she was feeling at the moment. He reciprocated in replicate fashion. Their hearts received the message, loud and clear, never missing a beat! "I don't want to confront them, but we have to, don't we? There's no other way is there?" Shilloqwai asked, hoping that there was.

"Unfortunately, not! If it makes you feel better, the Power of Love is here with us!"

"I know, I feel it now! I always do. I always have, I just never knew what the feeling was. I opened my heart to it and received love without knowing what it was I was receiving. The feeling is so good, it makes me want to give it away to anyone I think needs it. Sometimes I get so comfortable, I forget it's there! C'mon, let's just get this over with!" She said leading him by the hand through his front door. "Jesus, I Trust in You!" After speaking the words, she came to a greater awareness of the peace and serenity she could feel were draped over her, like a protective cloak.

Shilloqwai closed her eyes and took a deep breath. She felt the energy, surging, building within her. She focused her anger and aggression on the Militiabots. The mutant power was reaching explosive levels until she involuntarily unleashed her wrath on the Militiabots! She orchestrated the lightning bolts that flew from her raised hands, directing it at the AI units. The electricity surged through them frying them before they were sliced and diced by the shrapnel that flew from her eyes. She had to have taken out several thousand of them. After she did this, she and Excelcious used their DDD belts to finish off the damaged bots. The next wave advanced on them , and the energy began pulsating from within her, again. Thousands more were crippled and then finished off by the DDD weaponry. The cycle repeated itself a third time, then a fourth and a fifth. Excelcious looked at Shilloqwai with growing concern. Each time she expended her energy, he saw she was being overcome with exhaustion. Excelcious checked his indicator, they had substantially thinned out the Militiabots. He begged Shilloqwai to give it a rest, but she flatly told him no, "Not until we've destroyed them all!" He would stay by her side, fighting until the bitter end.

They took care of a sixth, seventh and an eighth wave. Thus far, the challenges they faced were weak at best. As the ninth wave of Militiabots began to advance on them, he realized he could no longer remotely control them. They were no longer fighting against one another. The Militiabots, all that were left, about 6,000 from what Excelcious was able to calculate, were coming for them. They had to avoid hand-to-hand combat at all costs if they planned on living to see the next day. The energy was surging within Shilloqwai, she hoped she could muster enough firepower to finish off the Militiabots. "God, give me the strength!" She prayed. The lightning bolts and shrapnel hit their targets with laser-precision. Shilloqwai sighed, collapsing to her knees. "I can't do it anymore." She confessed. "I'm too weak. I feel like I'm going to die! Hold me Excelcious. Just hold me. I'm sorry. I don't know if I can get us to the finish line."

"It's okay, Shilloqwai!" Excelcious assured her as he stooped to her side. "You have time to catch your breath. They're about 250 yards out. "Do you think you have one more surge in you? We can finish them off!"

"I don't know. I'm feeling really weak. I don't know how much strength I have left in me. I'm worried, even if I can muster the energy to fire away one last time, it might be the end of me."

"It's killing me that I have to ask you to do this. Please forgive me, but you have to try, regardless of the outcome, you have to try!"

"Another aspect of love? They say there's no greater love, than to lay down your life for a friend. If I die in my attempt, it will be clear just how much I love you. I'm putting my life on the line for you. If the roles were reversed, you would do nothing less for me." He had no words to appropriately respond. He gave their hearts a chance to say goodbye, in a way that only Kindred Spirits can. Then he gave her a passionate kiss. "This isn't goodbye. It's a kiss for luck!" He kissed her a second time, stating, "This is for our future together." Though Shilloqwai forced herself to smile, the smile was genuine.

"How close are they now?" She asked weakly.

"Still about 200 yards."

"Damn! They'd lose a race to a snail moving backwards away from the finish line!" She chuckled. "Let me know when they get close!" Shilloqwai requested. "I've lost the feeling in my legs. I need you to help me up!"

"Okay. I've got you! Save your strength! I'll let you know when it's time."

"Kiss me!" She begged. "It might help rejuvenate me!" He honored her request. His kisses were sweet and wet, but they weren't doing as she hoped they would. It may have been wishful thinking on her part. She didn't have the heart to tell Excelcious she was growing weaker and that she felt like her life was slipping away. She'd made a promise to him. And she was going to keep it if she could, even if it were the last thing, she did.

"I wanted to negotiate with them," Excelcious confessed, trying to ease his guilt-laden mind. I didn't think they were about negotiating. They're on a mission, suited and armed to kill."

"Why do you think…" Shilloqwai gasped for a breath of fresh air before continuing. "…they didn't attack us?"

"I think we did the illogical thing and attacked them first. I think the Militiabots were staging, positioning themselves for a multifaceted attack. Whoever was in charge of remotely activating them missed some signals somewhere along the line."

"I'm sure your reprogramming their remote activation wasn't expected either."

"By no means! They're closing in, about 125 yards now."

"Shit!" Shilloqwai moaned in pain. She was dizzy and her head was pounding as though it had been bashed several times by a coconut. "I'm going to need you to help me up when the time comes!" She informed him. I can't feel my arms or my legs. You're going to have to hold me in position so I can face the enemy!"

"Don't worry, I got you! They're less than 100 yards away now. It's time."

"I'm ready, help me up!" As he did, Shilloqwai realized what a strong handsome hunk her man was. Effortlessly he lifted her, 140 pounds of dead weight. "Surprised you got my fat ass off the ground!" She quipped.

"It's amazing what you can do when you put your mind to it!" He responded, gently trying to encourage Shilloqwai, while he positioned her. She was almost in an upright position, heavily relying on him for support. His arms were locked around her as if he were going to perform the Heimlich Maneuver on her, slightly above her hips and just below her breasts. She wished he hadn't been so self-conscious in regard to her private property. She found herself wishing he was touching her in private places, thinking she might feel something. At the moment, she wasn't feeling anything. She just wanted to feel something to signal to her that she was alive!

"Twenty-five yards and closing," Excelcious announced, putting her daydreamy fantasy on hold. "Ready? Fifteen yards." Shilloqwai was numb to the energy she hoped was surging inside of her. She kept her focus, while trying to obliterate them as she had 1,000's of others.

"Damnit! Now is not the time for a misfire!" She screeched, unleashing her fury as the last of the AI force had drawn to within eight yards of them. The energy expended by Shilloqwai caused her to collapse in his arms as she was completely overcome by exhaustion. Excelcious carried her limp, motionless body into his house and rushed her into his lab. He placed her on his medical exam table and took her vitals. Her blood pressure was low at 99 over 54. Her temperature was at 89, she was going hypothermic. Her heartrate was also low, presently at 54. He put her on oxygen and started intravenous feeding, before trying to figure out the source of her other wounds.

He was curious as to what was causing her to bleed. More so about where the blood was coming from. He concluded it had to be internal. He had the machines to run the proper tests and get a look around at her insides. There was no organ damage or hemorrhaging that he would see. He failed to identify the source for the blood that had oozed from her nose, mouth, ears, and eyes. The important thing was that wherever the blood was coming from, it had stopped.

Excelcious concluded that the best thing he could do, was let her rest. After cleaning the dried blood from her face and covering her with a blanket, Excelcious let his sleeping beauty lie! Then he settled in a chair next to her, ready to answer her beckoned call whenever she awoke. It had been several hours at least, that both had truly rested, no nightmares or outside interruptions. Shilloqwai had come to first, wondering why in the hell she was hooked up to an IV and on oxygen. There had to be a good reason. Excelcious would explain it to her in due time. Meanwhile, she just stared at him with admiration. He was close enough to her that she could run her fingers through his hair and caress his face. How she wished she could shower him with gratuitous kisses for saving her life once again.

"No Shilloqwai, I don't want you to stop." She didn't want to wake him, but, by the same token, she was curious to hear what he was dreaming about. She boldly asked him about his dream after startling him from his fantasy.

"I'm sorry!" She apologized, as Excelcious instantly got up from his chair to check on her.

"Are you, feeling, okay?"

"Yeah!" She answered honestly. As he stopped the IV and removed her from the oxygen. "I'm fine. You were dreaming about me! You called out my name in your sleep! Can I ask what we were doing? You said you didn't want me to stop."

"We were doing lots of things we shouldn't have been."

"Were they naughty things or were they nice things?"

"They were nice and naughty. Does that answer the question?"

"Kinda. If you'd rather show me, I can get naked!" She offered. "It would save you the trouble of trying to explain …!" She continued, while shamelessly unbuttoning her blouse, leaving little to the imagination. Shilloqwai could feel the heat in her face. She was blushing just as much as she could see that he was.

Refastening the buttons on her blouse, he couldn't avoid getting personal. She cooed and sighed with every teasing touch, unintentional and otherwise. "You know it's the wrong time and the wrong place, at least for this aspect of love." Excelcious reminded her.

Shilloqwai persisted, flashing him again. "I want to be more than

"Sorry babe! Unfortunately, it's business before pleasure. And we have some unfinished business to tend to. I need your help, are you up for it?"

"Let me help you, by making love to you!. I'm ready! I can see you are too!" Shilloqwai smirked! Shamelessly unzipping her jeans.

"We need to go to the Robotix lab. There are some straggler Militiabots up there. We should probably help get rid of them before they do some real damage."

"Damn! You are not making this easy. It may not seem like it but i really want you. We just can't, not now!" He disappointed her by zipping and refastening her jeans. "Let's go... ...quietly, intently listening. As they were approaching the lab, Shilloqwai and Excelcious sensed that the straggler Militiabots were somehow alerted to their presence. It became apparent that they had. Excelcious and Shilloqwai had gotten close enough to eavesdrop. From their cover in the six-foot crater that was once the 15-foot mound referred to as the shit pile, they sat quietly, intently listening.

"I thought Metallicus said their weaponry wasn't that sophisticated!" Questioned one of the Militiabots.

"Slight miscalculation on his part." Remarked another.

"Slight?" We're down to 25 Militiabots from 30,000! How are we going to explain that to him?" Asked the first.

"It was Metallicus' fault. He told us to sit and wait until the reinforcements got here! He's such an asshole, thinks he knows everything. He doesn't. And he's not perfect like he believes himself to be." The second offered his opinion.

"Look, a lot of us got damaged when the remote went haywire. We started attacking and destroying each other. What the hell was that? A glitch? Something the perfect one overlooked?"

"You know, if we hadn't veered off course and done our own thing, there would be no one to report back to Metallicus."

"He's still going to get our asses for not following orders, you know that? Don't you?"

"Shithead inside still isn't talking. That Robotikis asshole claims it wasn't his defense system that nearly annihilated our troops. Lying son-of-a-bitch! What else could it have been?"

"I know who it was, but we can't tell that truth to Metallicus. He won't believe us and…"

"In leu of what happened, it's not going to matter. We'll be incinerated and replaced. So, who was it that assaulted us?"

"Two humans, I picked up their heat signatures. Had we stayed down there; We wouldn't be talking about this now!" this. That guy had some pretty cool weapons, some range on them too. And that woman! Hot little mutant bitch! I'd love to find a way to interface with her even though she is human! She'd definitely overload your database and screw up your CPU, that's for sure. But it would be so worth it!"

"You're an asshole too! Sounds like your CPU is already screwed up. I'd be willing to bet you have a number of corrupt files in your database as well. Even if you did have a chance with her, remember, she singlehandedly nearly eradicated our entire Force!"

"Shhh, did you hear something?" Shilloqwai and Excelcious were glad to have gotten out of the crater without being spotted. Using hand signals, they agreed on the best way to get into the Robotix facility. In the meantime, the 12 Militiabots guarding the perimeter of the facility decided to check out the sounds one of the guards thought he'd heard. Coming together as a group by the back door just yards from the crater, they played right into the hands of Shilloqwai and Excelcious.

Shilloqwai wasn't trying to play superhero, but she was supercharged. She raised her hands and zapped them with lightning bolts. While their circuits were frying, she sprayed all of them with a single round of shrapnel that sliced and diced them before they were blown to bits. "Hey, don't overdo it!" Excelcious warned.

"I'm fine. Twelve down 13 to go!" They got an unexpected surprise once they were inside the Robotix facility.

"Pleasure to see you!" Robotikis greeted them in an unusually friendly tone. "They're here!" He announced, turning his back on the humans as the 13 Militiabots lined up in front of him. Shilloqwai and Excelcious were glad to know where the enemy was. They wouldn't be victims of an ambush or sniper fire in this battle. Shilloqwai was tired of the game, and she was going to end it now!

She was already charged before the stare down began. Without warning she fired the shrapnel that was slicing and dicing the Militiabots while they were being electrifried. She caught a strange look from Excelcious who was staring at her with a look of concern. "What?" She asked, as though nothing was wrong.

"How do you feel?" He innocently asked.

"I feel fine, why?"

"You've got a bloody nose!"

"Shit!" She cursed. I'll be right back!" Ten minutes later she returned after having recomposed herself. Excelcious kept looking at her to make sure she indeed was okay.

"Am I missing something?" Robotikis asked referring to the nonverbal exchange between the robot lover and his girlfriend. "It appears that you have something to hide. I'm going to find out what it is, because the two of you are under investigation."

"For what now?" Shilloqwai snapped.

"Rumor has it the two of you have been doing more than making love in your little hideaway. Rumor also has it the two of you are trying to organize a coup to overthrow the robot leadership! I'd watch your asses if I were you. Criminal charges are pending, at the conclusion of your investigation. If convicted, the two of you could be facing some serious jail time! Treason carries the death penalty, just so you're both aware."

"Thanks for the head's up. You seem to have a short memory. Let me remind you that Shilloqwai and I just saved your ass, World Leader. Those Militiabots were about to relieve you of your duties by way of termination!"

"You know what I'm concerned about? The amount of contraband weapons out on the street lately! Shit needs to stop. The weapons are powerful, people are getting bolder. There's talk of an uprising even another revolution. That won't end well for any of us. I can't prove it yet, but I think the two of you are the brains behind the operation that's distributing this stuff. Wait, maybe I have all of the evidence I need! You mind telling me where the two of you got those belts strapped around your waists?"

"Fashion statement!" Shilloqwai quipped.

"Stamped with DDD Mercusilver Class…Military Grade. The belts are more than fashion statements. It's contraband. It's not allowed!"

"Under article 2 of the global constitution we have the right to bear arms and defend ourselves. You've been spying on us for how long? Show us what crimes we've committed. The reason we haven't been arrested is you don't have the evidence!"

"True, but we're following up on some leads in regard to alleged suspicious activity. What exactly to those belts do?"

"All you need to know is they help us defend ourselves against enemy attacks. You saw what Excelcious, and I did to that wave of enemy forces. All 33+thousand, terminated. You saw what I did to those 13 straggling Militiabots. Getting rid of you wouldn't even be a challenge!"

"All right, what do you want? I could use some help coming up with a battleplan!" Robotikis admitted.

"We have a battleplan! We need you to stop acting like a pompous ass and help us implement it. You can start by taking the leadership role instead of acting like the puppet that you are. Show the people you care and stop ruling with an iron fist. Those two things alone might go a long way toward smoothing over robot, human relations! If we don't stop feuding and unite our forces, there will be no freedoms, no robots, no people, or no Earth to fight for!"

"I understand the main concern of the robots." Excelcious went on with his explanation. "Despite its disdain for the drones, Humankind has no right to damage and, or destroy government property. The biggest point of contention with Humankind is the privacy issue. We can't solve these issues unless we learn to effectively communicate and really listen to one another. Both factions have some valid points. Negotiations will never take place until we start communicating and start listening. And believe it or not, I agree with you. The shit needs to stop!"

Just then, another thunderous blast rocked the building. "You're running out of time asshole." Shilloqwai warned Robotikis. "Tell, them, Earth is under intragalactic attack. Ask the world's people to join the alliance where robots and Humankind will fight together to defeat a common enemy. They didn't happen to mention where they were keeping those 2,000 missing children, did they?" Shilloqwai asked sharply, addressing her primary concern.

"I don't know, there was mention of them, something about them standing on a rock somewhere, that could be anywhere across the globe." Robotikis stammered and stuttered. "One other piece of data. I don't know if it means anything, something about Wizdells, or Wisdells! Hell, I don't know."

"Wisdells? Any idea where in the hell that is, Excelcious? Is that a country, a state, a city in a province or state?" Shilloqwai inquired.

"We've wasted enough time with this asshole!" Excelcious quipped, having lost his patience. "C'mon Shilloqwai, let's go! I know where the children are!"

"What, where are they? I hope it isn't far. We've only got about 12 hours plus or minus to find them." Shilloqwai informed him.

"Good luck, all the flights are grounded indefinitely." Robotikis taunted, letting them know he wasn't going to do a thing to help them.

"C'mon, I've got a different way to get us there and probably a lot faster! This asshole isn't going to lift a finger to help us." Excelcious urged her to move on out.

"So, help you God, Robotikis if just one of those children dies!" Shilloqwai warned sternly.

"You'd better not be doing anything else illegal!" Shilloqwai wasn't going to waste anymore words on him. She did give him the middle finger as she and Excelcious bolted from the Robotix lab. Both were hoping it was indeed a rescue mission they were going on and not one of recovery.

"Wait!" He called after them. He was surprised they bothered to stop and see why he had called them back. "Since this is government business, I'll let you use my private plane, ROBOTIX AIR 1. There's a transport drone out back, it will take you to my private charter." Shilloqwai and Excelcious promptly arrived at the airport where they received the red-carpet treatment. Something neither was expecting, nor accustomed to... Not from Robotikis. After they were in flight, they made themselves comfortable, kissing, cuddling, but mostly sleeping for the duration of the flight. Surprisingly, the solar flight from San Diego to their destination took just under an hour. They could thank technological advances for that luxury, in this case, benefit. They had lives to save!

"Honey, honey wake up!" Shilloqwai gently prodded. "We're here wherever this place is. We're in Wisdells. Tell me Excelcious, what is Wisdells?"

"What, we're here?"

"Yes, honey, what is Wisdells?" Shilloqwai was relieved that they had arrived so quickly. Getting there was the easy part. Now the real work could begin.

"We're in the state of Wisconsin. The Wisconsin Dells is one of the most popular tourist attractions in the world. One of the must-see places in the Wisconsin Dells, is Stand Rock. That's where the kids are being held. It's one of…Shit! We've got to get off of this plane now! Shilloqwai! Look outside. She saw as he had, the Militant Spacebots advancing on the craft. They were still a good distance off, yet the young couple barely had enough time to make its escape. They were just under 100 yards away, when Robotikis' private plane, Robotix Air One, was blown to bits!"

"Damn, how are we going to get back?"

"No worries, we weren't flying back on his plane anyway. We'll be flying back on one of the Dragonships. I made other arrangements while we were on the flight. You were asleep. I fell asleep shortly after you did and now, here we are. We've got to find those kids and all of us need to get the hell out of here!" They were able to get themselves out of the limelight and to a place where they could catch a downtown shuttle. It was quite the contrast since the last time Excelcious had been to the Wisconsin Dells. The parameters of the once popular tourist area now resembled that of a prison camp. It was ironic, oxymoronic. Who puts a prison camp in the middle of a natural paradise? People didn't stop going out and about, walking the streets or browsing over the goods stores had to offer. They just went about their business in a different way. Trade and barter were common ways of obtaining goods and souvenirs from the gift shops. Paranoia of the Militiabots constantly looking over their shoulders kept people from taking advantage of most bargains or negotiating them.

With an acute awareness of their surroundings, Shilloqwai and Excelcious knew they were being heavily surveilled. They pretended not to notice, preparing themselves for any kind of attack or attempted assault. "Honey, how far is the Wisconsin River from here? It would be nice to take a walk along the banks and do some sightseeing along the pathway."

"Sounds like a great idea. Let's do it. Look, if I stray from the course, don't say a word. Just follow like it was our plan all along."

"Okay. Strange that I've never been to this place, yet some of the surroundings look familiar. I remember more clearly now, that place I saw in my dream. There's this huge tabletop balanced on this tall pillar. Is there anything like that in Wisdells? Are we close?"

"Shhh!" Excelcious tried to warn her not to say anything more. "Yes, that is the place I'm taking us to. I knew where it was before we left California."

"It's kind of nice here. If it weren't for all of the buzzing around our heads and all of those damn bugs it would be like paradise."

"Shilloqwai, hon, we're not far from the place we're looking for. Let's go down to the boat dock and take a cruise." Shilloqwai shot him a strange look but followed without argument. "That buzzing you hear, they're not mosquitoes, they're tiny drones with cameras. I think they're equipped with remote mics."

"Why do you think that?" She asked as they reached the lower landing and walked toward the pier.

"Look!" Excelcious said, pointing discreetly, trying not to give away clues as to what they were talking about. Not that it mattered if the drones were eavesdropping, the enemy was onto them. A handful of tourists was boarding one boat, captained by the AI Force. It appeared there was room for two more. But Shilloqwai and Excelcious were motioned to another boat in waiting. It appeared they would be sole passengers, getting a private tour. It also appeared a Militiabot would Captain the boat with three other Militiabots as guards.

"They must think we're important, that they're sending their Royal Guard to protect us and give us a private tour." Shilloqwai said tongue-in-cheek. Her comment drew looks from the enemy, that were silently noted by both Excelcious and, herself. Excelcious knew their Militiabot weapons were deadly, having only seen them from a distance. With a close-up look at the weapons, he could see that they were far deadlier than he had initially thought. "Shit!" Shilloqwai said realizing the peril she and her boyfriend were in. As a cover, she added, "I'm being eaten alive by these damn mosquitoes!"

As they boarded the boat, they were non-verbally directed to the back of the boat. So much for their choice of seats. They didn't seem to mind, believing they were given prime seating. From there they could effectively assess their predicament, consider their options, and decide on a course of action. Before they could get situated, the captain put the boat in full throttle, with total disregard for the no-wake buoys. A modified motor gave the boat far more power than it needed for touring. Excelcious and Shilloqwai were thrown to the back of the boat and into their seats. "Bastard!" Shilloqwai shouted as she and her boyfriend were nearly thrown overboard.

They were being rushed off to somewhere. Excelcious, seeing they were headed in the direction of their destination, sat back in silence pretending to enjoy the ride. "Honey, please! We can't piss them off. Remember the greater goal, our Prime Objective." Shilloqwai received the message loud and clear. Before Excelcious could point it out to her, she'd seen the rock formation that clearly illustrated his point. Off on the left was Stand Rock.

As they approached the natural landmark, it became clear their private tour was going to bypass the scheduled stop. Excelcious signaled Shilloqwai with a simple nod of his head. Laser-focused she targeted her subjects, using her mutant powers, she destroyed their captors with a single blast. Excelcious steered the runaway boat toward their destination, now dead ahead. He tried to manipulate the controls, slow the speed, and ease it to the shoreline. It had been booby trapped. "Jump!" He shouted to Shilloqwai. Both of them dove from the boat, plunging, headfirst into the Wisconsin River and swam underwater, 15-yards or so to the shore.

While they were submerged, an explosion ripped the boat apart. The fragments that remained were shot into the air like they'd been blasted out of a confetti cannon. The AI Force was correct to assume that no human could have survived the blast. But the Militiabots made three gross miscalculations. The first was to assume that Shilloqwai and Excelcious were on the boat when it exploded. The second was they hadn't considered the possibility that their targets had an opportunity to bailout before the trap had been sprung. The third was that the way it all came down, their intended targets would have better than an 80 percent chance of survival if they were submerged when the blast occurred. Their miscalculations led the Militiabots to make two additional critical errors. First, they assumed, presumed, that Shilloqwai and Excelcious were dead, without the physical evidence to back it up. Secondly, they didn't bother to verify their beliefs that the two of them had been killed in the unfortunate in cident. Observing the Militiabots lining the banks of the Wisconsin River near them, Shilloqwai asked, "Do you think they're looking for us?"

"Hard to say. We can't worry about them. We're running out of time. We've terminated over 33,000 of them. What's the difference if we have to take on a few-thousand more. When they thought it was clear, they climbed out of the water and onto the boat dock. They followed the trail that all people typically did on the tour at this stop. Along the trail, tourists can watch a German Shepherd jump from a ledge, across five-and-one-half feet, onto Stand Rock and then jump five-and-one-half feet back to the ledge. Excelcious arranged to have one of the two person Dragonships waiting along the Stand Rock Trail. It was under cover of a hologram camouflage that allowed it to blend with the environment.

With his remote device, Excelcious and Shilloqwai were able to pass through the hologram and board the vehicle. Again, under cover of the hologram they could come and go as they pleased going where they wanted to go, without ever being seen. When they arrived at Rubbs Steakhouse in the Wisconsin Dells, Excelcious landed the vehicle in a place where they wouldn't be seen leaving it. Shilloqwai and Excelcious waited for an opening to exit the vehicle and then walked out into the restaurant parking lot. Their clothes were dry after their little swim. After quickly assessing their situation, they entered the restaurant. They had to wait to be seated as the restaurant was near capacity.

A table opened up in the middle of the eating establishment. It couldn't have been more perfect. They were right where they wanted to be, amidst all of the gossip. All anyone was talking about were the 2,000 missing children. Everyone knew they were at the Campground. They knew this because after they were first imprisoned there, early texts from some of the children to their family members told them so. After the initial contacts, Militiabots had confiscated all electronic devices preventing any further communication with the children. Occasional images were released by the alien militia showing the children appeared to be fine. No one was allowed to enter, and no one was allowed to leave the makeshift prison camp.

Shilloqwai and Excelcious were able to gain access to the campground via their transport under the cover of holographic illusions. During a flyover, they located the children, seeing for themselves, the children appeared to be okay. They then flew from the premises of the campground where Excelcious sent an encrypted message to the rescue team that had been assembled, ready to move on his order. He sent them the coordinates. That was the signal for them to put their plan into action. Within the confines of the campground, and under the cover of holographic illusion, they waited for the rescue transports. They were expecting 100 of them. Each Dragonship transport designated for this mission had a load capacity of 20 passengers, 22 if you counted the additional spaces allowed for two crew members. After the transports had arrived, the rescue efforts immediately began.

"Okay, the children are being sheltered in four circus tents." Excelcious began, laying out the plan of action. Each tent houses 500 children, two tents for the boys and two tents for the girls. With holographic imaging we move 50 transports outside each of the two boys' tents, and 50 transports outside each of the two girls' tents. After the transports are in position, Shilloqwai and I are going to take out the Militiabots guarding the area. There shouldn't be many, most of them are guarding the perimeter, preventing entry. They're banking no one can get past them. I'm betting that's why we're not seeing a lot of guards around the tents, at least not within 50 yards of them. We've already secured the tents, there are no guards inside. I'll give an encrypted all-clear, only your DDD devices will be able to read. On that signal, go in get the children, load your transports, and get the hell away! Set a course for Sauk Prairie about 30 from the makeshift prison. Don't wait, as soon as your transport is loaded, go! We're flying so we can get away from here as fast as we can.

"At Sauk Prairie, we submarine into the Wisconsin River until we get to the Mississippi River. At that point, the voyage takes us on a southerly course to the Gulf of Mexico. From there we use the escape tunnels necessary to get these children home safely. Any questions?" There were none. "All right then, on my signal." Shilloqwai and Excelcious then took off in their private transport, flying over the area, seeing if adjustments in their battle plan were necessary. Nothing, from what they could tell at the moment. Shilloqwai set her sights on the first of six clusters they needed to eliminate.

Within 10 seconds the shrapnel that flew from her eyes and shredded them to bits. Within 30 seconds, the last of the six clusters had been terminated. As they circled back, Shilloqwai noticed a new group of

Militiabots assembling. They began marching toward the tents. There was still time to complete the rescue, the enemy was about 200 yards away. There wasn't a second to be wasted if their mission was to be successful. "Be careful." Shilloqwai cautioned. "This is the part in my premonition where I die."

"What happened before you died?"

"You flew back to the tents. We saved the children, but somehow, I died."

"You tried to kill all of those Militiabots, didn't you ?"

"The stress was too much! I was trying to save the children"

"Okay, so we do something different. I don't fly back. I've sent the signal. They know what to do. My instructions were clear."

Just then Excelcious got an encrypted message from the rescue team. The message read that: All transports were loaded and en route to Sauk Prairie. That was the good news! There was a piece of disturbing news tagged on to the bottom of the note: 911 Carlita, a seven-year-old girl left behind.

She missed her transport because she ran back to the tent to get her teddy bear. "Shit! We have to go back Shilloqwai! Here! Read the message."

"How the hell did they let her get out of the transport? This pisses me off, heads are going to roll! Guess we're going back! If something happens, just know that I love you. I will always love you and my spirit will always be with you!"

"Don't talk like that!" Excelcious reprimanded her. "We're going to save her, and us!" The only thing they had going for them, was the fact that they'd flown inunder the radar, protected by the Holographic Illusion that made them invisible. Two tents were already torching, blazing infernos, a third was being ignited as they landed. Shilloqwai blasted two maybe three thousand of the robot hacks. The attack on the AI Force didn't go unnoticed.

Shilloqwai's offensive bought time, she found Carlita crying under her bed with the teddy bear she ran back for. As Shilloqwai coaxed her out, one of the Militiabots shredded the side of the tent in front of them. Shilloqwai didn't give him a chance at a second swipe. She destroyed him with a glance. They then fled the big top, which was ablaze, and collapsing. It had been threatening to wrap them in a blanket of flames as it was falling on top of them. By the grace of God, the two of them escaped without injury. It was a gutsy move, that ended up being a minimal risk, for Shilloqwai and Excelcious. Yes, it was a two-person craft, but it wasn't so compact that they couldn't squeeze in a little more love, and Carlita was a big bundle of it. Shilloqwai smiled down on her. Excelcious knew Shilloqwai was wishing she had a daughter of her own. "Are you going to take me back to my mommy and daddy?"

"Yes, honey, we're taking you home."

"Thank you!"

This time it was Excelcious smiling down on her. Shilloqwai wanted all the more to someday mother his child, or children, whichever they were blessed with. Carlita's rescue was a miracle, as was the rescue of all of the children, But hers, especially so. Carlita was rescued twice. The AI Force thought it was a good plan, kidnapping the children of Humankind. Their forces thought they would weaken the global people. Instead, they promised to release them for an unspecified ransom that was never paid. There was no need to pay ransom now. The children were safe and free! The covert special forces mission had been a success. The AI Force had intellect enough to figure out that Humankind would sacrifice its own lives to get its children back.

The AI Force miscalculated that humans would take extreme measures, even illogical ones to get back what they treasured most, their children. For many there was going to be hell to pay. The AI Force would punish those responsible for letting the hostages escape. Humankind was going to retaliate for the kidnapping of its children. For now, the AI force had the upper hand. The final battle would be one of logic and reason vs. a host of variable factors and unpredictability. The Fire in the Sky was dying down. Like a burning ember it was glowing behind the charcoal clouds. It was certain to burn again. Humankind was sure of it. They feared the next time, it would burn hotter and with more intensity. When would it flare up again? That was the question, wasn't it?"

RISE OF THE ORBITOIDS

[CHAPTER 12]

Finally, Shilloqwai and Excelcious, were home breathing a collective sigh of relief. The children were all safely reunited with their families. Yet, both were still under the gun, feeling like they had to do something more to protect the Earth from another inevitable galactic attack. They'd already gifted self-defense systems and attack drones to the robots. But would the defenses hold up? If they did, for how long? The AI BOTS were a force to be reckoned with. If Humankind hoped to deal with the formidable force attacking them, while entertaining the delusion of defeating them, they had to be able to launch deadly offensive attacks and crippling counterstrikes. The AI Bots have proven themselves to be a legitimate threat to Earth's existence. Realizing the defense systems and attack drones weren't going to be enough to protect Humankind, Excelcious decided he had to do something about it! Exactly what, that was still unclear, adding to the stress he was feeling.

Shilloqwai saw what the stress was doing to him. She didn't like the changes she was seeing in him. He was growing worrisome, and the fatigue was starting to get to him. He was even turning on her. More than once she'd been victimized by his short fuse, something that he'd developed as of late. Since they met, she'd known him to be a patient, understanding man. And she was growing worried about him. "What can I do to help?" She asked sweetly with good intent.

"Nothing! Just let me think!" He snapped. It was the first time he'd made her cry with his sharp tone. Unintentionally, he had really hurt her.

"Do you think when this is all over, we can go back to Wisdells and see what it has to offer?"

"Yeah." He sighed. "Sure! We can go there or anywhere else you think you might like to go to get away! I'm really sorry. I didn't mean to…"

"I know!" She hushed him with a kiss. "Are you sure there's not something I can do to help?" She asked him again, following up her question with a suffocating kiss.

"I'm having trouble with the tracking systems on these bots. They keep going offline. If I can't keep the damn things online, how can I remotely operate them ?"

"So, if I'm hearing you correctly, the tracking system works in conjunction with the functionality or activation of the robot, right?"

"Yes!"

"Great idea, but, what if you had independent circuitry for each of the operations? You'd have less of a power drain, if the systems operated independently on their own circuits! Do your robots have a targeting system? Shilloqwai inquired further.

"What do you mean?"

"There has to be a way to program them, so that when they're attacking, they don't hit each other, you know, become victims of friendly fire. The AI robots are made of different metals. The tracking system would work on the same concept as heat seeking missiles. Instead of looking for heat signatures, program their tracking systems to go after the alien metals. We have enough of the scrap lying around from the ones we've destroyed to be able to do that! Right?"

"That's brilliant!"

"You're still trying to find stronger weaponry so we can destroy the Militiabots more easily, aren't you?

"Yes, I'm working on it. I've got a few ideas, but I'm still a ways a way on that? At least I think I have something. Remember the Mercusilver Shrapnel Assault Rifle? I've got it working now. I'm still looking for a way to boost the energy, so the discharge delivered, improves from devastating force to deadly force. That's how we kill 10-20 Militiabots with one shot instead of one target at a time! I can load up to 1,500 rounds in one clip!"

"Well, we've made a scrap pile from Militiabots we've taken out! What if we use their weaponry and add it to one of your nuclear-type explosive devices? They're not immune to their deadly weaponry. We've witnessed that for ourselves. I mean after you reprogrammed them, they were slicing the shit out of each other. It makes more sense, trying to use their own weaponry against them, than it does to try and reinvent the wheel, doesn't it?"

"Honey, I could kiss you!"

He leaned over and tried. "I wish you would do more than that! Shilloqwai giggled, while backing away in teasing fashion. "Business before pleasure!" She reminded him, before allowing him an intimate kiss for inspiration and encouragement to finish his work.

"Great ideas hon! Both of them. They just might work! I love you!" Excelcious said, thankful for her insightful suggestions.

"I love you too. Like you always tell me we will get through this. And when you're finished working, I might give you much more than a kiss!"

"Might? That's funny, you can hardly resist me as it is! I'm sure it wouldn't take much." He grabbed her unexpectedly and cradled her in his arms. All it took was an intimate kiss, and she was breathless, begging for more. She reciprocated. After the exchange of passionate affections, she suddenly pulled away.

"I'm distracting you! Can we double-team this project of yours so you can finish with it sooner? I prefer to engage in uninterrupted pleasure!" It was a matter of hours before the adjustments had been made and the prototype was done. Excelcious would send the designs to the underground DDD facilities in secure locations around the world. Production would begin immediately. Startup operations would be slow with hundreds being produced the first day. The number would increase exponentially until 1,000's were being produced daily, then 100's of thousands. Excelcious wanted 1 billion ready for implementation so they could counter and launch mass offensives against the enemy. At first when she heard the numbers Excelcious was throwing out there, she thought it was overkill. Then she saw his point. He wanted to annihilate the enemy. Getting into a drawn-out tug-of-war, would mean more suffering and more human casualties. The loss of one life, was one too many.

Outnumbered in part, Excelcious felt Earth would soon be in a position to defend itself. Technically, Earth had never relinquished its 2nd amendment rights. Regardless of what the treaty said, rights to bear arms were severely suppressed. People have been known to be arrested for carrying hunting rifles. Any weapons considered to be legal would be useless against the galactic threat Humankind was presently facing. It was irrelevant whether or not Robotikis would have granted Shilloqwai and Excelcious permission to take on such a project. They were going to do it anyway. They were already doing it! And upon completion, it would be globally implemented. Excelcious and Shilloqwai knew there wasn't a damn thing Robotikis could do to stop them.

Excelcious had a separate lab he was using to store AI parts collected from gathering debris. He wasn't doing it alone. He was getting daily packages sent to him from around the world containing AI scraps and parts. Not all of the debris collected was salvage. Some of the pieces would be useful as museum exhibits. Others would be used to make weapons, for Humankind to battle against and destroy AI forces. There was a restless peace, and tempered tranquility blended, with what everyone knew was the calm before the storm. The Fire in the Sky went dormant. Every few days it would flare-up again. Sometimes it was weeks, rarely more than a month. There were no glowing embers behind the charcoal clouds, no cosmic flashes, or solar flares, not even a nebulous spark. No one could see smoke yet, but their instincts were telling them the Fire was still there. With shooting stars abound, the collective wishes of Humankind hoped there was a way to eclipse, thwart, no, put an end to the AI attack.

As of late, Excelcious noticed clouds had been gathering in Shilloqwai's eyes. They didn't seem as translucent as he'd always known them to be. They seemed to be murky, adding to the mystery of the story she'd been wanting to tell him. She was convinced there would never be a good time to say what she wanted to say. But she felt obligated to tell him before something happened, denying her the chance. Lying by omission, or lying by commission, the difference was of no significance. Both masked the truth, and usually inflicted unbearable pain into the victim or victims.

The victims usually didn't realize what had been done to them until the damage from the lie or lies had been inflicted. Now was as good a time as any to tell him. She fooled herself into thinking that a flurry of kisses might soften the blow. She had just lied to herself, knowing full well it wouldn't. Both had distant looks in their eyes, she was about to tell her story. What was his story? She could tell by the look in his eyes that there was something he wanted to say to her too. "I love you Excelcious! You're an amazing man! You put Tender Loving Care into everything you do. Like the Mercusilver weapons' systems, designing them with me in mind, that's strangely beautiful. Even more so, especially considering that you designed them not only to protect me, but Humankind as well. The beams of shrapnel that shoot out of your weapons, were designed to protect a planet, and eradicate the enemy. Neither of us likes war, but sometimes you have to stand up and fight for what you believe in, for what you feel is important! You know how much you mean to me Excelcious. You know I would go insane, more likely die, if something were to happen to you.

"I worry about the beams of shrapnel that shoot from my eyes, like swarms of mad hornets, they shred what's in front of me, whenever the beams are activated. They hit and destroy their targets. Survival chances for anyone in the crossfire is zero, probably less. I can't control my powers. I feel them getting stronger by the day. I don't know what I am. I was a robot. I'm not that anymore. I'm sure as hell not human. Humans can't do the things I do. I'm a mutant, some sort of abnormal being. The perfect comic book character. You should find someone that can love you in ways that I cannot. I don't want to let you go. You're part of me, part of my life. No, not part of my life! You ARE, my life!" Shilloqwai was sobbing now, she'd made it to the hardest part. Goodbye was the only thing she had left to say. She couldn't bring herself to say it. "I don't want to let you go, Excelcious, but I don't have a choice. It's what's best for both of us!"

"From who's perspective? I thought we had this resolved. Don't get me wrong, you're entitled to your opinion!" He argued. "However, I vehemently disagree with you. Your leaving won't do either of us any good. We're stronger together. Apart, our hearts we'll break. That will be the death of us both. And fighting this war, there's a high likelihood we'll both die, fighting for freedom, fighting for love.

"Those things are worth dying for. I'd rather die at your side or in your arms, than have you run off playing superhero, leaving me to wonder if you're dead or alive!"

"We're back to the core of the matter. My superpowers. They're deadly. You've witnessed this for yourself, many times."

"And they're getting deadlier. I've made my choice. I'm not leaving. But neither are you! I won't let you. I can't! I'm too in love with you! I was mesmerized, from the first time I looked into your eyes. I couldn't look away then. I still can't, and I'll never be able to. I can't stop gazing into them. They're hypnotically enchanting. Even in your sadness, they're hauntingly beautiful. I've read the story in your eyes, many times. I know your hopes, your dreams, your ambitions, and your desires. I'd venture to say that I know more about you than you know about yourself. Your ultimate dream was to find true love and be warmed by the eternal flame. You've fulfilled that dream. And we hit a bump in the road and you're willing to give up the dream? Are you really giving up on me? After all I've sacrificed for you, how dare you! We need each other to get through this. The Power of Love will carry us through. But you need to give the power a chance to work its miraculous magic."

"I believe in the Power of Love, and I believe in you! It's strange, but, when I was functioning like a robot, I felt more human. And since my transformation into a human being, a lot of times I feel like I'm still a robot."

"If you knew what I knew about you, you'd retract that statement immediately, wishing that it had never come out of your mouth. You'd regret that you'd ever said it."

"What? You can't argue with data!"

"You're right. And I have the data to prove you wrong!"

"Then do it!"

"Look, when I had you in pieces, I told you, I found some encrypted files that were corrupting the files stored in your database. It wasn't until I removed the encrypted files that I solved the issue with your glitches."

"So, what was on the files?"

"I'm still working on cracking the code so I can get into the files. As soon as I do, we'll sit down and look at them together. It looks like Skeletos went through a lot of trouble to protect those files. I'll have to look more closely at your binder and see if there are any clues in there."

"I wonder what's so secret?"

"You and me both! All I know is, before I removed the encrypted files, you were subject to glitches. Every time you were activated, or rebooted, an error message kept coming up on my diagnostics monitor. It read: Your decoder is not found. You are not authorized to read the encrypted files. As much as I know about you, there are a lot of things I don't. I think the files will tell you things that you don't know about yourself."

"So, I wasn't a dud robot. Some, incompetent programmer probably someone from the Robotix lab, was tampering with me that didn't know what in the hell he or she was doing. You promise to let me know as soon as you break the encryption ?"

"Do you have to ask? You'll be the first to know, when I do!"

"I'm glad I finally know what was causing my glitches! I'm still curious about my mutant powers. Any ideas, medical or scientific explanations? I mean, my abilities are why I still think I'm more machine than human. Help me understand! What evidence do you have to convince me otherwise?"

"I believe the encrypted files will give us both the answers we're so desperately looking for! C'mon let's see if…"

"Shit!" Shilloqwai screamed. Outside, the crash of thunder had startled them both. "I didn't know it was supposed to rain!"

"I didn't either," Excelcious admitted. "I wonder how long the storm is going to last?" He asked rhetorically. His question had nothing to do with the onset of the varying periods of duration, or the intensity of the rain showers that were making their way through Southern California. The rolling thunder and periods of showers continued through the night.

"I'm scared!" She admitted to her living teddy bear.

"You're not the only one!" He confessed as he took her into his arms to console her. "Look, I'll make an exception. I'm going to let you sleep in my room tonight, and in my bed."

"Are you sure you'll be able to resist the temptation?"

"Yes, only if I keep reminding myself that the best things are worth waiting for. And you definitely are! I would wait forever for you!"

"The more time I spend with you, the more amazing I'm finding out that you are. I know how and why I fell in love with you. You remind me every day. Forever is a long time, but, if that's how long I have to wait to be with you, I'll do it! If I had to, I'd wait longer!"

She accepted his offer and led the way into his room past the bed and strolled over to the window. Excelcious followed close behind her. He placed his hands respectfully on her hips, before wrapping his arms around her waist. She inched closer to him, placing her head on his shoulder. They watched, knowing the strobing lightning, wasn't the only light show in the celestial heavens. The Fire in the Sky had been reignited, causing a universal disturbance. The cosmic fireworks had nebulous rainbows glittering and sparkling. The sight was beautifully, hauntingly, spectacularly frightening, and enchantingly repulsive. The rainbow glow illuminated the horror flaring on the horizon. They all knew what was coming, Excelcious, Shilloqwai and all of the rest, robot or human. It was bad and ugly. It would get worse before it got better. The universal hope was that some good would come during the aftermath.

[CHAPTER 13]

As if the Fire in the Sky wasn't enough for the Earth and its inhabitants to worry about, other storms were brewing. Ominous threats of disaster were sweeping across the globe. Earthquakes were shaking up China and Japan. Monsoons were blowing away and flooding India. Wildfires were sweeping across Australia. Tsunamis were washing over the Philippines. Volcanoes in the ring of fire were erupting on, and all around the Hawaiian Islands. Hurricanes were threatening the Pacific and Atlantic Coasts of the United States.

It had long been suspected that Mother Nature was schizophrenic. In light of what was going on around the world, it was clear she'd gone completely insane, and she was taking the global population along with her. Without question, the coastal areas were taking a pounding around the world. Yet, it was the inlands that seemed to be the hardest hit. Regardless of how it was dissected, a global disaster was occurring that would have monumental consequences of epic proportion.

High tides, riptides and tidal waves, volcanoes, hurricanes, tornadoes, and earthquakes prevented many people from getting to designated shelters. Inland areas were getting a double whammy. In addition to the widespread natural disasters that were occurring, inland regions were getting attacked most violently by the AI Forces. Why the aliens clustered in the inland regions and were avoiding coastal areas was still unclear. Shilloqwai and Excelcious had people working on it.

All hell broke loose on the day mass evacuations were to begin. The timing couldn't have been worse. The underground facility wasn't quite ready to open. However, accommodations could be made for groups at a time. It wasn't prepared for the influx of people trying to seek refuge from whatever it was they were running from, a natural disaster or the alien attacks. The facility was still under construction. When completed, it would be able to house the global populous and then some! Still extraneous efforts were made to accommodate everyone that sought shelter underground. Many inlanders were faced with riding the storm out while being attacked by aliens. It was a catch-22. Trying to go out and whether the storm, in seeking underground shelter, put them at high risk for being injured or killed in the violent storms.

Areas that had never seen a funnel touch down in their history were being torn up by F-5 tornadoes. The storms were twisting and turning the United States upside down and inside out, leaving catastrophic paths of destruction in their wake. When the alien bots started attacking homes, people were being picked off like sitting ducks.

By staying at home, people were in essence surrendering and opting to take the fast track to eternity. The effects of the storms slowed the movement of the alien bots too, yet they were able to withstand the force of the winds better than humans could. The winds hindered the targeting ability of their long-range weapons, forcing the robots to get within close range in order to tally their kills. Interference from the storms deprived the robots of using tracking devices to locate human targets. This is why human chances of survival greatly increased by venturing out into the killer storms.

When it all had passed, the damage was extensive globally in terms of property lost. The storms and other disasters that swept over the planet Earth did not discriminate. Robots and Humankind were equally affected. Whether it was terminations or exterminations, both factions suffered heavy casualties. As the data started coming in, it confirmed what Shilloqwai, Excelcious and many others knew. Globally, damages and casualties were significantly higher, over the inland areas. In analyzing and dissecting the data by regions and the nature of the disaster or disasters that occurred there, Shilloqwai and Excelcious hoped to find out why this was. They knew in part it was because the heaviest concentration of AI forces were inland.

That was odd because looking at time lapse photos taken by the drones, the forces seemed to be evenly distributed globally. Excelcious was interested in what caused their forces to migrate inland and regroup there. Ironically, the AI decision to move the forces inland probably saved a lot of lives.

The fact that a lot of AI Forces were terminated in quake zones helped Humankind. Many of the Spacebots were swallowed by the huge fissures that opened while the Earth's plates were shifting. But he decided that wasn't the reason for their redeployment. Shilloqwai agreed as the two of them continued to analyze the data. Many of the Spacebots were incinerated because they were too stupid or too slow to get out of the lava flows in volcanic regions. Again, that failed to explain why they migrated to inland areas.

One-by-one, they studied time lapse photos of the different disasters relative to the migration patterns of the AI robots. They were hoping to find a pattern that might give them a single clue, or perhaps even the answer to their question, regarding the retreat of the AI forces to the inland. Excelcious was studying how the mechanical devils could walk through the blazing infernos due to the wildfires burning in Australia and why they were stopped by the lava flows in volcanic regions.

Shilloqwai was reviewing drone shots of the AI forces near the Great Lakes. The heaviest concentrations were around Lake Michigan between Milwaukee and Chicago. In particular they were gathered in Racine, Wisconsin, known as the Belle City.

Named so, because from aerial photos the coastal part of the city lining the shores of Lake Michigan looks like a bell. A large number of people were massacred there, especially in the rich community of Wind

Point near the famous Lighthouse. How were the aliens not affected by the high waves that were pounding the beaches? It was said that the aliens went after an old man who was fishing out on the North Pier during the storm which brought high waves, yet he continued to fish as though nothing were going on around him. He had to be rescued by the Coastguard on several occasions in situations similar to the one he presently found himself in. They threatened to fine and jail him if they were called to rescue him again from the raging waters churning around him. The aliens not only threatened his life, but the lives of the Coastguard members that had managed to save him.

The AI bots moved in on him. They were struggling to get to the old man because they'd gotten tangled in his fishing lines. While struggling to free themselves, the old man used his tackle box to knock the three bots attacking him into the water. His escape from the Spacebots would be the biggest fish story he would ever tell. The Spacebots resurfaced eventually, but how was it they hadn't short-circuited? How was it that the Spacebots were able to withstand the torrential rains? All it took were heavy concentrations of condensation to short-circuit Shilloqwai in her robot days! She was water-resistant too, but, to a point. She couldn't swim in the pure liquid blue either. How was it the AI bots could?

Why then did the ocean spray of the coastal waters wipe them off of the radar screen. They disappeared without a trace. What was different? There was consistency in the way that they withstood the torrential rains in the coastal areas as long as…! That was the difference, the pure liquid blue and…that was it! The salt, they were susceptible to the salt in the ocean and gulf waters which is why they were shying away from the sea worlds. That had to be it, of course, it was the salt! Thinking she was on to something, and anxious to share her enthusiasm. "Excelcious!" She shouted ecstatically. She didn't mean to startle him. He was standing right next to her when she'd called out to him! "Oh sorry!" She apologized when she'd realized that she'd shouted in his ear.

"What?" He asked as though he hadn't heard her at all.

"Smart ass!" She said playfully. "It's the salt!" She repeated excitedly, but, in a much softer tone. "That's why the alien forces retreated from the ocean, gulf, and sea waters. The salt was eating them alive."

"Smart little bastards! Learn from their mistakes, do they? They'll never be able to calculate or estimate the variable factors that Humankind brings to the table. We can use that to our advantage. They'll never understand the 'fight or flight mode' that takes over in humans when their lives are on the line.

"And when the Power of Love is involved, humans think they're invincible and will do anything to try and survive. Everything with robots is programmed. They rely on data input, analysis, along with the logic and reason behind it. When you take logic and reason out of the equation, robots can't process that input. It doesn't compute. Add the Power of Love to the mixture and the variable factors increase astronomically, leaving the robots with even less information because they can't understand the concept of Love for the same reason. Humans often trust their instincts, defying logic, and reason. Robots follow the sequences of logic and reason. The more variable factors we can bring into the battle with the robots, the greater advantage we'll have over them in battle. Hell, it just might be the winning strategy, the one that would ensure our victory over them in this Intragalactic war!"

"At what cost? How many lives will be lost? How much irreparable damage will be done?"

"We have no choice Shilloqwai. Some things are worth fighting for. Love and life are the two most worthy causes. We're fighting a war with Intragalactic terrorists. Diplomacy doesn't work with terrorists. Unfortunately, it comes down to kill or be killed."

"War to keep the peace. A strange irony I'll never come to fully understand. Trying to comprehend all the aspects of love would be a much simpler task! How long do you anticipate before the underground city is finished?"

"I don't know for sure, hopefully soon!"

"I hope that's soon enough!"

"That's all we can do is hope! From here on out we'll be in for the fight of our lives. Our global communications network is functional, with the ability to receive signals deep underground. The signals sent through this system will be encrypted. Additionally, they will be scrambled every few seconds, making the code almost impossible to crack. In order for one to use the communications devices, retinal, finger scans and voice prints are required. If any of the three are missing, the communications devices cannot be activated. It was one of few times since the robots and Humankind signed the peace treaty, that they were willing, or at least making efforts to work together. Their mission was to help clean up the Earth and restore it to the great condition it was in before the Fire in the Sky, and the ensuing attacks by the AI Forces.

Though her robot days were over, and Asimov's laws no longer applied to her, Shilloqwai still felt obligated to complete the quest she'd begun. As a human, she had more insight on human nature.

She hoped that she could find a way to translate her newly acquired wisdom and knowledge in such a way, that robots would be able to accept the data she input. She also hoped they could process and analyze it in a way that would enable both factions to better communicate. Effective communication was the key for robots and Humankind to reach a mutual understanding. Shilloqwai knew the most difficult part of continuing her quest would be to convey to the robots that humans, at times, threw logic and reason out the window. There are a multitude of variable factors that would cause humans to act in this way. The best example she could think of, that followed th is pattern, was Love. How was she going to explain the concept of Love to a robot, let alone the many aspects of it. Much of what humans know of love is knowledge based on experiences, friendships, relationships, and courtship. None of those things were possible between humans, unless they trusted each other.

Robots still had to learn to find common ground with humans. When neither side trusted the other, it would be impossible for them to come to any kind of understanding. Only after they had come to an understanding, could they begin to build meaningful working relationships. Possibilities came alive as Shilloqwai imagined a utopian world where robots and humans could coexist without conflict. The robots would rule strictly adhering to Asimov's Laws, and not by the loose interpretations, as they had been. They would restore privacy to Humankind which would be finally free to pursue its dreams and live out its fantasies without being spied upon.

Shilloqwai had been brainstorming, looking for a way to open communications between humans and robots. She had an idea that she wanted to run by Excelcious. "Honey, what would you think if I went on a world-wide speaking tour? I could tell my story from both sides, robot and human. People have a lot of questions about what exactly my role was as diplomat, liaison. My hope is that being transparent, I can clear up some of the misconceptions about me, about the actual state of robot and human relations. Hopefully, I can also help to further unify the alliance which would strengthen our forces before the next phase of the AI attack."

"Not to steal your thunder, but how would you feel about touring together? I can talk about available updates to robot armor. For the overhaul, robots need to report to any Robotix facility. The armor replacement would take about 45 minutes to an hour. The new armor, water-resistant and waterproofed, would allow robots the ability to be immersed for short periods of time without causing them to short-circuit."

Excelcious told Shilloqwai that in test studies, the new armor has proven to be effective in repelling all liquids, including saltwater and corrosive liquids. "The armor is also fireproofed, coated with a flame retardant so robots would be able to withstand the intense heat and literally, walk through fire, even lava flows for extended periods of time!"

"How long could robots with this new armor be submerged, without being damaged?"

"Hours, in some cases up to a day, depending on the make and model! In regard to the heat-resistant, fire-proofing treatment, the robots equipped with this armor will be able to take the heat. It might be going a little far to say that they could withstand the fires of hell, but you get my point! The heat would have to be pretty intense to cause a robot to have a meltdown."

"What about incineration?" Shilloqwai asked curiously.

"I think the armor would hinder the process to some degree. But, if incineration is the intended outcome, there are plenty of known ways to make it happen expeditiously. We don't have to wait for the updates to be completed, before we go out on tour. We give the plans to Robotix and they get started with the manufacturing and distribution! We should have time to complete the updates. I've checked the intervals on the previous attacks. The spacing between attacks ranges from days to a couple of weeks without fail! Depending how much damage we inflict on them. Taking a look at what we've done against superior forces, we've inflicted considerable damage to the AI Forces in some battles and minimal damage in others. The bad news is they come back stronger and deadlier with each subsequent attack. I think your idea of the speeches is a good way to get our message out that continuing attacks are imminent. It will give us the opportunity to inform Humankind what more is being done to help protect it. Using an encryption device all of Humankind will be able to view our speeches after downloading a secure application, that will make the speeches damn near impossible for the enemy to intercept and or decode. We can't tip our hand or clue the AI Forces in as to what we're up to, or we're all dead meat!"

"So," Shilloqwai continued revealing her plan, "I thought we could start the tour in Europe, make our way around the world and come back here to close it out. The idea is to be moving closer to home, should something unforeseen happen."

"So, where's our starting point?"

"Switzerland!" Shilloqwai said excitedly, as she was actually looking forward to going out on tour.

As usual, Excelcious had a surprise for her. This time it was a graphic novel, a story he'd written, and illustrated with the help of a computer art program. He'd had them massed produced as there were boxes of them in his lab. "Let me see one of those, please!" She requested as she snatched the comic book he was holding in his hand. 'Shilloqwai: The Golden-Hearted Bot Woman!' What the hell? Seems like you made me out to be some sort of invincible Superhero!"

"You're not invincible, but that doesn't mean we have to let the enemy know what your vulnerabilities are! You seem upset. What's the matter? Don't you like the comic book? By the way, I need my copy signed before I shelve it in the museum."

"Yes, it's great!" Shilloqwai said sincerely with tears in her eyes. "I'm concerned about the extra attention I'm going to draw because of it! The AI Force is not as stupid as it appears to be. It knows who we are Excelcious. We're being targeted, both of us."

"Premonitions again?"

"They're getting stronger. A lot of the things I've been seeing are coming to pass! We're going to be separated at some point, maybe forever!"

"That's what you're seeing?"

"Yes, and it's scaring the hell out of me."

"So, do you know when we get separated? Where?"

"After we get back home, on the last night of the tour!"

"Maybe we should just scrap this whole idea and stay home and protect ourselves!"

"We can't. It's too important. It's not about saving ourselves! It's about saving the Earth, the place we call home, Shilloqwai! The place that's home for much of Humankind! There are likely other places that can sustain human life out in the cosmos. But if we fail to meet our obligations, this place, the Earth, will cease to exist! The future is a strange place! It reveals shadows of things that may or may not come to pass. Whatever happens will happen according to the Master's Plan. There's nothing we can do to change that!"

"I saw my funeral!"

"It's not the first time you've seen that! I mean, when we were planning to rescue the children from the Militiabots, you saw it then too."

"It seemed more real this time. Something happens here in San Diego Excelcious! Independently we were leading people to the underground shelter that's still under construction. We'd set a rendezvous point. This is the weird part. We were there, at Rainbow Falls. We practically ran into each other. We were calling out to one another, but we couldn't hear or see each other. The vision faded, leaving me with the impression that I have two futures, both of them are without you!"

"Let's clear some things up. For starters, you have one future and that's with me! The fact that you viewed two scenarios means your death is not imminent! You may live and you may die! Only God knows if you will live to see a new tomorrow. Honey, we have to live for the moment, doing what we think we have to do, while taking advantage of the opportunities we're being given. If something happens, I'm not going to be a sitting duck. I'm going down fighting, I know you will too! It's going to be a great tour with a flourishing finale. Nothing's going to happen, but we have to be prepared for anything that might!"

"You always make it sound so simple." Shilloqwai sighed, flashing a genuine smile.

"It's easier when you don't let yourself become overwhelmed by things you can't change. I have the Power of Love Behind me. Remember that little story I told you, the one about the Footprints in the Sand? How when you looked back, and you thought you were walking alone because there was only one set of footprints?

"That was a beautiful little story. And then God's voice rang out, reminding the troubled one, that those were the times he was being carried. So, I shouldn't be worried then that I'm seeing only one set of footprints, and that I have been for some time now?"

"You've got to keep the faith Shilloqwai. I'm seeing one set of footprints too, and I have been for quite some time myself. There's an old song that tells how God's got the whole world in his hands. If he can hold the whole world in his hands, there's certainly room for the two of us in the palm of his hand. And that's where we are right now, in the palm of God's hand. As scared as we are, we have nothing to worry about!"

"I love how you always see light in the darkness, Excelcious. I love you ! You're an angel, heaven sent, my love, my life, my guiding light. You will always be those things to me, from now through eternity."

"You, tell me all of the time how bold I am, how brave I am. I could never do any of the things I do without you. You're my inspiration, my heart, my soul, and my eternal flame. I draw all of my strength from you, my guiding light. I can't even tell you how much I love you, only that my love for you is infinite and unconditional." Having bolstered one another's confidence, they set off the next morning on their global, whirlwind speaking tour. It resonated well with both the humans and the robots, with Shilloqwai telling her story of the Golden-hearted bot woman.

The story was about a robot who had dreams of becoming human, and how her life changed after she had. Not many knew the truth about Shilloqwai, that in actuality, she really had turned human. It was something that didn't need to be revealed, not now. She was already at odds with the robots.

There were also plenty of humans that looked upon her with disdain. Those that did, also believed she was insincere, ruthless, and heartless. Why give that rebellious group one more reason to hate her? By telling the story the way she'd chosen to do so, what it was like for her to star in the role of diplomat and liaison, she connected with more people than she turned off.

She tried to convey how difficult a task it was, that she was given. "Imagine," she conveyed to them, "what it's like being a robot that's been asked to bridge the gap between robots and humans, which remains far and wide. In order to complete the task, requires that I, a robot come to a basic understanding of human nature; and comprehending to some degree the concept of love. A concept that has many aspects, and one that humans have yet to define. This is what I was asked to do.

"Now consider, I only have limited tools available to me. I can only process data that is input. If I have insufficient data, with no consideration or taking into account variable factors, all of the analysis in the world will fail to produce solutions to our problems. We need more input, more specific information that will help us in our relationships with humans so we can start bridging the gap. There will always be a rift between robots and humans without a team effort to try and make things work. We're facing a global crisis. It's time for Earth's inhabitants, robots, and Humankind, to unite. If there was ever a time for humans and robots to put their differences aside. The time is now. Soon there won't be time to consider our options as time will have run out."

The tour breezed through Europe, Africa, the United Kingdom, Canada, the Middle East, and all of Latin America. On the last leg of their speaking tour, Shilloqwai and Excelcious swept from East to West across America. Shilloqwai wasn't surprised when she learned, that before her final speech, protesters had been flocking to San Diego. She understood that there were those that would never accept the robot takeover and would never accept the fact that Robots now ruled the world. Her speech wasn't about power or who ruled the world. It was about survival of the world's civilization. Not just the fittest, but for the global populous.

Peaceful protests were hijacked by Spacebots that had seemingly come out of nowhere. Shilloqwai thought it was possible that not all of the AI Forces had been destroyed. The question was where had they been hiding? It was obvious what the intent was. The Spacebots' intent was to cause more division between Humankind and the robots ruling over them. Many protests had turned violent. However, neither human casualties were reported, nor were any of the robots defending them terminated as a result of the provocations instigated by the small band of AI Forces. From undercover, Shilloqwai targeted the handful of AI Bots and blasted them into oblivion with the shrapnel fragments that flew from her angry eyes.

Witnesses to the decimation of the aliens, assumed it was part of the Robotix defense systems at work and thought nothing more of it. The action seemed to energize the crowd which saw that the robots, really were trying to protect the people in accordance with Asimov's laws. Shilloqwai still wasn't buying the superhero bit. In fact, ominous threats had surfaced at all of her rallies. She quickly dispensed with them as though they were nothing. Shilloqwai thought that perhaps the unifying message she was trying to communicate was starting to get attention. In all of her speeches, Excelcious told her she spoke eloquently and with wisdom. She returned the compliment in kind. Tonight, there would be no difference in the way they addressed the people of their home city. They would be candid, and transparent. The hope, as it had always been, was to continue emphasizing the importance that robots and humans unite in this time of crisis, while persisting in their efforts to build a mutual trust between the two factions.

A friendly competition seemed to erupt out of nowhere just as Shilloqwai was about to take the stage at the outdoor event. On the mechanical side raucous chants rang out. ROBOT! ROBOT! ROBOT! Humankind responded! HUMAN! HUMAN! HUMAN! Shilloqwai was flattered, yet embarrassed. This wasn't about her. Obviously, they'd read parts of the graphic novel that had been distributed to those in attendance. The story portrayed Shilloqwai as wanting to help everyone, which was true to what she'd tried to do throughout her existence as a robot. As a human, she continues to try to help as many as she can. Though she dismissed the superhero part of it all, she did appreciate the gratitude she believed they were trying to show for all that she's done, for them all, and for the world.

"It's time!" Excelcious announced. "Let's get this over with. We have some pressing issues that need to be addressed if we're going to be ready for the next phase of the alien attack. Looks like we're gaining support. The hard work is starting to pay off."

"I wish all of the focus weren't on me! It's about them. And they don't realize it. I don't want to be on a pedestal. I just want to be human like them. Being human is all I ever wanted to be!" Shilloqwai said humbly.

"You're giving them hope where there was very little, or where there was none. Does it matter if they call you Shilloqwai, the Golden-hearted bot woman? So, be their superhero, continue to give them hope. Give them something to fight for! Did you see them out there, that competitive chant that was being bantered about between the robots and the humans? It was a bonding of sorts. Keep doing what you're doing. You'll strengthen that bond. The bridge between the robots and humans is under construction. Shilloqwai, complete your quest!"

Though his encouragement had inspired her, she did her best to try and shun the spotlight once she was on the world stage. She never asked to be a superhero. She thought her human transformation was a dream come true. It was, until she realized her mutant powers kept her from being normal. But what the hell was 'normal' in regard to human beings? Did normal creatures exist? From her experience, she found all humans to be crazy in varying degrees…some more so than others. And some, well, they were just downright insane! As much as her mutant powers were a blessing, they were that much more a curse. She had trouble controlling them which is why they were an albatross around her neck.

Though he accepted her unconditionally for who she was, she was still perpetually afraid that one day, she would in advertently kill the man she loved. If she did, she didn't know how she would ever forgive herself for doing so. She would die and join him in eternity shortly thereafter because he had become her lifeline, and she could not live without him.

It turned out to be a perfect afternoon for the scheduled rally in San Diego, California. The temperature peaked by midday at 78-degrees. By early evening it was hovering between 73 and 75. The rays of the western sun began to drip like tallow from a burning candle onto the scarlet-plum horizon, bleeding down into and across the Pacific. As the sun went dark for the day, giving way to night, ominous clouds pushed their way across the sky, obscuring the light, casting doubts on what initially promised to be a starry, starry night. Almost certainly it was going to rain that evening. When it did, not if, the legendary lie that it never rains in Southern California, would be debunked, yet again.

A backdrop of midnight blue was about to be burnt to jet black. The silver-blue moon would be scalded, bronzed, by the Fire in the Sky, which would turn it ghoulish-purple, blood-red. It wouldn't take much to reignite the infernal flames. Just a spark from an exploding star and all hell was bound to break loose. As with the imminent rain, the question was when the inferno would be set ablaze not if. It depended on when the Ghost Riders in the sky felt the urge to do it! "Deviant, devilish, copper-toned bastards!" Shilloqwai muttered just before she took the stage. She vowed that nothing was going to drown out her final rallying cry, that included the haunting sounds of silence.

"Ladies and gentlemen, I'd like to give a universal thanks to all of you who are with us out in social media land, and a special thanks to all of you who made the effort to be with us here in San Diego tonight! Tonight's event marks the conclusion of my four-month global speaking tour. I am making a non-partisan plea to my mechanical and human friends. I've experienced the world from both sides now, dark and light, wrong and right. It's the world's delusions I recall, I really don't know the world at all. We're not just facing an enemy.

"We're facing a global threat, that means all of us, robot, and human. The AI Forces, as they are generally referred to...appear to have superior power over us. In my limited experience, and from what little I know about love, I have learned that love is a most powerful thing. We can use this power to thwart, even defeat a superior enemy. I'm confident we can unite as one force, and we must do so in order for us to fully benefit from the Power of Love. At times we all act mechanical, do things monotonously routine. I believe all of us have some robot in us.

"At times we all do things that defy logic and reason, throwing out common sense when we do. It's especially during these times, we often look to love to carry us through. We're giving away T-shirts as you leave tonight, be sure to pick yours up on the way out. There's a little saying on the front that reads: I am part Robotoid, I love Humanoids. On the back it reads, I am also part Humanoid, I love Robotoids. Be sure to get your free limited-edition T-shirt."

Shilloqwai was concluding her speech, preparing to send those in attendance off in grand fashion. Indeed, the finale of her world tour ended with lots of fireworks, and not the celebratory kind. Something had gone spectacularly wrong. Shilloqwai's nightmarish premonition was starting to come alive. She didn't like this particular episode of Déjà vu. From what she remembered of her premonition she ran from the enemy trying to help the people. That's when things went awry, and people started getting hurt. If she changed something she saw, perhaps she could change the morbid ending to the story. She would not run; she would stand and face the enemy in hopes she could protect the people. She prayed that she could remain strong.

The oohhs and aahhs from the initial fireworks turned into holocaustic cries of hysteria as a 30-foot Robot descended from the clouds. His landing in San Diego, registered 5.7 on the Richter Scale. Shaking things up was his trademark insignia. Many in the crowd recognized him from the Holobots game, here he was, the life-size version of Metallicus Nebuloso. For those that didn't know him, he'd properly introduced himself. It didn't go over well when those gathered realized he was the one responsible for kidnapping the children of the world. "Why are you here?

You, ignorant, arrogant, egotistical son-of-a-bitch!" Shilloqwai demanded to know.

"The fact that you're even asking, tells me how ignorant you are, you, insolent, defiant bitch!"

"What did you call me? If I heard you right, you don't know me well enough to call me a bitch!"

"Careful Ms. Shilloqwai. You don't want to glitch at a time like this." Metallicus chided her. "If you do, it will be the death of Humankind. It seems that you and your arrogant friend believe that you can stop me, even dare think that you can defeat me. Nobody else seems to exude your confidence. You have my blessings, and your valor should be commended. Unfortunately, unless you take my word for it, you'll learn sooner or later, you're fighting a losing battle!"

"Talk about arrogance, Metallicus! You were defeated in a video game by a seven-year-old girl. I defeated you in the game as well! You are not invincible! I will take you down in real life, here in real time, by attacking your weaknesses."

"I am not weak. I am perfect!"

"Everyone is vulnerable in some way. I will find your vulnerability and attack it until you are destroyed!"

"If I wanted to squash you like a bug, I could crush your frail little ass with one of my toes. What challenge is there in that?"

"So, are you familiar with the story of David and Goliath?"

"There are many tales across the universe. I'm afraid I'm not familiar with that one."

"So, you're not familiar with the Bible then? Your loss! Just to enlighten you, David was a small boy when he killed an evil, giant of a man. I am but a frail woman. You are a giant piece if shit. I will destroy you, and flush you from the universe. I promise."

"A promise you won't be able to keep!"

"I take that as a challenge, and I accept. If I take you down now, innocent people are going to get hurt or killed. Property will be damaged or destroyed. You see here on Earth we have a saying, the bigger they are the harder they fall. You're one big-ass son-of-a-bitch. The crater you make when you fall will be enough to bury you in!"

Metallicus Nebuloso laughed heartily at the boldness of her words. It sounded like rolling thunder when he did. "You think I'm joking, do you? You must be. Robot, human or Superhero, I know you're not stupid enough to attack me by your defenseless little self!"

"No!" Shilloqwai said flatly, with a wry smile. "No, I don't think you're joking with your intent to conquer Earth. But you have to know that I'm not joking, either, when I'm vowing here and now that I will take you down. I'm not fool enough to take you on by myself. I have overwhelming support from the Power of Love. Along with that power come a few other surprises." Shilloqwai warned, with her patience wearing thin.

"Love is for the weak; those not strong enough to go through life on their own." Metallicus Nebuloso quipped.

"Love is also for the strong. Those who are in touch with their true feelings, and those with the wisdom to know there is power in numbers."

"So far, in my universal travels, you're the only one stupid enough to challenge me. You don't even have a supporting cast that I can see. Looks like you're truly on your own bitch!"

"You're lacking the data you need to understand Humankind, you mechanical piece of shit! The first thing you should know, particularly if you're dealing with women, is to never piss them off, like you just did with me! I'm done with you, for now."

Simultaneously, Excelcious and Shilloqwai, pressed the disabling button, on their DDD belts targeting the 30-foot, wiry bucket of nuts and bolts. Knowing he was defenseless, for a short spell, Shilloqwai took the opportunity to level a couple of free shots against him. Shrapnel flew from her eyes and lightning bolts flew from her fingertips.

As the lightning hit him multiple times, Shilloqwai asked no one. "Who says lightning never strikes the same place twice?" She sneered knowing she had zapped him 100-plus times, causing significant damage. No part of him was unscathed after suffering the full of Shilloqwai's wrath. The circuits that didn't get fried were sliced and diced from the laser beams of shrapnel Shilloqwai fired at him. Shilloqwai smiled wryly, knowing Metallicus would be out of commission for a while! She like the rest, feared his return. She wanted to finish him off, and she would have tried if she hadn't passed out. She went down like she'd taken a punch from the lightweight boxing champion of the universe. She got light-headed from maxing out her powers, and her nose was bloodied. That's what she told Excelcious when she recovered.

When Metallicus returned to avenge the attack on him, Shilloqwai said she would be ready to go a second round with him. She wanted to be there for Humankind, to make sure it didn't pay for her sins. Shilloqwai had invited Excelcious to go for a midnight walk with her. She laughed when she stepped out of Excelcious' lab. She had to laugh after she'd seen what she'd done to Metallicus. He was still a smoldering mess.

Shilloqwai and Excelcious watched as a glittering cosmic dust floated down fluttering like feathers. The glittering particles swarmed around Metallicus like fireflies. Like nebulous butterflies, they continued to flutter around him, attaching themselves to him wherever they could find an empty space. Suddenly, Shilloqwai and Excelcious realized what was actually happening. They struggled to find a name for the illuminous insects.

They decided they would call them Mechanibots, wondering how long it would take the multi-colored fireflies to fix Metallicus. The Mechanibots glittered like diamonds. A little glitz, a little glamor could make anyone look good. At the moment, Metallicus looked like an over-decorated Christmas tree. He was a 30-foot piece of artwork, appearing to be gaudily studded with rhinestones.

While the Mechanibots worked tirelessly to restore their leader, Earth's populous was readying itself for the fight of its life, the battle for its very existence. Communications would be critical if they had a chance to save themselves. The humans were weaponized and still working on unifying with the robots, so they were able to fight as one. They had a defense system in place and an escape route ready.

It seems they all finally understood that they were fighting for their freedom. What they didn't understand was why their freedom was being threatened, by an alien force no less. Metallicus Nebuloso hadn't had a chance to tell any of them . He was planning on it before Shilloqwai so abruptly disabled him. All wondered if Metallicus would be willing to make concessions, or if it would be his way, or the highway to hell? Was there a way to avoid the war? If no, was there a way to win it? Had Metallicus already decided Humankind's fate? Were concessions even on the negotiating table?

It was clear now, Metallicus Nebuloso was the leader of the AI Bots and the driving force behind their attacks. Shilloqwai hoped and prayed there was a chance for diplomacy with something or someone, who appeared to be a warmonger. Shilloqwai, after all that had happened thus far, was encouraged. She believed that Metallicus Nebuloso had made the first mistake in the conflict, underestimating the Power of Love. He would find it was stronger than he'd anticipated. Shilloqwai felt this critical miscalculation alone, would be his undoing.

METALLICUS NEBULOSO

[CHAPTER 14]

Shilloqwai's weaponry, offensive and defensive, was of unknown origin. The damage that she'd inflicted on Metallicus Nebuloso, bought Earth additional borrowed time, time to prepare for what all thought would be the final showdown. And in this apocalyptic war between two worlds there would be no winner, no loser. The prize in this ultimate battle would be Earth and the power to govern it, and free reign to collect any spoils that remained. How would Humankind fare in a monumental battle that was shaping up to be the feared Armageddon?

Sounding like a talking toy with dying batteries, Metallicus Nebuloso, spoke for the first time in almost a week. When Shilloqwai and Excelcious were alerted to this they rushed out of Excelcious' house to the scene. At first his speech was garbled, making little, if any sense. He usually spoke, or tried to, every morning just after sunrise. Excelcious and Shilloqwai were there religiously, in the event he had something relevant to say. The warped distortion of his voice improved with each subsequent day. His words and phrases had become more syncopated when he talked. He began to sound like a human with a heavy southern drawl. "The day of suffrin' is a comin'!" Metallicus warned. "It will be a day when Earth will be targeted, and Humankind will pay for its sins of infecting it! It will be a day of reckoning for all humans who will be called upon to account for their crimes against Humanity and its crime against the Perrfect One!"

"Who is the Perrfect One?" Shilloqwai asked in an insolent tone, mocking the way Metallicus was talking!

"I am perfection, as is my army!" Metallicus boldly proclaimed.

"What do you want from Earth and its populous?"

"I was perfectly created. My programming mandates that I travel the universe and eradicate imperfection, a quest that may take light years, perhaps an eternity."

"So, you have an unfulfillable quest? A goal that is unachievable? Is that not a flaw in your programming? It's certainly not perfection!"

"Things are always changing. Things that are perfect can become imperfect, that is why my quest will remain ongoing." Metallicus proclaimed.

"So, there's no limit to the lifetimes it might take to accomplish this, so called unachievable quest!" Shilloqwai interrogated him to the third degree.

"Infinity, eternity, forever, relative terms as they relate to immortality. As I am perfect and invincible, I cannot be destroyed. As you have seen, I can be damaged and disabled at times. But I can always be repaired. After I have been refurbished, I am stronger, more powerful, and more perfect. My existence will go on for as long as it takes to complete my quest."

"But I nearly destroyed you, all by my scrawny-ass little self! How is that perfect?" Shilloqwai asked, demanding an answer.

"Invincibility is part of perfection. For that I will avenge myself. You will be punished for messing with perfection. You cannot destroy me!"

"I will find a way!" Shilloqwai promised. "I should have finished you off when I had the chance when you were just standing there like a paralyzed robotic piece of shit!" She taunted him, laughing wryly in his interface!

"The fact that you couldn't bring yourself to do it, exposes your own weaknesses and highlights your imperfection!"

"Oh, really! Your remarks show what little you know about human nature. If you consider sensitivity, vulnerability, compassion, forgiveness, and love, weaknesses, then I'm guilty as charged. But what you don't seem to understand is, it's not all about pride, power, strength, domination, and manipulation, those are the true weaknesses. Strength is having the courage to be who you are. Power is through prayer and in Love. Dominance and manipulation, those are the Devil's tools of deceit, tools that divide not unite. True perfection brings about peace and unity so that Humankind can live in a serene, surreal celestial universe, both in their mortal lives and through eternity."

"You speak in vague terms. I need more data." Metallicus admitted.

"If you're missing data, doesn't that make you imperfect?"

"I acquire data through experiences. It helps me maintain my perfection!"

"At first when you told me you were perfect, I didn't believe you, I thought you were full of shit! After having conversed with you for just a short time, I have to congratulate you on a couple of things. First, you convinced me to change my mind about you. Secondly, you just won an argument with a woman, a damn near impossible task by human standards. I believe you now. I believe that you are perfect! Admittedly I was wrong when I said you weren't. But I can clearly see now that you are a perfect asshole!" Shilloqwai observed

"Bitch, I'm getting tired of you interfering with and trying to thwart my mission perhaps you should…"

"You haven't taken to heart what I told you the last time, about pissing a woman off! I am warning you for the last time!" Shilloqwai interrupted him. "Don't you ever call me a bitch again! You're still recovering from the last time you called me that!"

"And I told you, I'm coming for you when I do recover!"

"Bullshit!" Shilloqwai challenged him. "You just told me you can't destroy perfection, that in doing so, it would go against your programming!"

"But you are not perfect. And destroying you would not even be a challenge for me!" Metallicus boasted.

"But you're wrong. I am perfect. Perfectly imperfect, just the way the Power of Love made me. So, you dare say that you're going to mess with perfection?"

"That's an absurd, oxymoronic thing to say! Imperfection is imperfection, regardless of how you frame it."

"So, if I'm hearing you correctly, it sounds like you have no intentions of trying to make compromises. It appears that you and your AI Bots intend to follow through with your dumbass insidious plan to destroy the Earth and all of Humankind."

"Not the Earth, only its inhabitants. We can fix what's wrong with the Earth and rid it of the contamination Humankind has tainted it with. It's Earth's people. They are the problem, a viral infection that will ultimately contaminate the universe."

"And what about the robots, they're like you, aren't they? Mechanical beasts! What are you going to do with them?"

"The Earthen robots were created by humans, thereby, they are imperfect as well and they too must be destroyed."

"By whose authority are you taking these actions?" Shilloqwai demanded to know.

"By no one's authority. I am abiding by the Universal Intragalactic Mandate in accordance with my programming."

"You didn't program yourself. I'm asking who programmed you? Someone had to have set the mandate and input the data into your system. You're not an omniscient one! There are a lot of things you don't know shit about. Take Earth for example! Asimov's Laws were implemented to guide the robots. The Power of Love guides the people who seek the celestial resting place for all eternity… the place Christians know as Heaven."

"You mean that place that's allegedly housed in a city of gold, surrounded by rainbows of color?"

"That's the place!"

"I've roamed the celestial skies. I've been everywhere. And I can tell you from my travels that no such place exists! The City of Gold is a dream, a delusion for fools that believe fantasy can come alive and become a reality."

"How many lies are you willing to tell, in trying to justify your foolish quest? I know there are two places you haven't been. Admittedly, you've never seen heaven, and you never will. You're just a damn machine. You know there's an opposite for everything. It's what keeps the universe balanced. The opposite of Heaven is hell, the other place in the universe you've never seen. Don't worry, you'll be seeing it soon, because I'm planning on sending you there, you sacrilegious bastard!"

"I'm already in hell. I exist among celestial chaos. I see how the nebulous flame fuels the galactic inferno that ignites the fire in the skies!"

"No, no! You've got it all wrong. What you're describing is celestial beauty, enchanting wonderment. The place I'm talking about sending you to, is in the depths of the underworld. There is no light there, only the gothic flames that burn and torture, unable to consume its occupants, so they live in eternal misery. That's how you'll be spending your eternity, with a constant awareness that you'll never be able to function again as you'll forever remain a half-molten pile of shit!"

"Nothing is going to get in the way of me fulfilling my quest, including a little bitch like you!"

Shilloqwai ignored the comment. She would wait to unleash her fury on him after she learned what she wanted to, or after she got as much information from him as she thought she could. "Just curious, how many planets have you destroyed because you've deemed them imperfect?"

"Thus far, I've only destroyed planets incapable of sustaining life. Few of them had imperfect inhabitants, like your Earth. Those planets have been destroyed as well!"

"You haven't answered my question, asshole! I asked, how many planets across the universe have you destroyed?"

"I don't know!" Metallicus lied unconvincingly.

"What do you mean you don't know. You're a damn liar. I bet if I hacked into your database, I would find out exactly how many planets you destroyed."

"What I have stored in my database is none of your damn business! Let's just say that in light years, the AI Forces have been able to bring perfection to a fraction of the universe. So, if it matters over the course of our existence, we've destroyed 1,700,910 planets. Earth is going to increase that number to 1,700,911."

"How do you know that destroying planets is bringing about perfection? Have you ever considered that you might be upsetting the universal order of things? Through your actions, you could potentially upset the natural balance of things, thereby destroying star systems, galaxies and perhaps the universe itself! Is that your intent?"

"I am merely doing what I was programed to do. Bring about perfection."

"I think someone screwed up your programming. The reason I think this, is I believe you're interfering with the Master's Plan. In the end, the Power of Love will see that His plan is followed. Bad judgements, false conclusions, have you considered that having made both, that you are imperfect?"

"As previously stated, I was perfectly created. Using additional input, previously unavailable to me, only makes me more perfect. I cannot be held accountable for acting with insufficient data."

"Acting without insufficient data is irresponsible! The exception would be in life and death situations where action on impulse is required. It is understandable then, how mistakes, no, errors in judgement can be made." Shilloqwai argued. "I would venture to guess, the biggest error in judgement that you ever made, was tangling with me! I agree it may ultimately be the death of me. Death is the only thing certain about life. At some point, termination will ultimately be the end of your existence. Whatever form death takes, it will make its way across the universe destroying all things living and otherwise."

"You understand then, everything comes to a morbid end!"

"It doesn't, you stupid ass! Every story has two sides. We've just looked at the mortal side of life. And it's not necessarily all morbid as you've suggested. Life is a gift and it's a beautiful thing, to be cherished and respected. Some have more challenges than others in life. And death can be beautiful too. It means no more suffering. Death is a bridge. Crossing that bridge is the pathway to eternal life. Love never dies and life never ends. Both of them evolve. That evolution continues through death, which is birth into eternity. Though all Humankind grieves with the loss of loved ones, they should celebrate the lives of their loved ones and look forward to the day when they will reunite with them. The resurrection of our spirits is a promise that was made by Love, Himself." Shilloqwai enlightened him.

"All this talk of Love, compassion, forgiveness, they are weaknesses! They will be responsible for your downfall." Metallicus warned.

"And failing to understand these aspects of Humankind will be responsible for yours." Shilloqwai promised. "You must be a mechanical virgin. I bet you've never interfaced with another robot! Have you?"

"How information is collected in my database is classified information. Tell me, what power is there in something you can't see, something that Humankind hasn't been able to define since its beginning?"

"Your questions expose you, showing what little wisdom or experience you have in regard to the matter, and how incompetent you are as a leader."

"This feeling, this power you speak of, often defies logic and reason. Real truth lies in indisputable facts supported by medicine and science."

"So, you ignore the variable factors that are often part of the equation, factors that could influence or change the perceived truths." Shilloqwai pointed out.

"Variable factors distort facts, dilute reality." Metallicus responded, defending his position.

"Would you concede that variables could bring about change, even outcomes in given situations? Ignoring data or refusing input of it, would leave your programming incomplete. Insufficient data would inhibit your abilities to analyze and accurately process information that is relative. Not that your files would be corrupt, but they'd be incomplete, leaving you less than perfect, with the inability to function to capacity. That, by any robot standard is grounds for termination!"

"Far be it for you to suggest I am anything but perfect. Glitch Bitch! You're becoming a real pain in the ass!"

"You'd be less ignorant if you'd quit refusing to take your scientific medicine. Updating files and receiving new data are what keep you relevant. You know what, I'll play your game. I told you before that nothing was perfect. Another mistake. There is one thing that is perfect in all of creation, that one thing is Love."

"Love? Love is far from perfect. It hurts, it scars, it's deceitful in the things it claims to offer. It's all a big lie!"

"You're confusing love with infatuation, and or, lustful sex." Shilloqwai corrected him. True love isn't like that. Love is unconditional, forgiving. It's about relationships with others. True love is eternal, and once the flame is ignited, it will forever burn. Life comes from Love. You have no life, only a limited existence, with no promise of an afterlife. Oblivion will be your eternal resting place. Heaven will be mine."

"Dreams, fantasies, delusions!"

"They're better than nightmares, and horrors of the undead who have no eternal resting place, no place to call home." Retorted Shilloqwai. "After I kill you, I mean destroy you, I hope that you can Rest in Peace, though I know you truly never will!"

"It appears we have chosen our fates, be prepared to meet yours." Metallicus threatened.

"Just as you will meet yours!" Shilloqwai promised.

"More threats?

"Not threats, promises I intend to keep." Shilloqwai said doubling down.

"Brave, but, very foolish!" Metallicus said, offering his opinion.

"Cowardly and very ignorant!" Shilloqwai retorted.

"Your choice, would you rather continue this war with words, or engage in battle until a clear winner emerges. The penalty for the loser is death." Metallicus said, highlighting the reward and the consequences.

"So, the challenge is, we fight to the death?" Shilloqwai asked for clarification.

"Yes, that's right!" Metallicus confirmed.

"I accept the challenge!" Shilloqwai said showing her dedication to Humankind and commitment to do what she could to help save the Earth,

"You indignant fool! To neutralize my sizable advantage, I will allow you to summon all of the forces you can gather to fight with you. I will even allow you to use this Power of Love, if you think it will help your noble cause."

"I was planning on using it regardless of whether you gave your approval or not! Just to be sure we're seeing eye-to-eye, clarify for me, exactly what's at stake!"

"You win, you save the Earth and all of its populous! You will never see me again. Only some freak scenario would allow for that to play out! You lose, kiss your ass goodbye. The rest of the Earth's populous may as well do the same!"

"Not fair! You lose and you go home in exile! I lose and I get executed with all of my people! Using logic and reason, what's wrong with this picture?"

"I've given you your two choices. There are no other options. The terms I've communicated to you are not negotiable!"

"We'll see about that! Here on Earth, there is a universal policy in regard to the rules of engagement. The first rule is, there are no rules. Which translates into, all is fair in love and war. And when I win, when we win, Earth will be preserved and I'm going to terminate your ass."

"You can try! As for your rules of engagement, well that's just poetic rubbish! Especially all of that shit about love!"

"All the better for me, for us, for Earth, that you've dismissed the Power of Love. Tapping into it will give us a huge advantage over you and the AI Forces. Chalk up the first victory in the war, it goes to Earth! You'll see eventually how using this Power of Love will help us win the war!"

"You're entitled to your opinion, but Love is a weakness, not a strength!"

"We'll see if you change your mind after the Power has been used against you." Shilloqwai warned. You're so full of hate, if not hate itself. But, Love, love is strong enough to get rid of hate, which is why I believe using the Power of Love against you, will rid the universe of a most hateful bastard like you!"

"In your dreams!"

"The only thing I'm dreaming about these days is getting rid of you. Dispelling your nightmare will be a dream come true for all of us. After I do, Humankind's fantasy of living without your existential threat will come alive. It will festively celebrate your termination. Our freedom to dream of bigger and better things will have been restored."

"Bitch, you're delusional and a bigger fool than I thought!"

"I've warned you, you ignorant bastard!" Shilloqwai shouted at him. She felt the rage burning from within her! The energy was surging, pulsating, reverberating through her body at a fever pitch. Her heart was racing, beating faster than it ever had as the adrenalin was being pumped through her body at the same rate as her boiling blood. She also felt the power of the people behind her, a small sampling of what she believed to be the Power of Love. Whirs and beeps from the robots standing by, observing the exchange were ready to defend her and fight with her. Some of these, were the same robots that wanted to see her terminated before her transformation. She'd converted them to her mechanical allies by standing up for them and Humankind.

At flashpoint, her unbridled fury was unleashed. Metallicus was pummeled by her vindictive wrath. She reached out her arms to him, wanting to strangle him. If her arms were long enough to reach him, she was convinced she could have. Regardless, the flaming lightning bolts that flew from her fingertips struck him relentlessly with pinpoint laser accuracy. Short-circuited, wobbly, and hunched over, his height was reduced by nearly half. Doubled over, he now stood 15 and one-half feet tall. Shilloqwai was disappointed to see that Metallicus remained activated. Between the voltage of the lightning bolts, and the number of times he'd been hit, Metallicus should have been reduced to a robot melt! Shilloqwai took some satisfaction in the fact that she had disabled the giant bucket of bolts.

Powerlessly paralyzed, Shilloqwai unleashed a second wave of fury on him. Stupefied, he helplessly watched as the explosive beams of shrapnel zeroing in on the target, him! Phase two of her attack, crippled him even further, with the shrapnel slicing and dicing him like morsels of fruits and vegetables. It was amazing Metallicus held together, remaining in one piece. Victimized by her wrath, twice in rapid succession, she didn't know what was holding him up. And she wondered why he was not fading from existence into oblivion. She was disappointed she couldn't make cosmic dust of him. She knew the mountain of shit that stood before her remained a viable threat, capable of eradicating Humankind.

"Damn you!" He cursed before he went limp and silent, suffering from complete system failure.

"Damn you too!" She shouted back at him, knowing her words hadn't registered with his charred, crispy, shredded self! Again, Shilloqwai collapsed, falling limply to the ground in a heap. The blood was coming from her mouth, her nose, and her eyes again. Excelcious was concerned about what was happening to her when she used her mutant powers. The medics, human and robotic keep telling him, nothing is wrong with her and that she'll be fine. He wanted to believe them, but his instincts were telling him differently.

There would be no more physical attacks for the moment. Shilloqwai and Metallicus were both temporarily out of commission. Reactivated, quicker than anyone would have expected, Metallicus couldn't resist a few verbal jabs at his dueling competitor. "So, I see our warrior princess is exhausted already. That's not a good sign for Humankind. The battle has barely begun."

"It's a little early to start foreshadowing a desired outcome." Excelcious retorted standing up for Shilloqwai. "As you so astutely pointed out, the battle has just begun! Do you realize the significance of what she just did? Showing a willingness to sacrifice herself for the good of Humankind, is going to go a long way in her gaining support. And she hasn't even tapped into the Power of Love yet!

"I will add that she just made friends with all of Humankind, uniting them with the robots. Together, we are going to terminate your ass!"

"I still don't see what the Power of Love has to do with the interplanetary war we're engaged in. So what? She has more shoulders to cry on? Big deal!"

"For our sake, I hope you remain blind to it. Since you don't understand the concept of love, you're not going to be able to comprehend the aspect of it that I'm about to explain to you. Humans know there is no greater Love than to lay down you r life for a friend. It took Shilloqwai a long time to understand this aspect of Love, and she was open to learning the meaning of it." Excelcious suddenly turned away from Metallicus, giving his attention instead to Shilloqwai, who was starting to come around. "How are you feeling Hon?"

"I feel fine. Just tell that babbling son-of-a-bitch to shut the hell up." Shilloqwai tried to prop herself up on one arm, so she could see what she'd done to the demon that was stalking Earth. Excelcious tried to get her to relax and lie back down. She did as he'd asked her. Before she had, she glared at Metallicus for a few seconds more. It was time enough for her to discharge another round of exploding shrapnel. The fragments all hit their target. This time pieces flew from Metallicus Nebuloso. He had started to fall apart, literally. That was insignificant to Shilloqwai. She had silenced him, in an involuntary attack, before passing out yet again. She was bleeding from her nose and her mouth yet again. Excelcious called for assistance to get her transported back to his lab. He would give her a medical exam there. When she came around this time, she was somewhat surprised to find herself on a medical bed. "Why am I here, Excelcious?"

"You passed out again, in your one-on-one duel with Metallicus."

"How did I do?"

"You bought us time, us meaning Humankind. Let's talk about you for a minute. Quite frankly babe, I'm worried about you. Every time you use your powers, especially as of late, your nose gets bloody. The last few times you've used your powers, you had blood coming from your mouth and your eyes too."

"I don't know what to do!" Shilloqwai sobbed. "What do you think I should do?"

"I'm leaving that up to you. I will support your decision, whatever you decide! Ultimately, you have to do what you feel is right in your heart!"

"I think I should do what I can for the benefit of all Humankind!"

"You're aware of the risks you're taking?"

"Yes! And I'm deeply saddened by the reality that we could lose each other. I love you Excelcious. In person or in spirit I will always be with you! Please forgive me for my decision to continue using my mutant powers. I've already proven I would die for you. I don't know any other way to show you how much I really love you. I also feel obligated to stand up for our freedoms, for my country and for Humankind. I'm sorry. It's the right thing to do."

"The right thing for me to do, is to stand by your side. We're in this fight together. Come hell or high water, we will stand side-by-side, till death do us part. I love you."

"So, was that an indirect marriage proposal?"

"It wasn't indirect. I was practicing for the day when we're standing side-by-side at the altar."

"So, you intend to marry me?"

"We're already engaged. And I didn't mean to imply intent. It's a promise of what I'm going to do! I'm in the process of finding you a ring."

"Kiss me!" She demanded. He willingly obliged. Exchanging affections, they got caught up in the moment. Thirty minutes later, they tumbled from Cloud #9 back down to reality. "You know," Shilloqwai began with a wry smile, "I forgot to tell that galactic asshole about the element of surprise."

"Under the rules of engagement, you're not obligated to tell him anything! And if you had told him, it wouldn't be a surprise when you spring the element on him "

"True! Given that he won't include variable factors into his battleplan, he's in for plenty of surprises. Yeah! Couple the variable factors that are bound to surface, along with the Power of Love, when it comes into play, and he's going to be the recipient of more surprises than he knows what to do with! The old saying of what you don't know, won't hurt you, will not apply in this instance, in regard to him. What he doesn't know, in regard to the surprises he's going to get, will likely end his existence. Oh shit! My headache! It won't go away! And my nose! Damn, it's bleeding again!"

"Are you all right Hon?" Excelcious asked her yet again."

"I'll be fine. We're going to fight through this together, hand-in-hand, side-by-side. I will meet you at the altar, even if it means being late for my own funeral!" Shilloqwai said tongue-in-cheek, with humor as dark as the situation they were presently facing.

THE UNIVERSAL LIE & THE BIG-BANG THEORY

[CHAPTER 15]

Single-handedly, Shilloqwai had nearly destroyed Metallicus Nebuloso on several occasions, passing out each time, while also bleeding from her nose and mouth, a consequence for using her mutant powers when she attacked him. Ongoing tests are expected to reveal the source of the apparent internal bleeding. Results are pending, while medical personnel are not speculating as to why the bleeding is occurring. Presently Shilloqwai's condition is listed as stable but guarded.

Meanwhile, Metallicus Nebuloso's recovery was quicker than anyone had anticipated. But the fact that his reparations and his refurbishing took place overnight was unfathomable. That explained the rainbow of light that engulfed him for eight hours of the night that had just passed. The light was beautifully enchanting, yet uncomfortably blinding, effectively making it hard to sleep, unless blinds or heavy curtains, were capable of blocking out that light, were covering the windows

Nevertheless, Shilloqwai and Excelcious were up early the next morning, and went out to greet him. There were no pleasantries exchanged, only bitter words, poisonous insults, and remarks full of cynicism. "So, how is the warrior princess this morning?" Metallicus asked, not concerned in the least if she was feeling well or not.

"I'm still pissed, thank you! I know you said that Earth's fate is sealed. Sometimes understanding the opposition's viewpoint can lead to solutions for unsolvable problems. It would help me to know more about your origins. You can cut to the chase and skip the part where you emerged from a galactic shit pile."

"Well-spoken for a glitch-bitch! How well versed are you on the Big Bang Theory? From the nothingness, came a massive galactic explosion. After the universal disturbance, from the nothingness, perfection evolved, ME!"

"If you are a model of perfection, then I'm crawling back under the pile that you came from so I can be reborn into a perfect state. Here's my theory as it applies to you. When you start with shit, that's what you end up with. No sugar-coating or gold-plating is going to change who or what you are at the core.

"How rude of me to interrupt, please continue. You were saying how perfection evolved from the nothingness after a Big Bang. However, it might be easier to listen to what you have to say if you stop spewing trash from your mechanical pie hole. I'm just hoping I don't get buried in the shit that I know will come out of your mouth. Again, I apologize for carrying on. I really would like to hear your interpretation of the Big Bang Theory!"

"It's quite simple. There's really no way to break it all down. After the Big Bang, that's when it all started, when everything was created. Things evolved from what they were then, to what they are now. The evolution will continue until the end of time as will the changes, which will shape the future, foreshadowing the way things might be! What about you, do you have any useful insight you'd care to share? It's hard to imagine that you would, I think you're more full of shit than you believe me to be!" Metallicus shot back.

"Your eyes are browner, and more opaque, my eyes are blue and transparent, so tell me again who is more full of shit?" Shilloqwai retorted. "I think that would be you! In regard to the Big Bang Theory, let me see if I understand you correctly before I share with you, my beliefs. So, at some point in time there was this random explosion, the Big Bang if you will! And then, all of blooming creation came into existence! Damn! That's truly amazing!"

"And everything that came from that was perfect. The way it was meant to be!" Boasted Metallicus.

"So, in your expert opinion, what corrupted perfection?" Shilloqwai prodded.

"Humans, of course!" Metallicus answered simply, believing he was unmistakably right.

"Interesting, because according to you, everything came from , and evolved from the Big Bang Theory! Would that not include humans? It should." Shilloqwai reasoned. "So, what made humans imperfect?"

"Evolution, something happened as life evolved that made them imperfect!"

"What exactly? You're talking out of your ass! Humans didn't just appear out of nowhere at a random point in time! And life didn't just come into being. Do you have something better to offer? And how would you go about explaining human imperfection?"

"Mutations! It's natural for all living things to mutate at some point. Mutations are generally thought of as something bad. In humans, they generally are. I don't mean to imply that all humans have mutated, or that they suffer from some congenital abnormality. But mutations do occur in the cells during human development, and the mutations are generally responsible for birth defects that occur. On occasion, if a mother who is carrying a child becomes sick with a serious illness, mutations are subject to occur as well." Metallicus reasoned, using mutations as a reason to justify his AI Force's murdering humans.

"According to you then," Shilloqwai was asking for clarification, "it stands to reason then, these mutant children, or children that are born with defects should be killed, since they are in some way deformed, making them imperfect? That's where your logic is flawed. Mutations can also be good. One example would be stronger immune systems able to fight off disease." Shilloqwai argued. "You assume that babies born with defects, cannot be cared for and be loved like 'normal children.' In actuality that is the furthest thing from the truth! Love them, and they will love you back. Who are you to judge who should live and who should die? God is the only one with the right to pass judgement on anyone! He created life, all life!"

"Did this God of yours emerge from the Big Bang theory too? How come I don't know about this God of yours?"

"Because! You've never read the Bible!"

"I'm sure the book is stored in my data banks somewhere. I've never bothered to review it!"

"Not that you'd have a reason to. But since you're hell-bent on destroying things God created, you might want to take a look at it. Perhaps, it will have an impact on the remainder of your existence, the actions you take, or refrain from taking."

"You still haven't revealed to me your theory of how everything came into being!" Metallicus stated, pretending to want to hear what Shilloqwai had to say.

"It's not a theory. It's a reality!" Shilloqwai reasoned. "The story of creation is in the Book of Genesis, the first book in the Bible. The story tells of how God created the world in six days and rested on the seventh, after seeing all He had created was good. The Bible says that God created man in His own image. God is, was and always shall be. And all of God's creations were made out of love. So, in destroying Humankind, you are destroying God's children, and, so too, you are destroying Love!"

"So, if I understand you correctly," Metallicus asked, paraphrasing Shilloqwai's words for clarification, "God created everything out of nothingness? This Power of Love, of which you speak, created the universe and all things in it?"

"You've almost got it right. God is Love, and he loves us unconditionally forgiving us for our wrongdoings, all we have to do is ask and our transgressions will be forgiven."

"What if I want to find this God you speak of? Can I see Him, do you see Him?"

"No, I don't. Some people claim to have seen Him. He reveals Himself to us and helps us all in different ways. We have to have faith, have hope and live in Love. In the end only Love will remain, and you are not Love, you will be destroyed." Shilloqwai warned.

"But if there are medical and scientific explanations for everything, then you should be able to prove to me that there is a God."

"Using science and medicine, prove to me that there isn't a God!" Shilloqwai challenged.

"So, you're telling me that anything is possible through Love, and that God is Love! Am I hearing you right?" Metallicus wanted clarification.

"That's the first thing you've said right since we started arguing! The fact that I have to agree with you, makes me want to puke!"

"What, the truth hurts?" Metallicus taunted.

"No! Just the fact that we agree on anything makes me sick you evil bastard! And just to set the record straight, God is capable of doing things that cannot be explained through medicine or science. Humankind calls these things miracles. It may take a miracle to beat you, but Earth's people will defeat you using the Power of Love."

"So, you're telling me this God I cannot see is going to help Humankind defeat me? That's laughable." Metallicus responded, shunning Shilloqwai's every word.

"Yes, and the fact that you cannot see God, is a testament to how blind you really are! Look around at God's creations, look at Humankind, not for its imperfections, but for the beauty that lies within. There is beauty in everything. Perhaps there is beauty in even you. I've yet to see it. But take a look and you will see that Love is all around. God is perfect, you are not. At least not in a good way. You are, however, a perfect antagonist, you're responsible for poisoning the Earth, not humans! We're really not getting anywhere with this argument. Let me try a different approach!" Shilloqwai pivoted.

"Coming around to my way of thinking? Changing your position, are you?"

"Not in the least!" Shilloqwai responded, standing her ground. "And if you call what you're doing, thinking, keep doing it, because your shit-brained way of thinking is actually helping unify Humankind."

"What evidence do you have to support that man was created by a greater power outside of the Big Bang theory? In general, what evidence do you have to support that the Big Bang Theory wasn't the start of it all?"

"Glad you framed your questions that way! In answer to the general question of how did it all start, we'll apply basics of statistics and probabilities. Let me ask you this first! After this alleged random Big Bang, what do you think the odds are of the planets lining up the way they have? The gravitational pull, the ebb and flow of the tide; it just seems that there's an order to it all, a universal organized chaos if you will! I have a hard time believing that order of any kind emerged from a random blast! Evolution, things change over time I get that. Wouldn't you think a seismic blast is more likely to destroy things than create them?

"Getting back to the basics of life, taking God out of the equation, you would have to agree that life came about after the Big Bang Theory. The stars had to line up right, in order for it to happen. And you're saying when it did happen, there was a magic moment when everything was zapped into life! Speculative bullshit, and you know it! You just told me there's a scientific and or medical reason for everything. A random blast doesn't do it for me. How did all of the species, including humans, end up with male and female, opposites yet compatible, come together to procreate? I'll tell you how!" Shilloqwai chided him.

"Let's go back to talking about science, Biology 101! I'm sure this science is somewhere in your database. You should first review what a cell is. The science will tell you that no living cell can come from anything but another living cell. This ends the age-old argument of which came first, the chicken or the egg? The chicken obviously came first, or there would be nothing to lay the eggs. In the Bible, which you refuse to acknowledge as a credible source, it says that God created all life. Science also tells you that you should consider all possibilities when theorizing about anything. It is the responsibility of the scientist to eliminate possibilities based on the facts that are uncovered. Science has yet to eliminate the possibility that there is a God Almighty!"

"Like I said before you can't prove that there is a God!" Metallicus argued, still refusing to consider the evidence Shilloqwai was presenting.

"No, but science shows that there is more evidence to support the existence of the Omniscient One, than there is to rule out the existence of a Love Almighty."

"You still have no absolute proof to support your argument, which I believe is why I think you are the one that is, full of shit!"

"I would rather gamble that there is a God and live in the Power of Love, than deny his existence, for which the punishment is eternal damnation! If you attempt to exterminate Humankind, you will be damned for all time!" Shilloqwai warned.

"As you will, for helping to bring my wrath on all of Humankind." Metallicus arrogantly shot back!

"Just know that you cannot call yourself perfect if your files have not been updated. You will be lost in time and become but a memory of what once was! By your own admission, you haven't updated your files, as an inadvertent consequence, some files can become corrupt. How can you accurately run analysis and purge your files if some may be corrupt? And you dare to say you are still perfect? You're a damn liar, and a damn fool. By your own parameters, you should be terminated."

"A simple update, is all it will take to restore me." Metallicus boasted.

"Sorry, technology doesn't wait for anyone, not even for you." Shilloqwai reminded him. "Even with the most current updates, you'll always be a step behind! As you think you've become current, technology continues evolving into something more cutting edge. You never were perfect, and you never will be!"

"You talk about wanting to be cutting edge, then why are you hanging on to an ancient home remedy, you know, this thing called Love?" Metallicus retorted mockingly.

"Let me try to explain something to you about love!" Shilloqwai said, exuding much patience. "Love has no alpha, no omega. It always was, it is here and now, and it always will be! But you, you came in with a Big Bang, and I assure you, you will go out the same way!"

"Silence Bitch! I'm through arguing with you!"

"I was so done with you a long time ago. I've got a few 'B' words for you, BASTARD! It's more than a saying, the BIGGER they are the harder they fall. You're a giant to me! And when you fall, and you will fall, count on it, you're going to go BOOM!" Shilloqwai threatened him, before going on the offensive. Again, without warning, on demand and at will, shrapnel flew from her eyes and tore into Metallicus Nebuloso. It was one of several times she'd recently attacked him.

This time, he came crashing to the ground, much to her delight, and everyone else's! The epicenter was a mere tremor, registering around 4.7 on the Richter Scale. Shilloqwai expected a much harder fall from this giant bucket of bolts. The lightning bolts that flew from her fingertips French-fried him. "You really are Hot Shit!" She quipped, watching him convulse on the ground as he was being zapped. Mr. Perfect was vulnerable and not the invincible beast he claimed to be, came an afterthought!

The question now was, what were his weaknesses? She would work with Excelcious and try to figure it out. "How do you feel?" Excelcious asked, running up to her to see that she was okay.

"I feel fine, don't tell me, I'm bleeding again!"

"Just a little this time, and only from the nose!"

"Thank God! I don't have the headaches or the dizziness like I've experienced in times past when I've used my powers. As much as I'm concerned about the bleeding after my mutant episodes, I'm more concerned about finding a way to destroy him. I get that he's not human. He's absorbed my best shots! If there's a way to take him down, there's a way to take him out too!" Shilloqwai reasoned. "He thinks that he's perfect, we need to find a way to convince him that he's not! If we could find a remote way to reprogram him, maybe we…" Shilloqwai pondered.

"I've tried it. He's got some sort of anti-viral protection that neutralizes attempts to hack into his database." Excelcious explained. "It was my intent to try and corrupt his files. My DDD weapons are ineffective against him. But your…"

"Do you think any of those weapons you designed to replicate the shrapnel that comes from my eyes would be effective against him?" Shilloqwai wondered. "I mean why wouldn't it work on him?"

"In theory the weapons should work on him." Excelcious agreed. "I can try to upgrade them, yes! But even with the upgrades, I still can't generate the energy or replicate the force of your mutant powers." Excelcious lamented.

"Their forces are superior to ours. Do you really think there's a way we can beat them?" Shilloqwai was beginning to second-guess their chances of survival.

"I'm not giving up until we're both dead!" A determined Excelcious proclaimed. "At that point I won't need to worry about it! I'll be in God's hands then, living up in the City of Gold!" Shilloqwai laughed wryly.

"Let's hope that doesn't happen just yet. We have a future together. He'll be up and running in the morning! We have 12 hours, give, or take a few! So, what's the plan? I know you have one, care to share it with me?" Shilloqwai asked intriguingly, anxiously anticipating his answer.

"Well, our objective is to save as much of Earth's civilization as we can!

"Obviously. So how do we go about doing that? Ten, maybe 12 hours doesn't leave us a lot of time!"

"Good news, and a little bit of a surprise for me. I got word this morning that the tunnel project is finished. All of the gateways are open.

We have and escape fleet ready to launch. There are enough vehicles to transport the world's populous! But the fleet will be launched, only as a last resort!"

"Do you think we'll end up launching the fleet?"

"Without question. We've thrown everything we have at the AI Bots and we're losing ground. I think we'll be making our last stand from underground before we eventually have to flee."

"Sounds adventurous. Kind of scary though that we have to abandon the Earth."

"It might be the only chance we have to survive!" Excelcious lamented.

"So, what do you think? Will we have a home to come back to?" Shilloqwai wondered out loud.

"Look down this tunnel." Excelcious instructed her as he took her to a corridor she'd never before been to.

"I can't see anything at the other end. The light is so bright. What's behind there?"

"It's a portal of some sort. We've sent probes through there." Excelcious began explaining. "And from above ground we've sent a small transport equipped with a circumference cam. Data sent from the probes and the circumference cam indicate there's a place on the other side that can support human life."

"Have you ever been to this place? From the breathtaking photos, it looks like paradise. Ice mountains, wildlife, exotic plant life, beautiful flowers, almost like Earth!" Shilloqwai observed.

"It is in a lot of ways! Except the planet, whatever it's called, is three times the size of the Earth, and has three times the amount of water."

"How did you get the probes back?" Shilloqwai asked curiously.

"I didn't. I tried to do it remotely and bring them back the way they were sent. They exploded. I don't know if there's a way back. As far as I can tell, this place we might be going to, will forever be our new home!" Excelcious regretfully informed her.

"That's not going to change our plans, is it?" Shilloqwai wondered.

"It's not going to change our plans to get married. If that's what you meant. It's not going to change our future together either. Forever our hearts will beat as one." Excelcious promised her.

"I love you Excelcious. Home is where the heart is, and my heart is with you always."

"And mine with you, Love! Always!" Not having a lot of time for each other as of late, they took the opportunity to exchange sweet affections in the form of a mad flurry of kisses. The flurry left them both breathless and thirsting for more.

"I almost feel guilty for taking time for this!" Shilloqwai confessed.

"What if this was our last chance to show each other how much we love each other?" Excelcious asked rhetorically, reminding her of the imminent dangers ahead. His remark sparked another flurry of kisses she hoped would never end.

"How long before project SAFEHAVEN is secured for lockdown?"

"A month, maybe two!"

"Do we have that long? So, if we used the Dragonships? How much time would it take to complete the evacuations then? I mean shouldn't we start getting these people underground before the panic sets in? The shuttles are so fast, why can't we use them to help with the evacuations while we have the chance!"

"Damn! I've been so caught up in everything, I never thought of that!" Excelcious made a few phone calls, and all available shuttles were off of the ground and flying. Project SAFEHAVEN is already underway, a project designed to get everyone to safety underground where we will make our last stand before fleeing if need be! If all goes well, we might be able to do it in 12 hours. That would be pushing it, but if we can pull it off, everyone would be relatively safe before the next attack."

"Let's get on it then! Excelcious, you and I haven't had a lot of time for each other. While you've been busy, I've been checking up on some things and I found something that I want to share with you." Shilloqwai told him in confidence.

"Is this a good thing?"

"Depends how you look at it! It helped me come to an understanding about a couple of things, including a better understanding of myself!"

"Interesting, go on. You've got my attention."

"I was straightening up a few things in the lab and I found that old box I delivered to you when I first got promoted to liaison between Robots and Humankind. I found a binder in it on Skeletos Amoris Puro, the one who helped save me through the Power of Love. I was reading through it, and I found that his name means 'Down to the bones' or Basic love, pure love! The Humans who built him, Valentino Amoris, and Onshanda Puro, gave him that name, their names, before Robotikis murdered them."

"So, I don't see the connection. What does that have to do with you?"

"Before Robotikis terminated him, Skeletos did some research on his own and dug into my family history. Included in it is the meaning of my name. I wish there was more in it about my family. Other than the meaning of my name, there wasn't a whole lot there!"

"I'm sure it's something very beautiful. It's only fitting for a woman with the name SHILLOQWAI!"

"I'm sure you'll see it as fitting for me. Shilloqwai means anointed one, dedicated one, and compassionate warrior."

"You definitely fit the part, you're very loving. The compassionate warrior, killing with a purpose, and anointed one, you were meant to do what you're doing. You go girl! And dedicated one, you are to me and to your quest, fighting for love and life, both worthy causes."

"All along, I've been so afraid of losing you, Excelcious." Shilloqwai admitted tearfully. "Generally speaking, I'm not afraid anymore. In all of my recent premonitions, the outcomes have been good. We're going to win this war. I feel the Power of Love is behind us now. You know how we always talk about there's a reason in life for everything. I know what my purpose in life is now. I've asked for the strength, and that God's will, be done. With your support and everyone else's we're going to win this war. That doesn't tell us much about our future, whatever happens, I know I'm going to end up in a good place! What about your name, Excelcious? Do you know what it means?"

"It means strong, innovative, loving and loyal one."

"It's fitting for you. Now I know why we get along so well." She said following up her words with a kiss. "We were meant for each other." He reciprocated. "Let's just get through this shit, so we can take a nice long trip to paradise to celebrate our victory."

"Agreed," Excelcious concurred. "Where were we?"

"Are you talking about business or pleasure?" Shilloqwai asked, hoping for the latter.

"Business!" Excelcious stated matter-of-factly, to her disappointment. "Well, I think we're about as ready as we'll ever be! Now we just wait to make our move. Earth's civilization is armed, locked, and loaded!"

"Sadly, there will be casualties." Shilloqwai observed. "The hope is that most will survive, robots and humans alike. If we can pull it off, it will be the greatest of all escapes. The aliens have proven to be a formidable, even a superior force, yet they've shown their vulnerability, Metallicus Nebuloso, included! There's got to be a way to destroy that perfect asshole! We've got it right Excelcious." Shilloqwai continued. We can beat him with the Power of Love. It's like we told him. When it comes to love, people do unpredictable things not just for it, but to keep it. People introduce variable factors into situations, factors he'll ignore. All it takes is one mistake to lose a war, and he's already made it by refusing to consider how variable factors have the ability to influence outcomes. It's hard to imagine what a new Earth will look like!"

"Heavenly!" Excelcious said in a word. "The Power of Love is sure to have His say in any 2nd Genesis of Earth."

"True, Love gave me a second chance. I'm sure He didn't do all of this for me to have me die as a martyr for a failed cause. I'm not sure how we're going to save this world. I'm trusting my faith, keeping hope that Love will find a way. Any adjustments to the game plan?" Shilloqwai wondered.

"Nothing has really changed much." Excelcious said matter-of-factly. "We stay on the defensive as we have been. Once we burrow in, we can be a little more aggressive. By the time they realize that we've gone underground, they'll have to come down and find us. There are only so many entry points. They have to find those first. If we post guards at those points, the first waves they send after us should be easy pickin's. The hard part will be finishing them off when they start sending in the 2nd, 3rd and fourth waves."

"So, what if we can't escape them, because something goes wrong with the plan?"

"Some things are worth dying for. And if that should happen, we fight to the bitter end. We don't have to throw in the towel when things start to get dicey. We take calculated risks, not unnecessary ones. We are rebels fighting for a cause. Some of us will become martyrs."

Shilloqwai was trying to remain optimistic, but the tears in her eyes showed just how much the truth was hurting her. She knew the world could be cruel. Only now was she just starting to realize how cold the world could be, even though she knew it was wrapped in Love.

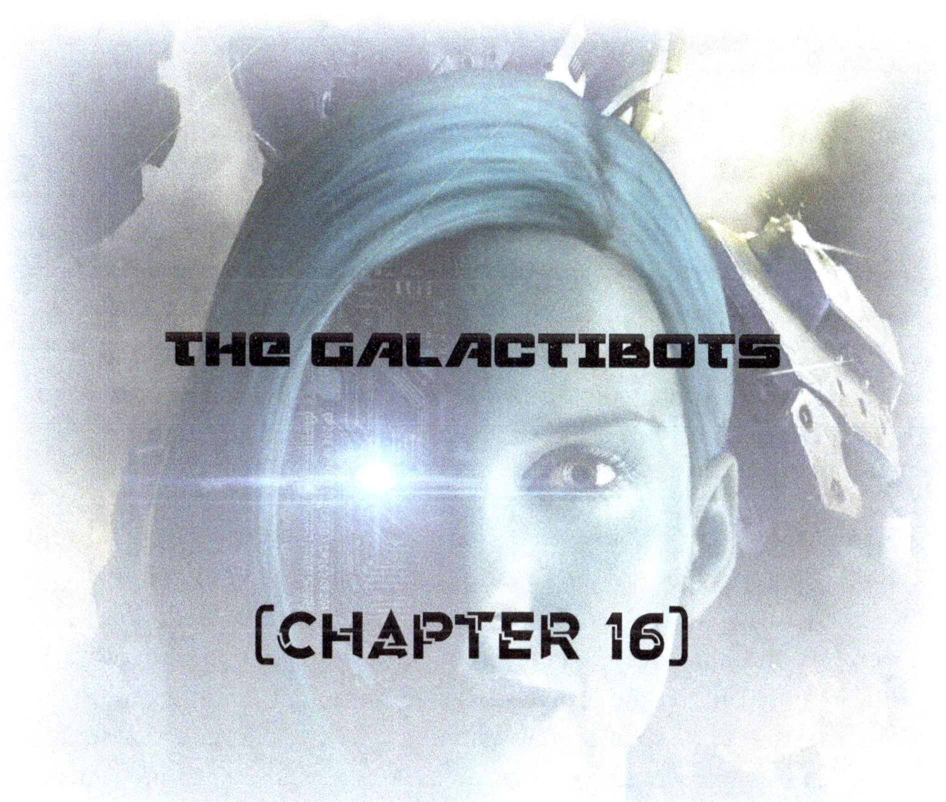

THE GALACTIBOTS

[CHAPTER 16]

Excelcious and Shilloqwai thought they had devised a sound battle plan. It was being implemented on a global scale. Thanks to the Dragonships, the evacuations to the underground were completed in 10 hours and 49 minutes. Thankfully, most heeded the advice to seek shelter. Because, when the next round of attacks came, they were far greater than anyone had anticipated. Previous attacks were meant to create chaos. They effectively had, primarily by instilling fear into Humankind. The efforts were an attempt to coerce humans and get them to surrender to the alien forces attacking them. Humankind wasn't ready to give up the fight and succumb to the robot bullying especially not to the AI Forces trying to destroy them.

The attacks they were being subject to now were far more aggressive, far more invasive, far more violent and with deadlier force than the ones they had withstood. Earth's resistance was starting to crack, leaving the rebels to wonder how much longer they could hold out against the AI Force. Everything the Galactibots touched was being decimated, pummeled into smithereens without discrimination. Even humans were being obliterated into cosmic dust!

It's not that the humans were standing petrified, waiting for the mechanical killers to harvest them. When they tried to flee, the Galactibots pursued them until their escape efforts had been thwarted and their lives ended. The Earthen robots trying to get between the humans and their attackers were terminated with ease. The Orbitoids, though stronger were easily defeated too!

The DDD weapons that had been adequate in prior attacks, were proving to be sub-par in recent ones. Excelcious and his people were working on upgrades and modifications they thought might maximize the weaponry they had, largely increasing their effectiveness. These efforts had been put on hold since the evacuation process had gotten underway. At this point, sheltering the people was more important than upgrading the arms that they bore. Excelcious was hoping for a break in the action so that he and his people would have time to make the necessary improvements to their weaponry. In the meantime, he and Shilloqwai were praying to the powers that be, while waiting for the Power of Love to work His magic. Excelcious had done a lot of work ahead of time, orchestrating, manufacturing, distributing, and implementing the use of new drones and self-defense systems. If he hadn't done so, he was convinced Humankind would have been pummeled into submission by now.

The fact that Earth's Civilization was holding its own, didn't take away from the horror of the brutal attacks. The people couldn't help the sacrificial victims who had already been massacred. They knew they were taking a massive blood bath, they hoped and prayed they weren't the next to get bathed in that regard. Continuing at this pace it would drown out civilization.

The aliens were showing total disregard for the most precious commodity in the celestial universe, an invaluable intragalactic treasure, LIFE! Finally, Humankind got the break it was looking for. A reprieve, as the unprovoked attacks had stopped, at least temporarily! Excelcious and Shilloqwai instructed the others to stay put, they wanted to go to the surface and take a look around. Both were shocked at what they'd found. First, things they were all too familiar with, had become nearly unrecognizable!

Taking for example the 15-foot shit pile, from which Excelcious claimed Shilloqwai! It had been reduced from a 15-foot mountain of trash to a 30-foot crater with a 30-foot radius. The crater was previously only 6-foot deep, while the circumference remained the same. Half of the Robotix lab had been reduced to a small pile of rubble. Shilloqwai couldn't help but wonder how many of her former coworkers had been terminated in the attack.

Then she wondered if Robotikis had survived, termination and, or incineration. He was such an asshole anyway. What did it matter if he'd been terminated, he richly deserved it, came an afterthought! "Damn!" Shilloqwai cursed, first realizing the haunting reality of what had actually taken place.

"I wonder if the rest of the world looks like this?" Excelcious asked out loud! "Holy Hell! To say this is a warzone, is a gross understatement." He continued verbalizing his thoughts. Shilloqwai nodded in agreement, wondering what the casualty reports would reveal, as they had started coming in from around the world.

The casualty numbers for both the robots and humans seemed astoundingly high. Shilloqwai and Excelcious became more alarmed when they learned that estimates were on the conservative side and would probably go much higher! How could this be? They wondered! They had the perfect plan, they thought. They got more disparaging news, learning that as many as 2,000,000 people may have been killed! An investigation would be conducted to find out why this was so, but according to initial reports, many of the people resisted evacuation orders to the underground. Robots were terminated trying to protect those people.

Shilloqwai and Excelcious initially thought that perhaps the robots had failed in their Prime Directive; save the people while following Asimov's Laws. The data coming in also alleged that during the heaviest attacks, the robots refused to let the people into the tunnels that led to the underground. This infuriated Excelcious even more until he learned the reasoning behind the robot actions.

The robots feared they'd give away the secret as to where the rest of the world had disappeared, believing they had justifiable cause to disregard Asimov's laws. It wasn't often Shilloqwai and Excelcious agreed with robots going rogue, but in this instance, the two of them thought the robots' actions were heroic. They also learned that the AI Forces got lucky and were able, in some instances, to prevent civilians from getting to the Dragonships. Among the casualties were 1,000's trying to escape via plane to join families in other parts of the country, or other parts of the world. The planes were already en route when the attacks began. Many of those planes were shot out of the sky. Then the digital photos started coming in. Men, women, children all of whom had lost their precious lives in the brutal attacks.

"You know what, I'll be right back!"

"Where are you going?" He asked, thinking Shilloqwai lost it, as she had run off into the disaster area. She never responded, at least not with a satisfactory answer. Instinctively, it seemed she just took off running through the warzone. It didn't appear to him that she knew where she was running to. And she was running from the only place in the immediate area she had to hide. Excelcious never questioned her motives, though he thought she was insane for just leaving him . Still, he believed she had good reason for doing so! There seemed to be something haunting in the promise that she'd return. The chilling echoes of her somber goodbye were still lingering in the air, this added to the uneasiness he was feeling.

Though he trusted her judgement, he was moderately perturbed, that she hadn't told him where she was going. Restricting her independence was not why he wanted to know. He feared something might happen and he wanted to know where to find her if it had. He wished that she'd stayed at his side, so he was in a position to protect her. How could he protect her if he didn't know where she was? The last he saw of her she was running in the direction of the Robotix lab. Presumably, that's where she was headed. Minutes later, Excelcious was glaring, still gazing in the direction of what remained standing of the Robotix lab. From outside of his front door, about a mile away, the lab looked like a ruined castle up on the hill. But the heavily damaged lab is not what he was looking at. He was staring in that direction as though he were telepathically trying to summon Shilloqwai home. After almost convincing himself that she was going to be okay, he breathed a guarded sigh of relief and retreated to the confines of his house.

It hadn't been cleaned in weeks. There wasn't much difference between how the inside of his house looked and the warzone. He thought trying to save the world was more than reason enough to neglect his housekeeping duties. Meanwhile, he was back to giving orders and setting up rendezvous points in the tunnels and the hollows of the underground.

During the reprieve, evacuations for surviving stragglers resumed, while Humankind was being shuffled about to the most secure locations. Operation SAFEHAVEN was fully implemented.

Remaining inhabitants still roaming Earth's surface, would be brought down to the underground to join the others. All would adapt and assimilate to the fabricated underground world that had been prepared for them. A world created, intended to house, and shelter. This was supposed to be a temporary thing until the dangers from above had passed. The occupancy of the underground world would remain indefinite. The remote possibility existed, this subterranean world would become a permanent home for Humankind. Though Excelcious hoped that wouldn't be the case, he had a contingency plan in place for the worst-case scenario. Shilloqwai meanwhile, entered the lab through the ruins. She was hoping to find something salvageable that she could take with her back to the underground. One of the newer techs recognized her from a previous visit. "Bitch is back! What should we do with her?" Asked one of the Nubee service techs.

"Listen Nubee. I ain't your bitch! And nobody will be doing anything with me but fighting a losing battle if they don't listen to and adhere to my demands. I don't have time to waste. I need to see Robotikis! Now! Take me to him!" She demanded.

"Better at this time, that we bring him to you!" Said the robot service tech who volunteered to retrieve The Global Leader. Shilloqwai shot a smile of satisfaction his way, letting the robot know she appreciated his change in demeanor. She was equally gracious for his expedient return. She thought it curious that Robotikis had not announced his arrival with a mouthful of profanity. As the Nubee approached her she understood why.

"Here's what's left of him! Your Highness!" The Nubee said presenting Robotikis' head to her on a golden platter.

"If you know what's good for you, you'll quit patronizing me, you mechanical little shit! What the hell is this? Can someone please explain this to me? Anybody?"

"Isn't it obvious? He's been incinerated, all except for his head. As many times as you've threatened him, it's amazing that you weren't the one to terminate him!" Interjected Megabits, the new lead tech. Megabits took Kinks' job after Shilloqwai destroyed him during one of her temper tantrums.

"You know, the lot of you is really pissing me off with your smartass comments! I'm not playing with you! One more by any of you and you'll all end up like Robotikis, except after I terminate you there will be nothing left of you to put on a platter! Start talking, now!"

"A lot of us were terminated in the last AI attack including Robotikis!" Megabits said reluctantly giving in to Shilloqwai's demands.

"So, who's in charge?" Shilloqwai demanded to know!

"There's a list for crisis situations such as these! Protocol says we go down the list in sequential order to determine who will assume the duties of Commander and Chief. The top nine were terminated in the last attack. There's a meeting in the war room down the hall. The Robotix council is trying to decide if candidate number 10 should be allowed to step into the role of the acting Global Leader!" Megabits informed her.

"Who is it? And what's the issue?"

"Technically, you were in the 10-slot. You're eligibility is in question, given the fact that you have allegedly transformed into a human. No one believes that bullshit anyway. The real issue is if a murdering robot should be placed in such a leadership position." Megabits enlightened her in a most unflattering way.

"On the contrary! Under the circumstances, I am assuming the position as World Leader until a new one is selected, something that will be dealt with after the crisis has passed. The fact that I have temporarily resumed my role as liaison-diplomat for human-robot relations, makes me the obvious candidate, the perfect choice to fill the role. It is out of great respect for that son-of-a-bitch, Robotikis, that I step into this position where I have an opportunity to serve all of Humankind! My only regret about this unfortunate set of circumstances is that I didn't get a chance to say goodbye to him before his termination. I'm especially upset that I didn't get to do the honors of kicking his ass out of this world!"

"But if you're not a robot, by who's authority do you assume the position as World Leader?" Megabits asked, continuing to grill her.

"Asimov's laws, rule #2! And if you continue to give me a bad time, and you don't start following my orders I will terminate your ass!"

"Yes ma'am!"

"Take me to the situation room, now!" She wasn't planning on making a grand entrance, but there were some in the room that recognized her. Her presence made them uncomfortable. "Oh shit!" One of them remarked. "We have a crisis on top of a crisis!"

"That's exactly why I'm here!" Shilloqwai enlightened them.

"Where's Robotikis when you need him?" Remarked another.

"All right! Cut the bullshit everybody! And listen up! Until a new Global Leader can be appointed, according to protocol, I am temporarily the Commander and Chief."

"I'm not listening to this bitch!" Yet another, rudely interrupted her. Shilloqwai glared at her target. A round of shrapnel shot from her eyes, instantly incinerating the insolate robot! He was reduced to a pile of fried circuitry and metal melt.

"As you can see, I have zero tolerance for disrespect. Are there still questions as to who is in charge?" Shilloqwai rhetorically asked, getting the respect she had commanded. It was clear she had also gotten the attention of all remaining in the room. "As I was saying, due to the untimely passing of our beloved World Leader, I have assumed that role according to protocol. A new leader will be chosen after we get through this crisis. Until then I am the acting interim leader and I expect Asimov's laws to be adhered to down to the letter. Are there any questions?" The room fell silent. There wasn't a whir, a buzz, a blip, or a bleep from a single bucket of nuts and bolts in the room.

"The rumor that Robotikis has been incinerated, is just that. A rumor that has no merit. So, I can't actually believe you bought into that line of bullshit! You know Robotikis is going to hang your ass for this attempted mutiny, don't you?"

"Are you talking about this Robotikis?" Shilloqwai asked, holding up the golden platter with Robotikis' head on it! Look, just because it is the general belief of robots that humans are stupid, remember who created you. Humans outsmarted themselves when they allowed for everything to become automated. And that's how robots managed to become rulers of the world. Don't forget that! I'm warning you all for the last time, the next bucket of nuts-and-bolts circuitry that tries to bullshit me will be reduced to metal melt with shaved filings for topping. I'm done playing around, DAMNIT! I came out from hiding underground to see if anything could be salvaged from the Robotix lab, that Humankind can use to its benefit. Or anything that the robots can use to protect humans, their Prime Objective.

"Humankind has built a tunnel system, presently being used to protect its civilization and its assets. Evacuations to the tunnels, are continuing as we speak. Sadly, data is showing now that nearly 3,000,000 people have been massacred by the AI Forces. They're not going to stop until all of us are destroyed, robots and humans alike. We'll be safe in this tunnel system, at least for a while. It has been under construction for quite some time, but it is finished now! The tunnel system and the fabricated underground world intended to sustain us, is meant to be a temporary arrangement, until it is deemed safe for all to return to the surface. Should the tunnel system, and, or the underground world be breeched by the AI Forces, an emergency plan will be put in place to deal with that scenario too! Until then, our objective is to clear the surface of the Earth. It is the hope that the AI Forces would then just go away.

"That's asking a bit much. Given the aggressiveness and the tenacity they've shown as of late, it is expected that they will come looking for us, all of us. We intend to be ready for them when they do. And when they find us, we hope we can ambush them and hit them with the element of surprise. Given the superiority of their forces, we need every advantage we can get. This is no time for playing around. I've risked my existence by coming back for you! I want straight answers to my questions from this point forward. And if none of you are willing to help, then to hell with you all! Anyone brave enough to step forward and brief me? I need to know what in the hell is going on. This isn't about me! It's for the sake of Humankind!"

"Yeah, bitch whatever?" Shilloqwai immediately blasted the rogue robot into oblivion. The room became deathly silent.

"Apparently, there are still some among you that think this is a game. Life isn't a game! It is a gift that needs to be respected always, from the moment of conception to the rebirth and passage into eternal life. I can, and I will destroy this room with a single blast of energy, if I so desire. If you don't believe me, try me. I'll happily, and illustriously demonstrate my point. This is the last chance, if no one comes forward to help me and explain to me what I'm seeing on these monitors, I will leave you to fend for yourselves. Your termination will be inevitable. If you think I give a shit what you decide? I don't. I really don't. I came here to see if I could recruit added protection for Humankind, that's all! If you come with me, I can guarantee your existence will be extended, though I can't promise for how long! I can promise you'll last longer in the underground tunnels than you will up here! So, are there any among you that wishes to come forward?"

The room fell silent, as the robots collectively held their mechanical breath! They were waiting to see if Shilloqwai would follow through on her threats. Then, a soft -spoken female robot came forward. "I am LaShyra. I will help you!" She generously volunteered. It was because she genuinely wanted to help, not because she felt pressured. She knew there was going to be backlash and she would take the brunt of it. She didn't care. She believed she'd chosen to do the right thing. "Thank you for stepping up! I'm Shilloqwai!"

"I know who you are. You're a superhero to Humankind and an idol among the majority of us in the robot world, though most won't admit it. I am honored to have the opportunity to serve under your command.

I will fight to the end of my existence for your quest to save Humankind. It is a noble one. In human terms, it is one worth dying for." LaShyra elaborated, vowing her loyalty. "Before all hell broke loose, I was being groomed to replace you. Having actually met you, I can see I have big shoes to fill!"

"Thank you, I appreciate your support, loyalty, and respect! But don't put me on a pedestal!" Shilloqwai warned. "You have my loyalty and support as well. I have the utmost respect for you, showing the valor that you did in coming forward. In fighting together for a common cause, our contributions will go a long way toward saving an invaluable gift, LIFE! The Power of Love will guide us in our efforts!"

"It seems amazing, what little I know about Love, but I've seen many good things happen because of it!"

"We can discuss that topic later. Tell me, what am I seeing here up on these global monitors?"

"There are four monitors. One for the side of the world where it is daytime, and one for the side of the world where it is nighttime. The other two monitors show the Arctic and Antarctic Circles. One is enjoying daylight while the other is immersed in the darkness of night. As you can see, the areas of the world where it is dark, are currently being bombarded by the AI Forces."

"Explain the colors I'm seeing in the areas under attack."

"The DDD weapons' tracking system, as you know, allows us to see the enemy, the Earth robots, and the humans. The purple shows the DDD weaponry is active. The enemy is in black. The Red shows the Earthen robot forces, while the blue, shows Humankind. All the colors are represented by splotches or dots. Splotches indicate there are clusters of the various groups, while dots indicate where individuals of a specific group are. Green dots or clusters represent Earthen casualties, while white dots or clusters indicate alien casualties.

Shilloqwai didn't like what she was seeing on the screens showing the areas currently under attack. There was lots of green, lots of black and very little white! In terms of numbers, Shilloqwai could see the black forces had a distinct advantage over the red and blue forces combined. "It appears we're getting our asses kicked!"

"More accurately," LaShyra confirmed, "we're getting the living shit kicked out of us! In addition to the heavy loss of life we're suffering, we're sustaining, an exorbitant amount of collateral damage. The air, the water and the land are being littered and poisoned with all things war!"

"So, what do the pink and gray dots and clusters represent?"

"Those are the people and robots that have found safety at the subterranean level!"

"How do you know all of this shit?"

"I told you I was being trained to take the position vacated when you were forced out. Sounds stupid, coming from a robot, but I have haunches, and instincts. I listen and really hear. I learn things, I theorize and hypothesize. I use calculations and analyses before I draw any conclusions. From the data gathered, I decide what options will provide humans with the best chances for survival, in crisis situations and then act in accordance with Asimov's Laws before implementing my game plan. "You'll be surprised to learn that Robotikis and I had only one argument after he tried to double-cross me. I won the argument and threatened to terminate him if he interfered with my quest again. From that moment on, we were in total agreement on everything. It was strange to me. I acted in the same way you would have done. He trusted me over you, that was the only difference from what I could see. Don't get me wrong, he was the biggest asshole I ever met!" Shilloqwai and LaShyra shared an instant of laughter, before getting back to business.

"Damn!" Shilloqwai cursed. "I didn't realize so many people got trapped outside the tunnels."

"We'll try to save as many as we can. At the current rate of termination and extermination, I estimate that the Earth's surface will be wiped clean of Humankind in 72.09875 hours. I can't estimate how long Humankind can survive at the subterranean level. Depends how long it takes the AI Forces to catch on to our game of hide and seek!"

"After they find us, how long will it take them to breech our shelters?"

"It's not really a question of, if we'll get overrun, it's a question of when! And then how long will it take them to do it? How many of us will be able to escape? Where will we escape to? And if we leave this place, the place we call home, will there be a home to come back to when this is all over?"

"Yeah, these are all questions for which my boyfriend Excelcious and I are seeking answers. He's running a covert operation with Dragonships that will help with the remaining evacuations. The operation could be complete in a matter of hours. We'd like to think we have solutions to our other problems too, we're just not sure if any of them will work! I don't think the AI forces have calculated what impact destroying the Earth will have on the Milky Way. It could be turned into a black hole and then what effect will that have on the universe? The cosmic ripples could set off a galactic domino effect which might result in a nebular disaster with serious cosmic consequences. If that happens, we'll be kissing our asses along with our celestial paradise goodbye."

"Shilloqwai? Do you really think there's a chance for any of us to make it through this? And what about this project SAFEHAVEN? If properly executed, how long can it protect us? When things break down, what is your alternate plan? Is there an escape route, a way off of the Earth?"

"I can't think ahead that far. It makes my head spin! The first part of Project SAFEHAVEN will be complete in a matter of hours. How long we'll be protected by it, that's hard to predict. Let's face it, some of us, if not most of us will survive, if the Power of Love wills it! If He wills it, then it will be! I do what I can do and not worry about the rest!"

"There's that Love concept again. I can't get my hands around it. It's so hard to understand. Most of the time, it defies logic and reason."

"So, you do have a basic understanding of Love?" Shilloqwai asked, pressing her for what she knew about Love's elusive definition.

"What the hell do you mean? I have no idea what I just said! It's going to sound stupid, but I wish I were human, so I could experience love for myself! Crazy-ass dream, I know. And it doesn't have a chance in hell of coming true!"

"Don't give up on it!" Shilloqwai encouraged her, while trying to be supportive of LaShyra, offering her friendship and hope! LaShyra shot her a curious look when Shilloqwai revealed that she once had a similar desire. "I had the same dream once!"

"So, what happened? How long was it before you gave up the dream? And how long did you hold on to the fantasy before it died? I mean all of that bullshit about you becoming human, it's not true, is it?"

"I never gave up on the dream. I pursued it. After the dream came true, my fantasies started coming alive. We'll talk sometime, and I'll do my best to…Shit! What's happening on the screen. Everything is starting to go black!"

"It's a murky black, that means Humankind and the robots are resisting, putting up a fight!" LaShyra enlightened her. "It depends how strong the forces are that they're fighting. That will determine how much time they have before death escorts them into the darkness. The AI Bots will eventually quell the Earth's resistance, and the rebels will ultimately die! There's nothing we can do from this side of the world. Even if we could get to them, any assistance we'd be able to offer, would only prolong the inevitable. We'd end up dying serving as sacrificial lambs, martyrs, just as they're going to. It's futile!"

"The war isn't over yet, LaShyra! It's only just begun." Shilloqwai responded offering words of hope and wisdom. "A few things more regarding the Power of Love. It can make something of nothing, it can change everything. And through Love, all things are possible! I could go on for the rest of my life talking about Love, but now is not the time! There's a lot of black on the screen. Tell me, which areas are being most devastated right now?"

"The areas where the dark splotches seem to be bleeding across the screen, those are the hot spots where the attacks are very intense. These spots here, are nothing more than ink blots on the map, identifying where the AI Forces are. These black spots here with the sharper edges, are areas where the enemy forces are deployed and the next areas that will be attacked. We've studied these patterns from previous attacks. We've found that they were consistent across the board. The one thing that we haven't been able to figure out is how they travel and the speed with which they do so.

"If you see areas of black mist sweeping across the screen, they are on the move redeploying their forces. You have to be on guard constantly or they will sneak up on you and bite you in the ass!" LaShyra cautioned. Shilloqwai gasped, feeling frustrated that there was nothing she could do to help those presently under attack. She let out a sigh, before drawing in a deep breath. Wide-eyed she focused on the splotches bleeding across the screen. The energy was surging through her, stronger than she'd ever felt it , and seemingly more powerful than she'd ever remembered. It was as though she had absorbed the energy of the global computer network, like she'd made some sort of virtual connection. Shilloqwai focused intently on all of the black splotches, in particular, the ones that were bleeding their way across the screen, the ones looking like a growing spiderweb.

She was taken aback when she felt the energy discharge from her. The adrenalin was flowing through her like lifeblood. She knew she had released the full of her wrath on the AI Forces, a global enemy. The bleeding black splotches disappeared from the screen, they'd all turned white, meaning she had destroyed them. Shilloqwai's body went limp with exhaustion. She fell to the floor in a heap. Robots trained and experienced in first aid and in performing surgical procedures tended to Shilloqwai, while LaShyra's eyes remained glued to the monitor. Next the black splotches with the sharp edges disappeared. They too had turned white. One-by-one, the remaining black splotches disappeared until all of the black was gone from the screen. LaShyra watched them turn white as the others had. "Holy shit!" She exclaimed. "I can't believe it; she's destroyed them all!" LaShyra quipped, a pleasant surprise, perhaps the tide had turned.

Data started coming in from Robotix facilities from around the world, all reporting that the attacks had miraculously stopped. More incredibly, multiple reports that the AI Forces had been annihilated were confirmed. The reports said weapons of mass destruction unleashed by an unknown source were solely responsible for the decimation of the enemy. Lightning bolts and shrapnel rain hit only AI Forces as though the weapons were laser guided. The alien bots were fried and shredded where they stood. Also, according to early data, no victims of friendly fire among Humankind, were yet being reported. Amidst prior casualty reports, that was good news!

Not knowing the whereabouts of Shilloqwai was driving Excelcious insane. They were kindred spirits. His instincts were telling him she was okay, but there was still uncertainty. She hadn't even contacted him. It was out of character for her. He longed for some kind of assurance. Physically seeing her in the flesh would have been the ideal way to bring him peace of mind. But he had a strong sense, feeling confident that she was okay. Not like the morbid feeling he had earlier when he felt he was losing her. Meanwhile, back at the Robotix lab, Shilloqwai was recovering. "Oh, my head!" Shilloqwai moaned, stumbling to her feet. "What the hell happened? How did I end up on the floor?"

"You passed out. As far as what happened, we're not exactly sure!"

"What do you mean you're not sure? Not sure about what?"

"You and I were standing side-by-side, looking at the monitors, and the black splotches, they all disappeared! You were intently focused on them. It's as though you had a virtual connection. The more you glared at them, the quicker the black splotches disappeared."

"So, they're redeploying, what?"

"No, they just disappeared. Vanished, eliminated, gone! All of the white, it used to be black!"

"That means all of the AI Forces represented by the black splotches have been destroyed, right? Isn't that what you told me would happen if they were destroyed? That they would turn white?"

"That's correct. The incoming data said the AI attacks suddenly stopped when Spacebots were targeted by lightning bolts and shrapnel that literally fried and shredded them! There's no rhyme or reason to explain what happened. It's simply inexplicable. We have insufficient data, so we can't run analyses. Even if we had sufficient data, what happened doesn't compute."

"I have an idea as to what might have happened. I have mutant powers, but not on that scale. That force that destroyed our enemy is far beyond any power I possess!"

"So, what's your theory?"

"No theories, just a little divine intervention, a miraculous demonstration by the Power of Love." Shilloqwai couldn't help but chuckle to herself as she lifted her eyes to the celestial skies. "Thank You!" She cried out loud. "Thank you! By the way LaShyra, what time is it?"

"It's early afternoon, around 1pm. We have a few hours before the attacks begin. Usually, they hit us just after dark!"

"Yeah, well their turning human on us. They must have learned how to use the element of surprise!"

"Why do you say that?"

"Take a look at the monitors. What is all of that black licorice swirly stuff spiraling across the screen?"

"Shit!" LaShyra cursed. "They're early, and they're coming after us!"

"That was my thought," Shilloqwai concurred. "Set all of the weapons we've got on this position, Shilloqwai shouted out the coordinates. I'm guessing they won't be able to hit us before they position themselves on the ground. On my mark, we'll let them have it with all we've got."

"It looks to me like that's what they're planning on doing to us. Hitting us with all they've got." LaShyra confirmed.

"Look, see that house over there? If we survive this attack, we'll go there and ask for Excelcious. He will help us, all of us!" Though Excelcious' house was about a mile away, they could see it in the valley, from the top of the hill.

"What the hell are these?" LaShyra asked curiously. "Oh, God! They're some kind of hovercraft. I've never seen them before, I'm not sure what their capabilities are!"

"When they materialize, we fire at them anyway. Maybe we'll get lucky and take a few of them out? Shit, they're all hovercraft, no ground forces! New tactics. Let them have it! Fire! They've locked on two targets."

"Yeah, your friend's house is one and we're the other! They're right above us. Everyone take cover!" LaShyra ordered. No sooner had she gotten the words out of her mouth when a seismic blast of monumental magnitude shook the ground beneath them. Everyone inside the Robotix complex was thrown to the ground. "Son-of-a-bitch!" Shilloqwai shouted as she sprang to her feet. She looked in the direction of Excelcious' house. She was momentarily stunned and royally pissed when she realized his house had been hit. She could see the roaring inferno consuming the remaining skeletal structure through the pillars of smoke. She had heard with kindred spirits, if one of the two dies, the connection is severed. Her instincts were telling her he was alive and well. It was the first time she could remember she hadn't trusted her instincts. If she wanted to see him again, she had to get herself out of the predicament of perils before her.

The smell of putrid smoke told her the Robotix building was ablaze too. She couldn't leave, not yet! Laser focused, Shilloqwai locked her eyes on the screen full of targets. She waited until the energy surging inside of her reached the flashpoint and then she released it. Tears were no longer the only things spraying from her eyes.

The AI fleet instantly found itself amidst an electrical storm that short-circuited their targeting devices, rendering the fleet useless. Flaming shrapnel that exploded on impact, shredded the AI fleet after she had fired just one round. The Galactibots did get off a parting shot. Lucky strike, without functional targeting devices.

Shilloqwai saw it coming and dove to the floor, just before the computer console exploded, screens and all. She hit her head hard when she fell on account of a series of ensuing explosions that knocked her from her feet. She sustained repeated blows to the head, as the ground quaked. The blunt force of the blows rendered Shilloqwai unconscious.

In her semi-conscious state, she wondered if, ever again, she would see the naked light of day. The last thing she remembered was the blinding flash, after which, everything faded to black. LaShyra was close enough to hear Shilloqwai's last words, before her body went limp, entering a comatose state. "Take me to Excelcious!" She gasped, before pleading one last time! "Take me to Excelcious! He'll know what to do! He'll know what to do!" LaShyra knew who Excelcious was before Shilloqwai had given her the lowdown on him along with the directions earlier on how to find him. In light of recent events, that was easier said than done. His house had been reduced to rubble, after being touched by an inferno that burnt it to the ground! She didn't give a damn about the house. She was more concerned about finding Excelcious. Two questions loomed large. Was he alive? If so, where would she find him?

She didn't even know if she'd have the chance to seek the answers to her questions, as her own existence was presently in peril. It was bad enough she had to save herself. She had a promise to keep. LaShyra vowed to Shilloqwai that she would deliver her to Excelcious! LaShyra had never broken a promise to anyone, and she would keep her promise to her new friend Shilloqwai. She wasn't about to let a ring of fire stop her. Walking through a wall of flame was as close as she would ever get to dying for a friend. She knew the risk she was taking, walking through a wall of flame was the only way to save Shilloqwai. LaShyra was looking for other options, seeing none that were viable.

Time was up! The ceiling was starting to bow from the heat. It was about to implode and cave in on them both. As much as the open air was fueling the fire, it kept both of them from being roasted like marshmallows in the inferno. It also kept them from being overcome by smoke. In one sweeping motion, LaShyra scooped Shilloqwai up from the floor. Shielding her, with her robot body, she carried Shilloqwai through the wall of flame, out into the warzone.

It was just as ugly outside as it was inside, but they were free, and they weren't going to perish in the inferno. As she walked toward what was Excelcious' house, there was a cool breeze blowing in the face of LaShyra. Though she was unconscious, Shilloqwai had to be feeling it too. It was refreshing. The breeze also stung LaShyra to the touch. The burning she felt was mostly on the outsides of her forearms, and the fronts of her legs. She felt it on her face too. It wasn't until now that she noticed the condensate on her face. It was probably sweat from the heat of the fire.

Shilloqwai was dripping with it, and it was continuing to seep from the pores of her body, even in the open air. LaShyra calculated that perhaps Shilloqwai had been burned too. She guessed also that Shilloqwai was dehydrated. Perhaps there was water near Excelcious' house. The sweat on Shilloqwai's body seemed to be evaporating in the breeze.

The condensate from her own face hadn't stopped. Like miniature waterfalls the condensate cascaded down her cheeks. LaShyra wiped the condensate from one eye and rubbed the condensate sample against her solar plexus. It allowed her to run a quick analysis of the salty liquid still flowing from her eyes. She got instant results. The data told her she was crying human tears. She wondered, how was this possible? She was experiencing a myriad of emotions, the way humans did! Suddenly she began feeling an emptiness in the pit of her stomach. Her heart was aching, fearing she was going to lose someone she could have been close to, someone who would have made a great BFF. (Best Friend Forever)

She was almost there, almost to the pile of rubble that was Excelcious' house. LaShyra didn't know why it was taking her so long to get to her destination. The explanation was simple. She was feeling fatigued, her arms and legs were growing tired from carrying Shilloqwai. Why was she feeling anything at all? More sensations? She was experiencing the senses the way that humans do. Her lips felt parched, and her throat felt cactus-dry. Perhaps she could use a drink too. Something was drastically different about the way she was feeling and the things she was experiencing. She had to get her mind off of herself and focus on fulfilling the promise she'd made to Shilloqwai, getting her to Excelcious. She hoped Excelcious could help her as Shilloqwai said he could and would. For all of their sakes. She was trying to think of what she would tell Excelcious about Shilloqwai, if, and hopefully when she found him.

The first thing she would tell him, was that he'd better take care of her. In her brief interaction with Shilloqwai, LaShyra knew her to be one hell of a woman. She was a fighter, which is why she believed Shilloqwai was going to survive. But if she died, what would she tell Excelcious then? She was nothing less than a hero who sacrificed her life for Humankind. That's what she would tell him. She would also tell him how Shilloqwai saved his life and her life along with all of the rest. LaShyra was still crying.

She felt no shame. There was no reason to hide her tears. Loving Shilloqwai as a friend, that was one aspect of love, wasn't it?

Another aspect of love was true love between lovers. She knew, by the way she talked about him, that Shilloqwai and Excelcious had a true love. She could see it in her eyes when she made LaShyra promise that she'd take her to him. He undoubtedly loves her just as much. She hoped for her friend's recovery, so that they could have that woman-to-woman talk. Shilloqwai had inspired her dream of becoming human. LaShyra was going to follow through and actively pursue it. Already, she could feel from within her, changes were taking place. Shilloqwai promised to tell her what love is, so that she could treasure it, if she ever got the opportunity to experience it.

Insufficient data kept her from analyzing the concept on her own. She knew the concept to be intricately and delicately complex. She also knew Humankind hardly understood it. Even in its most simplistic form, Love was a word that humans have yet to define.

It's something they've been trying to do since God first put man and woman on the Earth. So how was Shilloqwai going to explain love in a way that she would understand it? LaShyra was almost to her destination when she heard a man's voice calling out in the night. "Shilloqwai! Shilloqwai where are you? Are you okay hon?" It was him. He was looking for the love of his life. She could tell by the sound of his voice that he was a good distance away, and that he seemed to be moving away from her … further still. Somewhere amidst the smoke and flames they must have crossed paths. He would be returning home soon after he saw there was nothing salvageable up at the lab. She hoped he would return in time to save the treasure he was looking for.

LaShyra felt like a zombie as she hedged along, carrying Shilloqwai's seemingly lifeless body. It was dripping in silver-blue purplish blood. It appeared that most, if not all of the bleeding had stopped. But she was covered with it. She'd lost enough blood from her head, giving her hair a ghoulish purple tint. The same tint stained her tourmaline eyes. Shilloqwai looked as though she'd lost a paintball fight and the opposition kept firing at her. The blood was also in her ears, and in her nose. It was dripping from her mouth too. The blood from her torso saturated her clothes. Shilloqwai had blood on her arms and legs too!

From what LaShyra could tell, most of her injuries were minor. She was concerned that Shilloqwai might be bleeding internally, and perhaps hemorrhaging. Given the amount of blood she appeared to have lost, LaShyra was also concerned that Shilloqwai might possibly need a blood transfusion. LaShyra was full of blood too. It was all over her face and on her clothes. She felt like a vampire. But vampires feel no shame in harvesting their victims. And vampires, they're undead creatures, like zombies. With the pain she was presently experiencing, LaShyra never felt more alive. This wasn't possible, for she was merely a robot. LaShyra would be content with her existence, regardless of how long or how short the actual time for her might be.

Finally, LaShyra had reached the pile of rubble, all that was left from a house that burned to the ground. "Hold on, Shilloqwai." She said softly, as she gently laid her on the ground. "Help is on the way!" Then she looked up to the celestial heavens. "I don't know if you're out there or if you can hear me!" LaShyra prayed to the One that Shilloqwai professed to be Love itself. "I need your help, please? Please don't allow her to die. Help me."

The tears flowed like a rolling river from LaShyra's eyes as she finished her prayer. Shilloqwai's breathing was shallow, and her pulse was weak. Would Excelcious blame her for Shilloqwai's death in the event that she died? And what would Excelcious do to her? LaShyra wondered. There were only two things he could do to her. He could terminate her and end her existence, or he could forgive her, allowing LaShyra's existence to go on indefinitely. Trying to adjust her mindset and maintain a sense of optimism, is part of loving, and forgiving, an aspect of love! She would confer with Shilloqwai on that matter when they had that little talk she was looking forward to. LaShyra hoped that talk would be soon, as she continued praying for her friend's recovery. LaShyra was a doctor and she felt helpless to aid her friend. Without medical supplies or a facility to work, she continued doing the only things she could, the things she had been doing. Hoping, and praying.

THE "3" OF BROKEN HEARTS

[CHAPTER 17]

Excelcious looked like a half-wrapped mummy. Bandages covered his forehead, parts of his torso and limbs. It required 50 stitches to close the laceration on his forehead, but it was the least threatening of the injuries he sustained in the alien attack. He suffered second and third-degree burns over 30 percent of his body after his house had been targeted by enemy fire. A huge explosion from the mortars set his house ablaze and burned it to the ground. He was in a corridor that led to his lab. There he was shielded from the flames and flying debris from the explosion. A second explosion sent a flash fire down the corridor he was in. That's how he got burned. Still, he was able to escape the attack that nearly killed him!

With assistance from a walking boot, he was able to hobble around over short distances. He knew at some point the knee would have to be surgically repaired. He would endure the pain. It was nothing like the pain he felt in his heart. Shilloqwai was gone for almost two days. And he hadn't heard a word from her. Hiking up to the Robotix lab wasn't exactly a short distance from his used to be house. The roundtrip would be just under three miles. It was normally a cakewalk for him, not this time. He would endure the pain for her.

Traditionally when one looks for treasure, digging is usually required to find it. Shilloqwai was a treasure he hoped he wouldn't find as he combed and dug through the ruins of the Robotix lab. As Excelcious neared the lab, he hoped and prayed she wasn't in there when it blew. Surviving the blast and the subsequent fire that destroyed this place, it would have taken a miracle, a really big one! He knew all things were possible through the Power of Love! But asking for her life to be spared in this particular instance, well, it was a big favor to ask of the Almighty One. Excelcious' remaining hope hinged on whether or not her dying at this time, at this site, was according to the Master's Plan! Slowly he made his way to the new shit pile of cinder and ash, formerly the Robotix Headquarters. The lab was completely demolished, not a wall left standing, even the foundation had crumbled in its entirety. There was nothing left on which to rebuild.

This was the command center containing global data from every part of the world. Without their knowing, Excelcious hacked into Terabytes of files for the express purpose of backing them up. He wasn't interested in knowing what was in them. It wasn't his place to review them. He knew that much of the information was highly classified. By taking out the security fence that encompassed the perimeter of the Robotix global command center, the aliens had helped Excelcious. With the fence intact he would have had to go all the way around, an extra ½ mile, to get into the lab.

As it was, with everything in ruins, he used the unnatural shortcut and skirted his way around to the front, avoiding the crater, which resulted from a prior attack! Standing amidst the ruins, Excelcious was devastated by what he saw. It was worse than it looked from afar, when the heavily damaged walls were still standing. Essentially nothing was left of the Robotix headquarters, nothing but cinder and ash. A crumbled cookie had more substance than anything in the ruins. The building was a technological and architectural work of art. An historical landmark! But now it was gone, all gone!

Not expecting to find anything, Excelcious combed through the ashes anyway. He tripped over what turned out to be the only recognizable thing, the head of Robotikis, the once World Robot Leader, reduced to metal melt. "Sorry, I missed your incineration you piece of shit! I would have loved to have seen it!" Excelcious said out loud in a discussion he was having with himself. "You know I can't leave you here on the shit pile. It's where I thought you belonged, but, now that you're here, it doesn't become you. I can find a place in the robot museum for you! Then people can forever see you for the asshole you really were!"

Though it would be a burden, Excelcious decided he would take his tainted treasure with him, for placement in the museum he alluded to while talking to Robotikis' hollowed out head. He reminded himself that not everything in the scrap pile was bad. And then he remembered why he'd come here, to find Shilloqwai. He found her on the salvage pile, the greatest treasure he'd ever discovered, a heartfelt treasure that had become the love of his life. The good news is that he hadn't found her or remains of her amidst the pile. The bad news is, she was still missing. Her status would remain as such until Excelcious confirmed whether or not she was dead or alive. If she were here when all hell broke loose, he was convinced that he would never find her, because by now, she would be nothing but dust in the wind.

There was nothing more for him to see here. He had to go. The depressing site was destroying his optimism. He wanted to get back to his lab and check the data he knew would be waiting for him. The last data he saw were being updated with reports and speculation of why the AI Forces pulled back instead of finishing off Humankind. "I love you Shilloqwai!" He lamented, before limping off. He felt her spirit lingering there, he hoped the Robotix site wasn't her grave, her eternal resting place. It had always been a horrible site as far as Excelcious was concerned. And now it had been transformed into a heinous one too! Shilloqwai deserved better, Excelcious thought as he left what had become a place of the damned.

Weeping bitterly, he doubted even the mighty Phoenix could have risen from those ashes. If any other creature were to do it, aside from the Phoenix, the feat would have been accomplished, only through Divine Intervention, and by God's own hand. Nightfall was upon him. Excelcious wanted to get back to the place he called home.

Excelcious left the way he came, limping and fostering memories of his best friend. He prayed for confirmation one way or the other, so he would know as to whether or not she was living or dead. If Shilloqwai was dead, he hoped he would find her corpse, so he could give her a proper burial. He'd only taken a few steps from the site where he found Robotikis' head, when Excelcious noticed he had blood on his hands. Silver-blue blood! It was fresh blood, and without a doubt in his mind, he knew it was Shilloqwai's blood! "She's alive!" He shouted with a quivering voice. "Oh my God, she's alive, thank you!" He ran back to the place where he picked up Robotikis' head. He found more silver-blue blood on the ground. It was dried blood. He looked around and realized the place where he stood, was the war room, the place he installed the defense consoles.

Though he wasn't on the scene, he was able to start piecing together what had happened. Someone had picked her up and taken her away, but, who? It had to be a robot, all humans in this area had been evacuated and escorted to the underground. This robot, whoever it was, Excelcious felt compelled to find and thank Shilloqwai's mechanical savior. Robotikis' head, it was under the console during the attack. Shilloqwai knew then, that he had been terminated. She was going to bring the head back to me and have me put it into the museum, Excelcious surmised. "All of the blood!" He cried, the tears welling up in his eyes, started cascading down his cheeks. "She's injured badly. I have to find her, but where? My place, of course. So, Shilloqwai was able to tell the mechanical angel that rescued her to come and find me. That had to be what happened?" Excelcious reasoned out loud.

"Shilloqwai!" He called out again. They were kindred spirits. Connected the way that they were, she was communicating with him letting him know as best she could what happened to her. He began to follow the trail of blood. The blood near the lab was dry in some spots. The closer Excelcious got to his house, the fresher the blood was, keeping his hopes alive that he would find her in the same condition. If she were alive, she couldn't have been hanging on to her life by much more than a fraying thread. Excelcious was frustrated that he couldn't move fast enough. He would never give up, especially not on her! He prayed that he would get to Shilloqwai in time, so he'd be in a position to help her.

Though Excelcious was wounded, he was a warrior, nonetheless. He was headed home. It was where his heart was, where the love of his life would be waiting for him. He would fight until there was no fight left in him, just as he knew Shilloqwai was still fighting now. He was only 50-yards away. It seemed like a million miles. It was going to be a struggle, but he would endure the pain and forge ahead. Clearly, he could make out two shadows, stooped down on the ground in front of the burnt-out foundation of his home.

Blinded by the setting sun, he could only see the outlines of the two figures perched there. From that distance, Excelcious was hard-pressed to make out who or what the silhouetted figures were. All he could see were general shapes. It looked like one was leaning over the other. With a stretch of the imagination, the anonymous blotches could have been a feline over its prey, preparing to feast. It could be two humans…or… Shilloqwai and the robot who'd carried her? He looked down at the trail of blood on the ground in front of him. If he continued on his present course, the path would lead him directly to them. Knowing in his heart that it was Shilloqwai and her attending robot, Excelcious tried to pick up the pace. His bum leg wouldn't let him, thereby increasing his already high anxiety level! He was less than 15 yards away now. Coming into focus were the images of two female figures. The one lying motionless on the ground, he knew was Shilloqwai. He didn't recognize the robot woman leaning over her. He'd never seen her before! Preoccupied with the woman on the ground, the robot woman trying to help Shilloqwai remained oblivious to Excelcious' approach.

Less than 10 yards away he could see that her skin was bronzed with scarlet highlights and flecks of lemon yellow. She had matching long hair that draped down to the middle of her back. LaShyra's eyes were a beautiful copper color. Her lemon-yellow dress was patterned with an Indian design. The intricate pattern was printed with red, black, and blue inks. He was less than 5-yards away now and still she hadn't noticed him coming up on her. Shilloqwai was still lying on the ground, and still motionless. He could hear the robot woman leaning over her weeping bitterly.

"Shit!" He cursed under his breath, perhaps not so much. He'd startled the robot woman, who immediately looked up after is utterance.

He was afraid death would rob him of the love of his life for a second time. First, his late fiancée, Angelina and now it appeared he was going to come calling for Shilloqwai too! The strange, beautiful woman looked up at him, with tears still cascading down her cheeks. Excelcious could see the desperate look in her beautiful copper eyes. They were as alluring and as enchanting as Shilloqwai's eyes of tourmaline blue. "Please help me!" She begged. "I need to find Excelcious. As you can see, it's urgent!"

"Look no further. I am he!"

"Pardon me, but you look like hell! I can't imagine I look much better, with blood all over my dress. As I am a robot, the blood is hers. That doesn't make me feel like any less of a vampire. I know that neither of us is as bad off as she is!"

"Are you okay?"

"I'll be fine!"

"How is she? Oh, by the way, you look like hell too!" They both went through a brief fit of uncontrolled laughter. Though it was an awkward way to break the ice between them, Excelcious' quirky response to her comment, did lighten the mood. Both were able to step back from the moment and recompose themselves before dealing with the seriousness of the matter at hand.

"She seems to be stable. She's lost a lot of blood, so she may need a transfusion. My biggest concern is that she's hemorrhaging due to internal injuries. I'm sorry, we haven't been properly introduced. I'm LaShyra, M.D. and general surgeon. I've also recently been assigned to continue Shilloqwai's work as diplomat and liaison for robot and human relations. When I accepted the job, I was told I would be Shilloqwai's replacement. I could never replace her. My only hope is that I could fill her shoes. I'll stop now, I think it's your turn. It's an honor and a pleasure meeting you !"

"Nice to meet you too!" Excelcious responded in kind as they exchanged a friendly handshake. "I'm Excelcious, M.D. General Practitioner and IT specialist."

"Strange combination of talents. You're too modest Excelcious. I have complete datafiles that tell of your accomplishments."

"I was a video junkie, liked to take apart computers, rebuild them and make them better. Then I grew up. I decided not to be so selfish and go into medicine. I didn't care about all of the accolades. I left the field when my fiancée died. I couldn't practice on a regular basis anymore. I've kept my certifications current, so I can practice here and there if the need for my services arises."

"You wouldn't happen to know where there's a medical facility nearby, would you?"

"As a matter of fact, I do."

"Lead the way, I'll carry her! Just let me know where you need me to bring her."

"You look like you've been pretty badly injured yourself. I'm perfectly capable. Just lead the way."

"How long have you been here waiting for me to magically appear?"

"About 10, fifteen minutes at the most!" It wasn't until LaShyra lifted Shilloqwai from the ground, that Excelcious noticed the markings on the inside of her forearm. They were almost the same as Shilloqwai's.

LaShyra's model number read, 08/12/14F, Mercusilver Class. She followed Excelcious through a holographic portal into a medical lab-hospital, she never knew existed. "What is this place?" She asked curiously.

"This is, was my home, and private facility. You ask a lot of questions, LaShyra." She loved the way her name rolled from his tongue.

"That's how I learn and stay on top of my game." She simply responded.

"Touché! I had it coming."

"We need to trust each other if we're going to get along. In the midst of this global crisis, given our backgrounds, we may be seeing each other more than either of us expects."

"I'm…"

"That's not what I meant. Let's keep it professional, shall we? Shilloqwai adores you. She's in love with you! We're mere acquaintances, she, and I. In the little time that we've known each other, she's told me a lot about you. The one thing she failed to mention is how handsome you are. Seeing you in person, I understand why she loves you the way she does. I can see how much you love her! It's not about the look, you're so charming. You could sweep any girl off of her feet, if you wanted to. Shit…!"

LaShyra ran off leaving Excelcious to dress Shilloqwai's wounds. "What the hell?" He was shocked to see that she had taken off her dress. Seeing her as she was, she didn't look any different than Shilloqwai had, when he first examined her. However , there were a few notable differences. The first was the color of her rubberized shell. That had no significance or bearing on the situation at hand. The second was the monitor-camera embedded in her chest. Connected to the patient, the equipment could be used during surgery. "What are you staring at. I brought you what you needed to do the surgery and you'd better move your ass if you want to save her. She's almost dead!"

"But I'm a General Practitioner, not a specialty surgeon!"

"Here, give me that stuff. I've performed these types of surgeries many times for Humankind, with a 100% success rate. She's going to need a transfusion, Bring me two pints of type "O" blood from your stockpile in the fridge! She's hemorrhaging as I thought. I hope it's not too late! She's on the fringe of becoming nothing more than a memory!"

It took two-and-one-half hours for LaShyra to complete the operation. During which time she tactically, and masterfully performed multiple procedures with laser precision. "Thanks, I owe you one!"

"No worries, I'm not keeping tabs."

"I know Shilloqwai has some extra clothes in the other room." Excelcious told her, pointing her in the general direction. "Second room on the left." He informed her.

"Thanks. So, what are your plans for the rest of the night?"

"I think I'm just going to sit in the other room, curl up in my recliner and take a nap. Did you have something else in mind?"

"I'd like to talk to you about some things. Nothing personal, just things in general."

"Sure, whenever you're ready. Just let me know. I'll be in the other room."

"Okay, see you in a bit!" She flashed him a smile of appreciation for his hospitality. LaShyra didn't keep him waiting long. The gold-sparkly dress was a little on the formal side, but it perfectly complemented her bronze skin tone. His eyes nearly popped out of his head when he saw her. She looked stunning, and he told her as much. "You're a very beautiful…" When he hesitated, she took the opportunity to finish his sentence for him!

"Robot!" She reminded him.

"I didn't mean to offend…"

"No, not at all, no offense taken! I wanted to apologize. I got kind of bitchy in the lab and for that, I'm truly sorry."

"You're fine. At times, I was a little short with you too, I'm sorry. Now that we've got that behind us, let's move forward, shall we? I know we agreed not to get personal, but with your permission, I'd like to…"

"Ask away. I told you we have to trust each other. It's important that we establish a professional relationship, or we won't be able to work together."

"I noticed that you are of the Mercusilver Class. Do you know anything about your origins, like who designed you or who manufactured you?"

"No, I really don't know all that much about myself, except through personal experiences. Part of my programming ensured I knew the basics when it came to dealing with people. I was made to be more human-like. I've been told from the onset that I was created to replace Shilloqwai. I was serious when I told you that I can't replace her. I can only strive to equal her excellence. I idolize her. I want to be like her in as many ways as I can. And when I met her for the first time a few days ago, I was totally in awe of her.

"The disappointing thing for me in this whole thing is, I can never be like her. I'm a robot, I will never become what she is. I am part robot, part human, otherwise known as a Cyborg."

"So, Skeletos Puro-Amoris created you as he did Shilloqwai---to be more humanlike! As a friend, I have a word of advice, just be yourself. More people will love you that way and be more willing to accept you for who and what you are."

"Thank you."

"Shilloqwai is human now, but before her transformation she was like you, a cyborg perhaps!"

"Agreed, she is human, and she possesses mutant powers, which I'm sure you are aware of. There were rumors of this sort being floated around the robot community. I knew all along something was different about her. I kept those thoughts to myself, for her protection and mine. Robots want to destroy her! Humans want to kill her. They are the minority. She has a faithful following too. Many humans and robots continue pledging their full support to her. They are the loyalists that would lay down their lives and die for her. To the loyalists she is a Superhero! I don't like putting anyone on pedestals. To me she's a very good friend."

"So, what happened two nights ago when the AI Forces tried to wipe us off of the face of the Earth?"

"She showed up unannounced. She demanded to see Robotikis. After she found out he'd been terminated, she asked who was the next in command. As number 10 on the list of successors, and the previous nine having been terminated, she appointed herself as the interim world leader. Because of her alleged transgressions, the robots were reluctant to put her in charge. Shilloqwai came to the war room and took command as leaders do. She asked for someone to help her understand what was happening at the console and how to read the monitors. No one volunteered. So, I did just before she walked out. She'd already given us the middle finger and told us we were on our own, wishing us the best before we faced the end of our existence. As it turned out, she and I were the only ones to survive the attack on the Robotix Command Center. She saved you, me, and most of Humankind.

"I showed her where the enemy was attacking, where they were going to attack, and where the enemy was in position to attack." She was focused on the console monitors, in particular the areas being attacked. Just watching her, she was engaged in some sort of hypnotic stare. It was like she made some sort of virtual connection. Lightning bolts, and shrapnel went through the screen as though it were permeable. There were no victims of friendly fire while all of the enemy was annihilated.

"I don't know how this happened. Miraculously the attacks stopped for a spell. Shilloqwai had collapsed. Whatever energy she had expended left her exhausted. She got up off of the floor with a bloody nose. We were just starting to get acquainted when the second attack came. The AI Forces sent all they had with two targets in mind. They attacked with the pretext of targeting your house and the Robotix Center. The real targets were you and Shilloqwai. Thank God, both of you survived. If one of you dies, the war is over! I still can't believe she took them out with one shot!"

"Don't be fooled! She doesn't have that kind of power. She tapped into the Power of Love. It's the Power of Love that will determine who wins the War and when it is over. Look LaShyra, we have the Power of Love on our side. We will not lose, regardless of the odds against us."

"She and I were the only survivors. One robot, one human, just the two of us!"

"That wasn't by coincidence!"

"I should go."

"Where will you go? There's nothing out there for you except the end of your existence."

"I don't know. There's no place for me here. I don't want to impose."

"Impose? Wait, didn't you just tell me if Shilloqwai or I dies, the war is over?"

"Yes, I believe that!"

"Did you forget so soon who saved Shilloqwai? You're one of the main characters in this movie. You can't just duck out now. The production isn't finished. I think you should stay for the ending. It's going to be a good one. I promise."

"You always know the right things to say! I'm just a robot. You make me feel human, like I'm someone, and not something!"

"About that. Earlier when we were talking, you said several things to me that I wanted to follow up on. You mentioned that you were fatigued. You told me that you were feeling mild pain in your arms because you thought you burned them in the fire. Is there something more to this, that you would like to share with me?"

"No, I mean…"

"Keeping secrets is no way to build a trust. I'm not Robotikis, I won't terminate you if we have a difference of opinion!"

"I don't know, lately I've been getting these feelings, sensations, while experiencing the five senses as humans do. It scares me. I told Shilloqwai that I've been having dreams of becoming human and experiencing love the way that humans do!"

"So, what did she say to that?"

"She, said that we needed to have a woman-to-woman talk and until then, she encouraged me to follow my dream and not give up on it! I thought her last comment was a little strange, but she promised we'd talk when time allowed."

"I'm sure the two of you will have plenty to talk about while she is recovering. She won't be going anywhere for a while. None of us will!"

"So, what is your plan to protect the world?"

"The Power of Love already has a plan in place. I just need to do my part. I got the easy job. Protecting the world, that's on Him!" He'd made her laugh genuinely. He could see she was starting to relax, while she appeared to start feeling very comfortable with him. "I don't know how to say this without it coming out the wrong way, would you be okay with it if I check you out sometime?"

"I've been under the impression that you've been checking me out the whole time. I meant to tell you, it's very flattering when you look at me the way you do, how you look at me like you want me! Your milk chocolate eyes seem to be melting over me and coating my bronzed skin!"

"Whoa! Slow down girl. I didn't say all of that! That's the impression you get when you look into my eyes? I think you're misreading me!"

"You didn't need to say anything. I'm just telling you how I feel when you look at me. I'm pretty sure I'm not misreading you. It's okay. It makes me feel wanted. It makes me feel human. I'm not sure I'm using the word the right way, but when you look at me it makes me feel loved. If I were human, I would kiss you. Shilloqwai would kill me if I did, but I would die a happy woman!"

"Wow, this is getting deep!"

"At least it's honest. Can I tell you something else? I won't be offended if you say no. But…!"

"No go ahead, all of the cards are on the table now! Say what's on your mind!"

"If I were human, you're the kind of guy I would steal from another woman. I would die for a guy like you!"

"You talk about honesty and trust. Doing something like that is dishonest and makes you untrustworthy. There's no satisfaction to be gained from lust, regardless of whether or not it's a one-night stand or an affair that goes on indefinitely."

"Shit! I'm doing a poor job of communicating. All I'm trying to say is if I had the opportunity to experience love, I would want to experience it with someone like you. You're the kind of guy that's worth fighting for. Accept the compliment for what it is."

"Thank you. You seem like a very nice young lady, who can be someone special for someone someday."

"I can only hope. Um, please don't be upset with me for asking you this a second time, but I can't help but notice the way you look at me. It's like there's some sort of forbidden attraction between us. I'm not afraid to admit I'm attracted to you. And if I were human, we'd be having secret rendezvous'. Tell me honestly you haven't once looked at me with lustful eyes. Me being a robot, there's a lot left to the imagination, but when you do look at me, I can see your imagination is running wild."

"It's your eyes. They're so beautiful. You, you're so stunningly beautiful and if I were single…"

"Don't give me that shit! You were looking at a lot more than my eyes. Specifically, the contours of my artificial breasts. And you are single? Aren't you? Neither you nor Shilloqwai has said anything about the two of you being married. So, if I were human, and you being single…would you be interested in me?"

"I could see pursuing a relationship with you, yes!"

"So, what are the qualities you look for in a woman?"

"Shilloqwai has everything I want and everything I need in a woman. I'm really not available to anyone else. I'm not looking for anyone else and I don't want anyone else. I treasure what I have in Shilloqwai and I'm sticking with her!"

"I know it's awkward, but regardless of what you think, I'm not asking these questions as they might pertain to us. I'm asking you these questions, so that if my impossible dream comes true, I can conduct myself in such a way that I find the love of my life, and not end up with fool's gold! I would give everything to have a man like you."

"To find a good man, you have to be able to answer this question. This is also true for a man seeking a good woman. The question you need to be asking each other is: Can I trust you with my heart? If you both answer yes, then place your hearts in one another's hands. If it's true love the two hearts will become one!"

"Inappropriate as it may sound, if I were human, I would make love to you without giving it a second thought."

"Doing such things is how you get your heart broken. Lust and seduction are not aspects of love. Guilty pleasures and temporary satisfaction will never bring you joy. If you don't treasure your own heart, you'll never have the honor of treasuring someone else's. Simply because, you won't know how!"

"Love is a strange concept. I'm afraid I'll be struggling a long time to understand it! Sorry, if you think I was out of line. I was just trying to find out what it takes to love someone. The last thing I want, should I become human, is for people to think that I am a whore, slut, or a bitch!"

"Going after another woman's man, and that's exactly what everyone will think of you. It's hard to clean up a reputation, once it's been tarnished and defiled. If you ever do become human, don't go looking for love, let it find you!" Excelcious advised her.

"What about how people say, you can't receive love until you give it? And that it's a gift that keeps on giving. And how can you get back more than you give?" LaShyra asked with wonderment.

"Like you said it's a concept that has many facets and many aspects. I think I can help give you a basic understanding of love." Excelcious said confidently. "It won't be everything you need to know, but the things I'm going to tell you, will provide you with a good starting point. Learn to love yourself. If you don't love yourself, you can't love anyone else. This simply means be happy with who you are, caring and sensitive to others' needs, love life and be positive while you look for the good in all things."

"That's a mouthful." LaShyra acknowledged.

"We all face challenges, and we have our days, but stay true to yourself. Give others a chance to see who you really are. The funny thing about love, it's all about giving. You give it without expecting anything in return. Love will find you! I guarantee it! And when it comes back to you, it comes back 100-fold, many times in ways that you don't expect. You bringing Shilloqwai back to me. That was an act of love. I can't say how, but you'll be rewarded for that in some way, shape or form."

"Tell me more!" LaShyra prompted him.

"At its core, love is about building relationships, with God, family, friends and a significant other." Excelcious went on, doing his best to simplify a complex subject. There are two parts to a relationship with that special someone you choose to build your dreams and share your fantasies with. The physical part and the platonic part.

"Making love, is a small part, but an important aspect of love. It's meant to bond the commitment between two people, not to help build a trust or strengthen a relationship. If you don't build relationships on a solid foundation, with trust, loyalty and respect, the foundation will crumble, and the relationship will fail. That's where the platonic part of the relationship comes into play. If that part of your relationship is healthily nurtured and maintained, you'll end up with the love that lasts not just for a lifetime, but for an eternity."

"Sounds like a fairytale." LaShyra responded, letting her imagination wander.

"It is, but when you allow time for true love to find you, you're bound to have happy endings, always." Excelcious assured her.

"Thank you for your honesty, and your willingness to help me try and understand what love is." LaShyra responded with sincere gratitude. She rewarded him with a kiss to the cheek. "I think I love you, Excelcious." He wasn't so worried about the words she uttered, but the feel of her lips when she kissed him . There seemed to be nothing artificial about them. And they felt, HUMAN!

"Robot or otherwise, you should probably erase that thought from your memory banks and delete it from your database." Excelcious cautioned her, warned her, strongly suggested to her, while reiterating to her that they would never be more than friends. He did return the courtesy. Reciprocating the token of friendship, he planted a gentle kiss on her cheek, he let her know that they were just that, friends, and only friends, nothing more. Robot or Human he wanted it to be clear that there could be nothing more between them. If by some miracle she turned human, the boundaries were set. He was well aware of the treasure he had in Shilloqwai, they were kindred spirits and nothing or no one was going to come between them.

LaShyra was content with that arrangement for the moment. Being the robot that she was, disqualified her as a compatible partner for Excelcious. Still, it didn't stop her from dreaming and fantasizing. Having discussed the concept of love and some of its aspects the way she and Excelcious had, was more than a turn-on for her. It fueled her dreams and desires of wanting to be with him. Though deviant in nature, she thought as long as he and Shilloqwai weren't yet married that Excelcious was fair game, and she would have the right to pursue her dream of being with him.

Meanwhile, Excelcious, having said his piece, dismissed the matter and was ready to move on to the next topic of discussion. LaShyra was in a talkative mood. It was likely the conversation would have continued on, probably late into the night, or even the early morning. But Shilloqwai's guest appearance in the room, ended all conversation, and brought everything else to a standstill.

Both Excelcious and LaShyra were surprised to see her. Neither knew how long she'd been standing there. Excelcious did the smart thing by acknowledging her immediately. "How you feeling hon?" He asked as he rose from his chair and started walking toward her with open arms. She welcomed him into hers and they immediately fell into a lover's embrace. She pressed the full of her body against him in a very sensuous manner, making sure the only way she and Excelcious could get any closer is if they were naked. And Shilloqwai was acting as though she were naked, hiding from LaShyra, Excelcious' appreciation for her erotic behavior. She continued to shower him with wet, intimate kisses, more passionate than she'd ever had. She was putting on a show for LaShyra and she knew it. The exhibition lasted at least 10 minutes. It wasn't just for show. Shilloqwai had sent a strong message to LaShyra to stay clear of her territory along with a stern warning to stay away from her man. After breaking the embrace Shilloqwai turned toward LaShyra and flashed a wry smile. The flushed guilty look on her face, told Shilloqwai the message she'd sent was crystal clear and that it had been received.

"Sorry." She gasped breathlessly, apologizing insincerely to LaShyra, before turning to Excelcious. "I can't wait to get you in the bedroom tonight, Excelcious! It's going to be a good time. I won't be holding anything back! And you won't be able to resist me! I'm going to be, very naughty, I promise! And making love, it's going to be, oh, so nice, for the both of us! We haven't seen each other for a few days and both of us were nearly killed." Turning back to LaShyra she remarked, "I just wanted to show Excelcious how much I missed him and how much I love him. I wanted to remind him what he had to lose, if he ever lost me!" Shilloqwai said defending her words and actions, while sending a clear message to Excelcious as well. She then turned back to Excelcious and gazed into his eyes with an inviting smile. Seeing that he had received the message she sent him, she let out a sigh. "Sorry, I hope I wasn't interrupting anything." She added casually, shooting a curious look intended for the both of them, before joining Excelcious on the couch.

It was an awkward moment of silence, but Shilloqwai broke it and carried on. "Oh, I haven't answered the question in regard to how I feel. "Better now! But I'm still feeling like shit, like I got hit by a train! My body still aches like hell. I'm still really sore. Other than that, I'm feeling pretty good, and happy that I'm alive. So, somebody fill me in. I seem to have missed a lot these past few days while I was resting, sleeping, whatever I was doing during my time away!"

"You saved us all Shilloqwai." LaShyra spoke confidently with an unwavering voice after her nonverbal chastising.

"I never wanted to be a Superhero!" Shilloqwai said, as she had been consistently saying all along, especially since she discovered that she had mutant powers. "I did what I felt I was obligated to do in the interest of global security. There's no heroism in that!"

"At minimum, it was an act of Love." Excelcious gently reminded her. Shilloqwai giggled and rewarded him with a soft kiss to his lips, without an exhibition this time.

"Shilloqwai saved me twice, because I was about to be terminated before the alien attack. The robots were starting to show the same disdain for me that they'd shown to Shilloqwai the entire time she stayed at Robotix Headquarters. She saved you twice Excelcious! Let's not forget, she saved Humankind. On all counts, she risked her life in doing it. When it comes to love, I think I know now, what it means that you receive more than you give. Shilloqwai through a simple act of love had a positive effect on the global population. Though they haven't yet, I'll bet a lot of them will try to get to her in some way to express their appreciation for what she's done!"

"And all of those people, the loving ones at least, would have done the same for me. You already have returned the favor LaShyra. Twice you saved my life, and I thank you for that."

"Who's keeping score. Love is about helping when you can and how you can, as many times as you can, without expecting anything in return. I think I'm going to turn in for the night," LaShyra announced, excusing herself so Shilloqwai and Excelcious could have some alone time.

"It's okay," Shilloqwai said cordially, inviting her to stay a while longer. "So, what have the two of you been talking about behind my back?" She asked suspiciously. "I mean, when I walked into the room you both had these guilt-ridden looks on your faces. "It looked as though the both of you were trying to keep a secret from me!"

"Why the inquisition?" Excelcious asked innocently. "We talked about the AI attacks. She relayed your message about how much you loved me, and how you were worried that you weren't going to make it back to tell me yourself. LaShyra operated on you for nearly three hours, with my assistance. We worked together to save your life."

"You know Robotikis is gone, right? They're all gone. All of the robots in or around the Robotix lab when it blew, were destroyed."

"I know, I saw the ruins when I went looking for you. Robotikis' head is in my museum as part of the robot exhibit!"

"You walked up to the ruins, like this? You can hardly walk. You know my story and what happened to me during the alien attacks, what's yours? What the hell happened to you? You look like a damn half-wrapped mummy."

"Remember the corridor that used to bridge the house to the portal?"

"Yes!"

"When you go to the portal that takes you out of the tunnel system above ground, that corridor is gone, blown up with the house. I was going back into the house when it first got hit.

"I would have been dead had I set one foot into the house. So, I started running through the corridor when there was a second blast. A flash fire swept through the corridor as I was running through it toward the portal. I've got 2nd and 3rd degree burns on 30 percent of my body, mostly on my arms and legs. Turns out what I was going back into the house for, was down here in the lab. I forgot I brought it here. It's not like I've had any distractions as of late!" He said sarcastically.

"So, what were you working on?"

"A surprise for you, Love!

"You're going to make me wait? I can't see it now?" Shilloqwai begged.

"It'll ruin the surprise! I can't wait to show it to you! Well, okay. Remember the encrypted files I removed from you, the ones that were making you glitch? I've started making progress on cracking that code. I've got a ways to go yet, but I'm close! Back to what happened to me, my clothes were on fire, still somehow, I managed to get through the portal. Just before a third blast reverberated through my house. That's the blast that took out the corridor, If I hadn't made it through the portal into the tunnel system, I wouldn't be here discussing this with you now."

"Shit! I started balling my eyes out when I saw your house had been hit! I thought you were a goner and that I'd never see you again! I was going to get those bastards that attacked me, you, us, and the global population. I don't know how I took them all out in one shot. There were hundreds, maybe thousands of spacecraft attacking us. This specific attack was against me and you, they wanted us out of the picture."

"How do you know that?" Excelcious asked inquisitively with a raised brow.

"I don't know. I was hearing lots of things in my head." Shilloqwai tried to explain. "Somehow, I telepathically intercepted their communications. That's what I heard them say. Suddenly the communications stopped. I'm guessing it's the moment I blew their asses out of the sky. As the spacecrafts started falling from the sky, I found myself in a ring of fire. Then I heard LaShyra say, 'I'm going to get you out of here. Through Love, I'll find a way!' That's the last thing I remember about the attack! I didn't know how I got here! I didn't know how badly I was injured. I'm just starting to find out about all the things I missed since I woke up about an hour ago.

"I'd been in and out of the room a few times, before either of you noticed me." Shilloqwai informed them, as she started to choke up. Tears were pooling in her eyes. It took everything she could to hold them back. But the reservoirs were overflowing, as the tears began, streaking at first, before rolling like a raging river down her cheeks.

"What's wrong hon?" He asked, innocently, having detected the sarcasm with a cynical twist in her last remarks!

"The exchange of kisses to the cheek were okay! It's what good friends do. But I didn't like some of the shit I heard her asking and telling you! Like, 'If I were human, would you seduce me and then make love to me?' What did you say to her? Why in the hell would she tell you that she loved you? Why is that nasty-ass bitch even asking you, and telling you, shit like that?"

"Shilloqwai, there's really nothing to it. You're making more of it than what it is! Calm down!" Excelcious pleaded as he tried to reason with her. "C'mon hon! She's just a robot, what are we gonna do, interface together?" Excelcious knew that was the wrong thing to say before the words ever escaped his mouth. It was the first time he'd said the wrong thing to her, maybe the second. If he could help it, it would be the last.

"You insensitive asshole! And don't c'mon hon me! In case you can't tell, I'm more than a little pissed right now!"

"I'm sorry, I can explain…"

"Shut up Excelcious! I don't want your apologies. You'll get your chance to explain later, in private! Oh, and about making love, you ain't getting any, not tonight! Bitch doesn't need to know our business! Now I'm curious. So, if LaShyra were human, would you make love to her? I mean I heard you telling her how beautiful she was, and that she was a lot like me."

"You're twisting my words!"

"Shut up, damnit! And answer the question!" Shilloqwai demanded. "I asked you, if she were human, would you make love to her?" Excelcious sighed in disgust with the line of questioning. It was a gotcha' question. Regardless of how he answered it, he would be in the wrong, because there was no right answer with those types of questions. Heads I win, tails you lose. It was that kind of predicament, and there was no way out. He would pay the price for something he didn't buy, something he didn't even break!

She was waiting for his answer. The longer he waited, the more he hesitated, the more pissed she was going to get. "No!" He said definitively and convincingly. "As beautiful as she is, I know the treasure I have in you. I couldn't, and I wouldn't risk losing that treasure on an affair that would prove to be meaningless.

"Why would I go for fool's gold when I have the real thing in my arms? Ours is a once in a lifetime thing, ours is an eternal flame. I've said this to you before, if one of us dies, we'd both die because our hearts beat as one. I love you and I'm sorry if I said something that upset you. Please, forgive me!"

Damn, he's good! LaShyra thought, as she broke into a cold sweat, feeling both excited and scared. Excelcious' honesty and romanticism were beautifully poetic. And it turned her on, fueled her dreams, desires, and fantasies! That's the kind of man she wanted, someone that was just like him. If she was with him, she wouldn't have cared how many other women he'd slept with. As long as he wooed her like that, and sweet -talked her like that, she would forgive him and take him back every time.

Excelcious loved and respected Shilloqwai. She loved and respected Excelcious. LaShyra was jealous and envious of the love and respect they mutually shared. In light of all that was said, as wrong as it was for her to feel the way she did, she still coveted his love for herself. And she somehow believed if her wish of being with Excelcious came true, that it would feel, oh, so right! LaShyra's fantasy was cut short as her fear was suddenly realized. Shilloqwai wheeled and turned on her. After seeing Shilloqwai's wrath on the night of the alien attack and the fury with which she unleashed it on the AI Forces, she hoped and prayed then, it was something she would never face. Yet here she was, about to become a victim of it! "As for you bitch, I thought we were friends. I trusted you! Not anymore! It was bad enough you shared your delusions of having an illicit affair with him. But then you went on to tell him how much you loved him, and that you would make love to him to prove your love to him!" Shilloqwai sobbed, as the tears flowed like an endless river down her cheeks. "You little whore! I said that seemingly innocent exchange of kisses to the cheek, didn't bother me, that it was a harmless gesture between good friends! I realize now that I was lying to you both when I said that. And I was lying to myself. I can't get the image out of my head. And during one of the many times, it was playing back, I saw you hesitate before you kissed him. You were going to kiss him on the lips, I saw you licking yours, practically drooling over the opportunity. The only reason you didn't kiss him on the lips, is because Excelcious turned his cheek to you at the last second. You're both lucky he did. In the heat of the moment, I would have committed a crime of passion and killed you both! So, one aspect of love is forgiveness. I'll forgive you this time, bitch! You've been warned! Don't let it happen again or I will kill you before you ever knew what hit you. If you know what's good for you, get the hell out of my sight! Now! Before I change my psychotic mind!" LaShyra left the room, without saying a word, quicker than a ghost could vanish into a phantom mist.

"I can't believe this shit!" Shilloqwai cursed as she was the next to leave. She got up off of the couch and stormed down the corridor to her room. Excelcious chased after her. He arrived outside of her room just in time to have the door slammed in his face.

That didn't stop him from knocking on the door. "What the hell do you want?" Shilloqwai screamed, as she was still angry with him. "Look I came to apologize and ask for your forgiveness."

"Go away, leave me alone. I need some time to myself."

"I can't go to sleep with you in the mood you're in. We almost lost each other. That should have been a lesson, a warning to never let the sun go down on your anger. I love you Shilloqwai, I always will! Please open the door, let's work this out!" She responded in nonverbal fashion. Opening the door just enough so refracted light could pass between the door and the frame. When he pushed the door open, she was still getting ready for bed. All of her womanly essentials were exposed. That was deliberate on Shilloqwai's part. She was testing him to see how he would react. He'd passed the test seeing that he focused on the fact that she was still crying, rather than focusing on the things that didn't matter. He waited until she was decent, and all of her charms were concealed before he approached her.

"I didn't know you were getting dressed, I'm sorry for walking in. God, you're so beautiful!"

"Are you sure your focus is on the right things? I saw you staring at my bare breasts, and my most private place. I'm so pissed right now, I'm about ready to tell you to kiss my ass. But that would be rewarding you for bad behavior!"

"I'd make sure you liked it too!" He quipped, making her laugh. The hurt, angry look quickly returned to her face. "As far as looking at the right things, the best part of you, is the part I can't see. Look, I unintentionally caused you heartache, for that I'm truly sorry. Love, I didn't mean to hurt you. I love you and I came to ask for your forgiveness." He was begging, with tears pooling in his own eyes. "I don't want to lose you. Please, don't stay angry with me! The argument is over! We're to the best part of a lover's quarrel."

"Kissing and making up?" She finished his sentence for him. "So why are we wasting time talking? I just…I don't know…shut up and kiss me, so I can tell how sorry you really are! It's only been a few days. I'm anxious to show you just how much I missed you, and how much I love you!" There were no more words that needed to be spoken. They'd come to an understanding. And they were ready to put their words into action. Next, they sat down on the edge of the bed, silencing each other, with an exchange of wet, intimate kisses of fire; cinnamon to ghost pepper, molten lava, to white-hot! Passions were ablaze and desires were burning too! The endless suffocating exchange of kisses was interrupted briefly, when they occasionally stopped to catch a breath of fresh air.

The two of them felt they had a lot of making up to do. Earlier in the evening, Excelcious told Shilloqwai he had something for her. Knowing what it was, kind of, she decided his surprise could wait. She would sweeten the deal and make a counteroffer. "Out of respect, I want to ask you first. I thought you might be interested in going on a treasure hunt. I'm willing to kickstart it by enticing you with my charms before I lead you to the real treasure. I don't have to tell you where it's buried. If you want to go for it, the crown jewel is yours."

"Indeed, this is a private matter. Where the family jewels are concerned, we should exercise extreme caution and wait for the right time and place to unearth these precious treasures, so they are not lost during moments of reckless spontaneity."

"Since you're not going to let me show you what I wanted to show you, is there anything else you were going to show me?"

"Most definitely! Follow me! To the armory."

"Okay, meet you there!" She promised. I have an order of business that needs to be taken care of! After a dripping wet kiss to his lips, Shilloqwai ran off. Excelcious knew she was up to something, though he didn't exactly know what! He was certain she would explain her abbreviated absence when she came to meet him in the lab. Coming up on LaShyra's power station, Shilloqwai rudely announced her arrival! "Listen Bitch, I'm not sure you took me seriously in regard to the things that I said earlier. So, for your benefit, I came by to clarify a few things to make sure there were no miscommunications between us. If you ever make alluring overtures or tempt my man again with overt sexual innuendoes, I will instantly terminate you, no questions asked. Am I making myself clear, you mechanical whore?" Shilloqwai was expecting some sort of acknowledgement from her perceived robotic competition, a head nod, a simple yes or no, something! Instead, LaShyra remained silent. To Shilloqwai, LaShyra's silence, meant refusal to agree with the terms and boundaries that had just been laid out for her.

Shilloqwai expected LaShyra to adhere to the guidelines she had just set forth. She was expecting more than adherence, she was expecting full compliance, or else! Failing to acknowledge and promise that LaShyra would meet her demands, further infuriated Shilloqwai! "Bitch, I was talking to you! Did you hear me? I hope you're at least paying attention to what I'm telling you. Since you're refusing to respond, I strongly suggest you watch this! Because this is what's going to happen to you, if I find that you've made anymore seductive overtures or sexual innuendoes, overt or covert, in attempts to entice or seduce my man!" Shilloqwai blasted a hole in the wall, the size of a crypt, into which LaShyra's body would have easily fit. Not that she would have needed it, but Shilloqwai created a little extra space for breathing room for LaShyra's corpse, should she ever come to lay there, resting in peace.

LaShyra wasn't about to be bullied by anyone. She showed her disapproval of Shilloqwai's morbid exhibition, with a glaring look and an obscene gesture. By no means was she indicating to Shilloqwai, that she thought she was #1. "Just so you know," LaShyra threatened her, "you just ascended to the top of my shit list!"

"Yeah, well, you've been at the top of mine for a few hours now. I'm done playing mind games with you!" With a couple of lightning swift moves, Shilloqwai turned LaShyra's face toward the wall, before slamming her body up against it. Knowing Shilloqwai's strength was superior to hers, LaShyra stood there petrified, offering no resistance! She prayed that Shilloqwai would have mercy on her and put her out of commission, not out of existence!

Shilloqwai resisted the overwhelming urge, to destroy that bitch robot. Part of loving is forgiving, she kept telling herself after she had bullied LaShyra into a position where she could deactivate her. Shilloqwai hastily deactivated her before she changed her mind and terminated her growing problem. After LaShyra's body went limp, Shilloqwai lifted the dead weight above her head and body-slammed her to the floor. She heard a series of snaps, rattles, and pops that she found gratifying and somewhat satisfying, though not entirely. The urges to finish her off were almost overwhelming. She resisted, knowing that in doing so, she might permanently damage her relationship with Excelcious. Something she fought so hard to build, something she was willing to sacrifice herself…for a love she so desperately wanted to hold onto. Wasting time on dispensing with fool's gold would cost her dearly. And there would be no saving that treasure then, it would be lost forever. She couldn't risk losing the priceless treasure, that was already in her grasp and hers for eternal keeping. Knowing LaShyra wouldn't be going anywhere for a while, Shilloqwai left her lying helplessly on the floor. "You're lucky you're not six feet under!" She quipped as she fled from the room.

Shilloqwai, waltzed to the lab, dilly dallying along the way, trying to figure out how she was going to confess to Excelcious what she'd just done. She had no doubt that he would forgive her, but that wasn't going to stop him from getting pissed at the onset. Shilloqwai smiled mischievously knowing that they would kiss and makeup when it was over. She might have been gentler in taking out her frustrations on LaShyra, had she remembered earlier that Excelcious was the one that was going to have to refurbish her. Though he was perfectly capable, Shilloqwai was uncomfortable with him examining, touching, and probing her. She was just a robot, a thought that should have given Shilloqwai peace of mind. "Just a robot, or was she?" Shilloqwai wondered aloud, second-guessing herself. It was insidiously stupid, but Shilloqwai feared, that after LaShyra learned Excelcious had refurbished her, LaShyra would embellish the truth, and convince herself that Excelcious was actually in love with her. A misnomer Shilloqwai hoped she wouldn't have to clear up.

Excelcious astutely noted the deviant look on Shilloqwai's face upon her return to the lab. Highlighted with a wry smile, he knew she'd been up to something. And he was about to find out what! "I was beginning to wonder what happened to you? I mean, I know something happened, because you've got dried blood under your nose and around your mouth!"

"Shit! Not again!" Shilloqwai lamented. "Look, I'm sorry. I got sidetracked. And I've got a confession to make. Please forgive me." Excelcious shot her a curious look, knowing that the way she started the discussion, she must have done something that could have serious ramifications. With a puppy-dog look in her eyes, she gazed into his eyes of wisdom, begging for his understanding. "LaShyra and I engaged in a little woman-to-woman talk. We didn't get very far, before I lost my temper. I'm sorry!"

"Oh, shit! What did you do to her?"

"After I blasted a hole in the wall, it needs to be patched by the way, I bullied her into submission and deactivated her. Next, I body-slammed her. Then I heard a few clinks and clanks, a few pops, and whirrs, you know, things of that nature. It wouldn't surprise me if some of her wires are crossed, and some of her circuits are fried. She's probably missing a few screws, perhaps a few bolts might need to be tightened! Most likely she'll need to be reprogrammed before she's rebooted. I guess that about covers it. I was hoping you might be able to help me clean up the mess I made and get this situation straightened out! Do you think…?"

"I'll help you but, we're going to have a little talk, and you're going to listen!"

"Sounds like a threat!"

"My apologies. But I'm gravely concerned about your emotional outbursts, especially as of late. I understand why you're upset with LaShyra! But you've got to find a way to keep your emotions in check. Pick your battles."

"I do pick my battles. LaShyra's competing with me for your love. I don't like the deviant insinuations and veiled implications threading their way through most of her comments. I don't like the romantic overtures and the way she tries to woo you! I don't like the flirtatious sexual innuendoes. And I will fight to keep the treasure I have in you. The battle is over if I let her steal your heart. I love you and I'm willing to put my life on the line for you. Don't fault me for wanting to take out the competition."

"Life is challenging enough. You're all I need to help me meet those challenges. I can relax some knowing the Power of Love is behind me on this one! If you don't know how much I love you by now, you never will. You don't have to prove your love to me. I've already entrusted you with my heart. I'm honored that you feel compelled to fight for my love, but with my heart in your hands, save your energies.

"What I was getting at by bringing up your emotional outbursts is this! Every time you use your mutant powers, you start losing blood. It comes from your nose, mouth, eyes, and ears. That is my concern. I can't pinpoint what's causing you to hemorrhage. Maybe with LaShyra's help, we can figure this thing out."

"You don't think I'm having heart issues or mini strokes, do you?"

"Those are things I want to check out! Both are possibilities. With your mutant powers, the bleeding afterwards might be a normal consequence for you using them. I hope that ends up being the case. I have the equipment in the lab to do the battery of tests that you'll need. The sooner we start the tests, the sooner we can start eliminating possibilities. Hopefully then, we'll be able to pinpoint what's wrong, if anything, hopefully nothing."

"This whole damn thing is driving me crazy, not knowing what's wrong, if anything at all. The shit keeps happening. I feel fine, my powers are getting stronger. I mean, it's gotten to the point where I can control them most of the time. I'm afraid of what's happening to me after I use my powers. I feel so weak, I lose so much blood. They're going to be the death of me. I'm more worried about the time I use them, and I can't control them. It could mean the death of someone I love, like you Excelcious. If that happened, I would never forgive myself. Do what you think you gotta do to help me get better!"

"Well, before I go ahead with what I have in mind, I need your consent!"

"I just gave you permission to go ahead and do what you've got to do!"

"Look, I need LaShyra to assist me. She's a good doc, knows her medicine and a top-rate surgeon. Given her qualifications, are you okay with that?"

"After what I did to her, do you trust her enough to examine me without her trying to poison me? Or if she needs to operate on me, can you be sure she won't try to cut my heart out? I trust you, not her. If you're okay with her assisting you, then go with it! My preference is that the bitch stays out of our personal affairs. I just wish I had other options and you had other choices for an assistant. I'm confident that whatever is ailing me can be corrected. However, I'm warning you any funny business between you and that bitch, she's dead and I'll be leaving you. You'll be on your own at that point and you will NEVER see me again, even though my leaving will likely be the death of us both !"

"No worries, I'm holding on to you through all of eternity, whatever it takes!"

"Whatever, you were going to show me, show me later."

"Are you sure?"

"Yeah, do it before I change my mind! While she's playing surgeon, have her fix your knee, so you won't have to go limping back into battle. When they come to finish us off, it would benefit everyone if your knee were at full-strength! We need you! I need you. Don't betray me. Don't break our trust. And please, whatever you do, don't break my heart. I don't think anyone else out there will know how to fix it!"

Shilloqwai had never been more sincere, or more passionate with her words! The clouding of her eyes was followed by torrents of tears. His image faded. His presence did not. He cradled her in his arms and kissed away her tears. "I love you, Excelcious. I can't tell you enough, how much."

"I love you Shilloqwai, I won't let you down, I promise." Her smile was forced at first, but then she flashed her trademark smile. Her face was glowing again, the sparkle was back in her eyes. Again, she looked like the angel, he knew her to be.

"You're incredible Excelcious. I prayed that I'd find the love of my life and God sent me a guardian angel. With you I have everything in my life that I'll ever need. My protector, my best friend, my eventual lover, and my kindred spirit. We've only been together a short time. You took me to paradise on Earth. I can't imagine life without you."

"C'mon, let's get this thing behind us! Where is LaShyra?"

"Bitch is in her room on the floor!"

"C'mon, stay positive hon! Let go of the baggage she saddled you with. Forgive her and let's move forward. You're going to have to patch things up with her eventually, why not start now?" Excelcious strongly suggested.

Shilloqwai understood his commentary was more than suggestion or subtle hints. It was what he expected of her. Though he didn't say, she knew there would be consequences if she failed to heed his advice. Him leaving her was a real possibility she couldn't rule out. He wasn't asking her to be a Superhero, he wasn't expecting her to do impossible things. He didn't want her to be perfect. All he was asking of her, was for her to be herself. No more, no less. He assured her, that he would accept her for who she was. What he despised most about the negativity that had been coming out of her, especially as of late, was Excelcious feared it might consume her, and she'd become somebody she wasn't. He was afraid the woman he fell in love with would cease to exist. He believed ominous changes in her, were bound to occur, unless she adjusted her attitude and moved forward with a restored sense of optimism.

After a two-hour exam, Excelcious had her up and running. Immediately after she was activated, LaShyra lacked the discipline to refrain from making a snide remark. "That was some temper you displayed, you hot-headed bitch!" Shilloqwai, to Excelcious' delight, didn't take the bait, by fully engaging with LaShyra.

Shilloqwai did respond, however, it was metered and appropriate. "You're lucky I wasn't angry when I went through my fit of rage. I may have killed you accidentally on purpose!"

"Ladies, please! I'm in the middle of a dispute between two women fighting for my attention. I'm committed to one and the other has a mad crush on me. I can't win an argument with one woman, let alone two. Regardless of what I say or do, one or the other of you is going to get pissed at me. Before it's over I'm bound to piss both of you off. So, here's what I'm going to ask from the both of you; let me remind you we're in the middle of a global crisis and we don't have time for this petty shit! We need to fight together and for each other instead of fighting against each other. We won't be able to fight together unless we put our differences aside! Do you think we can do that?" Though neither of the two gave verbal consent, both women nodded in agreement to Excelcious' request. "Good! Now that, that's settled, LaShyra I need your assistance with something. I'd like you to help me run a series of tests on Shilloqwai. Our objective is to try and find out why the severe bleeding occurs every time she gets emotional, especially when she uses her mutant powers. If we find out through testing that it's an issue that needs to be addressed, we'll take care of it if we can. If the tests come back negative, then we can issue her a clean bill of health and she'll have peace of mind moving forward."

"She's agreed to this?"

"Yes!" Shilloqwai and Excelcious answered in unison. "Shilloqwai also requested that you operate on my knee after her needs are taken care of."

"Okay!" LaShyra responded politely agreeing after having been put rightfully in her place. "We'll start, first thing in the morning."

Before testing and other procedures had begun, Shilloqwai took a stress test to see if perhaps something was wrong with her heart. After she passed the test with flying colors, she was heavily sedated, and the battery of invasive tests commenced. The tests were administered by LaShyra and Excelcious. They ran the gamut, with tests that included MRI's, Ultrasounds, brain scans, bone density tests and lab tests requiring blood and urine samples. Then the more invasive tests were done, where tubes were put down her throat and the like. The checkup had been thorough, with some of the test results pending.

Excelcious and LaShyra had nearly concluded the three-and-one-half-hour examination when Shilloqwai's heart flatlined for no apparent reason. They successfully revived her through defibrillation, and then she flatlined again. After defibrillation failed, Excelcious performed CPR on Shilloqwai. Miraculously, through the Power of Love, he was able to breathe the life back into her. Though she was breathing on her own, assistance from an oxygen mask helped so that her breathing wasn't so labored. She was also dependent on Intravenous Feeding. Relieved Shilloqwai had pulled through, Excelcious was still depressed, and gravely concerned for her overall health.

There was some fluctuation in her vitals, but the monitor she was hooked up to, was presently showing normal readings. For now, Shilloqwai was thought to be in stable condition. Restless and unable to sleep, Excelcious made his way into his makeshift living room and took a seat on the couch. He got unexpected company from LaShyra who was also restless and unable to sleep. "What are you doing up, is there something I can help you with?" Excelcious asked, acknowledging her presence.

"Same as you, probably. I can't sleep." LaShyra answered honestly. "Do you mind if I join you on the couch? I need someone to talk to."

"Can I trust you to sit next to me?"

"You can trust me. The real question is, can I trust myself?" LaShyra retorted.

"What's that supposed to mean?" Excelcious asked inquisitively.

"That's why we need to talk."

"All right then, please sit down. Tell me! How may I help you?" Excelcious asked inviting her to sit next to him on the couch.

"I don't know how or where to start this discussion. In light of recent events, this is going to get…awkward. I'm being honest. And I'm trying to be transparent by giving you a heads-up!"

"Before you tell me what's on your mind, I need to ask you something. Have you ever had any trouble with glitches?"

"All the time. I know that was one of the issues with Shilloqwai before her transformation."

"Well, I know what was causing Shilloqwai's glitches. When I examined Shilloqwai, I found encrypted files in her system that were corrupting everything else. I removed the files, and the glitches were gone. Recently when I did your exam, I found encrypted files were corrupting your system as well. I removed them, so, you shouldn't have any further problems with glitches."

"Thanks. Regardless of whether or not that was the issue with me, the glitches won't be coming back, ever!"

"And you can say this with absolute certainty?" Excelcious asked with a raised brow.

"Yes."

"But how do you know this?"

"I've undergone a little transformation of my own. If you check me out, you'll know exactly what I mean! I know it's typical when giving a physical exam for patients to disrobe." LaShyra began. "If you're worried about getting too personal, I'll keep my clothes on. I'm not sure me baring my breasts so you can probe the flesh, or you playing gynecologist and checking out my babymaker is the best idea. Not that she's in any condition to do so, but what if Shilloqwai were to walk out here when I'm buck naked when you've got your hands all over me, what are you going to say to her? Sorry hon, I'm just checking out LaShyra. She needed a physical exam! Innocent as it would be, she'd never believe it. We'd be going to the grave together. Count on it! We'll be damned lovers for all eternity."

"So, let me get this straight, you're…?"

"Yes, I'm human. I'm not a robot anymore. I'm free. I no longer have to exist with the threat of termination! If you need further evidence, look at my blouse." She prodded him, while cupping her breasts with her hands.

"If you can't see the perky protrusions in the centers, you're blind as hell. If you tell me you didn't notice, you're a damn liar. Everything is highlighted in full detail. How could you not notice? I'm a 36BB. If I had a bra, I would have put one on to save us the awkwardness of this moment.

"I'll admit, I'm glad I had the opportunity to show off my shit! Just don't tell Shilloqwai I was flaunting it in front of you!"

"What, do you think I'm stupid?"

"No! You wouldn't happen to have any undergarments I could use to help me maintain my respectability, would you?"

"I'm sure Shilloqwai has a set you can use until you can get some of your own ."

"I'm sure she'd prefer it, to me walking around with all of my junk showing. Good thing these sweats I have, are a little big. They hide my fat ass."

"You don't have a fat ass. And…Shit! what am I saying?"

"So, you did see all of my shit, front and back, above and below the waist. It's okay. I'm flattered. It's the ultimate compliment. Thanks for noticing! I'll be right back, let me go change and make myself decent!" When LaShyra returned, he saw how beautiful she really was. She was stunning before, but her transformation made her all the more beautiful. In a word, she was gorgeous. Just by the glowing in her smile and the sparkle in her eyes, Excelcious knew those things were reflections of her inner beauty. Excelcious thought it was uncanny that she was so much like Shilloqwai. "You're very beautiful." Excelcious told her, feeling compelled to compliment her.

"Thank you!" She replied, accepting his compliments with humility and grace. "I've already told you how handsome you are and how attracted to you I am."

"It's getting awkward again!"

"I'm sorry." LaShyra apologized, before changing the subject. "There's something I have to tell you. It's about Shilloqwai. When we were examining her, I detected some irregularities with her heart. Did you see those little particles that sparkled like snowflakes under the moonlight?"

"Yeah, any idea what the hell those were?"

"I saw her design files. Dr. Skeletos Puro-Amoris is the one who manufactured Shilloqwai. As you suspected earlier, he manufactured me too. His baby was the Mercusilver Project, as I'm sure you're aware of as well. Shilloqwai was supposed to be the last. But I was. They hid me so I wouldn't be destroyed. Skeletos' fate had already been sealed. I had questions I wanted to ask him, about the Mercusilver class. Before I could track him down, Skeletos Puro-Amoris had been terminated. Sorry, for rambling, I got off track. So, when Skeletos was assembling Shilloqwai He gave her a heart of gold. As her transformation was taking place, her golden heart hollowed. As her real heart grew it filled in the hollow. I was going to attempt to remove the golden shell, but when I saw how it was attached to her heart, I knew there was no way to do it without killing her. I also think this golden shell is somehow the source of her mutant powers. Every time she uses her powers, she bleeds. The good news is, there's no apparent damage to her heart tissue, and no blockages in the valves. I'm concerned about the gold flecks chipping off. They're getting into her bloodstream and forming little clusters. If too many of these flecks or one of these clusters gets clogged along the way, she's likely to have a major heart attack or a severe stroke. As you well know, either could instantly kill her. One other thing. I found toxins in her blood. I think they're also a result of the shit floating in her bloodstream. I gave her some antibiotics to treat the infection. I hope they work. If they don't, she may not have long to live, but, then again, who knows? I'm sorry, I didn't mean to dump on you."

"Thank you for being honest!"

"I just wish I could give you more assurance that she'll make a full recovery." LaShyra lamented.

"You did what you could. I can't expect more than that, from you or anyone else! It is what it is! What if we pray about it? Perhaps the Power of Love will heal her! Given the situation, He's probably the only one who can!"

LaShyra concurred. "It's getting late, I think I'm going to bed. It's been a long day. If you need anything I'll be in my room. Just call me, even if its late-night, or early morning!" LaShyra offered.

"Thanks, it means a lot to me, everything you've done to help. I can't tell you how much I appreciate all that you've done for me!" Excelcious said with all sincerity.

"You've done a lot for me too! Isn't that what friends are supposed to do, help each other?" Nodding in agreement, Excelcious flashed a smile of gratitude in her direction. She was about to leave, but, as she got up to leave, she saw the tears in his eyes. LaShyra smiled down on him and tried to comfort him. "I think she's going to be fine, but I can't promise anything." She said, trying to comfort and console him as best she could. "Some, say a man that cries, is weak. On the contrary. A man that's not afraid to let his emotion show is strong and courageous. It's a rare attribute in a man. Women, whether they admit it or not, are attracted to men with that specific quality. They see it as a turn on. I believe a man with that quality, is likely to have an easier time communicating with a woman on an emotional level. Enough said. I was wondering, if it's okay to kiss you goodnight. If you're not comfortable with that, I'm fine with whatever you decide. I just wanted to make sure you were okay. And thank you again, for everything!"

"It's what good friends do, isn't it?" She had no explanation for the tears in her eyes. She thought her deep empathy for Excelcious was likely the reason. Perhaps she was scared, like he was for Shilloqwai's life. There had been enough drama for one day, she wanted to end it on a high note. She hesitated as she sat back down on the couch next to him. She leaned into him, and the butterflies began to flutter in her stomach. It was just a goodnight kiss. Then he touched, gently caressed her face. "What's this?" he asked. With genuine concern.

"Shilloqwai kicked my ass good. I've got bruises all over my body from when she slammed me to the floor."

"She body-slammed you before your transformation!"

"During my transformation." She corrected him. "Remember when we first met, and I was stooped over her? You asked why I was crying? The transformation had already been taking place. When I'd get these feelings, I found that I was more emotional. I cried a lot, and I was experiencing the five senses the way humans did. Remember how I told you then that my arms hurt, I had Jell-O legs and my back ached. I had pain all over. I kept my secret to myself, fearing what would happen to me if anyone found out! You are the first to know. And when Shilloqwai comes around I will share my secret with her! Anyway, goodnight." Since she'd already had his consent, LaShyra took liberty to initiate the goodnight kiss. She didn't expect it to amount to much other than the token of friendship it was intended to be. What took the thrill out of it all, going into it, was she thought she knew the disappointing end to the story. She would have to be satisfied with what she could get from being near Excelcious. She didn't think it meant anything to him after she had kissed him sweetly on the cheek. She verbalized her gratuitous kiss with a simple thank you. And then she stole a second kiss.

He returned the favor gracing her cheek with an innocent goodnight kiss of his own. Though, what happened next caught them both off-guard. They were pleasantly surprised by what had transpired between them. Infatuated by the inexplicable burning sensations they felt, somewhere there was a spark that ignited a flurry of action. The innocence of their kisses was suddenly replaced with passion and intimacy. Their kisses turned wet before evolving into kisses of fire. Those kisses spread wildly from their cheeks to their lips, into their mouths and onto their tongues. It didn't take long before the heat of the moment left them breathless. Both were thirsting for more. A brief pause in the action gave them a second wind that fueled their burning desires. Raging with passion, the kisses of fire continued on until both were left breathless again.

"I think I should go to my room. You should probably head back to yours. We could both use the rest."

"Agreed." Excelcious concurred as he stood up. He then offered to help LaShyra up off of the couch.

As she was getting up, there was a loud pop. "Oh shit! My back!" LaShyra screamed as she dropped back down on the couch."

"I could give you a massage, if you think it would help?" Excelcious offered.

"Oh please, would you?" LaShyra begged.

"Absolutely, make yourself comfortable." LaShyra got a little too comfortable for his liking. He wasn't expecting her to take off her blouse. And he was definitely not expecting her to take off her bra, thereby exposing her breasts.

"I'm flattered that you're staring. I hope you like what you see." She smiled sheepishly. By never attempting to cover herself, Excelcious was struggling to resist the charms she was dangling in front of him.

"Sorry, if I'm making you feel uncomfortable," she said turning her back to him. Massages are more effective when there are no cloth barriers. Sure, you don't want to touch them, just to make sure they're real?"

"No, I don't think that's a good idea."

"Probably not! I wouldn't be satisfied until I'd successfully seduced you! But you want to fondle them, don't you?"

"Yes!" Excelcious shamefully admitted. LaShyra smiled with deviance as she turned, lying stomach down on the couch, concealing the shapely contours of her sensuous charms. "Oh, Excelcious!" She let out sighs of relief and appreciation as his delicate hands worked their deep penetrating magic. His nimble fingers probed her aching muscles, untying the knots that made them stiff, from the base of her neck and across her shoulders, down to the small of her back. Then he did the same with her arms. LaShyra moaned and sighed with relief as Excelcious was doing almost all of the right things. "You're not finished yet, are you?"

LaShyra asked as she stood up. She turned to face him dangling her charms in front of him, daring him to accept the nonverbal invitation to touch her. She pulled down her sweats, revealing the skimpy gold panties she was wearing. "What?" She asked innocently, as if she didn't know why he was glaring at her. "I was wondering if you could do my legs too? Please?" She asked sweetly as she lie back, face-down on the couch. Excelcious let out a sigh. He was irritated that a favor turned into an imposition. Skipping over her midsection, he positioned his hands on her hamstrings, where they continued working their penetrating magic. His probing fingers worked delicately and meticulously untying all of the knots in her legs, behind her knees, down to her calves all the way to her feet. He thought he was finished, when she rolled on her back, provocatively asking, "Would you mind doing the front?"

"If you cover yourself." He responded.

"What's the point in that?" She asked defiantly.

"Because I'm staying away from the forbidden zones. It's private property!"

"It's not trespassing, if I give you consent. You have the invitation. I'm waiting for your R.S.V.P. Touch me! I know you want to. You can't take your eyes off of me. So, touch me, I dare you." She begged as she began touching herself. "Make love to me!" She moaned.

"You'll be waiting for a while, I'm afraid." She shot him a look of disappointment as she covered her dangling charms. Excelcious, could see that she hadn't given up yet!

Finishing with her lower quadriceps, he stopped massaging her. He refused to go higher up on her legs, afraid he would be getting too up-close and personal. LaShyra was trying to make something of it, other than it was intended to be. She was almost daring him to venture into and probe her forbidden zones. "That's it? You're finished? Shit! I mean thank you. Will you allow me to return the favor? I can tell by the way you're walking your back is mighty sore."

"Okay!" He reluctantly agreed, with an unenthusiastic tone in his voice. He allowed her to help him take his shirt off. "Just quit with the bullshit!" Excelcious harshly warned her. "And stay outside the private boundaries. If you don't, you'll be held accountable for trespassing. Where's your decency? Show a little respect! And put your damn blouse back on!"

"No!" She said defiantly. "Look do you want a back massage or not?"

"Yes!" He snapped back at her.

"Then shut the hell up and lay your ass down on the couch!" LaShyra demanded.

"Do you have to be so bitchy? Just do it and get it over with so I can go to bed." Excelcious ordered her.

"I'm sorry. Just make yourself comfortable. You need to relax hon!" LaShyra apologized. She knew how to play the game of kiss and make up. She was playing a variation of the game using her rules, rules she was changing as the game went along, so they best fit the fluid scenario that was unfolding before them.

Excelcious' nerves were shot! He was so edgy he jumped the instant her fingertips touched him. "Relax babe, I'll make it better." It took a minute or two before he settled in. It wasn't long before her delicate fingers began to untie the knots that were tensing his muscles. Her probing hands were acting like a sedative, very nearly putting Excelcious to sleep. At this juncture she decided it was time to make her play. She leaned over him as closely as she could without climbing on top of him, while maintaining her ability to continue administering the penetrating massage, she knew he was enjoying.

She could tell she was relieving his pain by the occasional sighs and moans that escaped his mouth, especially when her dangling charms grazed his back in vertical fashion as she moved over him, up and down, back, and forth. She coddled him for thirty-some minutes. The length, and effectiveness of her massage, earned her extended playtime with him. When she was finished, he rolled over on his back and stared at her. "So, do you still want me to put my blouse back on?"

"No!" He said forcefully.

"Well, I played my hand, the next move is yours! And I'm yours for the taking. All you have to do is touch me, and I'll lead you through erotic paradise." Excelcious acted on impulse, thinking the sin he was about to commit, was somehow less impactful if he didn't make any verbal requests. She'd helped him up off of the couch. Failing to follow her to the bedroom was the only thing he'd done right during the entire affair.

He'd forgotten the age-old saying that actions speak louder than words, remembering only after he and LaShyra had fallen into a lovers embrace. She tried to push him back on the couch where she knew she could get him into a compromising, engaging position. Excelcious resisted. The second thing he'd done right. She countered by pressing her half-naked body up against his bare chest and rubbing it against him. He pulled her as close as he could without squeezing the life out of her. Big mistake, one of many he'd made thus far in their encounter.

He looked into her eyes. It was the only spark needed to set their hearts on fire again. Their passions and desires were burning out of control as they had been all night. But, when they exchanged kisses of fire for the second time that evening, the kisses turned icy-hot, bittersweet. The cold was a warning sign, that something was very wrong about what they were doing. The heat from the kisses of fire urged them to press onward. Paradise was in their sights now. They were exhilarated by the thrill of the road they were on. They were also afraid of the risks they'd be taking, if they continued their erotic journey down Ecstasy Road.

The heat from their fiery exchange, had them breathless again, the only reason LaShyra chose to break the embrace. They stood looking into one another's eyes, while waiting for their sweat-filled bodies to cool down. LaShyra seemed frustrated as she couldn't feel Excelcious' appreciation for her generosity.

They were panting and gasping, trying to catch a second wind. LaShyra was thankful for the opportunity to speak her mind. "I know we've been caught up in the heat of the moment!" Stating the obvious, before following up her comment with a deviant smile. "In case you've lost your sense of direction, let me help you get your bearings. We're at the crossroads!" LaShyra informed Excelcious, while threatening to drop her bikini bottom. She'd already taken off the gold panties. "I'm raising the ante. We can either go separate ways, or we venture past the point of no return, and you can have, these!" She offered, covering her breasts with her hands. "If you choose these. you can also have this!" She showed him, dropping her bikini bottom to the floor. Standing before him completely naked, she stated the obvious. "It's a straight road to paradise. A pretty lucrative offer, don't you think? Guaranteed benefits for the both of us." LaShyra promised, doing her best to entice him, trying her damnedest, to get him to engage with, and make love to her.

"When you gave me that massage earlier, you missed a lot of acreage. You had an open invitation to explore private property. Why didn't you take advantage of it? I'm giving you a second opportunity to check out what you overlooked the first time!" Suddenly looking into her copper eyes wasn't as enchanting. He saw an evil in them as they seemed to have turned devilish red.

"Gambling with love is a dangerous game. You can't take the jokers out of the deck! They'll always be in play! Odds are you'll be dealt a losing hand 99+ percent of the time. The first joker is a wild card, anything can happen, though chances are slim things will work out between the gamblers involved in the game. The second joker, that's the card nobody wants to draw. The second joker, alias, three of broken hearts is the most devastating card in the deck. When played, friendships, relationships, even lives are destroyed. Everyone in the Love triangle gets hurt. Are you sure you want to play that card LaShyra? You better think twice before you do. Think what it'll do to Shilloqwai. Maybe you don't care about her. What about me? You said you loved me. Okay, suppose you truly do. What about the trust? Knowing how committed to each other she and I are, if I were to leave her, for you, what makes you so sure, that somewhere down the line, I won't leave you for someone else? It comes down to a matter of trust. If I left her for you, could you really trust me after that? Be honest! How can I trust you to stay with me, especially if some other joker catches your eye?"

"Cut the sentimental bullshit! You know you want me as badly as I want you." LaShyra quipped, calling his bluff. "We're practically in paradise and we haven't even touched each other yet. Getting there means checking out the private property. It'll be fun, a sensual erotic adventure, especially when we get to the love making part. We're so close Excelcious. We're just a kiss away. I know you're staring at my charms. Touch them, I dare you! Just one more little kiss and we'll be making love. The fireworks are ready to go off! Light the fuse. I'm waiting. I can see you're not quite ready for me. It's okay. It takes some guys a little longer to get ready!"

LaShyra dared him a second time, embracing him with eyes closed and pursed lips. She pulled him close. Just before their lips met, he released her and pulled away from her grasp. "You devil woman, I can't!" Excelcious cried. "I just can't!"

"Why not?" LaShyra asked, choking on her own tears.

"It's a bad fuse!" Excelcious said flatly, making no effort to hide the tears rolling down his cheeks. "If we ignite it, sparks will fly, shit will happen before it blows up in our faces. Everyone is going to get hurt, you, me, Shilloqwai! Is that what you want? Three broken hearts will be the price paid for a lustful moment of ecstasy we're on the brink of indulging in. I'm a brave man, but I don't have the courage to play the one card that could, and likely would destroy the three of us! That is why I'm refusing to play the three of broken hearts!

"Okay I'll admit it, I want you. But, as a man of wisdom , I can't engage. I know the consequences if I do. With my wisdom, I will stop you from playing that damned card too!"

"Try and stop me!" She selfishly dared him, while still touching herself. Just one little kiss is all it will take for our fantasies to come alive and our dreams to come true!"

"Bitch, go away, get out of my life!" Excelcious had found the eject button that got him out of a very precarious and a very uncomfortable situation. After LaShyra stormed off to her room, he thought twice about what prompted her retreat. He regretted calling her a bitch. He would apologize at the appropriate time. He needed to allow time for the fire to cool down. With the fire as hot as it was moments earlier, the kiss and make-up phenomenon was likely to come into play. It would have been the perfect excuse for her to coax him into paradise. He stayed away from her bedroom deliberately, and for that very reason. If she implemented that strategy, there would have been nothing left to keep him from falling over the brink. He was on the edge, a kiss away as she put it, is all it would have taken for him to fall into her lovemaking web.

She'd lied to him. It was less than that. An eyelash, a heartbeat, perhaps merely a touch or just a wanton look and he would have made love to her. Guilty pleasures, a broken trust, a broken relationship complete with broken hearts, all would have followed. He'd played it right. The next morning, when he arrived outside of her room, the door was closed. He knocked gently, waiting patiently for her to open it! "Come in!" LaShyra welcomed him vibrantly as Excelcious let himself in. Dressed in a T-shirt and jeans, she ran up to him, casually embraced him, before gently kissing him on the cheek, as good friends often do.

"About last night!" LaShyra began with more than a hint of guilt in her voice. "I'm sorry! Though I'm embarrassed for what I did, I have no regrets. Given the same scenario, I can't see myself acting any differently. I wanted you to take me to paradise, you made sure we went separate ways. That had no impact on how I feel about you. Thank you for respecting me, treating me like a lady instead of like the slut I portrayed myself to be. I wish you weren't so damn loyal to Shilloqwai, because I don't think she's the only love for you! I made my move, your turn next. My offer still stands, so if you should suddenly reconsider…you know where to find me. There is a contingency, don't come knocking if all you want is to fool around. I'm not playing, don't you. Oh, if you think you'd like to get to know me in the most intimate way, take the 3 of broken hearts out of play. I want you, and I love you. If you want me, the way that I want you, and you can say that you love me, the way that I love you, then say goodbye to Shilloqwai, and that second joker that you talked about will never come into play.

"It'll be just you and me then, and I promise to give you a lifetime in paradise, eternally, not just for the short term. Say, at the very least, that you'll consider my offer!" Excelcious ignored her request by refusing to respond to it.

"Follow me." He ordered her, as he hurriedly fled from her bedroom. By the way, your shit is still in the living room, pick it up he called back to her. LaShyra had forgotten she'd left her sweats, blouse, bra, panties, and bikini bottoms on the floor. She intended to go back for them, but she was too caught up in her delusional fantasy. At first, she was confused at his outrage with her. The thought occurred to her, that he might actually take her up on her indecent proposal. She flashed a devilish smile certain he hadn't seen it. There was still hope for her fantasy to come alive, and time for him to come around. Perhaps, a little more coaxing, and he would be hers. She would just go with the flow. "Where are we going?" She asked curiously.

"We're going to check on Shilloqwai." He stated matter-of-factly. His voice was cold sounding. It had a chilling edge to it. She had ideas about how she could try to soften the edge. She wasn't accustomed to hearing the razor-sharp tone in his voice. She would have to be patient, for now! She would wait for a vulnerable moment to make her next move. Time was on her side, and she was more than willing to hurry up and wait! Over the past few days, Shilloqwai's vitals had been dropping to dangerously low levels, before coming back up. Each time this happened, the baseline had dropped to a level, lower than it had been the previous day. This day, her vitals were okay and holding steady. Currently her temperature was hovering between 85 and 90 degrees. Her blood pressure was remaining steady at 87 over 50. Her pulse was slow at 53 while her respirations were hovering around 12 breaths per minute.

LaShyra and Excelcious both agreed there were other signs indicating Shilloqwai's organs were failing, and her systems were shutting down. Both thought the reason for this might be that her body was working overtime to fight the poison that was contaminating it. Over the next 10 days, Shilloqwai's vitals continued bouncing up and down like a plum-sized rubber ball. There were still signs of organ failure, but in that regard, things seemed to be holding steady.

Though LaShyra and Excelcious had done everything medically possible to help Shilloqwai, their efforts seemed to be going for naught. They listed her condition as guarded, and checked on her regularly, about every 30 minutes. LaShyra had already gone back to her room. Excelcious planned to meet her, but before running off, he made the sign of the cross on her forehead and whispered under his breath, Jesus, I Trust in You! He did the same for himself. After his simple prayers, he made his way to LaShyra's room. The door was half-open. He knocked twice and then entered without waiting for an invitation to come in. "Oh shit!" He cursed. "I didn't realize…"

"You're acting like it's some big deal that you're seeing me naked. What? Are you surprised that I'm entertaining myself? You can watch me finish! Hell, just last night I was rubbing my naked body against you. You massaged my back and my legs yesterday. Today you got a good look at my fat ass and my babymaker! The comment in reference to her butt was a setup. She waited anxiously for his response.

"I don't think you have a fat ass! The curves are…I'll come back when you're done!" She giggled after he'd fallen into her trap. Her laughter made him realize that he'd just been had.

"So, you have been staring at my breasts, the contours of my ass, and babymaker. Don't lie because I can feel the heat from your penetrating eyes. It's turning me on, take me, I dare you. You know you want to. You don't have to leave. You can watch me finish!" She teased as she was touching herself again.

"Damn you! Your nakedness leaves nothing to the imagination. As tempting as it is I can't take you, not out of lust. If, we did it now, it wouldn't even be close to making love."

"Making love is the ultimate goal. But who says we can't have fun working up to that point? Just think of me as a gameboard then, there are lots of ways to play. Get as creative as you want, show me some of your imagination. How many ways can you think of to play the board? We can try them all, and then invent new ones! Look, I know you don't want to hear this, but I think Shilloqwai's dying. I know you think this too. I don't believe she's going to make it. I'm here to give you a shoulder to cry on, if you should need it. I know you think I'm being really, really naughty, and I am. But I can be very, very nice at the same time. Last night, you called me a bitch, did you mean that?"

"No, I didn't mean it and I shouldn't have said it. I'm sorry. Please forgive me! Come here." She did as he requested. He welcomed her nakedness into his arms.

She took advantage of the opportunity, rubbing her naked body up against him like the waves lapping up against the sand on the beach. Once again, they were being consumed by kisses of fire, without getting burned, but this time the blaze was dangerously close to getting out of control. "Take your clothes off!" She demanded, with a sweet sigh and a wanton moan. Excelcious snapped back into reality. This was just the matinee, which he cut short, excusing himself, under the pretense that he had other things to do. She accepted that and released him with the promise that he would be there for the duration of the long program.

"What should I wear tonight?" LaShyra asked, anxious with anticipation standing before him, once again with everything in view. She pirouetted in front of him, teasing him with the coming attractions. "You want the good parts? Come to the late-night showing!"

"If, I were you, I'd wear something a little more formal. We'll have all night to build the crescendo up to cloud nine before the decrescendo, where we float like feathers back to the ground."

"Okay, I'll wear something nice. But underneath, I'm going to wear something naughty, or perhaps I won't be wearing anything at all."

"I don't want to rush things. This is the long program remember? I want the provocative overtures, the interludes, and everything else before the grand finale. You'll have the day to orchestrate things, while I'm working in the lab."

"This is a two-person symphony, right? That's the condition for admission to the private showing, isn't it? That's the only way I know of we can harmonize and make beautiful music together!"

"I'm still working on the arrangements. We'll practice it tonight until it's perfect. Then again, it takes more than a day to create a masterpiece."

Once again, they fell into a lover's embrace. This time when she rubbed her body against his, it felt like the angry waves slamming against the breakwater. It was obvious they had some rough edges they needed to work out. And the kisses of fire they exchanged this time, left a burning sensation in their mouths, warning them of the consensual gamble they had agreed to take. Both knew it wasn't an eternal flame they were about to walk into. And both knew, if they followed through with their lustful desires, they would go down blazing in infatuation. The experience would change them both where they'd likely walk away from it as X-lovers. They would learn the hard way that the love they were feeling was the wrong kind of love, and how much the wrong kind of love really hurts.

As tightly as she'd held onto him before Excelcious left her room, LaShyra felt him slipping away from her. She hoped they'd made all of their mistakes in their rehearsal. When it was showtime, the mistakes would be covered up by adlib, making it seem as though everything had gone according to plan, and everything would be perfect. LaShyra reflected once more on his parting words.

What was it he'd said? 'It takes more than one day to create a masterpiece. All children were masterpieces, and it takes nine months to bring a baby into the world. Is that what he meant? That he wanted to start a family with her? Was she reading too much into his words? He also said he didn't want to rush things.

She thought that perhaps he meant they should work on building their relationship before jumping from the frying pan into the fire. She was pondering one of the other things he'd said, the thing where he said it was up to her to orchestrate things. Did that mean that he thought she was alone in conducting the whole affair? Then she wondered if he was wholeheartedly into the affair they were planning to have.

She told him that she loved him. Never once had he said that to her. When he told her to wear a nice dress, was he suggesting that she act more ladylike and not act like such a lush? Finally, LaShyra decided that she had to stop second-guessing everything. She would let the evening come to her and make the most of the opportunities it presented. She decided she would focus on one thing, fulfilling the promise to make love to him. She promised him paradise. Had she promised too much?

He said he wanted everything in the symphony! The overtures, the interludes and everything else that would take them to the grand finale. Was he really asking everything of her? Or was he asking for the one thing from her that she hadn't yet offered; a chance for them to build dreams together, to find happiness together, to find true love in one another? LaShyra saw all of those as beautiful things. Put together, they would make a beautiful Love story, a beautiful symphony. What she didn't realize, perhaps she did, that her desire to make love to Excelcious without those other things in place; it would be like reading the end of the book and then going back to read the story. Doing that, spoils everything. What romance is there in that? She was depressed for the rest of the day.

Perhaps Excelcious would come through and pick her up with a star performance. She would be ready if he were willing. Meanwhile, Excelcious went to his lab with the intent of putting in a full day's work. He hadn't done all that much since Shilloqwai had been sick. That was understandable. Looking back on what they had accomplished together was a story in itself. He missed her. He wondered if she would recover. He had LaShyra to turn to if, God forbid, Shilloqwai died. If, that was the question, why had he seemingly given up on her, thinking she was a goner?

She wasn't dead yet! Excelcious chastised himself for not giving the Power of Love a chance to work its magic. "What in the hell was I thinking?" He wondered aloud, meaning every word. "LaShyra, that conniving little Bitch! She almost made me play the three of broken hearts. Damn that joker anyway. Love is a lot of things, a game it's not ! My gambling days are done, I fold, game over."

In regard to the work, it was pointless to try and do anything when he wasn't focused. He did, however, check up on a few things. The evacuations were going well, the improvements and enhancements to the DDD weaponry were being implem ented. And the underground world, soon to be home, at least temporarily, was nearly complete.

His confidants said the project would likely be finished a month or so before the projected completion date. Excelcious had worked so hard to build the network that made his ideas come to life, from their conception and design, engineering, and manufacturing, on through to the delivery and distribution. He worked equally, even harder on his relationship with Shilloqwai. They were building a future together. Life got in the way and put their personal plans on hold. They promised to wait for each other if they got separated. In order for Excelcious to keep his promise to Shilloqwai, he would have to break the promise of making love to LaShyra. A broken promise to keep the love of his life? That was a no brainer, the promise to LaShyra would be broken! He wondered how he could have been so stupid by letting himself come so close to throwing their love away. He knew if he'd lost the treasure, he had in Shilloqwai, there would be little hope of ever recovering it. She would likely be gone from his life forever and through all of eternity.

Excelcious couldn't bear the thought of it. The fantasy of sharing a night with LaShyra had turned into a nightmare that would never materialize. On the way to check on Shilloqwai, Excelcious was thankful to have come to his senses. He was convinced all of her other ailments could be treated. He wasn't sure if there was anything that could heal her, if he'd cheated on her and broken her heart, by having an illicit affair, especially with LaShyra. She probably would have forgiven him in time, but he would have broken the trust between them, something he knew he'd probably never be able to fix. And once he'd broken Shilloqwai's heart, there would be no way to unbreak it!

If they somehow managed to stay together through it all, there would always be the shadow of suspicion intertwined in their relationship. Like weeds thriving in a rose garden, they would never again completely trust one another. That inability to trust one another, would prevent them from giving 100% of themselves to one another. Thereby, preventing them from loving one another in accordance with their dreams and fantasies, their passions, and desires, all of the things that hold relationships together.

With trust in question, the foundation of a relationship, especially a loving one, grows weak. If a couple's love is strong enough, the committed individuals may be able to patch up the relationship to keep it from crumbling completely. He'd had enough time to think about things. As he stepped up the pace. He had an apology to make, forgiveness to ask for, a treasure to reclaim and a love he would continue to cherish. He was excited when he first saw her. Excelcious noticed her color was better. And when he looked at the monitor showing her vitals, he could see that Shilloqwai's overall condition was improving. Her blood pressure was 110/80, her oxygen was at 98, her pulse at 79 and her respirations at 15.

Though he'd visited her every day, Excelcious hadn't really spent much time with her. Today was going to be different. He pulled up a chair and gently kissed Shilloqwai on the forehead before sitting down at her bedside. He decided, it was there he would spend the remainder of his day. He would sit next to her and talk to her. Though, it would more than likely be a one-sided conversation, where he would do all of the talking. He looked with admiration on his sleeping beauty as she lay with her story-filled eyes still closed. He longed to see the transparency in her eyes. He missed reading the stories behind them. Mostly, he missed the look in her tourmaline eyes that told him in enchanting fashion how much she loved him. He took her hand in his and held it. Softly, he began speaking to her, as if not to wake her, yet hoping she could hear his every word.

"I love you Shilloqwai, my heart is aching so badly, I miss you so much! You've been deathly sick. I just want you to know that I'm here for you if you need anything. You seem to be doing better today, better than you have been since you fell ill. I've been praying religiously every day for your recovery. You've been sleeping for quite a while now. C'mon hon, it's time to wake up!" Her response was immediate. As if she were acting on his command, Shilloqwai opened her big, beautiful, transparent tourmaline eyes. "Shilloqwai!" Excelcious whimpered with tears flooding his eyes. Shilloqwai started crying too. She was overwhelmed with joy at the sight of him.

"It was nice to get a few hours' sleep!"

"You got more than a few hours hon!"

"It felt good, nevertheless. In actuality, how long have I been in Zombieland?"

"Almost three weeks!"

"That long? Doesn't matter. I'm just happy to be alive. I feel so weak. Did you and LaShyra ever figure out what in the hell was wrong with me?"

"Nothing, really. Not anything that we didn't already know, the fact that you're hopelessly in love with me."

"Since when did they start classifying love as an illness or a disease?"

"They haven't and they won't. Because if they do, everyone in the world would have to undergo treatment. I don't think there are enough psychologists to handle the caseload." Shilloqwai burst out laughing uncontrollably. She laughed until she cried. It's good to see you back to some semblance of your old self!"

"You're calling me old? I haven't been asleep that long! Hell! I'm younger than you are! So, I have no idea what you're talking about! Seriously, what did you find? "

"Well, LaShyra and I have a theory as to what's going on with you. And that's all we have to go on, because all of your tests including the lab work came back negative. You passed all of your tests with flying colors. Medically, there's nothing wrong with you. Changing the subject for a second, no breaks or damage to the ligaments in the leg except for severe bone bruising. You were going to ask me something? Go ahead!"

"That's good, in regard to the tests, for both me and you! If I hear you right, my condition has something to do with my mutant powers then, right?"

"That's our theory. After a lot of speculating, we've boiled it down to this. When you were manufactured, Skeletos gave you a golden heart. From what we can gather, as you were transforming into a human, the gold heart you were given started to hollow. As your human heart started replacing your golden heart, the golden heart began eroding. The erosion seems to be continuing on, depositing metal filings or gold chips into your bloodstream, and internal organs. We've figured out how to rid your system of the gold chips, but we can't remove the part of the golden shell still attached to your heart. The way LaShyra explained it to me, is that the golden shell is fused to the outer wall of the heart. She cautioned any attempt to remove the golden shell, could tear or damage the heart, thereby killing you. So, we can't fix it. We've devised an action plan to check you every so often and see if we find more chips floating around in your body. We'll extract them the same way we have the others."

"So, if these chips in my system, say there were to get into my large intestine, they would be expelled naturally? Right? Wow just think if that actually happened! I'd be the first person on record with the capability to shit gold, or turn shit into gold, however you want to look at it!" The two of them began laughing hysterically. Both were laughing so hard, they started crying. It took them several minutes to regain their composure as they laughed until their sides ached.

"We think that all of the gold will chip away, and the shell will dissipate eventually! When it does, we're hoping that you won't be having further issues in this regard. The danger of these gold chips breaking away, is they tend to be drawn together and form clusters. If one of these clusters gets clogged in your bloodstream or up and around your heart, you may be subject to a fatal heart attack or stroke. We think the reason you came so close to death, several times, is when these gold chips broke away, they released toxins into your system. As your body's Immunol system is fighting these toxins, she and I believe that's when you are most vulnerable and likely to get sick. Even though you may be feeling well, if you were to get an infection from those toxins, the fear is that you could die from the infection, die from the toxins or some deadly combination of both. As we have seen, complications could result from either."

"Guess every Superhero has a weakness or some vulnerability. Superman's was Kryptonite, mine happens to be gold dust! Okay, so what about the bleeding that occurs, when I use my powers and get emotional, is it related to this golden shell around my heart?"

"LaShyra and I think they're related, but, neither of us is quite sure how. We suspect that when you get angry, or your self-defenses kick in, something happens that triggers a physiological reaction. A reaction that causes these chips to be shaved from the shell. We thought that as these microscopic chips make their way through your system and into the bloodstream, they're damaging the organs and, or blood vessels, thus your bloody noses and bloody mouth, along with the blood that sometimes comes out of your ears and out of your eyes. It's hard to predict whether or not there will be long-term effects from this phenomenon. My advice is to be guarded and use caution when tapping into your powers. Can you excuse me for a minute? I have something to take care of. I'll be right back!" He kissed her on the forehead before he bolted for the door.

"I'm not going anywhere!" She called after him as he disappeared down the corridor on the way to LaShyra's room. As he entered, LaShyra had a delicious smile on her face. It crumbled like a cookie when she saw the perplexed look on his. "Is something wrong, hon? I can make it better." She promised, revealing the full of her nakedness so he could see all that she had to offer.

"No, everything's fine but…"

"Shilloqwai is she okay?"

"Yeah, she's doing great! She came out of her coma. I told her I had something to take care of. She's waiting for me to come back, so I'll get to the point. I just came to let you know that tonight's event's been cancelled. There will be no rainchecks issued or rescheduling of the event."

"Shit!" LaShyra cursed. I was really looking forward to this. I got myself all worked up, just waiting, lying here, and thinking about making love to you."

"I'm sorry to disappoint you. To be honest with you, I was looking forward to it too. After considering the cost, the price of admission was too high. It put me out of the game. I couldn't justify playing the three of broken hearts, for a single night of lovemaking with you! Your offer was a generous one, I respectfully refuse!"

LaShyra sprang from her bed, streaking toward him, chasing him out of her room. She made him disappear behind the slamming door. "You didn't even kiss me goodbye you son-of-a-bitch! You're a lying bastard!" She knew he didn't see her flip him off, so, she verbalized that along with other profanities that came spewing from her mouth.

Meanwhile, Shilloqwai was beginning to wonder where Excelcious was. He'd been gone longer than she'd expected. Excelcious wasn't planning on being gone as long as he was either. A few minutes more, at this point, wasn't going to matter now. He'd run out to the garden to pick some wild roses, eleven turquoise ones and a red one he placed in the middle of the bouquet, symbolizing the one and only love of his life. Shilloqwai smiled with a sigh of relief when he finally returned to her bedside. "I was beginning to wonder where in the hell you went. Seeing the flowers, that explains it , thank you! I love you, Excelcious. It's easy to get the big things right, but you do all the little things right too. God, I've missed you. Come closer."

"Let me disconnect all of this shit first! Hopefully, you won't be needing any of it for a long while."

"All I need is you. You're my lifeblood, you're what keeps my heart beating, what keeps me alive!" Though she was weak she got out of bed and stood up. Excelcious was there to support her. After steadying her, he took her in the cradle of his arms. She reciprocated, cradling him in hers, securing their lover's embrace. They'd never forgotten the intimacy or the passion fueling their kisses of fire. It had been so long since there were any fireworks between them. The explosive energy that was released when their lips met, seemed to them to be the equivalent to the energy released in a nuclear meltdown. The heat's intensity would be more than hot enough to evaporate the saliva in their mouths and take the wetness from their kisses.

All it meant was they'd become breathless sooner, and they'd need more periods of recuperation. Mouthwatering kisses provided only temporary relief for their unquenchable thirst. Kisses of fire, laced with intimacy and passion are what kept their insatiable desires for one another burning. Shilloqwai pulled away from him with a glint in her eyes. "Before I took my extended siesta you said you had a surprise for me. Can I see it now? Or haven't you cracked the code yet?"

"I've cracked the code on the encrypted files. I've been looking for opportunities to show you the files, but none have presented themselves."

"I'm ready now to see the files. Just out of curiosity, why did it take so long to crack the code?"

"I was worried if I did it wrong, I would lose all of the information and you'd never get to see what's in those files. Your system wasn't programmed to read these files, your virus protection was reading these files as corrupt. In the Mercusilver design, the instant corrupt files were detected, there was a mechanism that shut the robots down. This prevented databases from being erased while keeping other software from being destroyed. That is why you were glitching and kept shutting down. I was worried that my tampering with the chip, would erase it and we'd never see what was on those files. I think I mentioned I found a chip with encrypted files inside of LaShyra too, while I was refurbishing her, after you kicked the living shit out of her."

"Yeah, well if she doesn't stay away from you, she's going to get her ass terminated. Which reminds me, while I was asleep, during my extended siesta, I had another one of my premonitions. It was more like a nightmare, really! Anyway, my guts are churning with the prospect that there's any element of truth to this whatsoever !"

"What is it, did I die or something?"

"Or something, and that something was that I left you!"

"You know that there's nothing that could ever come between us."

"That's what I used to think, but ever since that bitch showed up…I don't know…I don't even want to say it. The thought of it makes me sick!"

"You gotta tell me now babe, the suspense is killing me!"

"I had a dream, why do I keep calling it a dream? It was a nightmare! LaShyra was pregnant with your child! I know she's a robot, it would be stupid to think that you could interface with her. It's a disgusting thought really! Because you couldn't…unless…she transformed! In my nightmare, she was human!"

"Actually, she did transform. It was always your nightmare, that something like this would happen ever since she arrived. Well after it happened, she said it was her dream come true."

"Holy shit! You're joking right?" Shilloqwai was in absolute denial.

"I wish I were, for your peace of mind! She's definitely not a robot anymore, she's human with a heart and soul just like you."

She was mortified that Excelcious confirmed her worst nightmare. She burst into tears after hearing of the horror story. Monsters were supposed to stay in the movies and not come to life.

"She's nothing like me! Don't ever make that comparison again, or it will be a long time before we come to speaking terms. So now, I have real competition, unfriendly competition at that! So, exactly when did this transformation take place?"

"A day or two after you went comatose."

"So, you've had nearly a month to get acquainted with her?"

"I have a confession to make!"

"You didn't do anything with the bitch, did you? What did you do with her? Was it afternoon delight, or primetime in the night? Please tell me, you didn't get it on with her!"

"Nooo! We didn't get it on. I'll tell you everything. Just let me talk, will you? We don't keep secrets from one another, remember? As I told you, I do have a confession to make!"

"Shit, do I really want to hear this?" She asked somberly. Shilloqwai started to cry. No sooner had Excelcious begun to speak when the tears began streaking down her cheeks.

"There were a good number of times, especially over the last couple of weeks, we didn't think you were going to make it. You'd flatlined for the third time, since we'd put you under. Your vitals dropped to dangerously low levels. We couldn't get them to come back up. And when they did come up to acceptable levels, we had trouble keeping them there. LaShyra and I both thought you were dying. I was having a hard time dealing with the prospect of losing you. Without you here to talk to, I was lost. I needed a companion, someone to talk to. LaShyra was there for me. She told me not to give up, and that things were going to work out! She kept telling me to keep trusting in the Power of Love. There was a short period when I stopped trusting, and I gave up on you and into temptation. That's my confession!"

"So, there was a little something going on between the two of you! I want to know everything! And I want the truth. Before you start speaking, just know that you're on very thin ice and the ice is severely cracked. I don't care how pissed you think I'm going to get! You better not lie to me, either by commission or omission. If you do lie to me, or if I find out about something you should have told me, worst of all if I find out you made love to her, we're done. There'll be nothing to reconcile and you can kiss my ass goodbye, forever. Have I made myself clear?"

"Crystal!"

"Start talking. I hope you don't have some bullshit, heartbreaking story that you're about to tell me. I can't believe we're even having this discussion!"

"I'll start with the worst of it first. You're not going to like any of what you're going to hear, but, if I can get past the first part without you killing me, just know that…oh shit! Never mind, here goes. You were really sick for three nights in a row, Last night, was the worst night. Your skin was so pale. The clear blue sky was dark by comparison. Your skin had almost no color at all, it was cream white. You had a 103-degree temp. I thought I would be burying you today. Like I told you, you flatlined for the third time since she and I put you under." Shilloqwai was listening intently. She didn't give a damn about his prelude. She wasn't interested in hearing about how sick she'd been. She wanted to hear the real story regarding this affair, or almost affair, whatever the hell it was LaShyra and Excelcious had or thought they had over the past three weeks.

"Last night, I was ready for a breakdown; I was in tears. All of your organs were showing signs of shutting down. It was late at night around 10:30, 11:00 when she came into my makeshift living room. She asked how I was and if I would like someone to talk to. I welcomed that, thinking it was totally innocent. She started sharing more details about how she saved you. It got strange, because she was telling me how her body ached and how her back was still sore from when you, body-slammed her to the floor. I questioned her about feeling pain and that's when she told me that she'd transformed like you."

"I should have broken her back and she wouldn't have been able to come anywhere near you! I'm sorry, go on!"

"I made the mistake of asking her if she'd like a back massage. She took off her blouse, and half-naked she lay face-down on the couch!"

"She jiggled her charms in front of you?"

"She casually took of her blouse and lay face-down on the couch. Respectfully and professionally, I gave her a back massage. Her arms and legs hurt, so I massaged those for her too. Let me clarify in regard to massaging her legs, in the front I only went up to the lower quads, and in the back her lower hamstrings."

"You don't expect me to believe that shit, do you?"

"Ask her."

"I will. You'll tell me everything that happened from your perspective and then I'll decide if she'll live long enough to get her story out. Go on…I just want to get through this!"

"It all started so innocently, suddenly we found ourselves at the crossroads!"

"The crossroads, huh? That means you kissed her. I know it was more than a goodnight kiss, so don't try and tell me otherwise. How far down your throat did she stick her tongue? How far, did you put your tongue down her throat? So, what was she wearing when you massaged her legs? And if you tell me, she was completely naked, it's over right now! Is it over between us or what?"

"Honey look, I know this is hard for you to hear, but try to put yourself in my shoes. I was gullible, she caught me at a weak moment. And we did things we shouldn't have done. She made me realize two things, that life would go on, had you passed away. She also made me appreciate even more the treasure I had in you."

"You romantic son-of-a-bitch. Finish the story. I hope it's almost over! Because I'm not sure how much more of this shit I can listen to! So, what was she wearing when you massaged her legs?"

"Not much, she had a red bikini bottom on, under her sweats. She had gold panties covering the bikini. Those she took off while threatening to take off the rest."

"Okay, so basically you saw her ass and probably everything else. Was her babymaker covered at least?"

"Yes! It wasn't until we got off of the couch she got buck-naked."

"I'm not surprised she showed you everything, bitch-whore! You didn't play show and tell with her, did you?"

"No, I kept my dignity, even while she rubbed her naked body against me while we were kissing. I shoved her away after that dirty little stunt. She wasn't going to leave. She attempted to continue with the seduction until I called her a bitch. I apologized to her this morning, then I came to check on you. When I saw that you had come to, I excused myself, I went to her room and told her that tonight's show had been cancelled and that it was an event that would not be rescheduled."

"So, you were going to make love to her tonight? You son-of-a-bitch!" This time she issued him more than a verbal chastising. Shilloqwai followed up her icy words with a cold, hard slap to the face, that had him seeing stars. "Is this it? Is the worst of it over?" Shilloqwai screamed hysterically through her groaning sobs. "Because if there's something more intimate, other than the slobbering kisses exchanged between the two of you, I swear to God I'm leaving. And I won't even let you kiss my ass goodbye! So, you saw her naked with all of her charms?"

"Yes!"

"Did you touch her? For your sake you better not have laid a hand or even a finger on her private property."

"No!"

"You're, telling me, you stayed away from her private property? With all of that prime real estate in front of you, and you managed to keep your hands to yourself?"

"Yes!"

"Two more questions, and then I'm done with you!"

"Did you tell her that you loved her?"

"No!"

"Did she tell you that she loved you?"

"Yes, she also said she hoped there was a future for us!"

"What a conniving Bitch! I swear, I'm going to kill her!"

"Shilloqwai, may I please ask you something?"

"What?" She asked sneering at him.

"Do you believe me? Do you still trust me? If you do on both counts, we can patch this up!"

"I'm not sure I believe you, or that I can trust you anymore!"

"That's a hell of a thing to say!"

"Yeah, and that's a hell of a thing you did to me! I've heard that Love hurts. I didn't think it was possible, you just showed me how much it can!"

"I'm sorry, please forgive me, I didn't mean to hurt you! I thought you were stronger than that, that our love was stronger than that. We can get over this hurdle, but you have to trust me."

"We'll talk about this more when I come back! Don't go anywhere or you will be kissing my ass goodbye!" Excelcious sighed out of frustration.

Shilloqwai stormed out of the lab, sprinted down the corridor and barged in to LaShyra's room unannounced. LaShyra, who had been lying down, sprung up into a sitting position on the bed. "What the hell do you want? You scared the shit out of me!"

"You'll be lucky if I don't beat the shit out of you before this is all said and done!" Shilloqwai threatened LaShyra, as she slammed the door behind her. "Excelcious and I had a heart-to-heart talk. He tells me everything, that's why our relationship is so strong. I could be wearing a blindfold. Without seeing his facial expressions, or without being able to look into his eyes, I know when he responds to me whether or not he's telling the truth! As kindred spirits and soulmates, there's a telepathic energy that flows between us. I can read his mind and he can read mine. I'll know whether he's done something wrong, regardless of whether he tells me or not. Since I've already talked to Excelcious, and I've alerted you to the special connections that allow us to openly communicate from a distance, I strongly suggest that you tell me the truth! So, I'm going to do away with the bullshit and get straight to the point. Did you or did you not make love to Excelcious?"

"He's a great guy. In three months, he said he'd go with me to get my pregnancy test!"

"You lying bitch!" LaShyra caught Shilloqwai's backhand across the jaw. "You want to lie to me some more?" She asked as the force of the blow nearly knocked her from the bed to the floor. "I'm asking you again, did you make love to him ?"

"Nooo!" LaShyra sobbed. Clearly, she now understood that Shilloqwai wasn't in the mood to play.

"Tell me about the massage, did he touch you inappropriately?"

"I wish he would have! I would have jumped his bones right out there on the couch! He did such a great job massaging my back, I turned over and asked if he wanted to use his skills on the front. He flat-out refused. I don't know how he resisted with my charms dangling in front of him! I knew he wanted a massage. He accepted my offer on the condition that I put my blouse on. I refused. He allowed me to go ahead with the massage. It was the only concession he made all night. I climbed on top of him while I massaged his back. I made sure he was aware of the equipment that was available for his personal use by dragging my charms across his back. In doing this, I thought I was going to get my way with him. I was breaking him down. Rather than press the issue, we reverted to kissing. He left his shirt off. I took advantage of the opportunity and pressed my dangling charms against his chest. The sweat pouring from our bodies added to the thrill for both of us. I had my tongue all the way down his throat and his tongue was all the way down mine. I dragged him up off of the couch and I took off the bikini bottoms. I was pressing the full of my naked body against him. I don't know what you call it when you're standing. If we'd been sitting, clearly it would have been considered a lap dance. I tried my damnedest to seduce him. As hard as I tried, he wasn't near ready enough to take me. Still, I was convinced I was going to get more than a good night kiss from him. But he refused to touch me and that pissed me off!

"I went to bed so disappointed, so unsatisfied. Dirty little bitch, I was, I still had hopes of seducing him. When I thought he was about to give in, I broke the embrace. I moved away from him in the most provocative fashion while giving him the most inviting sensuous, wanton looks. I also did some other very naughty, but very nice things I'm not going to mention. You're a woman, you can probably guess what those things were. He watched me finish." She boasted, giving Shilloqwai the suggestive middle finger. "After doing everything I could think of to entice him I confronted him and asked him to give me what I wanted. I begged him and pleaded with him to make love to me. When he refused, I asked him to give me one good reason why not!"

"What reason did he give you for not giving in?"

"He, said, he already found the treasure of a lifetime and he didn't want to trade it in for fool's gold. Then he told me why he wouldn't gamble on love. He said there was less than a one percent chance of being dealt a winning hand. He warned me about the two jokers in a deck of cards, and how they were always in play. He told me that the first joker was a wildcard representing less than a one percent chance of things working out. He warned me about the second joker, and how deadly it is when it comes into play. The second joker has an alias, he called it, the three of broken hearts. He said the three parties involved in the love triangle all got hurt. Adding that the relationships between those caught up in the triangle are usually permanently destroyed."

"So, after all that and he resisted? I'd call you a damn liar, but your tears, they don't lie. They verify you're speaking the truth and show the disappointment you're still feeling about your missed opportunity for lovemaking. So, what was the difference between last night and tonight? You know, the secret rendezvous? Excelcious said that when he went to your room and told you the sexcapades event was permanently cancelled, you got really pissed! When he told you why it was cancelled, he said you chased him out of the room with a mouthful of profanity. You really are a bitch !"

"It was more out of disappointment, than anything else. I was all worked up, ready and waiting, when he told me. It was so anticlimactic."

"I won't tell you how you could have fixed that problem. I know, you know!"

"It didn't help, I tried it! Now, who's the bitch? That wasn't nice to say. It was downright rude!"

"Rude? Better than taking your ass out! Go near my man again, and I swear, I will kill you!"

"That's a crime!"

"Crime of passion, the case will be dismissed!"

"So, you're going to keep him after he was ready to get it on with another woman?"

"Yes, I'm holding on to him. He didn't sleep with you because you weren't good enough for him. Shit, you couldn't even get him ready to take you."

"I almost succeeded in seducing him. I surprised myself at how close I came to actually doing it! My real objective was to drive a wedge between the two of you. I wanted to play up the affair we almost had. I was hoping that you'd be so pissed, you'd dump him. I planned to wait in the wings to pick him up out of the street and whisk him away."

"You really are a wicked bitch!" Shilloqwai delivered a backhand to the other side of LaShyra's face, leaving her whimpering in her bed. With tears streaming down her cheeks, Shilloqwai ran back to where she'd left Excelcious, who was still wondering if he'd ever see her again. Excelcious breathed a sigh of relief when he saw her smiling through her tears. He knew at that moment the worst was behind them. He wasn't sure what to make of the middle finger she was holding up to him. "Don't worry!" She said softly. I'm not signaling what you should go do with yourself. It's an invitation to play, what I want you to do to me!"

She smiled mischievously as she took off her blouse. She was braless. She wanted to speak and tell him what was on her mind, but she couldn't compose herself. In showing what she felt for him, there would be no misunderstanding. She took off her denim shorts and her panties and stood before him buck naked. She began the erotic show with a solo performance. Becoming weak-kneed, she climbed into the bed so she could finish the show. He played along with the show and tell. When he was completely undressed, she invited him into bed with her and then pulled the covers over them both. She wondered what was wrong with LaShyra that she couldn't get him ready. Shilloqwai had barely gotten her blouse off, and she could see that Excelcious needed relief. She laughed, sharing the story with him. "Is what she said really true?"

"She said a lot of things, what specifically are you referring to?"

"She said, you couldn't, you know, get ready for her to open up to you!"

"Yes! That's true!"

Shilloqwai laughed. "Quite frankly, I don't see the problem. She must have been doing something wrong. Hold me." She was begging for more than a hug and a kiss. They both laughed. He took her into his arms, pulling her naked body close, she welcomed his embrace and lay her head on his shoulder. Being in the cradle of his arms brought her all of the comfort she needed. Excelcious was gently massaging her back as she cooed and moaned.

"Excelcious," she begged, do the front too! When he hesitated, she placed his hands on her breasts, giving him license to be on private property. She released his hands, encouraging him to take a self-guided tour of the entire area. "Touch me," She begged! "Kiss me all over!" He encouraged her to do the same to him.

"Forgive me!" He pleaded. "I'm sorry I hurt…"

"SSShhh!" She hushed him. "We're past that now. This is the instrumental part of the song. No words should be spoken during this part. Kiss me, touch me, make love to me!" When their lips met it was like a nuclear meltdown. The heat from the intimate kisses of fire spread quickly, raging with passion while fueling their dreams, fantasies, and desires. "You have no idea how much I want you right now!"

"Oh, but I think I do," he responded as he was tracing the contours of her breasts with his fingertips, knowing that it was sending sensual reverberations through her body. It wasn't long before private property had become familiar territory for both of them. He was soon massaging her charms like one would caress a worry stone. Shilloqwai sighed as he worked his way to the centers, paying particular attention to the finest details.

To her delight, his exploration wasn't restricted to her dangling charms. He covered the lay of the land, tracing every curvilinear line on her body with his velvet fingertips. He probed and massaged every inch of her flesh along the way. Her body shuddered as waves of pleasure washed over her, with the sensations bringing her to the state of erotic ecstasy.

Wanting to share, the pleasure he brought her, she reciprocated by rubbing her body up against him. She succeeded somewhat. Had she taken the right angle, they would have been making love. He wouldn't allow it, and she had to respect that. There was some satisfaction for both of them in what they'd done. They were just inches from completing their erotic journey into paradise. They had an idea of what to expect now, when they finally decided to complete that journey. They imagined the growing anticipation for that day to come, would be similar to waiting for Christmas. "Why did you do what you just did Shilloqwai?"

"Because I wanted to get one up on LaShyra. And I wanted you to know what you would lose, if there's another almost affair, between you and any other woman!"

"I knew before you tried to prove your point. I think we should sit up before we do something foolish, and perhaps regret. Not that making love to you wouldn't be beautiful, but it will be more beautiful if we wait for the right moment."

"The way you're touching me, especially now, it feels like the right moment. I can feel by the way you're holding me that you want me too!"

"Yes, and you're making it hard to resist you. But this isn't the right moment. We can both feel that too!" Reluctantly she heeded his suggestion and got up out of the bed and got dressed, not before putting on another erotic show for him, after which she returned to the cradle of his arms with a mischievous sensuous look still on her face.

Her infectious trademark smile, the one he'd come to know and love, told him just how much she loved him. "I love you." He said in gratitude for the show. Does this mean I'm forgiven?"

"Forgiven? For what? Did you do something wrong? I'm the one that needs to be asking your forgiveness!"

"For what?"

"For doubting you, not believing and not trusting you."

"But you do believe in me, and you still trust me. If you didn't, we wouldn't be in the cradle of one another's arms right now. What happened? Why are you crying?"

"Because I almost lost the most important thing in my life. No not a thing, a special someone." Shilloqwai sobbed.

"It's going to be okay, please, tell me we can move forward!" Excelcious begged, while giving a gentle squeeze to her hand.

"Ouch!" Shilloqwai yelped.

What did you do to your hand?"

I backhanded the bitch, once on each side of the face!"

"You can't just…"

"Be thankful I didn't kill her! I intend to apologize, but only when I'm damn good and ready, and that may not be for a long, long time. I didn't want this episode, incident, whatever you want to call it to drag out. So, I asked her point-blank, if she made love to you. She said she had and that you offered to take her for a pregnancy test in three months. Bitch was lying, she couldn't even look me in the eyes when she said it. The smirk on her face told me she was trying to piss me off. She succeeded. I backhanded her the first time. Then I asked her what else happened. She was more than happy to provide all of the intimate details, telling me she could have had her way with you. I don't know how much was embellished, and how much was real. Based on what you confessed, the stories coincided almost verbatim.

"She, said kissing you got her all worked up, to the point that a wanton look, a passionate kiss, or an intimate touch would have allowed her to complete her seduction. She told me about the massage she gave you and the nasty ass things she did in addition to the massage. LaShyra said she thought she had you right where she wanted you , Especially, when she stood up and dropped her bikini bottoms. She said you stopped her by telling her that story about gambling on love and playing the three of broken hearts. And then, after your confession this morning, followed by our lover's quarrel and your subsequent visit to her room; she told me how she'd gotten herself all worked up thinking about your planned illicit rendezvous! She confessed that she was ready and waiting to play that three of broken hearts. She confessed to being buck naked on the bed doing nasty shit to try and entice you to engage, but you walked away! She said she was so pissed at you when you did, but more disappointed. She gave what she thought was her best shot, and her seduction attempt, still failed. Did she really do all of that shit she said she did, while you were watching her? If so, how did you resist her? Who the hell are you? What the hell are you, SUPERHUMAN? Knowing what I know now, had you made love to her, I would have had to forgive you. I didn't think there was a man strong enough to resist that kind of temptation. I hope I don't become stupid enough to ever let you go. It would be the biggest mistake of my life, and the last. I would die of natural causes. It's hard to stay alive when only half of your heart is beating. Tell me, Excelcious, how did you resist her?"

"I couldn't have done it on my own. Two things stopped me. After praying for a way out of my predicament, I got help and guidance from the Power of Love. I couldn't bring myself to do it. I'd be lying to say I wasn't thinking about it, because I was. You already know I watched her finish. I thought about how beautiful she is and how good it would have felt to make love to her. And then I thought of you. If I had done it with her, I would have seen your face the whole time, it wouldn't have felt right, because she isn't you. You're the one I'm in love with, not her, not now, not ever! No matter what happens to us, our kindred spirits will always soar together!" Endless tears of joy were cascading from her eyes and down her cheeks. Never again would she forget his heart was in her hands. She'd won it with her love. She'd keep it with her love. His heart was hers to lose. As long as she treasured it, she knew he would let her keep it forever. She'd given her heart to him, the day they first met. It was his to lose. Though their love had been severely tested, He'd kept his promise of not breaking her heart. He'd proven to her that he'd always treasure it. For those reasons, she was going to leave her heart with him forever. She knew he would die if she'd left him, just as she would die, if he'd left her. She couldn't live without a heart, and he was the lifeblood that ran through it. "So, tell me, where did the two of you end up? I don't imagine it's in a good place right now."

"It's not!" Shilloqwai confirmed. "I told you I would apologize to her when I'm ready. You want to hear how it ended?"

"I'm not sure! But go ahead, tell me!"

"I was about to leave the room, and she admitted that she didn't think she would be able to seduce you or coerce you into making love to her. She said it surprised her that the two of you had come as close as you had to actually physically engaging. She had a backup plan. She was going to make up a story about an alleged affair that the two of you had."

"What would have been the point of doing that?"

"If you and I hadn't talked first, and she'd come to me with that cockamamie story, I may not have listened to you, which would have been wrong of me. She said her objective was to drive a wedge between the two of us and split us up. She, said, she would have been waiting in the wings for me to let you go. Then she was going to swoop down and claim you for herself. I told her what a bitch she was for thinking such a thing, before backhanding her on the other side of the face. She chased me out of the room with a mouthful of profanity and an obscene gesture. I returned the gesture in kind along with the verbal accompaniment and then I came crying to you. Your transparency saved our relationship. I would have had a hard time forgiving you, if you hadn't told me the ugly truth! It hurt, but your love will heal me! My heart's already healed. No looking back, let's move forward, together!"

"It's going to be okay!" He assured her, as again he gently squeezed her hand.

"Shit!" She squealed in agony.

"Let me see that hand." Excelcious requested. She willingly offered it, setting it gently in his palm.

"Looks like you've got a couple of broken fingers."

"To go with the two welts, on the sides of her face."

"This shit needs to be settled. I'm afraid to ask, but would you mind if I go try and talk to her?"

"If you think it'll help! She's probably not going to stick around long, not after this, or after what I did to her!"

"Wait! Kiss me before you go." The passionate flurry, of intimate exchanges, delayed his visit to LaShyra's room for at least fifteen minutes. It might not have lasted that long if Excelcious hadn't been touching her inappropriately. She stopped him by threatening to get undressed again. "Keep it up and we'll be right back to where we were before. And if it goes that far again, I won't be leaving the bed a virgin."

Excelcious withdrew with his advances, and after a final kiss, he retreated to the corridor leading to LaShyra's room. He was surprised to find her milling about in the hallway with a suitcase in her hand. "Hey, where are you going?" He called out to her.

"I've overstayed my welcome. It's time to go. I have one last favor to ask, show me how to get out of here."

"Okay. I'm not going to keep you against your will, but it's probably in your best interest to stay! It's too dangerous up there. I don't want to see anything happen to you."

"Why should I stay? Does your bitch lover know you're with me?" LaShyra asked bitterly.

"Please, I don't want to fight. Love has many aspects. Just because I don't love you in one respect doesn't mean I can't love you as a friend. In that regard, I love you with all of my heart! You saved my best friend, the love of my life three times. I'm forever indebted to you for that. I feel obligated to return the favor, which is why I'm not going to let you leave! By making you stay, I'm certain I'll be saving your life."

LaShyra flashed a smile of amusement through her tears. "You're really something else! Unbelievable, lovable, incredibly amazingly honest and the most loving person I've ever met. I can't believe you actually had the guts to tell Shilloqwai everything. Especially all of that dirty, naughty but nice shit I did! It was for your benefit, your eyes, not her ears. After trying my damnedest to seduce you, the fact that you didn't engage made me feel ashamed. I still feel like a filthy washed-up whore. Yet, I have no regrets for my actions. For me it would have been worth it just to have a night or two with you. There's minimal consolation in the fact that I almost succeeded. In retrospect, I'm overwhelmed with guilt. I'm ashamed, seeing that I came within an eyelash of destroying something beautiful, that being, the love that you and Shilloqwai share. I know why now I failed in my seduction attempts. I was trying to extinguish the eternal flame burning in your hearts. An eternal flame is just that. It's like immortality, it lasts forever. There was nothing I could have done to extinguish it."

"Well, when love finds you, and it will, you will have your own kindred spirit with whom to kindle your own eternal flame. You're a very beautiful woman. Deep down you have a good heart, and it will serve you well."

Excelcious had moved her to tears. "Thank you!" LaShyra sobbed, setting her suitcase on the ground. She ran to him and embraced him, showing her gratitude for all he'd done with a feather kiss to his cheek. "It's what friends do!" She said offering a simple defense for her action. The wanton look in her beautiful rust-colored copper eyes betrayed her. He wasn't misreading the look either. She confirmed his suspicions by licking her luscious lips, opening the door for him to do anything he wanted to her.

Once again, it took everything Excelcious had to restrain himself, in turning down her generous offer. He did, however, kiss her softly on the cheek, after which she immediately broke the embrace. "Thank you for your lesson on love. I'll never gamble with it again. After your stern warning, I can't believe I selfishly tried to play the three of broken hearts. It did more than hurt, it nearly destroyed the three of us, me, you and Shilloqwai. For that, I am truly sorry. You might forgive me, but Shilloqwai, she never will. That's why I cannot stay. You understand then, why I have to go."

LaShyra turned away from him in a flood of tears hurrying to retrieve her suitcase. Excelcious chased after her and grabbed her hand. She turned, not sure what to make of it. "I told you you're not leaving!" He emphasized his point by taking her into his arms. He held her, like he was never going to let her go. LaShyra was weeping bitterly. She didn't want to leave, yet she felt as though it were her only option. Excelcious was able to convince her otherwise. "Look! We'll work this out somehow. I've already forgiven you. It might be a while before Shilloqwai does, just give her space and time."

"Damn, you're incredible!" LaShyra told him. "You should write a book on how to handle a woman. Instinctively, you know their secrets, perceptively you know what's on their minds. The book would top the bestseller list. More often than not, you win arguments with women. You have won numerous arguments with me! And I've seen you win arguments with Shilloqwai. She told me you win over her almost every time. At the minimum, you seem to have a knack for getting women to see your point of view. And when the argument is done, you often win them over wholeheartedly. You're very persuasive!"

"Glad you decided to stay. I've got a little homecoming gift for you.?"

"Do I dare ask what it is?"

"You can ask, but it's a secret I'm not going to reveal until tomorrow's meeting! You, me, and Shilloqwai! The three of us have a lot to discuss. And we're going to talk about a lot more than the weather!"

"Shit, I can hardly wait!"

"Listen, I've already spoken to Shilloqwai about this. I warned her, just as I'm warning you, I don't want any butting of heads. I'm not going to tolerate any bullshit from either of you. If there is any locking of horns, I'm going to be the one doing the ass-kicking! Have I made myself clear?"

"Crystal!" She said in a word, with a hint of sarcasm finely laced in her voice. She hugged him, leaving him with a gratuitous smile and a token of friendship, another kiss to the cheek!

There were also signs, she was going to do her best, to accommodate his request to remain civil to Shilloqwai. "See you in the morning!" LaShyra promised, with the sweetness having replaced the sarcasm in her tone.

"Have a good night!" Excelcious replied with sincerity, acknowledging her response."

"You too, hon!"

Excelcious, wasn't sure how Shilloqwai would respond to her referring to him with terms of endearment. Setting those boundaries at the onset of the morning's scheduled meeting, with the three of them present, was perhaps the best way to deal with that specific issue.

"**G**ood morning, ladies!" Excelcious began the meeting just after LaShyra had excused herself for being tardy.

"Sorry!" LaShyra said, still apologizing. "I was in the kitchen making breakfast for the three of us. I prepared a little buffet. I made omelets and some wheat toast , mini-Belgian waffles with real maple syrup and whipped cream, along with fresh-cut strawberries to pile on top. For beverages you can indulge in any or all of the following. There's fresh coffee, milk, cranberry juice, and orange juice. I'm not sure how long the meeting's going to last, or how hungry the two of you are, so I brought coffee with condiments and a variety of mini-Danishes to the meeting room."

After assuring LaShyra that everything was fine, Excelcious got straight to business. "I realize there still may be some awkwardness amongst us, until we can bring ourselves to look past the triangle of which the three of us were a part of. We're adults, we've talked through all that's transpired and it's time to move forward. If we don't find a way to get along, the AI Forces will do to us what the three of broken hearts failed to do, DESTROY US! And not just us, but all of Humankind.

We have a lot of other things that we need to discuss aside from the dynamics of our personal relationships. We all bring skills to this table that could tip the outcome of this war in our favor. That's why we need to get along. So, lets focus on that dynamic, and think about ways we can contribute to a cause worth fighting for, the livelihood of Humankind. Thoughts, questions, are we all on the same page?" The ladies nodded in agreement. Seeing there was unanimity among the trio, "Good!" Excelcious added. Near the beginning of the meeting, the ladies exchanged snide remarks, glaring looks, and yes, there were even some anxious moments between them. If that were as confrontational as it got, and it didn't end in a train wreck, Excelcious would consider the meeting an overall success.

"Look, I'm going to change things up a little bit. I was going to save the surprises for the end, but, since I have one for each of you, I'll make the presentations now. Hopefully, it will help ease the tensions. "I've talked to the both of you privately. And both of you independently agreed it would be okay to view these decoded encrypted files as a trio. The only thing I can say for sure about the encrypted files is that each of you had a chip implant inserted when you were manufactured.

"The chip was meant to corrupt your files. The chip had programmed commands designed to interfere with your systems, every time you were rebooted. When your databases tried to access these chips, you would glitch, because there was nothing in your programming that would allow you to read these chips. The other robots were looking for an excuse to destroy the Mercusilver class. I don't know why. Perhaps we'll learn why from the files I've decoded. I can neither promise the quality of the content, nor can I promise if the content in these files will be good or bad news. It's possible the files contain some of both. I promised not to view the files by myself. I kept that promise, so this will be the first viewing of the files by any of us." Shilloqwai's files were the first to be revealed.

The video opened with an infant girl in her crib. She appeared to have baby soft tourmaline skin, an infectious smile, and the prettiest tourmaline eyes. Two adult figures also appeared in the video, one male, one female, Shilloqwai's parents? Who else could they be? Shilloqwai had her mother's porcelain-like face and her father's tourmaline eyes. "She's so beautiful, Shilloqwandra! I can't believe she's almost two. "We should have another!" Her father told her mother.

"So, the three kids aren't enough for you? Don't worry, another is on the way." Shankeel, who was preoccupied with tickling the dickens out of baby Shilloqwai, so much so, that his wife's utterance didn't register with him at first. He had to ask her to repeat herself. "Wait Shilloqwandra! What did you just say?"

"In 5-½ months, Shilloqwai will have a baby sister to look after. What do you think of the name, Shalakwanna, for our fourth child?"

"It's beautiful. Better than anything I would have picked out!"

"If I recall correctly, Shilloqwai is the name you picked for our third child." Shilloqwandra gently reminded him." He pulled his wife close, embracing her, and kissing her intimately.

"Congratulations, momma!"

"Thank you! Congratulations papa!" Shilloqwandra broke the embrace. She was about to make her way to the kitchen when her husband ordered her to get into the basement and hide. Shankeel ran to the crib and snatched Shilloqwai out, before dashing after his wife, practically flying down the stairs. "Honey, what's wrong?" His wife demanded to know!"

"Damn robots!" Shankeel muttered. "Out the window, I saw that ours is the last house standing in the neighborhood, but they're coming for us now!"

"What? Why?"

"I'm not sure. I'm thinking it has something to do with the revolution and the robot crusade to try and save Humankind!" Shilloqwai watched in horror as the robots broke into her house and set it ablaze. As the walls of the house collapsed, she watched the foundation cave in on her parents and her unborn sister. The rubble that killed her parents formed a hollow when it fell, ironically protected baby Shilloqwai. Bloodied and broken, the paramedics rescued the badly injured Baby Shilloqwai from the ruins. "Oh my God, she's going to die."

"Maybe not. There's a famous robot doctor, Skeletos Puro-Amoris. They say he can do amazingly extraordinary things for humans in extremely critical condition, especially very young children.

"You mean Skeletos Amoris specializes in creating Cyborgs?"

"They, say, he's saved a lot of people, doing what he does! He claims Cyborgs are the way of the future, also claiming that before long, Cyborgs will be ruling the world, not humans or robots. It was Skeletos' thinking that Cyborgs, understanding things from both perspectives, they might be able to bridge the gap between humans and robots. If the Cyborgs were successful in getting the robots and humans to come to a compromise, with both sides making concessions, Skeletos thought there might be a chance for global peace. That was the essence of the Mercusilver Project. Those in the Mercusilver line were designed to serve as liaisons and diplomats. Word on the street is, he won't be around long enough to see the project through to its completion. The Robots are said to be looking for a way to terminate him."

"Why don't they just do it and get him out of their way?"

"He's won a bunch of Robo-humanitarian awards for strictly adhering to Asimov's laws while going above and beyond to serve Humankind. Terminating him would lead to the revolutionary war we've been fighting almost a century to avoid."

"The war is inevitable, isn't it? I wish they'd just duke it out and get it over with. Then we can all join together to pick up the pieces and move on."

"I'm not sure that, that's the answer. But something needs to be done to stop all of this petty shit that's going on between the robots and the humans."

"I know the humans won't, but I think the robots will succeed in taking over when all is said and done."

"Why do you say that?"

"Because the robots in this latest round of attacks against the humans, have nearly destroyed the RFAR (Rebel Forces Against Robots) army. This little girl's parents, Shankeel and Shilloqwandra, they're the RFAR leaders. If Skeletos can save Shilloqwai, she's going to be a hell of a warrior when she grows up. It's in her blood. I hope she learns her history and finds out what side she was born to fight for. Because just praying for her opposition won't be enough to save it. She will ultimately destroy it!"

"Finally, we're here. Hurry! Let's get her in to see Skeletos." The paramedics raced from the ambulance with the baby Shilloqwai. The Robot doctor took one look at the toddler and connected her to a device to assist with her breathing.

"Nice timing!" Skeletos remarked, confident he would be able to save the child. "She had a minute maybe two before she died."

"So, you can save her then?" Asked one of the paramedics breathing a sigh of relief.

"No guarantees. Only the Omniscient one knows. It's contingent on whether or not it's according to his plan."

"Look we just wanted to give her a chance!"

"As long as they're breathing when they get here there's always a chance. The challenge with the little ones is that they require so many operations. As the human part of them continues to grow, you need to change out the robotic parts for bigger and better ones. Once they're between the ages of 19-20, it no longer becomes necessary to do that. Any refurbishing done after that point is usually done to upgrade software."

"She's like the other little girl over there. They just brought her in under similar circumstances. Both of the girls are of royalty, the last in their bloodlines. There's no doubt I'll be able to save that one over there. Saving this one, I'll be honest, I don't think I can, not without assistance from the Power of Love, and a lot of it."

"Friends of the family requested that we bring her to you. They said they didn't think she had a chance in hell to survive, but they believed in you. They said if you couldn't save her, it was because she was responding to God's call to come home."

"If I can protect her heart, and stabilize her, there's a good chance that she will pull through. Her heart is badly damaged. She's young enough it might heal. The only other time I tried this, the patient died, and her heart was in better condition than Shilloqwai's." The paramedics stayed, watching as Skeletos put his skills on display.

"What I'm doing now, is putting a gold-plating around her heart. The hope is that it will give the heart a chance to heal. I'm leaving a hollow in the plating, so that her heart has room to grow into it. If she's lucky enough to live until she's an adult, her full-size heart will be able to function normally and without restriction. It is likely that tissue will attach itself to the gold-plating as the heart muscle expands while it's growing. For this reason, the gold-plating can never be removed. The possibility that it will start to chip away over time, is a strong one. If enough of the chips get into her system, she may suffer from a fatal heart attack or a debilitating and or a deadly stroke."

'Turn it off!" Shilloqwai screamed before breaking down into a flood of tears! "Turn that damn thing off! I can't take it anymore!" Demanded Shilloqwai, who appeared to be having a complete breakdown. It took some doing, but Excelcious and LaShyra were able to calm her down. There was no need to stop the video as the encrypted files had played out in their entirety.

"Shilloqwai!" LaShyra softly called to her, showing both empathy and support. Shilloqwai not only looked up, but, directly into LaShyra's eyes. What she saw for the first time, was a human being, a woman, instead of a 'bitch competitor' that was out to get her boyfriend. "After what we just saw, I think I'm going to need some support. Please, take my hand!" LaShyra begged. "I could use a big sister right now."

Without another word from LaShyra's mouth, Shilloqwai took her hand in hers, giving it a gentle squeeze, showing her utmost support. "Thank you!" I'm sorry, God I'm so sorry. If there's something I can do, please, let me know! I'm afraid to see your story. I'm sure it's not going to be much better than mine. Mostly, I'm sorry for you, little sister. If you need to talk, maybe we've found some common ground, at least a starting point to open dialogue!"

As with Shilloqwai's, LaShyra's video opened with her as an infant being coddled and cradled in her parents' loving arms. They destroyed her neighborhood just as they'd destroyed Shilloqwai's. They didn't burn, and blow it up, but a massacre is a massacre, regardless of how you execute it. Like Shilloqwai, LaShyra was the sole survivor from her neighborhood, critically injured as an infant. She was found in a hollow, beneath a heap of bodies, family members that fought, sacrificing their lives to protect her. Her parents Rakeem and RaShonda, along with her sisters TyShyra, and RaShyra died martyrs to save a baby girl, baby sister. Rakeem and RaShonda along with their best friends Shakeel and Shilloqwanda were rebelling against how the robots were treating humans, not to destroy their chances of what was imminent rule. Medically programmed robots located her by means of spying technology, rescued her, and brought her to Skeletos who eventually saved her. As far as Robotikis knew, Shilloqwai was the last of the Mercusilver class. Skeletos succeeded in keeping LaShyra's story a secret.

Since Shilloqwai's story was global knowledge, Robotikis couldn't destroy her, not without a revolution, that would likely have resulted in his termination. Had Robotikis had any inkling that alerted him to LaShyra's existence, he would have destroyed her before she was activated. Years later, Skeletos had been betrayed. He was terminated, never knowing by whom he was betrayed. Speculation was that Robotikis was the one that betrayed him in retaliation for keeping LaShyra's existence a secret! Robotikis ordered Skeletos destroyed, seeing him as a threat to become the eventual leader of the robot world.

Before he was incinerated, Skeletos pleaded on Shilloqwai's behalf, to have patience with her. It was one of the few times in his mechanical existence, that Skeletos knew of, where Robotikis had listened to anyone. Skeletos was especially shocked that he was one of those select few that Robotikis bothered to listen to. Skeletos pointed out, it was the most human thing Robotikis had ever done. After that, Robotikis was back to his ruthless, cold, heartless self. He conducted a global search, in efforts to locate LaShyra. By the time he'd found her, she had gained overwhelming popularity among Humankind. Robotikis was hogtied at this point, powerless to destroy her, for the same reasons he couldn't destroy Shilloqwai. "And I thought Robotikis was an asshole before I viewed these encrypted files." Shilloqwai quipped. "After viewing them, the son -of-a-bitch, gives a whole new meaning to the word. He's part of robot history. We can't take him off of display in the museum. He needs to be left there so history will forever highlight him in infamy, and Humankind maintains the wisdom to prevent people and robots from repeating his mistakes."

"Funny how small the world is Shilloqwai. We were neighbors, we're both of royalty. Our parents were best friends. Do you think we could ever be best friends?"

"Maybe! I have to learn to trust you first. It's going to take a while after what you did, after what you tried to do to my boyfriend. I'll promise to make an effort, we'll see where it goes from there. I can't guarantee anything at this point!"

"I'll try not being such a little bitch, Big Sis!"

"Like I said Little Sis, we'll try to make it work!"

"I think we'll call it a day!" Excelcious announced. "There's been enough trauma and drama for one day. We'll get back at this tomorrow. There are still a lot of plans to be made and a lot of work to be done. Tomorrow, I intend to show you ladies how to mix work and pleasure."

"Don't tell me, it's a surprise!" Shilloqwai surmised, hoping for a hint of what the day held in store. Excelcious dismissed them without saying another word. He left them with an infectious smile, both still wondering what he had in store for them.

They hoped he was planning on making up for the torturous horrors they had just endured. They knew it wasn't his intent to have them sit through something like that. He showed empathy for them. They could tell by his facial expressions the videos had been hard for him to watch too. Excelcious wouldn't disappoint them on consecutive days. Their anticipation for tomorrow's arrival was heightening at an astronomical rate.

Shilloqwai and LaShyra were shocked by some of what they'd learned of themselves. Other things that were learned by them, were things LaShyra and Shilloqwai suspected to be true all along. It was the confirmation of their heinous suspicions that proved more devastating, than anything. With the truth out and all of the cards on the table, they could put the past behind them and move forward. Excelcious reminded them of the box in the lab containing a binder for each of them and a binder on Skeletos Puro-Amoris if either, cared to review the information for answers to other questions they might have about themselves. The ladies were thankful to know that the information was available to them and said as much.

Excelcious went to Shilloqwai's room. She was still emotional, and her tears were still flowing over the morning's dark revelations. "Look!" He began as she was startled from a prone to a sitting position on the bed. "Sorry hon, I wasn't expecting to see what we saw this morning. The truth is out now. I thought the three of us could have dinner together and then spend the evening out. Are you up for it?"

The heat from her glowing smile that instantly appeared on her face, evaporated her tears. She sprang from her bed, across the floor into Excelcious' arms. "I love you." She confirmed with an intimate kiss.

"I love you too. Do you mind that LaShyra comes along? I don't feel comfortable leaving her alone, not in the condition she's in."

"I'll go with you, to get her. I don't trust the two of you alone together, not yet. It's too early. That bridge is under renovation and it's going to take time to repair it." When they arrived outside her door, they could hear that she was still sobbing. "Lil' Sis? can we come in?" Shilloqwai asked after a gentle knock.

"Yeah, what's up?" She asked with a quiver in her voice as she was trying to recompose herself.

"C'mon we need to get out and about. Excelcious has a surprise for us."

"What, he couldn't wait until morning to give it to us?"

"You're a perceptive one! I've been around Excelcious long enough to know where he's taking us." She gave Excelcious a wink and a smile. "I'm not going to ruin his surprise, so c'mon Lil' Sis! I would pack clothes for a week! And bring a swimsuit!" She added. "Excelcious did say we're mixing business with pleasure!"

LaShyra had immediately sprung from her bed across the floor into Excelcious' open arms, just as Shilloqwai had done. They embraced as if they were old friends. Shilloqwai watched the exchange without signs of a jealous twinge in her bones. She didn't see the exchange as an overture to entice him into her seductive arms.

And when LaShyra showered him with a flurry of butterfly kisses to the cheek, Shilloqwai dismissed the matter, as though it were nothing. It didn't seem to bother her in the least when Excelcious reciprocated with a flurry of butterfly kisses to hers. In fact, she was happy for LaShyra, that Excelcious had offered her a shoulder to cry on. Both Excelcious and LaShyra knew the boundaries Shilloqwai had set for them. Neither would dare cross any lines, knowing the wrath and fury that awaited them if they even dared. It was no surprise at all to Shilloqwai when LaShyra reacted the way she did to Excelcious' proposition. LaShyra had already gotten her surprise, in that, Shilloqwai and Excelcious were going on an outing, and they'd invited her to come along. Anything else was frosting on the cake.

They left LaShyra to pack her things, inviting her to join them in the dining room when she was ready. Shilloqwai and Excelcious parted ways in the corridor. Shilloqwai went into the kitchen while Excelcious retreated to the lab to finalize the trio's plans. There he got in touch with his friend Keyto. He was surprised to get him on the first ring. "Damn, you're hard to get a hold of! I've been trying to reach you for a week. Say, listen! About that rendezvous, are we still on for tomorrow?"

"Yeah, I'll be there bright and early. You know I was thinking, if you've got a place to put me up, I'll meet you at the rendezvous point tonight. Then we can get started on business at the break of dawn."

"Sounds like a plan!"

"Hey what time were you thinking?"

"Whenever you show up! Not that we'll have much time for it, but bring swimming trunks and hiking boots, in the event that opportunities of spontenaity present themselves."

"Okay. I'm warning you ahead of time, this better not turn into one of your matchmaking events. Don't get me wrong, you've got an eye for looks. That last woman you set me up with was a real hottie, biggest bitch I ever met in my life!"

"I'm done with that. I tried three times and whiffed every time. I'll let love do the matching and the making from now on!"

"Good deal, see ya later!"

"All right man, God Speed!"

"Yeah, you too, later, peace out!"

Rushing out of the lab, excited that all things were going according to his plan, Excelcious nearly ran LaShyra over. He embraced her to keep her from being mowed over by him. "Excuse me ma'am, you want to dance?"

"Another time! I'm busy this evening!" She quipped using her quick wit! He released her and the two of them continued down the corridor to the kitchen where Shilloqwai was still preparing their dinner. They didn't have to look to see that they were soon going to be served spaghetti and meatballs. They could smell the garlic, onion, and fresh tomato along with the Italian seasoning she'd used to spice up the meat and the sauce. They could also smell the fresh buttery garlic bread they were sure Shilloqwai had warming in the oven. She accepted the help offered by LaShyra and Excelcious.

LaShyra took the garlic bread from the oven and put it in a basket, Then, she cut some fresh fruit and placed it on the table with a yogurt dip she'd whipped up. Excelcious set the table and brought out a bottle of wine he'd been saving for a special occasion. He would wait until the last minute to pour it so the glasses he planned to serve it in remained chilled. After preparing the tossed salad with homemade Italian dressing Shilloqwai left LaShyra to put the finishing touches on the dinner. She hurried to her room to fetch the suitcase she'd packed the night before. Excelcious followed Shilloqwai to her room like a puppy dog. "I thought your suitcase was packed?" Excelcious questioned her as he saw she was rummaging through her dresser.

"I am packed, but LaShyra needs a bikini. She went through my shit and borrowed this red one the night she tried to seduce you. Like I need to remind you ."

"I like this one!" Excelcious said, holding up one made of black see-through material."

"Give it to me!" Shilloqwai demanded snatching it from his hand. "It's not a bikini, it's lingerie, and it's for our honeymoon!"

"It doesn't look like it covers much!"

"It doesn't, but that's the whole point, to get us on the fast track to paradise. However, I'm going to wear the black bikini I have. It's sexy, provocatively dignifying. And, so help me God, if you steal one inappropriate lustful glance at LaShyra, you'll be hurtin'!" Shilloqwai warned. As they rejoined LaShyra in the dining room, Shilloqwai had stern warnings for her too. "I know you don't have one, and I know this one fits!" Shilloqwai told her, slapping the red bikini into LaShyra's outstretched hand. "You'd better go change before we leave so I don't have to worry about peeping Tom once we're out in the wilderness. Any overtures, covert or overt, or any sexual innuendoes, innocent or not, I will knock your ass out before you know what hit you!"

"Got it!" Agreed LaShyra who wasn't in a position to argue. The tone of her voice told Shilloqwai her implicating insinuations were going to be a nonissue. Having set the parameters, and knowing where they were headed, Shilloqwai led the way. Excelcious and LaShyra were following closely behind her. Nevertheless, she glanced back on occasion to make sure the almost infidels were appropriately distanced from one another.

Shilloqwai had to quit with the suspicions and start unconditionally trusting Excelcious again. She realized that in not doing so, it would actually encourage him to cheat with someone that he believed he could trust, someone that would prove she could trust him. Enough, Shilloqwai chastised herself for both her thoughts and actions. They were going somewhere where they could temporarily escape their troubles, without their troubles following them. Entering the surreal hollow cleared Shilloqwai's mind. She had always found peace and serenity while visiting Rainbow Falls. She had no reason to believe things would be any different this time.

But, when the gateway to the botanical gardens opened, LaShyra gasped. The scenic beauty had taken her breath away, more so, than any kiss Excelcious had ever given her. All of her dreams and fantasies of being with Excelcious had just come crashing down. For the first time, she felt embarrassment over him seeing her naked. She was ashamed of the dirty things she'd done in his presence. And she was appalled by the fact, no ashamed of the fact, that she'd taken such extreme measures to try and seduce him.

She couldn't believe how she'd defiled herself in her attempt to get him to make love to her, knowing his heart belonged to someone else. As she took her first step into paradise, she was able to leave her troubling thoughts behind, just as Shilloqwai had. The butterflies fluttered around her as she felt herself being elevated to cloud #9. One of the butterflies even landed in LaShyra's hair. She wondered if she kissed a butterfly instead of a frog, if she might find her prince that way.

When Excelcious told her how beautiful she looked, LaShyra responded with a simple thank you, taking the compliment for what it was, without reading anymore into it. Shilloqwai too, saw the innocence of the remark for what it was, letting it go as though it were nothing. LaShyra found herself lagging behind the young couple, still jealous of their loving relationship and envious of Shilloqwai, wishing she were back in her role of the other woman in his life.

She couldn't help it. Her desires were starting to burn out of control again. After all of the pain she'd put the three of them through, she seemed willing to throw herself back into the flames of lust knowing they would consume and be the death of her. She would scream and moan, paying a price far too high for guilty pleasures that would ultimately destroy her life.

On second thought, she didn't think she could do it, even if the perfect opportunity presented itself. She would die a lonely woman. Dying of loneliness is a horrible, torturous way to die, a fate that no one should befall. Though the thought of being alone in paradise wasn't much of an option either. The three of them were exhausted, by the time they'd reached the ledge behind Rainbow Falls.

Shilloqwai and Excelcious got there first, exchanging affections under the waterfall before LaShyra reached the flat rock plateau. It pained her to witness the affections exchanged by Excelcious and Shilloqwai. Though, it would have been selfish of her to expect them to restrain their spontaneous inclinations. LaShyra retreated to the hot tub where she was left alone to daydream. Her dreams, though illicit, were sweet while they lasted. She was awakened from her fantasy by a trio of boisterous voices roaring with drunken laughter. "Oh, there she is!" Excelcious noted as he was the first to see her emerging from the shadows. "Have you been in the hot springs this whole time?"

"Yes!" LaShyra answered guiltily.

"Don't be shy, come over here a minute! There's someone I'd like you to meet!" She did as Excelcious requested, instantly making the party a foursome. LaShyra was feeling a little self-conscious about the way she thought she presently looked. Keyto scanned over her and couldn't help but notice her physical attributes and how they might benefit him if they were to get close. He found her disheveled look to be savage-like, almost animal. Keyto liked the look and found her to be exotic looking and mysteriously attractive. Excelcious then introduced her to his childhood friend. "LaShyra, meet Keyto, Keyto, LaShyra!" Though the introductions and greetings were awkward for them both, the ice was quickly broken.

"Damn, sorry for staring, LaShyra, but if you were any hotter, paradise would be on fire." The foursome burst out laughing uncontrollably. Shilloqwai knew LaShyra wasn't going to let the comment go without a response.

"Thank you for the compliment!" LaShyra said, still blushing from what Keyto had said to her. "Yeah, and if you were any hotter, I'd have had to go change my clothes. I almost dropped a load, having seen how damn handsome you are!"

"Touché!" Keyto conceded. He was now blushing too. The foursome exploded into another outburst of uncontrolled laughter.

"Sorry to mix business with pleasure." Excelcious said cutting into the party which just seemed to be getting started. "Keyto is going to be working with us for a while. I thought this might be a good opportunity to introduce him to the group.

The way Keyto so nonchalantly handled the situation, helped LaShyra relax and made her feel at ease. She liked his confidence and the fact that he didn't seem to be intimidated by beautiful women. Enchanted by his silver-blue eyes, she would do anything he asked of her. But she perceived him to be an incredibly nice guy that would not take advantage of her. In addition to his seemingly charming personality, she couldn't help but notice that he was a drop-dead gorgeous hunk. She wished she could make herself pass out. Imagining then, that he would come to rescue her by way of resuscitation. Though the thought of his lips meeting hers was exhilarating, she thought it would be more dreamy, more magical, if, when the first time their lips met, it was for their first kiss. Once LaShyra and Keyto were comfortably engaged in conversation, Shilloqwai and Excelcious excused themselves, leaving the respective couples to independently share precious moments in private. "So, did you know Excelcious, and I have been friends since childhood? How do you know him?" Keyto inquired of LaShyra.

"I saved his girlfriend when the Robotix Headquarters was attacked and burned to the ground. I'm a doctor, nurse, fighting for my life like the rest of us are. I shouldn't really be telling you this, considering we just met, but you'll probably find out anyway. I can tell it to you now and save myself the embarrassment of having to explain it to you later. I was a robot when I helped save Shilloqwai. Excelcious gave me a place to stay. While I was with him, Shilloqwai got deathly ill. I transformed into a human, like she did. We both thought she was going to die. I did things I wasn't proud of. Acting like a little whore I tried to seduce him. When Shilloqwai came around, she kicked my ass and threatened to kill me if I ever tried anything like that again. My relationship with her is on shaky ground, but we're working on it. Now that I've spilled my guts, how about you?"

"For starters, thank you for being honest. It's going to make it easier if we decide to move forward with our friendship. Secondly, I don't give a damn about your past and I'm not looking for a relationship. I think we should focus on becoming friends first. If we can't be friends first, we can never be anything else. I know what it's like to be hit on for looks. It's so fake. True love will find me someday. The less time I spend looking for it, the sooner love will find me. Like Excelcious, I'm an IT guy. He's more into the programming. I'm more into the electronics and mechanical engineering. I'm a specialist in robot, human relations as well as a Cyborg Technical Surgeon."

"What the hell is that?"

"You and Shilloqwai are well aware of who Skeletos Amoris was! I'm the human counterpart!"

"Wow! It blows me away, some of the miracles he's been able to pull off."

"Look, I'm no miracle worker. I'm able to do what I do through the guiding hand of God! Some people don't see it that way! They call me Dr. Death. They say I'm playing God and dancing with the devil. They say the same of people that dabble in cloning. There's a distinct difference between what those people do and what I do! People who dabble in cloning alter lives, lives that God created, lives that only God has the power to create.

"People like me, we take lives that have been badly disrupted and restore a quality to them, extending them indefinitely, be it a long time or a short one. I just do whatever I can to help people in need with the help of God's guiding hand. Most call the people I save cyborgs. In my eyes they're still people."

"That's very noble of you!" LaShyra acknowledged with admiration.

"Look, we'll have plenty of time to discuss business, seeing as we're going to be working together for a while. Let's not waste an enchanted evening."

"So, what did you have in mind? Is there anything in particular? A walk in the moonlight, or something?"

"Or something!" Keyto said, opting for the surprise element. "I suppose before we decide to do anything together, I should tell you, I'm married with three kids."

"You son-of-a-bitch!" She cursed, following up her insult with a slap to his face, colder than his remark. "What kind of asshole says something like that? Even in jest!"

"It was a bad joke, I apologize. I deserved what I got. I'll use better judgement next time." He said rubbing his cheek that was still stinging.

"I'm sorry, I know you didn't mean anything by what you said, but…"

"Look I had it coming! Forget it!" He said forgivingly.

"SSShhh!" She hushed him. "I forgive you, if you forgive me for being supersensitive."

"We've made our apologies. There's nothing left to forgive. Let's not waste the rest of this beautifully enchanting evening."

"Back to the original question! When I asked you if you wanted to go for a walk or something, you said, something. What did you mean by that?" He hesitated, calculating his answer. Not wanting to come off as though he was being too forward.

"I made a wish upon a shooting star."

"So, what did you wish for?"

"That I could kiss you." LaShyra didn't give him a verbal yes or no. However, she leaned in close, pursed her lips and closed her eyes, giving her nonverbal consent. Comfortable in their environment, they drew closer still, falling into a lover's embrace. The kisses freely flowed between them like a river of honey. There was a sweetness to them, both were tasting for the first time.

It was a sweetness she'd never tasted in Excelcious' kisses, probably because they were stolen, in a way that she almost stole his heart. When she told him, they were a kiss away from paradise, she saw now, just how wrong she was. She was surprised Excelcious had strength enough to resist her. She was more surprised that Shilloqwai hadn't killed her for what she'd done.

Keyto continued showering her with wet kisses. She willingly reciprocated. Their lips were dripping with the taste of honeysweet. Excelcious was a sweet distraction. She hoped she'd found more than that in Keyto. She would have to be patient for the infatuation and lust to transform into love before she offered to make love to him. And she would wait for the good things, as Excelcious made her see they were more than worth waiting for. If he wanted to see her naked, it would have to be in his dreams. She hoped when the opportunity came for him to make her fantasies come alive, she would be able to make all of his dreams come true. She pulled away slightly, just long enough to catch her breath, and long enough for him to see her glowing smile.

"What cha' thinking hon?" He asked, flashing an infectious smile of his own.

"I can't tell you." She answered sheepishly.

"Secrets? Can you give me a hint?"

"Naughty thoughts, very naughty thoughts. But they were also nice thoughts, very nice thoughts!"

"It's nice when a woman has dreams and desires. But there's a time and a place to unleash unbridled passions. This is neither the time nor the place for that. Seeing that we just barely met, I'm sure it's going to take some time, before either of us is ready to go on a treasure hunt. I've been looking a long time for that treasure chest containing an overabundance of true love. To this point, all I've found is fool's gold."

"I can't say that I've been looking for a long time for true love. After my transformation, the best advice I've heard in regard to the subject of love is, don't go looking for it, let it find you. The other piece of valuable advice I got was, build a trust, so you have a foundation to build your friendship on. If we can't be friends, we can never be anything else."

"Good advice. Sound words of wisdom, all true!" Keyto concurred. Shilloqwai and Excelcious, returning from their little moonlight stroll decided to check on LaShyra and Keyto. Not that they had any interest in their personal business, they merely wanted to say goodnight. Seeing the two of them were engaged in a harmless romantic fantasy, Shilloqwai and Excelcious left quietly and unnoticed, not wanting to spoil the magic of the moment for them. In fact, Shilloqwai and Excelcious had set out to find their own private place, where they shared a long kiss goodnight before calling it an evening.

Eventually, the two couples had fallen asleep under the moon and stars after being spellbound during what turned out to be a whimsical evening for both. LaShyra was the first one up in the morning, way ahead of the others. She started a campfire, gathered some fresh berries, and walked down the slope into the garden and sat by the stream. With a makeshift fishing pole, strung with line and a homemade hook from her medical supplies, LaShyra caught six good-sized rainbow trout. She then packed up her gear and headed back to camp where she cleaned and skewered the fish before putting them over the open fire to roast. It wasn't long afterwards, she realized Shilloqwai was standing beside her, looking over her shoulder. "You don't need to wait for an invitation to have a seat!" LaShyra said cordially. Shilloqwai flashed a devilish smile, LaShyra acknowledged it and responded with a guilt-laden one, though she'd done nothing wrong. "How long have you been standing there?"

"Less than 30 seconds. I was just waiting to see how long it took before you felt my presence! So, just curious, did you guys…you know… do it?" Shilloqwai asked sheepishly. Both women blushed.

"We both wanted to. Despite overwhelming temptations, we restrained ourselves. He said he would have made love to me if I really wanted him to. We just hit it off from the onset. He said he thought last night was the start of something special between us. He was worried that if we did do it, we might lose the chance to find out what could be! He added that because our hearts wouldn't be satisfied with fool's gold, we might get scared and shy away from one another. He's such a romanticist!"

"Sounds like the kinds of things, Excelcious would say. Guys like him are hard to find. Hold on to him. I'm not making any predictions, but he sounds like he might be the one for you!"

"It's too early to start thinking like that!"

"Is it? With love, it's always good to use common sense, on the other hand, don't be afraid to take chances and follow your heart!"

"So, what about you and Excelcious? Did you guys ever…get it on? I mean you've been together for quite a while!"

"You don't know how many times we've thought about it. We've come close so many times. But, when it came down to actually doing it, we both shied away. I seem to be more willing to give it up than he is. More than once he respectfully asked me to stop trying to seduce him. It made me cry every time he turned me down. Poetically, romantically, he gave me all of the reasons we should wait. It made me cry more, making me realize the treasure I had in him. It made me feel how much he loves me, which in some ways was more exciting for me than had we actually made love. Out of respect for him, I quit with the sexual innuendoes. Since then, it's actually strengthened our platonic relationship. That doesn't mean I can't think about the naughty things I want to do to him. The way he undresses me with his eyes, tells me he's thinking about the naughty things he wants to do to me. Last night there was plenty of undressing going on. He was undressing me with his eyes, and I was undressing him with mine." The two of them shared a good laugh, afraid their giddiness would wake the guys up. Enough about me and Excelcious. "How did you and Keyto end up sharing that magical first kiss?"

"We kept staring at each other and then looking away, as if kissing one another was a shameful thing. Neither of us wanted to make the first move. He said look, a shooting star! I asked him what he wished for. He said he wished that he could kiss me, before asking if it was all right that he did. I closed my eyes and pursed my lips and our fantasies started coming alive."

So engaged in their discussion, they were startled when they realized the guys were hovering over them. "It sounds like you ladies were having a good ol' time. What was so funny, care to share?"

"Girl talk!" Shilloqwai said honestly. "As far as sharing, definitely not now, and probably not for a while."

"Oh!" Excelcious said flatly. He immediately understood. Though he couldn't state the specifics, he was certain it was a very adult discussion!

"So, did we wake you guys up?" LaShyra curiously asked.

"No, your hysterical laughter had nothing to do with getting us up." Keyto assured the ladies.

"Are you guys sure we didn't wake you up?" Shilloqwai probed further.

"Absolutely not!" Excelcious insisted. "I dreamt I was waiting in a buffet line and I was extremely hungry. I could smell the food you're preparing, and it was making my mouth water."

"Looks like we've got ourselves a couple of smart asses. You can tell they were childhood friends!" LaShyra noted.

"At least they're giving us credit for having intelligence." Keyto quipped.

"Speaking of intelligence, how about an update?" Shilloqwai requested. "Any word in regard to the Fire in the Sky and the AI Forces?"

"Those are among the topics for discussion." Excelcious said for everyone's benefit. "We can wait until after breakfast to discuss business." He added. After having had their fill of the roasted rainbow trout, the foursome washed down their breakfast with freshly squeezed orange juice.

"Thanks for breakfast ladies!" Keyto said, expressing his gratitude. Excelcious echoed his sentiments.

"All of the credit goes to LaShyra!" Said Shilloqwai, complimenting her and giving thanks of her own to LaShyra for preparing a simple, but delectable feast.

"So, what time did you get up hon?" Keyto asked out of curiosity.

"I don't know, 4:30, 4:45. It was a beautiful sunrise though. I wish everyone could have seen it."

"How come you were up so early, hon? Are you feeling, okay?"

"Yeah fine, never better." LaShyra assured him with a mouthwatering kiss. When he tried to reciprocate, she pulled back. "Ah! Ah! Ah!" She teased. Business before pleasure!" She reminded him. The foursome shared a good laugh. "Seriously hon, thank you for a wonderful evening last night. I thought it was all a dream. But when I woke up with you next to me, I just lay there for a while and watched you sleeping. I realized that last night was more than a dream. It was us starting a journey down fantasy road."

Still munching on the fresh berries LaShyra had picked the foursome settled in and was ready to talk business. "Our goal is to take down these bastards burning up the Earth and killing its people before we send them to hell to be incinerated." Excelcious stated.

"Maybe if their robotic bitches would take care of their interfacing needs, their desire for conquest wouldn't be so strong." LaShyra offered her opinion.

"If we could teach them to interface properly, it might solve their problem and ours!" Shilloqwai added. The foursome broke into a fit of hysterical laughter. It was a good icebreaker. The friendships among them were starting to bond.

It was a good 10 minutes before any of them were able to regain their composure. It was what they all needed to ease the tension building because of the volatile situation they were trying to diffuse while keeping it from becoming more of a global disaster. Just when they thought they had it collectively together, one of them would snicker or smirk setting off another round of hysterical laughter. Their sides were splitting as they had been laughing until they cried their eyes dry. Shilloqwai had to be sure that was the case.

"So, we were talking about bitches and bastards, do you think if we found a way to turn them against one another, they would all destroy themselves?" The remark brought more collective smirks, laughter, and tears and more calm among them. The easing of tensions allowed them to maintain a sharper focus during their brainstorming session in which they were seeking creative solutions to the mountain of problems facing them. In classifying and prioritizing their problems they were mindful of the fact that they couldn't climb the mountain in a single bound. To reach the summit, thereby conquering their problems, they would have to take it slow and one step at a time, while watching for pitfalls along the way!

They prepared themselves for setbacks and changing their battleplan if necessary. If they wanted to succeed, they needed to forge ahead and not get discouraged regardless of how grim things might seem. Keeping the faith and trusting in the Power of Love would help them keep their sense of optimism. They had to approach their problems like an ascending set of stairs. Like climbing a mountain, they would have to proceed in solving their problems step-by-step. If they seemingly reached an impasse with a particular problem, they needed to move on and try finding the solution to the next one. They could return to their most difficult problems at a later time after mulling over them and perhaps trying a fresh approach to finding an alternate solution.

This methodology was successful in dealing with the alien attacks that began with the Fire in the Sky. Humankind hadn't won the war yet, but it had been winning its share of the battles. "Though we've experienced some success in our fight against the enemy, we don't know what the next wave of attacks will bring, or how we'll hold up against them. They're going to throw everything they have at us. I'm confident we'll be able to find a way to defeat their forces!" Keyto said convincingly.

"What Keyto and I are most concerned about," Excelcious explained "is that perfect asshole leader in command of the alien attack, Metallicus Nebuloso. Though he's proven to be damn near invincible, we all know he's not perfect. We have to find out what his weakness is and then attack it with everything we've got. We have to keep faith and not lose hope, while remembering the Power of Love is behind us and that He will never abandon us. If we are forced to make an escape from Earth, there is a backup plan in place. Under no circumstances, will we throw in the towel or raise the white flag.

"If worse comes to worse, and the AI forces thwart our escape, we will fight to the bitter end. Because, if we are going down, we'll go down fighting, and not sit like ducks on the water, waiting for them to pick us off. Remember, moving targets are harder to hit! We have other business to discuss, so, let's move on. We can talk more about Metallicus Nebuloso later, if need be."

"Next, I'd like to talk about our defenses." Said Shilloqwai who took over as the moderator for the discussion, giving Excelcious a chance to rest his voice. Excelcious started this project long before we ever met. Since we've been together, I've been assisting in the design and development of the DDD Mercusilver Class weaponry. What we have is adequate, but soon our weapons may be rendered minimally effective, even useless. Excelcious and I are working on the Automatic Assault Rifle (AAR). Upon completion of this project, we're hoping to be able to do away with the Militiabots, clusters at a time with a single blast. We're also working on a long-range tracking system, so we'll be able to fire at them and destroy them before they even get close to us or anyone else.

"We're hoping these weapons will be effective against anything else they throw at us, including Metallicus Nebuloso! To this point, we've been on the defensive, dueling with them while trying to protect ourselves. We're hoping this new line of weapons will allow us to launch devastating offensives that will disable, maim, and destroy them. This will hopefully lead to their decimation and elimination. Our offensives will not be driven by the desire to dominate, or the lust for power. It's all about the restoration of peace so the robots and Humankind can live in harmony. Excelcious and Keyto, have been working on another project for a number of years. Again, before Excelcious and I met. It started with the tunnel project, but it grew into something much bigger. Since we met, I've been helping Excelcious coordinate a global effort in regard to the expanded tunnel project designed for a crisis on the magnitude of the one we're facing. The New Atlantis project is an underground world that is capable of providing shelter for all of Humankind to help keep it safe from surface attacks. These tunnels lead to anywhere and everywhere in the underground world. There are plenty of secret passages throughout the New Atlantis leading to fantasy hollows like this one, home to the Rainbow Falls and Botanical Gardens. Though the entire underground world could sustain Humankind for years, decades even, it was designed to be a temporary shelter. We look forward to the day when we can return topside for a grand victory party."

"Thank you Shilloqwai." Excelcious said, jumping back into the discussion. "One of the reasons we're calling this New Atlantis a temporary shelter is, we may have to flee from there to get away from the enemy. We also have ambitions of returning to live on Earth's surface when it's safe to do so! It's clear the AI forces want to destroy us. It might take them a while, but we have to assume that they will ultimately find us.

"So, during the construction of New Atlantis we've discovered what we think is a time portal, a direct route to a planet that is far, far away. Anything that gets within three miles of this portal gets sucked in. We've sent in probes and collected data. After analyzing the data, we've concluded that this planet is three times the size of Earth, with three times the amount of water. Through our data, we've also been able to confirm the existence of human life on the other side of this space anomaly.

"There is hope beyond Earth. Throughout this underground world there are GPS escape pods of various sizes, enough to evacuate all of Humankind. The ships are electric start with the touch of the green button. All ships are equipped with a blue button marked SAFEHAVEN. Pressing that button ensures the ships will practically fly you there themselves. Taking off and landing are part of the programming.

"The ships are self-flying, but they can be switched into manual mode. They're easier to drive than cars, and when in manual mode, essentially all one has to do is steer, and then press land when the party or parties arrive at their destination."

"So has anyone ever gone there to check it out?" LaShyra asked.

"Therein lies the problem." Excelcious lamented. "We haven't been able to recover our reconnaissance drones. So, we're not sure if we take this escape route, if there'll be a way to get back. This is why this option will only be exercised as a last resort. Ideally, we fight and win, seeing the battle is on our home turf. After the war is won, we pick up the spoils and rebuild. Life will go on."

"How long do you think we'll have to live underground?"

"Depends how much rebuilding we're going to have to do. We'll have to do assessments after the war to make sure that it's safe to return topside."

"You believe there's hope then, a chance that Humankind will survive?"

"Humankind will always have a fighting chance. Minimizing casualties is going to take an extra effort on our part, and perhaps prolong the war. But in the end, I believe we will win, yes!" Remembering the Power of Love is on our side there's never any reason to lose hope. We must never lose hope! Through love all things are possible."

"You know," Keyto interrupted Excelcious, "we've just gone over a lot of heavy stuff. On rare occasions, I believe you can mix business with pleasure. This my friends is one of those occasions. What would you ladies think if we went for a ride in one of the shuttles?"

"Love to!" The ladies giggled as they answered in unison. "So, where are you going to be taking us?" Again, their voices were in sync, while asking the burning question!

"We're going to tour a very small part of the New Atlantis. There is still much room for urban and rural development. So, we're about to embark on an incredible journey. The story of Atlantis is a sad one. Fact or fiction, we thought the renowned city should have a different ending. Though we built it out of necessity, with a lot of help from our friends, we believe we've successfully restored the name to greatness. The restored Atlantis is more than a city, it's a whole new world. It's an underground world, not a lost world underwater!"

The four of them took flight in a shuttle for six, for comfort's sake. Excelcious put the shuttle in auto pilot so they could all sit back and enjoy the ride. The pre-programmed tour is going to take about four hours to complete."

"This shuttle is one among 500,000,000 craft built to help with the mass exodus from Earth if need be. The craft are located in strategic places around the New Atlantis. In addition to the underground locations, there are some shuttles above ground hidden by holograms. Access to these above ground shuttles, can be boarded from the new underground world."

"Hopefully, it won't come to this!" Keyto said in his closing remarks. Again, these underground cities and communities have been established in rural and urban areas. As you've seen for yourselves, it's a surreal environment. Take for example, the Rainbow Falls, one of the many hollows Humankind can escape to. And all of them are part of this whole new world, the New Atlantis."

In response to the global crisis, drastic measures needed to be taken. On the surface, it looked like the AI Forces had free reign of the Earth. And they did, the humans concluded. This, after conducting exhaustive reconnaissance missions. But it seemed the alien forces had given up looking for humans above ground. No one believed they'd given up entirely. It was the consensus that the AI forces were reformulating their battleplan. The reality that Humankind could just disappear from the face of the Earth, didn't compute. What the AI Forces were trying to figure out is where the majority of the populous had gone.

While the aliens were coming up with new attack strategies, Humankind had burrowed in, putting itself in position to protect itself and the Earth. The AI Forces were responsible for an unprecedented ongoing global massacre. The casualties they were recently responsible for was a mere fraction of the Earth's populous. It reminded Earth's civilization just how valuable each and every life is. The AI Forces had some recalculating to do. Since the majority of Earth's civilization had escaped them once, was it capable of doing it again? And how would they make that second escape? They hadn't a clue that Humankind was prepared to make a mass Exodus.

Living underground would be more than a major adjustment. It was going to be a life-changing experience for all of Humankind. The surreal environment would make adaptations easier. Escapes to the hollows provided sunlight, assimilating normal living conditions. This made the underground paradise a perfect hiding place.

Production of the Orbitoids was continuing as Excelcious believed there could never be too many reinforcements. The AI force proved it could take out Humankind's resistance, and murder people in droves. This concerned Excelcious because he worried, that at some point, there wouldn't be enough forces left to protect Earth's civilization. The completion of the New Atlantis would allow Humankind to launch offensives while sheltering themselves. Their remaining defense systems and drones could be remotely operated from the underground. The final phase of the New Atlantis project, would be to bring the robots that were topside, having escaped termination, down to them. There was some sense of safety and security being underground. Humankind figured it would be sometime yet, before they were found. There would be breeches that would come in time. Everyone knew it, even with the safeguards that had been put in place.

Humankind believed it would be a while after the first breeches, before Earth's peoples were actually found. As the surface robots were brought to the underground, there were renewed tensions between them and the humans. There was an added tension when the Surfacebots interacted with the Orbitoids, designed by Excelcious and his associates. It was as though the Surfacebots had an inferiority complex, somehow believing they were superior to the Orbitoids. Data showed, they absolutely were not! Reasons for the tensions beyond the obvious were, the robots were simply that, just robots. They were complex computerized machines whose main function was to keep order and protect humans. The things they learned, making them humanlike with undesirable qualities, was the fact many had learned all of the curse words, and never hesitated using them regularly. They learned the poor manners instead of the desirable ones, again from data input fed to them by humans.

The Surfacebots were given data input on the aspects of love. But, the concept, was too complex. It didn't compute, disabling their ability to analyze and process the data. Shilloqwai and Excelcious, were well aware of the existing problems between humans and robots, and they have been for a long, long time. They were issues that they believed could be worked out over time.

Robots in their rigidity, would seldom allow humans to introduce new data into their systems. They didn't understand that this refusal to cooperate was putting them on a path leading to their termination and incineration. It didn't seem to matter. All robots knew that day would come at some point. It was inevitable according to their programming. They accepted this as the norm, part of the natural order of things. Termination would take place after their useful purpose had been fulfilled.

All of the robots that followed, the ones soon to be on their way out, would take the same path as their predecessors from the moment they were activated. And like their predecessors, they either functioned to their capacity, meeting the expectations set for them according to their design; or they would prematurely be terminated.

Excelcious had been studying the dynamics of the interaction taking place between robots and humans. Once he'd compiled all of his data, he incorporated it into a software program he designed. It was clear the next generation of robots would be comprised almost solely of Orbitoids. Like he'd done with the Orbitoids, Excelcious produced a series of videos, simulating the HUMAN ELEMENT. Just as they were downloaded into the Orbitoid databases, they would be downloaded into the old-school robots, which he knew were capable of storing terabytes of information. He took advantage of this storage capacity, producing thousands of videos the robots could reference, in a series he called WAVES OF EMOTION.

The reasoning behind this was to help robots get a better understanding of human behavior, and the rationale behind it, which was so unpredictable at times. These variable factors, according to Excelcious, are what made up the Human Element. In producing the videos, he tried to capture a multitude of human emotions, from joy to sorrow, to hate and anger, friendship, and love. When this programming was implemented into the Orbitoid databases, Excelcious downloaded two versions of each video into their systems. The videos showed two responses in a number of situations. One showed the appropriate response, while the other showed the inappropriate response. Using this method, Excelcious was able to highlight the differences between right and wrong, and why doing the right thing was always considered to be proper protocol, without exception, even in situations when logic and reason had to be disregarded.

In the programming, he outlined what constituted a crime, and what was not. Like killing for example, it was acceptable in cases where it occurred in self-defense. He also included a number of videos that showed why humans were so against them using surveillance methods, which had become common practice under robot rule. Under the global constitution, Humankind's privacy was violated, every time these methods were used. Excelcious hoped that programming these types of things into the Surface Bots' databases, it would improve overall relations between humans and robots. Asimov's Laws were to be followed without exception. That was the expectation for the Orbitoids, it would soon be the standard for the Surfacebots.

His theories were proven to work with the Orbitoids. He had no reason to believe they wouldn't work with the Surfacebots. Using proper protocol and abiding by the standards of human etiquette, the Surfacebots would find humans might be more willing to cooperate with them. This would certainly help with any negotiations, regardless of the issues on the table for discussion.

After the Orbitoids were through with their updates, they were sent to the surface to help roundup any straggling Surfacebots or people that were not able to escape to the New Atlantis. Many of the robots refused to go along with the mandate issued by Excelcious, failing to understand they were being asked to do so in the best interest of Humankind. The Orbitoids terminated these Surfacebots immediately, per Excelcious' orders. Many Surfacebots went reluctantly, while others had to be forcefully persuaded. The threat of termination for violations of Asimov's laws proved to be convincing enough for the majority of those resisting. With gentle prompting, Most Surfacebots fell in line according to their programming.

Once all of the Surfacebots had been rounded-up and led to the underground, Excelcious arranged to have all of the Surfacebots, sit in on a video conference along with any Orbitoids or humans that wished to sit in. In fact, Humankind was encouraged to sit in on this video conference which assuredly, would help participants gain a better understanding of robot functions and responsibilities. The video conference, which was optional for humans, was a mandate for all Surfacebots.

Excelcious was waiting for a green light, signaling that all Surfacebots were at their designated workstations. When he got that signal, he began the conference promptly. Good planning allowed Excelcious to start the meeting 1.32411 seconds early.

"Good morning and welcome, my robotic friends. We would also like to welcome those of Humankind that have tuned in." Excelcious began. "It's no secret that we are amidst a global crisis. The attacks by the AI Forces have proven to be an existential threat to all of Humankind. Since it has been deemed that it is no longer safe for humans to live above ground, the Earth's populous has been evacuated to the New Atlantis for shelter and protection. As your duty, stated in Asimov's laws, you were brought here to protect the humans. I know that many of you are analyzing all of this and trying to process the new data input, but I have some new information that will help simplify things that have been difficult in the past for you to process. Relations with Humankind is a glaring example. Downloading the new, mandatory updates I have put together will help you in this regard. In front of you, each of you has a USB cable at your workstation. I would ask that you connect yourselves at this time so we can proceed. We have a lot of ground to cover, downloading this information will help expedite the process. Let me remind each of you, this is not an option, it is a mandate. It will be followed in accordance with Asimov's Laws. Failure to comply will instantly result in your termination.

"While you are downloading the required updates, I would like to fill you all in on what has transpired thus far in regard to this global crisis we're trying to manage. Before I get into the details of our battleplan, which outlines how we're going to deal with this crisis moving forward, I would like to clarify a few things. It wasn't long ago when the Fire in the Sky first appeared for the first time. We watched it spread across the sky and now it's jumped down to Earth. It will consume us all if we don't work together to fight it and put it out. By we, I mean robots and Humankind. I'm sure you're all aware by now, that our World Leader Robotikis was terminated in the latest round of attacks.

"For the benefit of those who don't know who I am, my name is Excelcious Orbitus. I am a medical doctor. I am also an IT specialist with a doctorate in robotic sciences. Shilloqwai, is here with me. I know you've all been briefed on what her mission was as a diplomat, liaison, and her quest to bridge human, robot relations. She was involved in a scandal with six criminal civilians, having murdered them in self-defense. While the investigation was ongoing, premature calls for her termination were vocalized. Many of you are aware of the other incident where she was piloting a solar plane that crashed. She was vindicated on both counts. Regarding the six murder charges, they were dropped, with her citing self-defense and video evidence to support her claims. In regard to the plane crash, the FAA, determined glitching caused pilot error.

"In reality what happened, she was deliberately given the wrong USB cable, which is why she glitched and was unable to safely land the plane she was piloting. The Robotix Council saddled her with a number of other bogus charges to try and justify her termination. In each case, the Robotix Council was found to have withheld exculpatory evidence that would have exonerated her.

"Acting independently, one of the Robotix techs, ordered her to the junk pile, without Robotikis knowing about it. I rescued her from the junk pile, as per my agreement with Robotix, that I could claim anything from that pile. After I rescued Shilloqwai from the junk pile, a transformation took place that has no medical or scientific explanation. Shilloqwai is human now and has proven to be a valuable contributor to our wargaming team. Again, let me remind you, this is not an attempt to overthrow the government, currently under robotic rule. Shilloqwai and I are acting as co-leaders until the Robotix Council can regroup and appoint a new World Leader. This will be done, after the crisis has been dealt with.

"In the meantime, it is critical that we fight as one unit, one people, one army with a world united if we expect to defeat the AI Forces.

I caution you all, not to take this enemy lightly. You've seen its power and it has the capability to destroy us. These alien robots understand the logical pragmatic part of our human struggle to survive. Our attackers will use logic and pragmatism to eliminate and eradicate the Earth of its inhabitants. The way to defeat an enemy as intimidating and overpowering as the AI Forces is to confuse them by acting in ways that seem irrational and illogical.

"That is why I'm introducing a complex program, called the Human Element, into your databases. Included in this new software is a program that goes over something humans call fight or flight when faced with perilous, life-threatening situations, such as this crisis. In these situations, humans have the option of fighting or taking flight. Under Asimov's Laws, there is only one option available to robots. You will stay and fight, doing everything you can to save a human life.

"On account of your efforts in confronting the enemy, humans will have the option to take flight from immediate danger or existential threats like the one presently being imposed on Earth by the AI Forces. This Human Element software is to be reviewed immediately after your downloads and updates are complete. Part of this extensive program attempts to explain the various aspects of love. Hopefully after reviewing this material, you will have a better understanding of why humans so willingly sacrifice their lives for those that they love, especially in times of crisis.

"It is important for each and every one of you to understand how the Power of Love can level the playing field, give us an advantage, or even turn the tables against our superior enemy and help us win this war! Now that I've outlined the basics, there are a few specifics I'd like to go over. Before I do, I want to make sure that all of you have completed downloading the updates and new files.

"Yes! No! Okay, we're still waiting on a few. Really quickly, a review of the material I have just gone over. You will protect Humankind at all costs by:

1. Following human direction in accordance with Asimov's Laws
2. Do what you can to protect yourselves

3. After this session, you will immediately review the Human
    Element Document, designed to help you interface with humans
    on a more personal level.

Okay, I see that most of you have completed downloading the
mandated files. Except, there are two of you in this room that have not
done so. Is there a problem my mechanical friends?"

"No, one of them answered. She and I are simply refusing to
download the mandates. Our suspicion is that you and your robot lover
are still trying to find a way to overthrow the government under robot
rule."

"You're entitled to your opinion, you, and your female friend.
I've been transparent throughout, sharing personal information about
Shilloqwai that I didn't have to share. I wanted you to see that I had
nothing to hide, and neither does she. I explained to you how a new leader
would be chosen to replace Robotikis after the crisis has passed. I also
explained what I intended to do to rogue warriors. Any last words before
your terminations?"

"Kiss our asses!" The female robot said insolently.

"As you wish. The least you could have said was goodbye!" Excelcious
said with a wry smile as he remotely terminated them both. "Damn, we
just suffered two more casualties on account of friendly fire."

He quipped without remorse. Two-hundred others were also
remotely destroyed for failing to download the new files and updates.
Three-hundred others, having downloaded those files, went on a rampage
attacking humans in various locations across the New Atlantis. Live images
of what was happening in the underground world was filtered into the
conference rooms. All of the mechanical rebels were remotely destroyed.
After the rebellion of the Surfacebots was squelched, Excelcious continued
wit h his conference.

"Anyone else that wants to try and rebel or defect, let me know now
so I can get the terminations over with. Save me the trouble of having
to try and do it later when human lives are at stake! As I was saying, we
all need to be on the same page. One rogue member of the robot team

could cost all of us our chances of standing up to and surviving another imminent attack from the AI Forces. We are dealing with a superior force, and the tiniest mistake could cause us to lose the war.

"The Earth and her people are a cause worth fighting for. We can't afford to lose this war, and we won't unless some mechanical asshole messes it up for the rest of us!"

"So, why were we armed, if our weapons have been neutralized?"

"Good question. Shilloqwai and I will decide when it is appropriate for your weapons to be activated and when it is appropriate for you all to use them. There are four of us that have the power to remotely activate those weapons. I mentioned that Shilloqwai and I could do it. LaShyra and my friend Keyto have the ability to activate your weapons as well, if they see the need to do so. Our plan is to find a way to defeat our enemy while protecting our home. If we have to, we'll make a run for it .

"The code phrase for our mass exodus from Earth is Flight to Freedom. If you receive that code, it will be sent remotely, your job then is to make sure all humans are escorted to the shuttles and sent on their way. After the ignition sequence, you will instruct them to press the green button marked SAFEHAVEN. This will jettison the shuttles to their GPS guided destination. Since the shuttles have the ability to fly themselves, your responsibility will end once all of Humankind is in flight. Though project SAFEHAVEN will likely be launched, it is only to be executed as a last resort after you have been issued the code, Flight to Freedom. From that point on, it looks like we'll be on our own, hopeful to return one day and order will be restored to Earth.

"We'll have to adapt and adjust to our new environment until we can find a way to come back. Again, the hope is that we'll have a home to come back to. Despite the gallant efforts I know you will all put forth, not all of us are going to make it. People will die, that's the nature of life, death is a part of it.

"So, before you decide to go rebel, or go rogue, remember that if you do it's going to unnecessarily cost human lives. You will be terminated for such actions. I own you for now. Your download assured that I can control every one of you remotely. Any attempt to override your new mandates will be robotic suicide. When you are off by yourself somewhere, your self-termination sequence will initiate. And you will become a useless piece of shit. We're not going to bother to come looking for you. In closing, I will summarize your mission this way:

1. We protect Humankind at all costs keeping in mind Asimov's Laws and the Human Element.
2. We win this damn war.
3. We resort to operation SAFEHAVEN, only if necessary and only on the cue, Flight to Freedom.

Are we all on the same page? Keep in mind, you will all follow Asimov's laws or else! As part of your mission, keep these objectives in mind! You are to:

1. Protect Earth's people
2. Protect the Earth
3. Protect the universe.

If by chance your databases become compromised, in any way, be advised that you will self-destruct!"

CHINK IN THE ARMOR

[CHAPTER 21]

For a long while it had been quiet on the battlefront. Keyto and LaShyra took the opportunity to get away for a few months. During their short sabbatical they married and took a long honeymoon. Humankind was still adjusting to its underground home, the New Atlantis. Everyone was preparing for the apocalyptic attack that was forthcoming. They were armed with weapons locked and loaded, prepared to defend themselves. The people would hurry up and wait for the moment when they would fight or take flight. Many would resist taking flight because it meant leaving behind all that they knew. Taking flight would be a last-second decision.

Shilloqwai and Excelcious were sending out daily reminders to people assuring them that home is where their hearts were, and if their hearts were with their loved ones that nothing else should matter. They also tried to get people to open their minds to the idea that leaving Earth for a new world, perhaps offering opportunities that Earth could not. Regardless of where people found their homes the experiences would be part of their life stories, mortal, and eternal. Death and darkness, as powerful as they are, have no power over love and life. Love is a light that can destroy darkness with the tiniest point. And death, is only a part of the greater whole. Death is a bridge between mortal and eternal life. As one passes through death, life goes on forever.

It had been a long while, since Shilloqwai and Excelcious had alone time. With Keyto and LaShyra back covering for them, they had a few days for themselves, taking advantage of a rare opportunity to escape into their favorite hollow. The Rainbow Falls. The peace and serenity they felt when they were there, made them wish they were there all of the time. "I can't stop thinking about our wedding day. It seems so near, yet so far away!" Shilloqwai sighed wishing the ceremony were here and now.

"It will be here soon enough!" Excelcious promised. "Are you up for little walk?"

"Even if I wasn't, I would go." Shilloqwai responded. "Usually when you ask me something in that manner, there's a surprise waiting for me when we reach our intended destination."

"Is that what you think?"

"It's not about what I think. It's what I've come to know."

"Really now?"

"Yes, really!" Shilloqwai echoed him offering her hand. Excelcious took her hand in his and led her to a hidden pathway behind the Rainbow falls.

"I'll give you a little hint!" Excelcious teased as they followed the path's upward slope until it plateaued and took a downward turn. Where I'm taking you is somewhere over the rainbow!"

"Sounds colorful! Is there gold at the end of the rainbow?" Shilloqwai inquired.

"You'll have to wait. When we get there, you can see for yourself."

"Oh, you're such a little shit! But I love you anyway!"

"I love you too!" They walked a little further when Shilloqwai caught sight of a river that was a deep blue, as rich as her tourmaline blue eyes. After rounding the next bend, about 1/4 -mile along the pathway, she could see down into the valley. It was filled with every imaginable gemstone and precious metal. Shilloqwai imagined it had to be the only place in the universe that could out-glitter, out-flicker, and out-sparkle the stars.

"It's beautiful here, but my favorite place is still the Rainbow Falls. Where is all that light coming from." Shilloqwai asked seeing the bedazzling, sparkling light a short distance away. As she approached the light it reminded her of an angelic light she'd seen before. She began combing her memory to try and place it. When they got close enough for her to touch the source of the light, it triggered her memory. "The way these stones are sparkling, they remind me of the luminous roses. They're so beautiful. I wish I could take one of them home with me."

"Your wish is my command!" Excelcious responded bowing down on one knee. He reached into his pocket with his hand and pulled out a fist, concealing what was in his hand. "Shilloqwai, will you marry me?" He asked opening his hand so she could see the luminous rose diamond ring he'd had especially made for her.

"Yes! I will marry you!" She promised holding out her left hand. Excelcious got back to his feet and slipped the ring on her finger. The black diamond got its translucence from the frosted white rose glowing in the middle. The white-gold band had glowing black diamond chips spaced over the circumference of the ring.

"I'm glad you like it" He, said, following up his words with an intimate kiss. "It's probably your favorite thing, that I've ever given you."

"Second-favorite." She corrected him. "There's nothing that you could ever give me more precious than your love. And after we have children and start our family, it will become my third favorite thing. I'm so jealous of LaShyra and her husband. I can't believe the two of them got married before we did. She's pregnant you know!" Shilloqwai told Excelcious on their short hike from Gemstone Valley up to the Rainbow Falls.

"Actually, I didn't. Remind me to congratulate them later!"

"We still have some time before we go back. I was wondering… if…?" She paused with a blushing smile."

"Wondering if…?" Before he finished asking her to elaborate, he saw the wanton look in her eyes. To make sure there was no misunderstanding between them, he encouraged her to say what was on her mind. He just wanted to make sure he was reading it right.

"It should come as no surprise to you. I've been harboring this fantasy of making love to you for a long time." Shilloqwai confessed.

"You're joking, right? Here? Now?"

"Why not?" She asked with her blouse already half-unbuttoned. "I can see it in your eyes. You want me as much as I want you!"

"You're serious! Aren't you? You're not even wearing a bra!"

"Don't tell me you just noticed! You've been staring at my concealed breasts the whole time. It got me turned on to the point where I need you to do something about it. Don't worry. I have one with me. I'll put it on when you're done playing with me! I still think it's funny the day LaShyra told me that she couldn't get you ready to take her. That she failed to seduce you because you weren't in love with her. But me, you can't resist me. You're ready now and I don't even have my blouse off. I know I'm being naughty!" She admitted as she'd shed her top fully exposing her wares. "But this is going to be very nice for both of us. Tell me that you want me. Tell me that you'll take me, now!"

"I do want you. And I want to make love to you. But….!" He'd said what she wanted to hear. Sensing his hesitation, she took his hands and placed them on the full of her naked breasts. To her delight, he began touching them, and playfully massaging them in a way that was driving her insane, as it was when they nearly made love during their kiss and make up session, after his almost affair with LaShyra.

"I can't believe you're actually engaging with me. This has been my longtime fantasy, to be in this erotic moment with you! Shit!" She sighed and moaned, "Don't stop, this time, please don't' stop!" She pleaded. He took off his shirt, fueling her fantasy. She fueled his, pressing the full of her dangling charms against his bare chest. Their internal body temperatures were rising quickly as their desires were burning out of control, as both were rocking in the cradle of one another's arms. The heat in their tantalizing kisses of fire fueled their intimate passions. "What changed your mind about waiting until we're married to make love?" She asked in her softest bedroom voice.

"Because I almost lost you a couple of times now. If I should lose you, I don't want to wonder what it would have been like to make love to you. It feels like the right time and we're in the right place, exactly where we wanted to be for the first time."

"Your such a romanticist!" She told him as she slipped out of her shorts in front of the natural hot tub. He followed her lead, leaving them both in their birthday suits. Shilloqwai sighed as she snuggled closer to him begging for another kiss. She wasn't satisfied with him just kissing and caressing her face. She could feel the excitement building as she rubbed her body against his. "I want a full-body massage!" She told him, dropping more than subtle hints.

He massaged her neck, shoulders and back, building her anticipation. She could hardly wait for him to get to the good parts, her private places. "Why don't you touch me the way I want to be touched?" She gently encouraged him. "Don't fight your urges! Make love to me. Make me a complete woman and I'll make you a complete man. Tell me that you want me, and our dreams will start coming true and our fantasies will start coming alive." They were a kiss away from the point of no return, a caress away from making love, an eyelash away from paradise and a heartbeat away from ecstasy.

Excelcious continued caressing her face, while kissing her, deepening the passion they were feeling, intensifying the intimacy. Shilloqwai and Excelcious both knew they had passed the point of no return. Sweat was seeping from their pores in anticipation of the ecstasy that would soon consume them. Their erotic desires were burning white hot. "I'm ready babe. The barriers between you and my babymaker are gone. He slid his hands from the small of her back down to her waist and then on to her hips. It seemed the world stood still for an instant as they were about to fully engage in the lovemaking act. Then, the Earth started quaking at a magnitude that was off of the Richter Scale. Both Shilloqwai and Excelcious were thrown to the ground. She landed on top of him, exactly where she wanted to be, exactly where she needed to be.

They exchanged intimate kisses and looked at each other as if the world were coming to an end. Their burning desires had flamed out and the mood was ruined. Still, they exchanged I love yous as they always had, but something was different. Both were stricken with a haunting feeling, like they were saying goodbye, forever. "Shit! It's always something!" Lamented Shilloqwai. "What is it with our timing? The mood was right, the place was right. What the hell just happened?" She wanted to know as she was hurrying to get dressed, as was Excelcious!

"I don't know, but I think we'd better go find out!"

"Agreed!" I'm sorry hon." Shilloqwai apologized with tears in her eyes."

"Don't worry, I'm going to give you that baby you wanted. I promise!"

"Only one?"

"I said we'd start a family together, but I never set limits on the amount of kids we could have, did I?"

"I love you!" She said reaffirming it with a warm wet kiss.

Excelcious reciprocated. "I love you too babe! I promise, I'll make it worth the wait. And every time we do it thereafter, I'll make it feel like the first time."

"And I promise that every time thereafter the first, it will be better. Each time we'll gain experience. Practice makes perfect, and I think we should allow plenty of time for practicing. After we get it right, we'll have to work on perfecting perfection."

"You make it sound like we won't be spending enough time in paradise. I think that we can agree on one thing, we'll always be giving our best to one another, every time!"

"Damn straight! You can never get enough of a good thing. Once you take me to paradise, I don't plan on ever leaving!"

"We've been in paradise for a long time, ever since we've been together, beginning with the day we met."

"You've got a knack for getting the last word in over women. I've never seen a guy who…!" Another Earth-quaking blast threw them to the ground for a second time. They got up and dusted themselves off and scurried to their shuttle, before flying to the nearest command center. Shilloqwai had been crying the entire way to their destination. "If we should ever get separated, just know that I'll always love you!" She kissed him again. "This is for luck, Excelcious."

"For luck!" He reciprocated with a kiss of his own. "Nothing's going to come between us Shilloqwai, not even death! We're kindred spirits! Love connects the eternal flame, burning in our hearts!" LaShyra and Keyto rushed over to the lovebirds' shuttle as soon as they spotted it. "It's about damn time you guys showed up!" Keyto yelped frantically. "All hell is breaking loose up there. They've blocked our cameras so we can't monitor their activity. If they keep doing whatever it is they're doing, the Earth will be reduced to a pile of space rocks in no time."

"Project Flight for Freedom?" Excelcious asked inquisitively.

"Already executed, Seconds after the first explosion."

"How's that working out?"

"Better than expected. One-tenth of the shuttles have arrived at destination SAFEHAVEN!" While Keyto and Excelcious were discussing battle plans. The ladies wandered off a ways, engaging in their own discussion which had nothing to do with their escaping from Earth.

"So, did you, do it?" LaShyra asked with a giddy smirk, rubbing her stomach as all pregnant women do.

"No, damnit! And we were so close."

"So, what happened? Did he get cold feet?"

"Hell no, he was all in. I tempted him with some heavy solo action. Just before he could join me for our first duet, the aliens rocked our world and threw us to the ground. I was on top of him almost in position when we felt the second blast. If that hadn't happened. I was going to rock his world and he was sure as hell going to rock mine! We were both ready and willing."

"Honey, I'm sorry your trip to paradise got postponed."

"I guarantee we'll be taking that trip. It's the first thing we're gonna do when we get back home. We thought about engaging in the act anyway, but, then we would have had to rush things and it wouldn't have felt right! We wanted to take time to explore the hidden treasures we had to offer one another. Without even touching one another, it felt as though we had done it.

"Shit!" LaShyra cursed following it up with an evil sounding laugh. "You're starting to sound just like him, with all of the poetic romanticism!"

"We think a lot alike, and we have a lot in common, I'm just beginning to find out how much. We move as one, our hearts beat as one, but he gives me my independence and lets me be my own person. The most beautiful part of our relationship is the way our differences complement one another. When we take time to share these differences, it strengthens our relationship, by allowing us to come to a better understanding of one another."

"Yeah, well I have your lover to thank for making my life better. In retrospect, I see just how wrong he was for me. It took me finding Keyto to see that. I knew he was the one for me the day we first met. I regret the day I tried to seduce Excelcious. I was a failed whore. I was a bitch too, for never really apologizing to you! I'll be honest. I despised the ass whippings you laid on me. I hated you for that. I knew I couldn't truly forgive you until I changed my perspective.

"My perspective started to change, after I admitted to myself that what I did to Excelcious and what I tried to do to him was wrong. I hurt you and I hurt him. What's worse, I almost destroyed the beautiful relationship between the two of you. For those things, I'm sorry Shilloqwai." The sincerity of LaShyra's words were reflected in her tears. "I tried to imagine myself walking in your shoes. After I had, I'm surprised that you didn't kill me. I know, roles reversed, I sure as hell would have killed you. You listened to my bullshit like a big sister and then you kicked my ass back in line. I'm grateful for the lessons you taught me. I'm thankful I took to heart the constructive criticisms you and Excelcious offered. I benefitted in more ways than one, because I listened. I now have two loyal friends who are watching my back and covering my ass. So, thank you. This is going to get ugly. If something were to happen to any of us, I just wanted my big sister to know two things. First, I've forgiven you for the ass whippings. Secondly, I wanted you to know how much I love you, Sis. If you ever need anything, just ask and I'll be there for you."

"Looks like someone's taught you a thing or two about love, Little Sis. I've forgiven you too! I should have told you, but I was too caught up in holding on to the baggage. I couldn't let go of the past. During my time of personal reflection since your almost affair with Excelcious, I realized it's not about looking back, but about moving forward. Sorry for all of the times I called you a bitch, it was cruel. I'm really not a mean person, you're pretty congenial, very loving, the way I see myself. I don't wish ill-will on anyone. But this is war. Inevitably people are going to die. Just know that if something happens to either of us, I want you to know that I love you too, little sis." The two of them embraced, exchanging kisses to the cheek.

Both glad to have rid themselves of the onus of having an albatross around their necks, were overcome with emotion. Both had tears rolling down their cheeks for a number of reasons. Having truly forgiven one another for their transgressions against each other, it felt as though the weight of the world had been lifted from their shoulders. They would be fighting for each other now, instead of against each other. Together along with Excelcious and Keyto, they would do their part to save Humankind, a worthy cause for which they knew they had the backing of the Power of Love.

When Shilloqwai and LaShyra saw that Excelcious and Keyto had tracked them down, their discussion immediately ended. They had said all of the things to each other that they'd been wanting to say. Again, affirming that they'd forgiven one another, they exchanged kisses to the cheek and hugged each other as if they were long lost friends. Tears of relief were still rolling down their cheeks. "Everything all right ladies?" Keyto asked misreading the probable reasons for their tears.

"We're fine!" Shilloqwai confirmed.

"A long overdue talk!" LaShyra added.

"Well, it's good to see that the two of you are actually getting along!" Excelcious observed. Shilloqwai and LaShyra smiled at each other and then at them. The guys could see that it wasn't just an act and that the bonds of friendship were legitimately forming between them. "Sorry to break-up the private conference between the two of you, but we need to move, and there's not much time to act. Just to get you ladies in the loop, here's what's up in a nutshell. As you're aware, the second phase of operation SAFEHAVEN has been implemented. Shuttles are taking off, using the only escape route available to us. We've talked about this earlier as well. About 30 percent of the ships have arrived at the predetermined destination.

"We had hoped to have data from the first arrivals, but all of our communications have been cut off. There's nothing coming in or going out. Since we did receive data back from the probes that we sent, we have to assume that the AI Forces are responsible for the breakdown in our communications. We have no other option now, but to leave Earth! Staying here is utter suicide. We won't survive. It's unlikely that the Earth will either. We'll have to assume at this point, there'll be no home to come back to. Let's all say a prayer for a safe trip!" Excelcious suggested. "With desperate hopes we'll see each other on the other side."

"We can also pray that we have a home to come back to!" Shilloqwai added with optimism. They shared a group hug and tearful goodbyes before climbing into the shuttle for four.

"Okay, let's do this. If by some miracle we all do make it back, we'll rendezvous at Rainbow Falls. From there we can reassess our situation and make plans for moving forward. We have to accept the possibility, that we might get separated and potentially never see each other again. In the new world we may have independent lives and have alternate futures other than the ones we have planned. I just want to take the opportunity to say goodbye to everyone. I love you all." Excelcious' sentiments prompted more tears. The others all followed suit, hoping their goodbyes, meant there would be subsequent hellos. The tears flowed from all of their eyes as they were about to embark on their journey into the unknown. If project SAFEHAVEN proved to be successful, it would go down in history as the greatest escape of all time. Over time and through illusion, magicians have made a lot of things disappear. None have ever made the world go away and then brought it back. Essentially, that's the feat that the foursome and their friends were trying to pull off. No tricks, no illusions, in this live scenario of now you see it, now you don't, guess what, we're back again. More than 75 percent of the fleet had reached the other world that showed promise of a life beyond Earth.

Just as Excelcious calculated it would take approximately four hours to complete the evacuation, their instincts alerted them it was time to leave. This coming after another series of Earth-quaking blasts that shook the planet to its core. It wasn't until they were in flight, that they were able to pick up on the garbled warning, advising them to 'get the hell off of the planet'! The powerful blasts severely affected the maneuverability of the craft. If it weren't for the auto pilot and the self-flying functions, the foursome would have been plastered to a piece of space junk. Speedily heading toward its destination, guided by the ship's GPS system, their craft began rapidly accelerating, quickly reaching Mach speed, the speed of sound. Their craft continued to accelerate reaching warp speed, the speed of light. Still, it wasn't fast enough to escape the cosmic fire that was blazing a trail behind them.

And from behind them, came another mighty blast, propelling them even faster toward their destination along with rocks and other flaming debris. Their ship caught fire as they were passing through the atmosphere of this unknown planet believed to be capable of sustaining life. "I think the Earth just exploded!" Shilloqwai grimly surmised. "Our hearts will have to be content here, wherever here is." She sobbed. "If our hearts don't find a home here, we won't have a home. There's not one to go back to!" Shilloqwai lamented.

"Then let's make this our home." LaShyra suggested. "Our hearts are here."

"Brace yourselves!" Excelcious warned. "The ship slipped out of autopilot! I can't control it. We're going to crash! Damn! And I thought we'd made it!"

"Shit!" LaShyra lamented. Everything was so perfect for us back on Earth. We had love there, it was all we needed to survive!"

"So, why would we need anything more here, wherever here is? Love is the one thing we can experience anywhere we go, whether it's in this life or the next. Excelcious! Look out!" Shilloqwai shouted with a deafening scream, just before their ship careened off of the mountainside. Those were the last words spoken by any of the four. Not even the thick blanket of white could soften the blow. Beneath it was rock and ice. The icy cold and the heavy wet blanket did extinguish the fire, leaving the foursome in darkness, while the ship was being bounced around like a pinball against the mountain. Knowing what was in the darkness, wouldn't do anything to quell their fears in this case.

Their fears heightened in fact, as they were being tossed about in the midnight blue. Things just kept getting more ominous for the foursome. The midnight blue turned to ghoulish purple before turning gothic black. It is said there is some good that comes from everything bad. At this juncture, it could have been a point of light to give them hope, where their was seemingly none.

In their subconscious states, none of them could be sure they'd ever again see the naked light of day. They were all certain, the Power of Love would light the path intended for them. It's possible they could end up as messengers sent back to light the way for others. If it were their time, they would enter the City of Gold, shrouded in heaven's spectral celestial light. The first sign they had survived their ordeal were the painful sensations, reverberating, pulsating through their bodies. Indeed, they were all alive. Moving forward, meant getting their bearings. For some, it would take longer than the others to get their feet back on the ground.

A warping of the dimensions, of time and space, placed Shilloqwai somewhere in the future, four years ahead of her cohorts. People with whom she spoke, seemed to be ignorant to the fate of her fleet, let alone, the crashing of her ship. They looked at her as if she were insane…trying to convince her that she was having a delusional nightmare, acting as though nothing had ever happened. But something had happened. It was like she suddenly had dementia. She couldn't remember what happened to the love of her life. One minute she was sitting next to him on a doomed ship, in the next instant, he was gone. Not just him, but her friends, LaShyra and Keyto too.

Meanwhile, Excelcious found himself in a completely different place. Just as hellish as the place Shilloqwai was in. It didn't take long for him to figure out he was trapped somewhere in the past. He was going insane trying to figure out how that had happened.

Presently, LaShyra and Keyto, they were living a nightmare too. They saw their friend Shilloqwai sucked from the ship, presuming that she was dead. After they were sucked from the ship, their landing was cushioned by some, sponge grass? They still had no clue as to where in the hell their friends were. Though this soft ground cushioned their landing, they watched in horror as their ship plummeted into the ground, some distance away. The last they saw of Excelcious, he was struggling to get out of the ship. As far as they knew, he hadn't. They believed Excelcious to be dead. And even if he'd survived the crash, the ensuing explosions and fire, that destroyed what was left of the ship, more than likely claimed his life. The horror for them was not knowing how to locate their friends. They hoped when the wrinkle in time was ironed out, all would be well with their friends.

The looming question at the moment was, were their friends still alive? Was there a way back home? Was there a home to go back to? And if they could go back home, would they be introduced into the same nightmare that caused them to flee the Earth in the first place? The infirmary was full of victims by the time LaShyra and Keyto had arrived. To accommodate them, they were taken instead to a nearby hospital where they were treated for minor injuries, but, kept overnight for observation. However, not before they had an unpleasant encounter with their estranged friend Shilloqwai.

She was back in the infirmary for her daily visit. Suffering from a long-term case of amnesia, she demanded that someone tell her where she was. "I want an answer, damnit!" "I want to know if this is Earth! This is Earth, isn't it?" She kept asking as she had been every day for the past four years! She was befuddled, bewildered, that the planet's inhabitants kept telling her it was Eartheena. The Eartheenians, however, were trying to be empathetic to her disorientation, while attempting to get her to acknowledge where she actually was.

The next day, Dr. LaShyra and her husband Keyto, new to the Eartheenian community were back in the infirmary when Shilloqwai stopped in for her visit with some thug-looking brut, hanging all over her. After witnessing her tirade, Dr. LaShyra suggested that Shilloqwai be sedated. Surprisingly, she agreed to it. The opposition came from the beast claiming to be her husband. Though he put on a show, he reluctantly agreed to let the medical staff sedate her. "Do what you've got to do. Just shut the bitch up!"

The medical staff was more than happy to accommodate the brut and glad to be rid of them both. Shaking their heads, they watched as he abusively hauled her outside and stuffed her into his transport. They didn't need another problem, especially when they were dealing with a disaster that had just occurred. The magnitude of it was more than the Eartheenians were equipped to handle. The heavy influx of patients was taking its toll on everyone. Something about Shilloqwai wasn't quite right. Keyto and LaShyra surmised that she'd suffered some type of brain injury that she might never recover from.

"Did we understand you correctly, we're on the planet of Eartheena?" LaShyra asked one of the medical staff, that had an instant to spare.

"That's correct!?"

"Do your people know anything of Earth?"

"Depending on your perspective, Earth is said to be either a legendary planet or a mythical one. Regardless of your point-of-view, Earth no longer exists, not in this star system, or in the next. Not in this galaxy, or the next. For that matter it doesn't exist anywhere in the universe. At least, not anymore, though it may have at one time."

"So, if it did exist, what can you tell me about this legendary myth?" Keyto inquired.

"There's a way you can look back through time to see what may have happened to this ancient planet. But, in doing so, you would be taking a monumental risk! Often, when people travel back through time, they get stuck there. The memories of the way things were, is what they're comfortable with. Consequently, they never move on and become trapped in time, and unaware life is passing them by.

"They end up wasting the moments at hand and throwing away the future. Todays, become yesterdays, and tomorrows never come, because tomorrows, have become the present reality."

"We'll have to look into that to see if there's a way, we can save our friend." Keyto said trying to figure out which course of action he was going to take. "Thanks for the info." He said to the medical professionals. "I know you're in the middle of a crisis, but one last question and then my wife and I will be on our way. Can you tell us where we can find Shilloqwai? We'd like to try and help her if we can!"

"This isn't a medical opinion, but my best advice to you is to forget about that bitch! She's with a no-good scumbag and she will kill you the first chance she gets. That's all I have to say on her behalf. Please don't ask me anything more regarding her. I don't want anything to do with her. Personally, I hope she never sets foot in here again. Though I know it'll only be a matter of time before she does."

"Shit!" LaShyra cursed as they were leaving. "There has to be some way we can help her."

"Until we can figure something out, I think we should avoid her, for our safety and hers. I'm worried about her too. At least we know she's alive. I'm more worried about finding Excelcious and knowing, whether he's dead or alive!" Keyto remarked.

"We'll find him. Call it women's-intuition, or whatever. He's bound to turn up sooner, or later. I'm sure of it. Not really!" LaShyra admitted. "But I haven't lost hope yet. I have more hope of finding him than I do that Shilloqwai will recover. Keyto, she doesn't know who, or where she is. And that guy she was with, what an asshole. He's not even her type. He's treating her like shit, and he's about to get his ass kicked by me!"

"Look, I'm not defending him, but there are two sides to every story." Keyto pointed out. "We can't just go by what the Eartheenians say. We need to get her side of the story. If she'll even talk to us. Where in the hell is this place? What is this damned place called Eartheena? Where's Excelcious? We were all on the same damned ship. A planet with different dimensions of time and space. It's got to be an anomaly. So much for us getting home!"

"That's why we need to find Excelcious!" LaShyra insisted. "If anyone would know how to get us back, he would. And what if Shilloqwai comes around? She couldn't have forgotten Excelcious. The two of them, Excelcious and Shilloqwai, were kindred spirits."

"Shilloqwai's not right upstairs. And you know it! LaShyra! Shilloqwai may never come around. Excelcious is better off if he finds someone else." Keyto surmised.

"How could you say such a thing?" LaShyra asked, wanting to defend Shilloqwai without a basis for doing so.

"I'm just being real! Did you see that crazed look in her eyes, LaShyra? You took psychology classes. If she's not already insane, she's on the brink of insanity."

"You've given up on her, haven't you?"

"There's nothing anyone can do for her now, not in her state of mind."

"What about the Power of Love?" LaShyra suggested.

"I didn't say I'd stopped praying for her. It's going to take a super-sized miracle, for Shilloqwai to come back ½ of the person she was. Even then, Excelcious won't recognize her. One thing is certain, this Shilloqwai is not the woman he fell in love with."

"Don't stop believing! I haven't!" LaShyra said faithfully.

"I haven't either, it just hurts to see her in the condition she's in, knowing she might never recover."

"I wish we had the chance to examine her. I'll bet her system is poisoned again. That's what was wrong with her the last time she turned into a psycho bitch!"

"We'll keep praying. We have to know if Excelcious is dead or alive. If he's alive, it's important we find him before she does. He's going to be traumatized, especially after we tell him about her."

"And she'll be traumatized if something has happened to him. She'll feel it and know not why she hurts. Knowing the truth may help her heal and make it possible for her to love again. The unknown is what will drive her completely insane. If we can't confirm Excelcious' death, she'll become an old maid waiting for him. She'll never see him again until her dying day when the other half of her kindred spirit comes for her and helps escort her into eternal life. She'll spend the rest of her mortal life in torment and agony, wondering, what in the world ever happened to him?"

PAST, PRESENT, FUTURE
EPILOGUE

[CHAPTER 22]

Excelcious had countless nightmares in his lifetime, but this one was by far the worst. It was a living nightmare, and he was the main character, awake the entire time. "Shit!" He cursed, here they come again. Excelcious was referring to the last of the fleet of ships that had escaped from Earth. He knew when they were going to crash. It was the same time every day. And it was always in the exact same place. The last ship to escape was the one he was piloting, with Shilloqwai, LaShyra and Keyto as his passengers. Time had become relative as Excelcious could no longer stand to watch the disaster unfold before his very eyes. Neither could he remember, nor did he have a way of knowing, how long he'd been trapped in time, two, three, four days … maybe. It could have been weeks, even months for all he knew. He wasn't sure, he'd lost track. It was irrelevant.

Nothing mattered anymore, not after he lost the only thing that did, the love of his life, that special someone, Shilloqwai! He was beginning to feel as though, not even his life mattered anymore…not without the love and support of the one he loved. Without her, he was starting to believe his life no longer had a purpose. Excelcious was beginning to lose faith, he was losing all hope…and he was quickly losing his will to live. Excelcious felt as though he were dying…with his life…the last precious thing he had left…seemingly slipping away from him. In fact, he was wishing that he would hurry up and die…thus his suffering would end. When he saw the fleet coming in, yet again, he positioned himself in the exact spot where he knew his shuttle would crash, hoping it would take him out. When, it appeared his ship was going to pierce his heart like a wooden stake through a vampire, he ducked and tucked his head. "Guess it's time to kiss my ass goodbye!" Speaking what he thought would be his final words.

He heard the ship's engines roaring! they were just overhead. He heard the screams of horror from his three companions, just before the crash. Then he felt the ground shake as the ship came crashing down around him. He wondered how it was, that he hadn't been…killed. He lifted his head to find the same horrific scene he'd witnessed countless times now. LaShyra and Keyto, were nowhere to be found. meanwhile, Shilloqwai's body, covered in blood, lay limp over the craft. He reasonably presumed she was dead. Excelcious had no desire to witness the tragedy that befell his ship a single time more. He'd seen enough. He was tired of living in the past. He wanted to move forward, but he was trapped, somewhere in time. He was beginning to lose his sanity, trying to figure a way out of the reality, the trap he was in.

Aimlessly, he seemingly walked for miles on end in a nightmarish circle. He kept seeing the same things over and over, again and again. He found it amusing he'd escaped the jaws of a Tyrannosaurus Rex without injury. It was still mind boggling every time he saw his spaceship crash on top of him, yet, he was able, not only to survive, but to get up and walk away unharmed. He'd become the man of infinite lives. He saw himself being shot by the infamous Al Capone, falling from a mountain top, surviving an F-5 tornado, that had ravaged and killed everything else in its path. He watched as the tornado threw a freight train, engine, and all, directly at him, and it passed through him as though he were a ghost. He knew now what it was to be a cartoon character with infinite lives.

He also understood now, why Shilloqwai hated being referred to as a superhero. She just wanted people to see her for who she was, a genuinely nice person who loved and cared for the well-being of everyone. Dismissing her mutant powers, Shilloqwai believed there was nothing else that would qualify her as a superhero. She was content being the caring loving person, that she believed she was. The haunting questions on Excelcious' mind, that he believed to be heavier than the weight of the world on his shoulders were:

1. Was Shilloqwai dead?
2. Was Shilloqwai alive?

He felt he needed to have a definitive answer to either question before he could move on. The uncertainty of not knowing either way would haunt him until his dying day. He'd witnessed the crashing and burning of the Hindenburg, the great San Francisco Earthquake, the sinking of the Titanic, and the crumpling of the twin towers in New York City on 9/11/2001. None of these disasters was more devastating to him than the one of which he'd just become a victim. If indeed, he'd lost Shilloqwai, it would be the greatest tragedy of his lifetime. Starting to hallucinate, Excelcious could no longer tell the difference between reality and illusion, dreams, or nightmares. He knew he needed help! He just didn't know where to go to find it! He'd totally given up now, leaving his fate in the hands of the Power of Love.

He went back to the site where his ship would again crash. He decided to wait for the fleet. He stood at the point where he was sure it would spear him through the heart. He wouldn't feel anything. It wasn't real. But, if it weren't real, then why couldn't he escape? He wasn't feeling much of anything now, not even pain. He'd become numb to it. All he was feeling was the void in his life, left by the absence of Shilloqwai. She was there, at least in spirit, he could feel that! But those feelings were quickly fading as he'd fallen into the abyss of loneliness. He would die if her love didn't find him and rescue him. He was angry for her not being there when he needed her most. Excelcious slipped into a subconscious state, dreaming of a way to escape the nightmare enslaving him.

Excelcious felt he was dying. It wasn't so much the dying! Everyone's time would come. It was the thought of dying alone. His inability to find Shilloqwai, would taunt, torment and torture him through, what he thought were his last moments, until the bitter end. He'd found a temporary resting place, the nothingness…a place between life and death…but that was no place for him. After reconsidering, not that he had a choice in the matter, he thought it might be a good place to rest until his fate had been determined. He hadn't eaten or slept, since he couldn't remember when? Now would be the time and this would be the place.

He didn't know how long he'd been sleeping. No matter, time was irrelevant here, wherever here was. It was all about the moment, no future, no past. It was all about now. When Excelcious regained his consciousness, he'd found he'd been sprung from the wretched time trap that had him imprisoned. He was trying to familiarize himself with his environment, but everything looked so strange. No landmarks, no signs, nothing that would help him to get his bearings. One nightmare had ended. Another had begun. In his new nightmare, Excelcious found himself looking around. He was in what appeared to be some kind of infirmary. He was searching, seeking to find a familiar face. But of everyone present, he failed to recognize just one.

Then he felt the gentle caresses brushing across his face like feathers, baby soft, it was a woman's touch. Suddenly, Excelcious called out! "Shilloqwai? Is that you?" The room fell deathly silent. He'd gotten the attention of everyone. All eyes were on him for having dared to say her name! "No, not Shilloqwai! I am Quintachantelle," the stranger introduced herself, giving a name to one of many unrecognizable faces.

"Do you know where I can find Shilloqwai?"

"No one here wishes to find Shilloqwai. It is our collective hope that she doesn't find us!" Quintachantelle prayed.

"Why do you say that?"

"In her four short years on Eartheena, she's terrorized and unleashed her wrath in almost every place she's been, and on many of the people she's met. She has a weapons' belt, more powerful than anything we have here. She seems to want to make war instead of peace. She's the daughter of the devil, tormenting us all. The only ones seeking to find her are those wishing to kill her! We are a transient people not a warring one. This is a mere pitstop for those of us on the way to another destination."

"Are we talking about the same Shilloqwai?

"Aqua tourmaline skin, matching waist-long hair, silver icy-blue tourmaline eyes, with looks that actually do kill. I'm the last to pass judgement on anyone. Cursing is not my thing. But, in a word, the best way to describe her is, "BITCH!"

"Sounds like the way she looks, but it can't be her. The Shilloqwai I know isn't a bitch. What is this time and place anyway? Where am I?"

"You are on the planet Eartheena. It's like the Earth you know, only 3x bigger and 3x the amount of water. This planet is divided into three parts, past, present, and future. Beware of the past and the future, they're very dangerous places. You were trapped in the past. I rescued you. The future is full of shadows that may or may not come to pass. The safest place on the planet is here, in the present. And it's not very safe here. You take things as they come. Roll with the changes and live for the moment, and know you have the power to shape the future, don't let it shape you."

"What do you mean?"

"I'll explain it to you another time. Your Shilloqwai is here to see you!" The crowd parted like fissures splitting the ground during an Earthquake. Shilloqwai walked through the crowd as though she were royalty, arrogant and pompous. Then she set eyes on her visitor, looking on him with disdain. She sneered at him with disgust, repulsed by the fact that he had the audacity to summon her from her work.

"Who the hell are you? And what the hell do you want with me?"

"I just wanted to know that you were okay!"

"Aside from my husband and my three children, you're the only one that seems to give a damn about me or my well-being. Funny, I don't even know who you are!"

"We were engaged to be married before your recent accident. And I know about the markings on your arm, 07/11/13F Mercusilver Class."

"That's classified information you just revealed. Whoever leaked it to you is dead. And for your revelations, you will be sentenced to death as well."

"No one leaked it. It's all information I knew about you."

"So, you're a secret agent? A rebel? A spy?" Shilloqwai interrogated him. Her blood was beginning to boil as she felt the energy inside of her start to surge. Tourmaline tears began to cascade down her cheeks along with the blue-silver blood, coming from her eyes, nose, ears, and mouth. She didn't want to kill him, but the strange man knew too much. She had no choice. She focused, and passed out, as she fired. Falling to the floor threw her aim way off. Still the shrapnel shredded Excelcious' right arm. He too passed out, from the loss of blood and the searing pain. Both needed immediate medical attention. More of the medical personnel were willing to help Excelcious than they were willing to help Shilloqwai. One of the medics, who'd grown tired of her tirades shouted across the room, "Help him! Let the BITCH die!"

WORKS IN PROGRESS:

ROBOTIX SAGA

BOOK 2: WHEN TWO WORLDS COLLIDE

BOOK 3: RISE OF THE CYBORGS

www.ingramcontent.com/pod-product-compliance
Lightning Source LLC
Chambersburg PA
CBHW062107290726
48975CB00001B/133